Can one small note give her the courage to find a new path?

Kate gave up her dreams of being a painter years ago. But six little words pinned to the noticeboard of her local café might just give her the inspiration she needs.

'To be, or not to be...' – printed on orange card with no explanation – appears one morning.

Each day, a new line is added, sparking curiosity throughout the café. Among the regulars is Bardy, a retired English teacher grappling with writer's block.

As Kate and Bardy follow this breadcrumb trail, they discover a local community group encouraging people to rediscover their own creative spark – and the long-lost courage to chase it.

For Kate, their new group might just offer a second chance at happiness, if only Bardy can find the strength to share his story too...

After studying history at university, Sally moved to London to work in advertising. However, in her spare time she studied floristry at night school and eventually opened her own flower shop. She soon came to appreciate that flower shops offer a unique window into people's stories and eventually she began to photograph and write about this floral life in a series of non-fiction books. Later, she continued her interest in writing when she founded her fountain pen company, Plooms.co.uk.

In her debut novel, *The Keeper of Stories*, Sally combines her love of history and writing with her abiding interest in the stories people have to tell. Sally now lives in Dorset. Her eldest daughter, Alex, is a doctor and her youngest daughter is the author, Libby Page.

@SallyPageBooks
@bysallypage
sallypage.com

26 February 2026

PB | 9780008767495
EB | 9780008767501
EA | 9780008767519

For publicity enquiries, please contact
libby.haddock@harpercollins.co.uk

UNCORRECTED PROOF COPY.
NOT FOR SALE OR QUOTATION.

'This book is simply joyful'
☆☆☆☆☆

'A warm embrace when you most need it'
☆☆☆☆☆

'Another delightful book by Sally Page. She has the ability to get into the heart of a character and expose it to the reader'
☆☆☆☆☆

'I laughed and I cried and didn't want it to end'
☆☆☆☆☆

'A rich and well-written book which touches so many issues. With vivid descriptions and wonderful characters, this book is a true page-turner'
☆☆☆☆☆

'The absolute definition of a feel-good read'
☆☆☆☆☆

'If you're looking for a delightful, thought-provoking read with a cast of lovable characters, this is it'
☆☆☆☆☆

'Sally Page is a master at describing human nature'

'What a wonderful story! I already think this will be one of my favourite reads of 2025'
☆☆☆☆☆

'Friendship, life and love in one absolutely joyous book'
☆ ☆ ☆ ☆ ☆

'A celebration of second chances, self-worth, and the joy of pursuing your passions, no matter your age or circumstances'
☆ ☆ ☆ ☆ ☆

'Adore Sally Page's novels and this did not disappoint'
☆ ☆ ☆ ☆ ☆

'A heartwarming page-turner that gives all the feels'
☆ ☆ ☆ ☆ ☆

'A delightful, thought-provoking read with a cast of lovable characters'
☆ ☆ ☆ ☆ ☆

Six Little Words

After studying history at university, Sally moved to London to work in advertising. In her spare time she studied floristry at night school and eventually opened her own flower shop. Sally came to appreciate that flower shops offer a unique window into people's stories and she began to photograph and write about this floral life in a series of non-fiction books. Later, Sally continued her interest in writing when she founded her fountain pen company, PLOOMS.

Sally now lives in Dorset. Her eldest daughter, Alex, is a doctor and her youngest daughter is the author Libby Page.

Sally's debut novel, *The Keeper of Stories*, was a *Sunday Times* bestseller, has now sold over 500,000 copies and has been translated into 29 languages.

Also by Sally Page

The Keeper of Stories
The Book of Beginnings
The Secrets of Flowers

Six Little Words

SALLY PAGE

*To Kristy,
I hope you enjoy it!
Sally Page*

HarperCollins*Publishers*

HarperCollins*Publishers* Ltd
1 London Bridge Street,
London SE1 9GF

www.harpercollins.co.uk

HarperCollins*Publishers*
Macken House, 39/40 Mayor Street Upper
Dublin 1, D01 C9W8, Ireland

First published by HarperCollins*Publishers* Ltd 2025

1

Copyright © Sally Page 2025

Sally Page asserts the moral right to be identified as the author of this work.

A catalogue record for this book is available from the British Library.

ISBN: 978-0-00-876749-5 (PB)

This novel is entirely a work of fiction. The names, characters and incidents portrayed in it are the work of the author's imagination. Any resemblance to actual persons, living or dead, events or localities is entirely coincidental.

Typeset in Berling LT Std by HarperCollins*Publishers* India

Printed and bound in the UK using 100%
Renewable Electricity at CPI Group (UK) Ltd

All rights reserved. No part of this publication may be reproduced, stored in a retrieval system, or transmitted, in any form or by any means, electronic, mechanical, photocopying, recording or otherwise, without the prior written permission of the publishers.

Without limiting the author's and publisher's exclusive rights, any unauthorised use of this publication to train generative artificial intelligence (AI) technologies is expressly prohibited. HarperCollins also exercise their rights under Article 4(3) of the Digital Single Market Directive 2019/790 and expressly reserve this publication from the text and data mining exception.

This book is produced from independently certified FSC paper to ensure responsible forest management.
For more information visit: www.harpercollins.co.uk/green

*This book is dedicated to
Stephen & Judith Cutting
and
Nigel Done
my fellow Norfolk travellers*

*and with thanks to
William Shakespeare*

Prologue

Bardy

I was adored once too

She was a golden yellow.

That luminous tone that sits between the glistening hue of honey and a wheatfield caught in the slanting rays of an August evening. He saw it as soon as he met her. He wonders sometimes if he glimpsed it, turned to the glow, even before she walked into his classroom: dull-red exercise books held in the crook of her arm, spines nestled against her hip.

She had introduced herself – Miss Anderson… Hana – a new teacher, like him. She laughed at his name. Most did. Then she left for her own classroom, his life changed forever.

He dips into the memory of the colour like the painter he isn't. She was the artist, had taught him so much about colour. But she never quite understood when he tried to tell her how he saw certain people. Instead she laughed and later – weeks, months later – had turned her head towards him on the pillow and asked if he experienced things in colour. He smiled and shrugged a nod. Sometimes.

'Sex?' she asked, stretching like a cat beside him.

He just reached for her, unsure if she would laugh at him again.

But he knew that sex with her started with the blue of a Slovenian lake made turquoise with the richness of lime, that it strengthened to ultramarine until there was a purple so deep he was lost in it.

THIRTY-NINE YEARS LATER

North Norfolk

Spring

Chapter 1

Kate

To be or not to be

To be or not to be...
That is all that is written on the orange card. Six little words. Nothing more. Kate scans the rest of the noticeboard for a clue. There are the usual advertisements for toddler groups, RNLI bake sales and pilates. A testament to the customers who gather in this small Italian-style coffee shop. Locals, in the winter months; incomers, in the summer months or when the sweep of migration draws the birders in their flocks. She turns her attention back to the noticeboard.
Reflexology.
Yoga for Dogs.
Kate smiles.
But there is nothing that sheds any light on the orange notice. She glances over her shoulder to the young girl behind

the counter, tempted to ask her. But she has her head down, texting on her phone. Or is she filming herself?

The owner, Luigi, appears from the back. 'Phone!' he barks at the girl who flicks it into her apron pocket with a fluid twist of the hand.

'I wasn't!' she declares, eyes wide, head shimmering with indignant shakes.

'Tay, you know the rules.'

'Chill out,' she mutters, head ducked low. But her voice holds the suspicion of a grin that Kate cannot see, although she spots the answering ghost of a smile on Luigi's face.

I bet he likes having her around. I bet it makes him feel alive.

Kate looks around at the café, with its speckled marbled tabletops circled by chairs painted duck-egg blue or teal. Along one wall is a long bench filled with orange and turquoise patterned cushions, a long wooden table set in front of it, ready for larger groups. On the wall in pale ash frames are retro posters of colourful houses, spilling into Mediterranean seas, and behind the counter, a large, square oil painting of lemons, their skins flecked with sunshine. She fleetingly wonders if there will come a time when the café will start to look dated and tired. Luigi has not changed a single thing in here since his wife, Tina, died four years ago. The espresso cups she collected, still hang from hooks below a shelf stacked with the café's terracotta and white china.

If the time comes, perhaps Tay – she thinks that's what Luigi called her – will sort it out for him.

'Now that is the question.'

'I'm sorry?' Startled, Kate turns to the woman who is standing beside her. She didn't hear the woman, and a man she presumes to be her husband, come in.

'To be or not to be, that is the question,' the woman repeats, smiling at Kate. She looks to be in her late seventies, wrapped up against the wind and squally rain – it's late March – but not a birder, Kate decides. Smart mac and black boots.

'Ah, Shakespeare,' her husband proclaims, joining them.

The woman raises an eyebrow at Kate, 'Yes, Leonard, I think we gathered that.'

'I was wondering what it—' Kate starts.

Leonard's words roll over hers, flattening them. '*Hamlet* of course. He is talking about life. "To BE or not to BE" coffee and cake?' he continues all in one breath.

He doesn't wait for an answer and his wife's eyes follow him as he bustles towards the counter.

'Are you married?' she asks Kate, still watching him.

'Divorced,' Kate replies, with more relief than regret.

'Wise,' the woman comments, looking at her husband who is gesticulating at each cake in turn.

'Coffee, or blueberry and almond? Or there are brownies? Don't much like the look of the carrot cake,' Leonard calls, oblivious of Tay's eye roll.

'Coffee,' the woman responds, smiling at Tay. She continues, reflectively, 'When you were married did you ever have dreams where you were hitting your husband over the head with a frying pan?'

Kate laughs. 'No, can't say I did.'

She had thought a lot of things about Doug, or Dougie as he

now likes to be called. But that hadn't been one of them. 'Do you?' she enquires.

'Oh, yes, I often dream that,' the woman says mildly. She leans in closer as she moves away. 'And sometimes, I'm not even asleep.'

Kate smiles at the memory of this as she collects her bicycle from where it is propped beside the café wall. She takes the narrow road leading from the square at the top of the town, down to the harbour. The rain has stopped – as she hoped it would – and as she sails past the fishing boats lining the quay she can see that the sun is doing its best to break through. She steers her bike between the boat sheds and the lobster hatchery, snaking between the puddles. Then she is out, following the creek, leaving the town behind her, heading into the world she loves – the marshlands.

First comes the freshwater marsh protected from the sea by the great shingle banks and seawalls so ancient they are protruding green ribs within the body of the landscape. Water in the pools and reedbeds rise and fall with the breath of the seasons and in time to the creak and clank of the dyke sluice gates. But saltwater is crafty and it creeps in through the creeks and tributaries. Still, it pays its dues for this invasion – the saltmarsh that it brings protects this lowland like nothing else does from its sister the sea.

Within this land and rising above it in the vast skies are the birds. Some are true home-birds that will never leave until death claims them; some are visitors, happy to stay awhile. A few have got lost and made their home here, accepted neighbours – only exotic to the birders. While others are passage migrants, journeying through on their way to far-flung lands. Today the pink-footed geese are leaving, the long lazy V that drifts across the sky a mirage masking the hard honking work of leaders constantly changing places at the tip of an arrow pointing north.

Kate watches the retreating silhouettes through narrowed eyes and wonders if she is now a home-bird. This is where she has lived since her daughters were little. Three mud-spattered creatures that quickly evolved from city-park-dwellers to creek-dwellers. As they grew in confidence, they eventually managed their own small rowboat, *The Rose*. It was named by the girls' aunt – Kate's sister, Alice, who had declared this with a grin and a knowing look thrown in Kate's direction. Jess had insisted on being the captain, but it seemed to Kate they usually ended up doing what the second in command demanded – Bella. Kindness on Jess's part or giving in to a stronger will? Kate was never quite sure. Ellie had just bopped along, life jacket bumping the tip of her nose, happily turning the three of them into orphans lost on the Mississippi. Ellie had always had a taste for the dramatic and, as it turned out, for travel.

Kate passes two elderly walkers and her thoughts return to the couple in the café.

To be or not to be...

To be or not to be... *alive?*

That is what Leonard seemed to think it was all about. Well, she would take that. She has come close enough to the alternative and still feels like she 'got away with it'.

Kate stops the next thought that naturally follows from this and feels the wind whip away her tears as she pushes down hard on the pedals.

Birds are nestled, half-submerged in the sea blight and sea lavender edging the creek, and as she passes a small flock of gulls lifts as if swept up by her momentum. They twist erratically in the wind, filling the air with their staccato song of the seaside.

She slows and pulls up beside a long patch of grass. This is where her cottage sits, one in a row of small, redbrick houses, set looking out over the creek, and beyond that, the marshes.

To be or not to be…

Pregnant?

Could Jess be pregnant? She turns to this thought with a sense of relief. On their last call her eldest daughter had sounded… Was there suppressed excitement in her voice? She knows Jess and Matt have been trying.

To be or not to be… *a grandmother?*

She smiles. She thinks she would go with 'Granny'. What would Doug want to be? He would probably insist the child call him 'Dougie'. She can't imagine 'Grandad' would sit well with his Californian lifestyle. Her husband had left her for a girl (you could hardly call her a woman) who was crewing on one of the yachts moored here twelve summers ago.

In the café when she had told the woman that she was divorced she had genuinely felt more relief than regret. But it doesn't take much to stir the waters and be washed in old memories.

When Doug had told her he was leaving she had been hollowed out by the shock of it. She had been numb for weeks and then felt more like someone suffering from flu than a wife facing a husband's betrayal. During all of this she had had no option but to hold it together for the girls. Her husband had morphed from a man in his forties into a teenager – a teenager who had just lost his virginity. He swaggered and grinned, apparently oblivious of the carnage and the hurt he was inflicting. He had even told Kate that she would get on well with his new love.

'You *really* would.'

Did he expect her to sail away on their love-yacht with them?

Now she suspects he hadn't thought any of it through, was swept away on a cliché. She sometimes wonders if he regrets it. But mainly she cannot be bothered to think about him at all.

In the end there hadn't been a final goodbye. Just a gradual leeching of his possessions (and some of hers) and one day Doug had receded like the tide. She was left trying to stop seventeen-year-old Jess obsessing about how the dishwasher was loaded and had taken the axe from her hands when she tried to split the logs. Jess was amazing at maths, rather than being hands-on or practical; Kate remembers the injuries Jess had once inflicted on her hand with a lino knife. Bella had been bloody in a different way and it seemed she wanted (but didn't really want) Kate to show the same degree of rage. While Ellie, at twelve, had regressed into cuddly toys and made Kate feel sick with how frightened she could look.

But they had survived. When Alice visited she made them laugh like no one else could. And eventually Kate and the girls became a team of four, Kate part-confused, part-incredulous with the realisation of how little Doug had actually done for his family. Still, she had encouraged the girls to contact him and he had responded with an alacrity which she suspects was fuelled by guilt as much as gratitude.

Kate takes off her helmet and leans forward on her bike. The wind eddying across the creek tugs at her hair. Not that the strands of grey move much in the sharp breeze, her hair had grown back bristle-brush tough after the chemo. Her girls tell her it suits her. That it looks good. Kate's never sure. She *is* sure there are easier ways to a new hairstyle.

The last treatment was over four years ago now.

By then, Doug long gone.

So much other loss.

But not her.

And during all of it her girls had been incredible. Even Ellie, who was just eighteen when she was first diagnosed. Popping back from uni with every sort of Haribo (which seemed to be the one thing that curbed the sickness), holding her hand and chatting, as Kate sat on the sofa, head flung back, eyes closed. Jess had organised the online rota for friends and family to take her to hospital, and had been there for weekends in-between her teacher-training. Bella had returned from the States for a prolonged visit – she was taking a course in sports physio in Florida. And on the good days they had pretended everything was normal. Picnicking on the beach, the wind tugging at the ends of the soft silk scarf Bella had brought her back from the Keys to wrap around her head. Returning home via the creek, Kate wedged between them in *The Rose* as the girls tucked a rug more securely around her against the cold that only she could feel. She had read about the reversal of roles in old age – children looking after parents. She just hadn't expected it as she turned fifty.

Looking back, it is the thought of her girls that always makes her cry. Not the fact of her cancer and the surgery. Or even how unfair it sometimes seemed. Nor the nights of pitch-black terror or the crippling, clammy nausea and exhaustion that seemed to want to wring the life out of her.

But seeing her girls as the women they had become?

The memory of that, will *always* make her cry.

Kate gazes across the broad breadth of the creek, at the exposed sand lying in plump pockets as if quilted by the outgoing tide. The piping trill of oyster catchers rises above the clinking halyards of yachts stranded at tipsy angles in the sand. The water within the creek bed is a shallow stream – a shoal of ripples breaking the surface. This habit of pausing and checking, grounds her in the place she calls home. Today it doesn't come with the usual contentment.

To be or not to be... *happy?*

Kate's eyes travel across the sweeping saltmarsh beyond the creek to the thin line of indigo that is the sea. Against the horizon the wind turbines appear tiny – white cocktail-stick angels, arms and wings spread wide.

She knows she has much to be happy about. That she should be grateful just to be standing here.

But knowing it doesn't make it so.

Kate wonders when it was, she lost her way to happiness.

Chapter 2

Bardy

I would that I were laid low in my grave

'Oy, Jon, you going to order something or just sit there looking pretty?'

Bardy responds automatically, even though he isn't hungry. 'Sorry mate, a bacon sandwich and a large black Americano.'

'So the usual,' Luigi replies, shrugging, as if bemused Bardy has wasted so many words. Luigi is one of the few people who call Bardy, 'Jon'. They had met long before Hana. Long before her nickname for him caught and stuck. They had been classmates at the local school. Luigi, the newcomer, had told class 3B his family were Mafia. Eight-year-old Jon had believed him. Kept close to him. Well, you would, wouldn't you? And even back then Luigi was a big lad. Jon has always been middling in pretty much everything. Middling height. Middling at sport. Middling at schoolwork. The only thing he was good at was English. So he helped Luigi when he struggled with the language and it had become, 'Jon and Lou'. Lou hadn't laughed at his surname. Just nodded. Pursed his lips, with what Jon Shakespeare likes to think was respect. Well, even the Mafia had heard of Shakespeare.

Now, years on, it's 'Jon and Lou', men in their early sixties. He mentally rephrases. Two lonely old buggers. He glances at Lou behind the counter. Still friends. At times still sticking to the code of omertà. Even if Luigi's dad had, in fact, been a bus driver. A mild-mannered man from Pisa.

Bardy goes back to staring out of the window and contemplating the best way to die. He dismisses a gun. Doesn't have one. Too messy. Drowning? He's heard it's a horrendous way to go. He's just considering some of the deaths he's read about in novels when Luigi dumps his order on the table.

'What is it?' Lou snaps.

'What? Nothing.'

Lou injects a suitable level of scepticism into his grunt before heading back to the counter.

Bardy knows the scales are tipped against him saying anything to Lou. The man whose wife died versus the man whose wife left him. What's he got to moan about? After a marriage of thirty years, Hana had finally got gut-achingly bored of him and decided she'd had enough. He's surprised it took that long. Maybe if lockdown hadn't happened she might have stayed. But being shut up in a house with just him? The boys gone, all the kids they'd fostered grown and scattered. Her departure had shredded his heart and stripped the most important colour from his world, but he couldn't honestly say he blamed her.

He remembers the day she left as one of those bright warm days of early lockdown. How could the whole globe be in crisis he world glowed like this? As the sun set on the garden he had not moved from for hours, he realised that all ore him was a mirage, there to mock him: his inadequacies, is blind stupidity. How could he not have realised how she felt? He tried to reach for her colour, but despite the golden yellow of the evening taunting him... it was gone. He saw himself as a stick-man drawing sitting on his bench. A scribble of grey on a white background. No colour. No substance. He had closed his eyes and dipped his head, unable to bear the warming rays on his skin. He wondered if Hana was now basking in the relief of that sun. A long overdue decision made. Did the boys know? Had they always known? This was too much shame to shoulder.

In his mind's eye he saw the stick man reach in his pocket for his phone. So that is what the man on the bench did. He phoned Lou.

He looks at his friend now. This is not something he should bang on about. Not five years later. Still unable to move on. He knows Lou would have sucked the leukaemia from Tina's body and swallowed it whole if he could have done. So, no, on that scale, it was time for a different sort of omertà. He should just shut the fuck up. Anyway, he wasn't really serious. Wasn't really thinking of killing himself. Had just been wondering – what was the point? Lou *would* understand that.

Bardy finishes his breakfast and goes to pay.

As he waits in line behind a young couple he spots an orange card on the noticeboard, just two lines written in the centre.

To be or not to be...
If music be...

Reflex finishes the line for him: ...*the food of love play on.* Jon Shakespeare has taught enough of the Bard over the years to do that one in his sleep. *Twelfth Night.*

He reaches the counter.

'Tay in today?'

Why had the card made him think of her?

'Later,' Luigi replies, studying him.

'How's she getting on?' It was Bardy's idea that Lou offer her work. Late afternoons and some weekends. He knew Tay was struggling, that her job in customer service paid badly, and although she still lived with her mum, it was Tay who made sure there was food in the fridge. She might only be seventeen, but Tay was a born fixer. A coper. Always had been. Had to be.

'Doesn't listen. Always on her phone. Doesn't think timekeeping applies to her.' Luigi shrugs. 'But apart from that.'

Bardy breathes out, 'So you like her.'

'God knows why.'

Bardy nods his understanding and leaves. Tay: heart-shaped face, cynical eyes; thick wavy hair, tied back tight with short-cropped fringe; slight body in oversized clothes. A girl of contrasts. She could alternate between monosyllabic and mouthy. But in the space between, there were moments of surprising, considered conversation that Bardy relished. He had thought Lou might too. There's just something about Tay. If she lets you see it.

For Bardy, Tay is red ochre.

Maybe she had started life as ochre – that soft, earthy yellow – but by the time Bardy met her at three years old, the oxidation process had started. Tay had been exposed to too much. Seen too much. Her mother, Toni, had been fostered by

Bardy and Hana, on and off between seven and fourteen. Toni was the product of a mother with a serious drug habit who was an easy target for abusive men. At seventeen Toni had given birth to Taylor.

'At the end of the day, T-Swizzle may be an icon,' Tay had later commented, 'but WTF.'

Bardy knew that Toni loved Tay, but it was with the same intensity that made her such an obsessive Swiftie. She wore early motherhood on social media like her rancid-bright clothes that exposed flesh and vulnerability in equal measure. Then nothing for months. Periods when addiction re-emerged. A gift from her own mother. Then Bardy and Hana would do what they could. Which was never going to be enough. But Tay had become a kind of foster granddaughter. Close to Hana. She was the only person Tay would spontaneously hug. Bardy, she wanted sitting close to her but not touching. Talking. And he loved those times. Brushed by her red ochre. An organic crimson tinged with yellow. He hoped Tay would stay that rich tone. Not harden over time to an iron-coloured rust. Sometimes he thought he detected streaks of it within her. Her comments could be brutal. But he stayed steady. Still. Kept faith.

And it wasn't just him, he thought his boys had seen it too. Maybe not the colour. But the *something*.

They hadn't started fostering until their boys were in their teens and Hana was only working a few evenings a week, running adult art courses at the local college. There had been a family discussion. His eco-warrior, quasi-charitable, we-all-have-too-much-stuff sons were initially dumfounded.

'What, *here?*'

'In *our* house?'

So much for 'ownership is bondage'.

But Hana had persisted. Persuaded. He had reassured. And eventually Tom and Ned had turned to each other and nodded very slightly: 'Okay, we'll give it a go.'

Big of you, Hana had mouthed silently behind their backs.

In the main the fostering had worked. Some experiences definitely better than others. The nuggets of real hope hard won in the layers of trouble, piled on trouble. Problems laid down years, sometimes generations ago. The boys had connected with some, avoided others, and Bardy thought that was their right. He thought they handled it well. Was proud of them. They barely knew Tay's mother Toni, as they were out or away when she was with them. But one Christmas Eve they came home – young men in their late-twenties – to find four-year-old Tay on the sofa wearing a hand-me-down dressing gown and an expression of deep suspicion on her face. She would not let Bardy sit near her, and her eyes followed Hana around watchfully. When the boys entered the room, she drew her knees up close to her chest, wrapped her arms around them and tucked her head down until only her eyes were visible. At the time Bardy thought he saw flecks of iron-rust in her dark pupils. From then on, the only time her eyes left the boys was when they flicked to the table laid with their normal Christmas Eve feast of favourite foods. A family tradition of eat-what-you like picnic, a kind of *MasterChef* meets Walmart.

In a hurried aside in the kitchen, Bardy explained about the emergency placement and then realising his boys were old hands at this, he asked their advice. After all they still seemed like children to him, despite their qualifications and jobs, and in Ned's case, live-in-girlfriend.

Then followed their normal conflab. Brothers finishing each other's sentences.

Ned: 'What she doesn't need is all that Christmassy, you've been a good girl for—'

Tom: '—Santa bollocks. She'd be freaked out. But she looks—'

Ned: '—hungry?'

Tom: 'Yeah. Takin' in all that—'

Ned: '—food. Me too. Bloody starving.'

Bardy (trying not to plead): 'Still, I'd like to make it special for her. Hell, she's only four.'

Tom (serious): 'No idea what her Christmases have been like. Don't want to set the bar too high. Make everything else that comes next look shit.'

Ned, nodding: 'Chernobyl.'

Tom: 'Yeah... right bro.'

Bardy: '*Chernobyl?*'

Tom and Ned in unison: 'Yeah, all those rich Americans having kids from Chernobyl over for a week. Feed 'em up. Throw toys at them. Then send 'em back.'

Ned: 'Fucking cruel.'

Silence.

Tom: 'She just needs to chill, feel safe.'

Ned (tentative): 'Jolabokaflod?'

Bardy and Tom: 'Not with you, mate.'

So, Ned explained. It was something his Icelandic girlfriend had told him about.

Bardy, thoughtful: 'Yolbukflud?'

Ned laughed, shook his head and headed up to his old room, followed by Tom to collect what they needed.

After that, until the boys left for good, they had celebrated the Icelandic Christmas Eve tradition of Jolabokaflod – or in English, a book flood. Everyone gives presents of books and you all sit around in silence reading. And in Bardy's family, also indulging in a crazy kind of picnic. The loss of it is the main reason he now hates Christmas. But he can't ever regret the introduction of this tradition as it brings back memories of their first one. Tay eventually curled on the sofa by Hana as she read her *The Cat in the Hat*. Wide-eyed like it was something out of this world. Which reminded Bardy that it *really* was. And made him sad. But also hopeful. There were so many more books for Tay to enjoy.

His favourite recollection of that evening was when she let Ned read her *Hairy Maclary* with Tom joining in the chorus. They had sat on the floor by the sofa so she could lean over them. But not touching. His boys their normal earthy tones: Ned the colour of a worn grey pebble washed by the sea; Tom the colour of marshland mud, flecked with sand. In the soft glow of the Christmas tree lights, a skinny four-year-old, with yellowing bruises on arms and legs, had shone a rich red ochre.

So yes, with Tay, even years on, he continues to keep the faith. As in that beautiful deep ruby he detects such hope.

Why is it then, that he feels something has gone wrong between them? That she is hiding something from him?

Chapter 3

Kate

The short and the long of it

The list is growing.

> *To be or not to be...*
> *If music be...*
> *The short and the long of it...*

The orange card now even has its own Instagram account – tagged at the bottom of the notice. Kate finds it on her phone, but there are only three posts repeating the quotes, each on a different coloured background. The profile simply reads, *Create.* Which leaves her wondering... *create what?* Over coffee and croissant, she looks up the quotes: *Hamlet* – she knew that – *Twelfth Night* and *The Merry Wives of Windsor.* Maybe a Shakespeare company is coming to town? But it doesn't look that professional. Maybe a school production?

She puts her phone away and turns back to her laptop. Luigi doesn't mind people working in here when it's quiet, as long as they buy a steady stream of coffee and cake – which suits Kate just fine. She re-reads the financial report she has just finished before pressing send. An analysis of sales for a national furniture company that is based just outside the town. She can't say she loves the work, but it pays the bills. This was particularly important when Doug left. He made a big thing of telling people, 'I'm leaving Kate and the girls the house'. Which was in her name anyway. But he had cleared out their joint bank account. This, he forgot to mention. So, she had upped her hours and taken some accountancy qualifications to up her salary, working with people who in the main she likes very much. It was the thought of the people that kept her going in each day and it was the same people who supported her when she got the breast cancer diagnosis and had to undergo surgery and months of chemo. Now she works three days a week, packing in as much as she can in those hours. Still not loving it and increasingly restless but feeling it would be ungrateful to leave.

The café is starting to fill up so Kate puts her laptop aside and orders another coffee. She adds a blackberry and apple Danish pastry to her order. Since she has started running again she has been able to eat what she likes, although some things still taste strangely metallic. The nurses said this would go in time. Luigi delivers the coffee and pastry with the nod that he reserves for locals. Not that he is unfriendly to incomers, if anything he is more effusive, sounding more 'Italian'. Kate notices he reverts to a more nondescript accent with the regulars.

There is a mix of people in today. A familiar family with two young children and a baby. The mum has thought to bring books and pre-snack snacks to keep the toddlers going until their order arrives. A group of birders are on the big table. Binoculars beside them, serious all-weather gear hanging on their chairs – no fashion brands there. They have the look of people who have known each other for years. Probably retired, Kate thinks.

Perhaps she could retire? That would be easier to say to her bosses. But she is only fifty-six and she doesn't think they would buy that. Plus she still needs to bring some money in. Anyway, what would she do?

Over the years she has seriously thought about taking time out to learn to oil paint. It has been a secret dream. But these days she barely even does any drawing. There was a time when she always had a small sketchbook in her backpack. Would keep a visual diary of the life of the creek, her walks punctuated by the turning over and smoothing of a page, pens pulled from her worn green leather pencil case. Then came the stillness of looking, as if for the first time. Burrowing into and becoming part of the landscape she loved. Her hand would flow and flick over the page and this combination of seeing and sketching would soothe her like nothing else did.

Now she looks at the world around her and can never quite decide what to draw and she feels she has lost something, not simply inspiration. She is too unsettled to draw, and she cannot force herself to make a start, despite knowing that drawing would be the one thing that would ease her.

Her thoughts are interrupted by the café door opening. A

man in dark jeans and a grey down jacket slips into a newly vacant spot at a table by the window. She recognises him from years of parents' evenings. Mr Shakespeare. He taught all three of her girls. She thinks he was Jess's tutor for a while too. His feedback had been professional, well observed – sometimes humorous. She remembers liking the man, thinking there was something about him.

Rather attractive, she decides, studying him surreptitiously over her coffee cup. Other mums had thought so too, she recalls. Kate has seen him around over the years. Although she doesn't think in this particular café – maybe they came in at different times? But she knows she has been conscious of him when she has spotted him out walking, or shopping with a woman who she presumes is his wife. Long dark hair flowing back from a high brow. It always seemed there were kids around. Maybe they had a big family? Kate never said 'hello', not wanting to embarrass him. There was no way he could remember all the parents he spoke to. But she was aware of him. Is aware of him now.

And he is on his own. Hadn't someone said his wife taught art at the local college? She can't recall the last time she saw the attractive dark-haired woman. It has been a while now…

At that moment he catches her eye. Before she can look away he smiles and something in her stirs.

'Do you mind if I share your table?'

Kate looks up at the woman standing beside her, relieved to be diverted from thoughts that are spinning ludicrously off track.

'Of course.' She nods invitingly to the chair beside her.

'Do you mind dogs?'

'Not at all.' Kate glances down at the delicate mushroom and cream dog that seems to have curved its body in an arc around the woman's booted legs (very nice boots too). 'Oh he... she is beautiful.'

The woman smiles, sitting down, the dog tucking contentedly under the table by her feet. 'I think so, but I know whippets aren't everyone's choice. They are a bit of a Marmite dog.'

The familiarity of 'Marmite' said with a slight accent makes Kate wonder where this woman is from. A visitor?

'What is she called?'

'He,' the woman says apologetically as if not wishing to correct Kate. 'He's called...' She then says a name that Kate thinks might be 'Noohhaaai.'

The stranger smiles in response to Kate's expression. 'It is from a book I read when I was little.' She adds, 'I'm Danish.' This is said with the same lilt of apology.

Kate thinks this woman has nothing to apologise for. She is open and friendly, besides being one of the most elegant women Kate has ever seen. She's dressed in muted tones of cream and soft browns, her clothes clearly not from any high street brand, and Kate suspects they were very expensive. It makes Kate want to rush home and throw away most of her wardrobe. Kate also recognises that she is a very beautiful woman.

'What can I get you?' Luigi asks, appearing at their table.

He pointedly ignores Kate's glance of incredulity. Everyone else has to order at the counter. Not that she blames him. The woman's ash-grey hair is sculpted to an exquisitely shaped head and she has cheekbones that look as if they have been chiselled from ice. Her eyes are a glowing amber, flecked with coffee-bean brown. Kate guesses she must be early fifties but she doesn't think age is ever going to mar this woman's beauty.

It wouldn't dare.

Despite the gentle, apologetic tone Kate gets a sense of something edgier underneath. She is intrigued.

Once Luigi leaves, the woman returns to the subject of dogs, oblivious of Luigi's flattering attention. Kate presumes she must be used to it. 'Most people call him Noy.' A tiny grimace wrinkles her face. 'Although my neighbour will insist on calling him Noy Boy.'

Kate laughs. 'I'm Kate by the way,'

'Pia,' the woman responds, holding out her hand. Pia's light clasp feels cool and dry against her skin and Kate is conscious of how gnarled her knuckles look compared to Pia's long tapering fingers. She spots a ring of what look like perfect diamonds on her forefinger.

'Are you visiting?' Kate enquires.

'No, I live here.'

'*Really?*' Kate rushes on, worried this sounded rude. 'It's just I haven't seen you in here before.'

'Well, I used to spend a lot of my time in London...'

This makes more sense.

'...but now I do more and more work from home. I live about five miles out of town on the coast road.'

Kate wonders which house Pia lives in. She is imagining something modern with a lot of glass. 'What do you do?'

'I'm a lawyer. I presume you live here too?'

Kate nods. 'I have done for years. We first came here when our children were little. My ex-husband got a job as a manager with the wind turbine company, but our girls are grown up now and have all moved away.'

Something in Pia's expression of polite interest decides Kate against expanding on this. Instead, on a whim, she says, 'Have you noticed that orange card on the board? Each time I come in something new is added to it.'

Pia leans forward with real interest now. 'Yes! I've been wondering what it's about. I thought it must be something people knew about.'

From this Kate gathers that, despite living here, Pia feels like an outsider. That she suspects she is one of the few people not 'in' on this. This glimpse of vulnerability surprises Kate and she thinks there is something else tucked in there too. Loneliness? Kate determines that together they will find out what's going on. Even if it turns out to be a teaser for a school play. Surely Luigi will know?

As if the room is reading her thoughts she hears someone at the counter ask, 'Lou, you must know what that notice is about? Who put it up?'

So, Mr Shakespeare is a friend of Luigi's. She doesn't think she has ever heard anyone call him 'Lou' before. And he wants to know about the card too. She is aware that Pia's attention is also fixed on the conversation. They share a conspiratorial glance and edge a fraction closer as they listen.

'You'll have to ask Tay about that,' Luigi comments.

'*Tay*? What's she got to do with it?' Mr Shakespeare asks, suspiciously.

Kate leans towards Pia and mutters under her breath, 'Young girl who works here.'

'As I say, ask Tay about that. I've got no bleedin' idea what she's up to. She's in later on.'

'What time?'

'Your guess is as good as mine, mate,' Luigi responds with weary resignation.

As Mr Shakespeare turns to leave, Kate catches his eye again and they hold each other's gaze for a moment. Kate, flushing, looks away first.

'Interesting,' Pia comments significantly.

Kate nods. *You're not kidding.*

But she's not sure she and Pia are thinking of the same thing.

Chapter 4

Bardy

Age cannot wither her

He makes a dash for the newly vacated table by the window. He nods at Lou above the heads of those queueing at the counter. Lou knows how he likes his coffee. Will get to him in time. He's in no rush.

No Tay today. But then it would be too early. She would be at work at the call centre.

The coffee machine blasts and screeches, and then comes the sharp rap of old coffee being discarded, the squeaky, metallic scrunch of new coffee being loaded. Did anyone ever use a coffee machine as a musical instrument? People used dustbins didn't they? Vacuum cleaners. A mother pushes a toddler in a buggy past the steamy window. Hard work against the wind. The child straining its body against the straps like an angry starfish caught in a net. The boys had been like that. Fighting against everything. Often without considering if they might like what was on offer. Stubborn.

God, he misses them.

He scans the café's customers. There is a face he knows. A nice face. What was her name? He had taught her girls. All three of them. Husband was a bit of a twat. He remembers that. Had wondered what she was doing with him. But then he often wondered what Hana saw in him. What *was* her name? He'd heard something in the staffroom about Mr whateveritis going off with some young American... or was it Canadian? The girls he can remember: Jess... Bella... and... Ellie. She'd been fun, Ellie. Taken A level English. Could have done something like journalism but had gone for art... textile art, something like that.

Oliver! That's it. Mrs Oliver.

Bardy's triumph quickly fades, and he is left with the dregs of disappointment. He'd really like to know what her first name is.

Some of his colleagues would never live where they taught. And he could understand that. Could never get away from the kids. And the families. Some of those families! They were enough to make you want to emigrate.

But he thought it had its advantages. You *did* know the families. The good and the bad. Gave you some feel for what their home life was like. Getting an English essay in on time might be the least of their worries. And it wasn't always deprivation that caused the problems. Some of the richest, poshest kids he'd taught had parents who were the biggest cokeheads. Wanting to hang out with their kids' friends. He didn't need Tay to tell him how deeply uncool that was. At least he hadn't inflicted that on his boys even though he had taught them.

Bardy catches Mrs Oliver's eye and smiles. He hopes she's okay. The hair tells its own tale. He's seen her around town, head wrapped in a silk scarf. He turns away and returns to thoughts of his boys. He hopes that having him as a teacher wasn't too hard for them. He's never really asked them, fearing the answer. Still, when Ned came back during lockdown it had been okay. Tom smug in New Zealand. Hana gone back to Wales. He wasn't glad when Ned split up with his girlfriend, but he was pleased he came home to him. His girlfriend, Freyja, had wanted to be home with her family in Iceland. Hana had never been quite sure about her – too needy, she'd said. Hana didn't have much time for needy. Which was odd when she was such a good foster mum. So, Ned had come to him and they'd had an okay time, all things considered. He sometimes wonders if Hana had put the idea in his head: 'Your dad's not doing so well'…

Bardy looks up, glancing in Mrs Oliver's direction.

Then he sees the woman beside her. He experiences her like a physical blow in his guts. No time to tense. No time to prepare. How can such a petite woman pack such a punch? But she is simply stunning. He tries to catch at her colour. A way to calm himself. To combat the ridiculous heart-hammering clamminess that has swept him.

But there is no colour.

Instead, his mind is suddenly filled with the memory of a painting he once saw of a woman dressed entirely in cream, face half in shadow, light falling on just such a cheekbone. He had headed into the gallery to escape the heat of the street. He can't recall where it was. Cairo? Istanbul? The light diffuse apart from pinpoints at his feet. A scattering of stars from the grille set in the ceiling above his head. Then through the playful light he had seen the painting. The line of that cheekbone. Had wanted to reach out and touch it.

He starts to imagine the feel of this woman's cheek under his fingers and is shocked by the sick sense of intrusion it brings. Like some sad stalker. Instead he stares deep into the cappuccino that Lou has just brought him. He looks up quickly. He always drinks Americanos. Lou is there at the women's table, all Italian bonhomie.

The bugger is sucking his stomach in.

Lou won't catch Bardy's eye. Doesn't even realise he has delivered the wrong coffee.

Silently laughing at Lou – and himself – helps Bardy. It calms his breathing. He sips the wrong coffee. What are he and Lou like? Acting like teenagers just because she is so… He chances a quick glance at the woman. She is talking to Mrs Oliver, smiling, leaning in. He hasn't felt like this since Hana walked into his classroom all those years ago. It had made some kind of sense then because the experience had been suffused in that glorious golden yellow. It had been as if the colour was signalling to him. He lets his mind go blank. Searches. But still there is no glimpse of a colour.

There are many people who Bardy meets who have no link with a colour. In fact, most of them. For those that do, the colour doesn't come as an aura but something clean and clear – distinctly knowable in his mind's eye. His head is simply flooded with their colour. The colour he experiences may change over time, but it is what it is. It isn't something he chooses and it certainly has nothing to do with a person's skin or hair colouring. Knowing how 'I see people in colour', might sound, he has only ever told two people about his dubious gift.

It started around puberty. As if he didn't have enough to deal with. One day he was letting a friend of his dad's into the house and the man brought with him a flood of lilac. He was a big bloke too. Great bushy beard. Then it was his English teacher, Miss Abbot. A rich warm caramel. That hadn't surprised him. But it didn't help with the other stuff that came with puberty. Lou had spotted it. Well, not the erection. But the fact he carried his bag slung in front of him 'like a girl'. Which was ironic. Fuck. But what could he say? One look at Lou told him not to go there. Best mate. Yes. But 'Do you ever see people in colour?' was not a conversation he wanted to have. Well not then. Not at thirteen. He had tried a few tentative enquiries with his art teacher, but he just thought he was taking the piss. Maybe he should have tried Miss Powell, the biology teacher. No chance of a boner in her class.

Dead slug grey.

He can't imagine even Farrow and Ball wanting that one.

Over the years he has researched synaesthesia and knows it is often linked to music – has read that the composer, Sibelius, told his decorator to paint his stove F Major. Green, apparently. He once heard a woman on the radio talking about how each day of the week was a particular colour – she seemed surprised that others didn't see it that way. He does remember that Monday was French navy. And another time he caught the end of a documentary where a musician said that when he was young and had gone to concerts he presumed that when the orchestra started, and the lights were turned down, it was so the audience could see the colours. Bardy knows he's not musical. Just an ordinary bloke with a love of words. With a weird way of seeing people. Still, he wishes this woman had a colour. It might help.

She looks his way, and he quickly lowers his gaze, but not before he catches the gleam of an amber eye. He is forcefully reminded of a curlew. Eye bright. Feathers, lying soft, interlocking, layer upon layer of subtle, beautiful browns, creams and sand. A natural camouflage against the muted tones of the marsh. Out there on the mudflats she could disappear from view. Would be hidden.

Bardy feels shaken. He has no idea what is going on so hangs on to the one thing he does know. He has had enough of his cappuccino. Remembers why he doesn't ever order them. He pushes the cup aside and goes to pay. In the queue he wavers. He could go up and say hello to Mrs Oliver. Would that seem odd? She did smile back. Seemed to recognise him. Before he can teeter one way or another off his tightrope of indecision he spots the card. The brightness of the orange breaks through his distraction.

He asks Lou.

Who doesn't know much, but seems to think Tay might be behind it.

Bardy is just turning to leave when he hears the woman speak. The slight accent fits. Scandinavian? He slows. Maybe he'll say something. He could mention Jolabokaflod. *What the hell is he thinking?* Maybe he should just nod and smile. But like the eight-year-old Jon he was – he bottles it. Instead he catches Mrs Oliver's eye. Looks at her for far too long and then bolts for the door, sure that Jess and Bella and Ellie's mum must think her daughters' old English teacher is completely mad.

Chapter 5

Kate

The game's afoot

Pia's text is short:

Have you seen the Instagram post?

They had swapped numbers at the café, planning to meet for coffee again soon. Another text arrives, this time with a link and a note:

Sorry you might not know what I was talking about. 😊

Kate clicks on the link. There is a post against a bright green background. It reads:

> *To be or not to be… an artist*
> *If music be… your thing*

The short and the long of it... want to write a poem,
a short story or the next Harry Potter?
Then you need to know about the MACKL competition.

The what? Kate has never heard of it.
Below this post is:

Just get on with it.
Just do it.
Follow this link NOW!!!

Brief and to the point, Kate grins. She wonders if it does have something to do with Tay in the coffee shop. It is how her teenage girls would have talked to her. All exclamation marks, no proper explanation. 'Mum!!! No brainer!!'

She clicks on the link.

A new text arrives:

What do you think?

Kate quickly types:

Just reading.

The link takes Kate to a website with a very different tone. She switches to her tablet to see better. Professional, but with a definite community feel to it. It depicts photos of artwork of all descriptions, some photography and links to prose pieces and poetry. Images show people of all ages gathered in groups. She quickly gets the answer to what the MACKL competition is.

It seems that Shakespeare wrote rather a lot while in quarantine for the plague: *Macbeth*; *Antony and Cleopatra*; and *King Lear*. Hence MACKL. The competition started when people had similarly been quarantined – this time in lockdown. The idea being that stress and worry could inhibit creativity (she knew that one well) and that this collection of prizes would be an incentive to get people writing or painting – or whatever. Open to pretty much all forms of expression, the clear implication was that it would be something positive to concentrate on and help with mental wellbeing during lockdown.

But why is it still going?

Kate reads on.

Ah, so this is not so much about the competition – which *is* still running – but a community group designed to support people who want to enter the competition.

Her phone rings. 'It is interesting, is it not?' Pia says. She clearly got tired of waiting.

'Yes,' Kate responds, still reading. 'It looks like this group meets every week for eight weeks in the run-up to the deadline for the competition, so people can support each other.'

There's a pause, then Pia adds, 'It says here that they get in experts if someone gets stuck… It seems mainly writing, art and some sculpture.'

'I think there's composing too,' Kate comments, looking at a photo of a young man playing a classical guitar. 'Have you seen the picture of that guy, Sam? He was a runner-up a few years ago.'

'So not an art class. More like a...' Pia then says something Kate cannot understand. 'I'm sorry that is how we refer to this type of community group in Denmark.'

Kate gets sidetracked. 'How long have you lived in England?'

'Since my twenties.'

'You've not been tempted to move back?'

'Sometimes. I did for a few years. Now I spend a lot of my summers at home seeing family...'

So this is not her home.

'...but I really love the English and how you are...'

This makes Kate smile.

'...and now I am spending more time here in Norfolk, I *am* happier.'

Pia says this in rather a forlorn voice and it makes Kate wonder even more about her life.

'I grew up by the sea, so it feels good to be settled here.'

There is a pause. Kate is aware that she is talking to a relative stranger. And vice versa. Nonetheless she leaps in, 'What do you think? Should we join and try and enter something?' Is this the push she needs to start drawing again? Could she try and do an oil painting? And maybe Pia needs something in her life too?

The gurgle of laughter at the end of the phone stops her in her tracks. It is so unlike the sophisticated, slightly hesitant woman she met in the café.

'What is it?' Kate queries.

'Kate, I'm as creative as a *stone*.'

'But you can't be,' Kate blurts.

'Why not?' Pia laughs.

'I'm sorry, I hardly know you. It's just you *look* creative,'

Kate says, grinning. She finds she is imagining Pia as a sculptress, effortlessly stylish in a studio looking out to sea.

The vaguely apologetic tone creeps back into Pia's voice, like she doesn't want to disappoint Kate. 'It is not that I don't appreciate beautiful things, and what others can do. I enjoy visiting art galleries and the ballet. In London and in Denmark. I love that other people can do these things. It is just not me.'

This last sentence is delivered with a firmness that hints again at a steelier side to Pia.

Kate is a bit lost. She realises she would like to join this group and thinks it would be far easier to go with someone. Not that she couldn't go on her own or ask one of her other friends. But she would like to get to know Pia better.

'Is there nothing you've ever fancied doing? I just thought it would be a good chance to meet new people…' Kate leaves that out there. She feels sure she detected a loneliness in Pia, a desire to be part of something. 'Do you draw, or write or… how about pottery?'

Pia's response is despondent. 'Not really.'

'How about music?'

'I play the piano.'

'There you go,' Kate says encouragingly. She wonders if she is being a pain in the arse. Like people who love golf and insist you should love it too.

'*No.*'

There is such finality in the single word that Kate is silenced.

'Look, I'm sorry Kate, that was rude. What would you do?'

'I'd like to try oil painting.' Kate recognises a wistful note in her voice and she wonders if Pia hears it too.

'I can quilt,' she says with resignation. 'Do you think that would do?'

'I'm *sure* it would. My youngest daughter did textile art at uni and she made the most amazing pictures out of embroidery and fabrics for her final exhibition. I've got loads of stuff of hers here, and her sewing machine.'

'She doesn't use them in her work now?' Pia asks. And Kate feels Pia rather wishes she did.

'Ellie's travelling. Has been for the past few years. She's in Patagonia at the moment. I don't think she has plans to come back anytime soon.'

'Do you mind?'

It is a direct question. None of her friends have come out and asked her this. She wants to say 'Yes' and 'No'. But it is too complicated, because the 'No' is so linked with her sister, Alice. And thinking of her brings so much with it, like the storm tide that leaves beautiful driftwood, but also detritus on her shore. So, instead she says, 'Sometimes,' which is sort of true.

There is a pause on the phone and Kate wonders if Pia knows she is prevaricating. She is a lawyer after all.

'What do we do next then?' Pia asks, moving on. Obviously resigned to joining, along with Kate.

Kate grins and scrolls down the page looking for contact details. No mention of Tay.

Pia spots it first. 'It says here to book into the first session, which is next week, we need to email a guy called, Shakespeare: JK Shakespeare. It seems he runs this group.' Kate can hear the smile in Pia's voice as she adds, 'Well, Mr Shakespeare certainly has the right name for this. I wonder if he's a writer.'

Kate hears the answering warmth in her own voice. Maybe it was a sign seeing him in the café? Not that she believes in things like that. But still. 'He taught English at the school my girls went to. I think he's married to... or was married to...' *Why did she add that?* 'An art teacher.'

'Maybe they run it together,' Pia suggests.

Oh, I hope not.

Kate can't stop this last thought.

After the phone call Kate goes to the cupboard under the stairs to unearth Ellie's sewing machine – she is pretty certain she still has it. After bullying Pia into this, it is the least she can do. Peering into the cupboard on her hands and knees, she spots the cream case and as she pulls it towards her a box topples onto the carpet spilling threads, ribbons, embroidered patches and a scattering of sequins. Kate collapses back on her haunches transported to another time.

Alice was ten years older than Kate and left home at seventeen. Alice. Bright as a dragonfly. And just as elusive. They never quite knew when Alice would come to visit – either when Kate was a child or as an adult. Except with Kate's daughters – she had never failed to appear for their birthdays and important dates. Kate picks up some stray sequins and sprinkles them into her open palm. Alice had always been able to sew. Whenever she popped up she would make a bee line for Kate's wardrobe, rummaging and commenting on the good, the bad and the ugly, until she found what she was looking for.

She would then fall on this 'chosen' garment and sitting cross-legged – usually on Kate's bed – she would settle down to chat and sew. She would swap buttons around, add colourful stitching to a collar, even change the lining of a jacket. It did not occur to either of them that Alice should ask Kate's permission. That wasn't how it worked. These transformations were Alice's gift. And Kate loved them. As a child she would find butterflies and birds embroidered somewhere on her jeans; as a teenager Alice's embellishments made her walk that bit taller; even as a middle-aged woman she loved the off-beat style her sister lent her. The clothes Alice sewed would become favourite pieces, and Kate felt as if her sister was with her when she wore them.

'And what would you think of all this, Alice?' she asks aloud, thinking of painting, new friendships and an English teacher called Mr Shakespeare.

All around is silence. Even the wind and water outside are still.

Kate exhales and starts to gather the jumble of haberdashery. She boxes it up and closes the cupboard door on it. As she walks back down the hall, a shaft of sunlight gleams through the glass of her front door catching a lone sequin lying there. It winks at her – an iridescent peacock blue.

Dragonfly bright.

Chapter 6

Bardy

I never knew so young a body with so old a head

Bardy sits on his Ikea sofa staring at the plain walls of his rectangular sitting room and re-runs his morning in Luigi's. He creates different scenarios. Her settling at a table next to him and ordering a cappuccino. Then it's an Americano. His imagination doesn't get beyond that. Instead, he finds himself staring at the sitting room walls wondering why he bought this flat when he and Hana sold the family home. It was about the time Ned was heading off to visit Tom in New Zealand so it was logical to buy something small. But why a box? Easy to keep? Ground floor so if he ever needed to, he could get a wheelchair in? Or a coffin?

The doorbell rings. He immediately thinks delivery rather than visitor. But he's not expecting anything. The only person it might be is Lou. But he always texts first. Bardy does have other friends, mainly ex-teachers, but they tend to meet in the pub. As he heads for the door he glances at his phone. He has some unread emails and realises his phone is set to silent. He has also missed some calls.

Tay stands there.

'Well!' she demands.

'What?' He is bemused on so many fronts. 'Toni?' he demands, suddenly worried,

'Nah. Pissed, but not using. Off with some dickhead.' She dismisses her mother with apparent brutal unconcern. A shard of bright rust. 'Why aren't you answering your fucking phone?'

Bardy had thought since working in customer service Tay was swearing less. Maybe not.

Then he gets it. She was worried when she couldn't get hold of him.

'On silent.'

He is about to apologise but remembers for some reason this really pisses Tay off. And she's angry enough.

'Do that with your large arse?' she demands, pushing past him into the flat.

This fails to hit the mark. Bardy knows in all things he is middling. Neither fat nor thin. In fact thinner since Hana left. Weird when she was so into healthy eating. 'Ah, mate,' he can almost hear Lou say, 'but you do actually have to remember to eat.'

He decides, like the middling man he is, to go for a middle ground. 'No. Just a mistake. But, yeah, stupid thing to do.'

Tay grunts. Which he thinks may be acceptance of his apology that isn't quite an apology. She throws herself on to his sofa. All baggy clothes, big boots, but delicately boned hands, the sight of which snags him somehow. He checks her. Still red ochre. He sits the other end of the sofa to her. 'Get you anything?'

'Yeah. Vodka shot.'

She doesn't drink. Won't take any drugs. Just vapes sometimes.

'What you doing sitting there?' She draws a line with her nailbitten forefinger across the sofa cushion, chipped varnish, bright blue. 'There.'

Suppressing a smile, he budges up to the right space on the sofa. The required distance apart. 'You heard from Hana?' he asks.

She nods but doesn't say anything. And Bardy wishes he hadn't asked. Wants to know. Doesn't want to know. Wants to be sure she is keeping an eye on Tay too, that it isn't all up to him. That feels too heavy a load. The last few texts from Hana have thrown him. They've made him feel even more isolated from her. And telling himself, *it's been five years, mate, of course she's moving on...* well, it didn't help. He knows now he's well and truly on his own. Is that why he wanted Tay working at Lou's? Someone else to have her back? He sees that Tay is watching him. God, she is so young and yet so tough.

'You know you're a mess,' she comments, conversationally.

He glances down at his clothes. Not too bad today. Quite trendy for him. Wilfully misunderstanding her, 'It is what it is,' he responds, parroting one of her favourite sayings.

'Bardy, get a grip!' She's cross. Knows he's being intentionally obtuse. She changes direction. 'Have you checked your emails?' She bounces up from the sofa and wanders into the kitchen where he can hear her rummaging in his fridge. He half glances towards the open kitchen door. This foraging is normal. The eat-when-you-can habit of a feral childhood.

He looks at his phone. There are four emails from people enquiring about the MACKL competition and the group he runs. Except he doesn't run it anymore. Last time he did, not a single person turned up. He remembers the relief. Sinking into the inertia of bingeable Netflix able to say: *well I did try.*

Light dawns and he's up and at the kitchen door. 'Is that what that orange card's about?'

Tay, mouth full of ham, hand grasping a slice of last night's pizza: 'You've got an Instagram account too.'

He thinks she's grinning but it's hard to tell.

'What?!'

'Well, you weren't doing anything,' she says sitting back on the sofa. Boots on, cross-legged. Munching.

'I did,' he says, defensively, staring down at her.

'You're joking me,' she flashes back. She points to his spot on the sofa with the bitten end of the pizza and he collapses into it

'Last year I set it all up and no one came,' he says, lamely.

'Yeah. Just like basketball club.'

He stares at her. She stares back. She twists her head with a funny sort of nod. He knows it well. Point made. Point won. He has to give her that one.

He skim reads the emails. One name he knows. One name he hopes he might get to know. If it is her. Sounds Scandinavian. He brightens. But will there be enough of them? That never worried him in the past.

Flippin' hell! Tay has even set up a new timetable of meetings on his website. How did she do that? How does she know his password? Ah, of course! He may be divorced, but he types

Hana's name several times a week. Won't use autofill. He knew it was a useless password, the same one he's used for years. And one that's easily guessed. *Obviously*.

Boy, he's a sad arse.

'So?' she says, watching him. Wiping her hands on her jeans.

He senses now that she is nervous. Anxious about his reaction. Her knee is bouncing. He looks at her, considering for a moment, then says, 'Thank you, Tay.' She doesn't smile, but he can feel some of the tension leave the small body beside him. The knee stills. Something threatens to tear inside of him. He focuses and adds, '"I never knew so young a body with so old a head".'

She snorts and gets up from the sofa. She never sits still for long. She heads for the door. He expects her to say nothing more, or maybe to cheerfully tell him to piss off. Neither would surprise him. It is only when she is opening the front door that she does say something. '*Merchant of Venice*.' That does surprise him. How the hell did Tay remember that the quote he used was from *The Merchant of Venice*? But then Tay was a remarkable girl.

Red ochre.

He can tell by the way she jubilantly slams the front door that she knows she has scored yet another point.

Basketball club. He had started it at school in the lunch break. First session, only two people came. Tay and a guy… what was his name? Bardy sits on the sofa, his mind reaching into the past. Chad! So just Tay and Chad, who had a basketball player's build and had stood looming over her.

'So, that's it sir? No point is there.' Chad was already looking towards where his mates hung out, regretting having come in the first place.

Tay had just watched Bardy. She had recently arrived at secondary school but Bardy knew her of old. Ever since Toni brought her to the house as a three-year-old; then there was the Christmas placement; and afterwards, visits with or without her mum, Toni. Also, picking Tay up from school, squats. Once from the police station.

'Ah, you don't get off that easy, Chad,' he had told him, thinking of coffee and the marking he could get done in the staffroom. 'We can do some practice passes and shots. Then when others turn up next week, you'll have them beat.' So that is what they had done. Tay quick and crafty on court despite her lack of inches. And others *had* come and eventually they really did have a basketball club.

In the following weeks Bardy had seen Tay watching him. An odd look on her face. Perplexed and considering. Eventually, she had been in the car with him. He can't remember why he was giving her a lift. Staring straight ahead not looking at him, she suddenly asked, 'Why didn't you cancel that first basketball club session? Why not wait until more people came?'

He had been taken off guard, but he knew what to say. And what not to say. He kept staring straight ahead, like Tay, and said, with no great emphasis, but so she had no chance of misunderstanding him.

'If I say I'm going to do something, Tay, I do it.'

She hadn't said anything else, but that evening – they must have been going home to their house, looking after her for the night – she got him to sit on the sofa with her. Close, but not too close. Just where she wanted him.

What he had not said to Tay in the car was that he kept going for the full forty minutes with her and Chad because they had expected him to bail. Say it didn't matter. Let's do it another time. And he knew from teaching and fostering that some kids have had a lifetime of that until they don't expect anything else. Adults not turning up. Not bothering to explain. Full of hot air and promises. Full of shit.

Bardy gets up from the sofa and heads to the kitchen. So now he is going to be running his creative group again. *Thanks for that, Tay.* He finds he means it both genuinely and sarcastically.

And she obviously won't take any excuses for him not keeping at it.

He finds he is grinning as he heads back to the sofa – beer in hand, ready to respond to some emails.

The Merchant of Venice. Who'd have thought.

WEEK 1

Two redshanks step neatly, bills dipping. Orange legs at the edge of the creek, moving in time to the rhythm of feeding. The water flows past carrying the rippling reflection of a spring sky. It is now April. A few hours later the tide will turn and it will return holding the moonlight within it. On a post near the water's edge a solitary redshank calls. The piping whistle part of a growing symphony. It is time to be looking for a mate.

Chapter 7

Kate

Nothing can come of nothing

Kate is waiting to pay. It feels like the café is becoming a second home. Does she keep popping in because she hopes to bump into... Before she gets any further, Mr Shakespeare rushes in and she feels caught out. As if, somehow, he must realise she was looking out for him. Her hand instinctively moves to her chemo-hair, before she stuffs it into her pocket with a self-conscious jerk. She knows from his email that his name is Jon, but she still finds herself thinking of him as 'Mr Shakespeare', and this makes her feel at a double disadvantage.

She glances at him. Is she imagining things or is he looking frazzled too?

He nods distractedly at her. 'Hi, Mrs Oli... Kate... sorry, d'you mind if I push in and have a word with Tay?'

'If you can,' she replies, cryptically.

The couple in front of her have been there for some time.

'Now do you make the tea in a pot?' the elderly man is asking.

'I'll make it any way you like,' Tay responds.

'Well, my wife will have her coffee as she explained, you remember that? Half the water you'd normally add, and only half a shot of coffee...'

Kate wonders how this would be different from just drinking half an Americano.

'...and for me, tea, leaf tea made in a pot, but only half a spoonful of tea...'

'D'you think they're glass half-full or half-empty?' Mr Shakespeare murmurs beside her.

Kate stifles a laugh.

'And the milk...' the elderly man begins.

'Would that be semi-skimmed?' Tay asks blandly.

'No! *Oat* milk! You do have oat milk?' the man demands, flustered.

'Of course. I'll bring it all over.'

As they turn towards their table the elderly woman leans towards Tay. 'I'm sorry to be so fussy, dear.' She drops her voice to a whisper. 'It's my bowels.'

Kate wonders what her husband's excuse is.

Bardy leaps in, 'Tay, did you check the community hall was free when you came up with that timetable?'

Tay looks at him blankly, 'Nice to see you too, Bardy.'

What did she call him?

'Yeah, yeah, but have you booked it? It shows online it's bridge club.'

Ah, that's why he's hassled. Kate can't help feeling foolish.

Tay studies him, 'What's with the trauma dump, Bardy?

I can't do everything, I did the rest.' She turns away to start on the order of half drinks. 'Get a shift on,' she says without looking at him. Then, when he doesn't immediately move, adds, 'Best crack on, Bardy.'

He throws Tay a look of frustration and heads for the door, calling to Kate, 'I'll be in touch. We won't be meeting tonight in the community hall, but leave it with me, I'll find somewhere.'

'What did you call him?' Kate asks.

'Oh, Bardy. You know as in The Bard... Shakespeare. I think Hana came up with that one. Luigi calls him Jon, but he's the only one.' Tay offers Kate the card machine with one hand while loading a tray with the other. 'Unless it's "Mr Shakespeare", or if he catches someone messing about, then it's, "sir".'

Kate would like to ask who Hana is but feels it would be too obvious. 'Did he teach you?' she asks instead.

Tay considers her for a moment, an inscrutable look on her face, 'Yeah, you could say that.'

Kate cycles along the short road that connects the town with the beach. The bank rising to her right has a path on the top of it that looks out over the channel leading to the harbour. She often takes this path when she goes running. To her left is an expanse of heath and pine woodland. In the beach car park there are a few cars – but not many considering it is the school holidays. Mainly walkers making the most of the lighter evenings.

Ahead of her, beyond the beach café, is a large modern building of wood and glass, the rounded roof reminiscent of the lazy swell of the ocean. This is the lifeboat station, and this is where she is heading. The local crew are already out on the water for their weekly exercise, and the large lower door is gaping open like a cavernous mouth. In a town where most people know someone you know, it seems Bardy has persuaded a connection in the RNLI to let him use their training room for their first meeting.

Kate opens the double doors at the top of the stairs and is met by a panoramic view over the beach. The whole end of the room is glass. She has never seen the beach from this height before. Lemon, cream and blue beach huts alternate in a long arc, set against a backdrop of pine trees – liquorice black in the shadow cast by the low-slung sun. It is approaching high tide, and the water washing the wide expanse of sand appears glazed – palest peach and dusky blue, striped with ripples of dark grey. A reflection of the sky above. The steep ladders leading to the beach huts gleam white, and on the shoreline, people and dogs come and go dragging long shadows.

Oh, to be able to paint this.

It is then she notices the figures silhouetted against the scene. Four people standing at the far side of the window. Bardy turns and smiles, beckoning to her.

'Come in, Kate. We've just been admiring the view.'

'It rather takes your breath away,' another person adds, and Kate realises it is the woman from the café, who dreams of hitting her husband with a frying pan.

It seems Leonard is still in one piece.

'Wish I'd brought my bins,' he frets, casting a covetous look at the telescope set up on the other side of the room. 'I'm sure I saw a pallid harrier a moment ago. Almost certain.'

Bardy nods towards the telescope. 'Leonard, you can have a look later.'

It seems Bardy and Leonard already know each other.

'Bins?' Pia queries as she walks towards the long table in the centre of the room.

Kate acknowledges her with a smile and half-wave.

'Binoculars,' the older woman informs Pia, joining her at the table, 'Leonard's a twitcher.'

This does make her husband twitch.

'*Not* a twitcher, a *birder*. I do keep telling you Linda. There is the world of a difference.'

'Oh, is there, dear,' Linda says, vaguely. But from the shadow of a smile Kate is quite sure Linda already knows this.

'Anyway,' Linda continues, smiling, 'we're Leonard and Linda Cowland.' She pauses as she looks at Kate. 'Now, I'm sure we've met before.'

'We chatted briefly in Luigi's,' Kate responds, mouthing silently, 'frying pan'.

Linda laughs. 'Ah, that will be it.'

But for some reason, Kate doesn't think that *is* it. She's sure Linda was thinking of something else.

Kate then introduces herself and Pia follows suit.

Bardy looks up from the table where he has been leafing through some papers. 'Great, you're all getting to know each other. I'm Jon but most people call me Bardy. Please call me whatever you like, except Mr Shakespeare—' he grins '—or "sir".'

Kate can feel the three people beside her relax. So, she wasn't the only one feeling nervous about coming tonight.

Bardy gestures to the table. 'Shall we all take a seat.'

They settle, Pia drawing up a chair next to Kate's.

Pia glances towards the door. 'Is this all of us?' She sounds anxious and Kate hopes she doesn't feel she has been badgered into attending.

Bardy replies, looking more at Kate than Pia as he speaks – which she can't decide is nice or slightly odd. 'Don't worry, Pia, more may come once they know about it. But I think this is a good start.' He continues in the same friendly tone, addressing all of them this time, 'I know I asked you to bring in something that gives a hint of what you would like to do for your entry for the MACKL competition. But we will come to that.' He holds up a hand. 'And please don't worry if you haven't landed on something yet or feel like people will judge you. It won't be like that. This is about giving each other encouragement and being somewhere we can chat ideas or problems through. I can also organise to get some experts in if you think it will help you. Much better than struggling on all alone and then giving up. I entered the first of these competitions during lockdown. Never got anywhere, which didn't surprise me.' He laughs. 'Or anyone else.' He continues more seriously, 'But the hardest bit was doing it on my own...'

What about the art teacher wife?

'...and that's how I came to start this group. First online, and later when we could, meeting up.' He smiles and Kate thinks not only is Mr Shakespeare probably a very good teacher, but that she would have had the most enormous crush on him.

What does she mean, *would have had*?

'So this group is for my benefit as much as yours, and in the past it's turned out to be fun. One of our group, Sam, even got placed for a piece he composed for the guitar.'

He looks at their faces and seems to sense their unease. 'Look, I'm not suggesting you have to be a "Sam" – you may be, who knows. But I can tell you one thing. Life without creativity can feel a lot like just getting by. You know you're doing all the stuff you should, but something's missing. Start to draw or write or make something and things feel more in balance.' He laughs self-consciously. 'Sorry, it's a bit of a bandwagon of mine. And don't get me started on what we teach in schools and how we underestimate creativity. We judge ourselves by how much work we achieve in a day... in our lives. And we measure this on a scale that is getting laid down in the classroom. Anything else is often seen as "wasting time". We don't seem to realise the act of creating is a wonderful and essential end in itself. And that without creativity mankind wouldn't be pushing forward and solving problems.' Bardy is blushing. 'Well, enough to say, I think we all need to embrace our creative side. Look after it, give it time. Let it out to play.'

Kate thinks she may be in love.

Then she wonders if he is thinking of his artist wife.

'And another thing – creativity can take so many forms... writing, music and the arts, obviously, but also cooking, gardening, even conversation...'

Sex.

She's got to get a grip.

'...so why not start here? You've got nothing to lose. I also think one of the benefits of this group is that we often do very different things, so we aren't comparing what we produce with others.'

'Fifteen bunches of bananas,' Linda says, nodding at Bardy.

'Fifteen what?' Leonard demands, looking confused.

Linda carries on, 'I once went to a local art group...' She pauses reflectively. 'Well, if I'm honest, over the years I've tried pretty much everything, sketching, painting, pottery. I once tried to decoupage the whole of our downstairs loo. Thank goodness I knew a good decorator. Anyway, the still life group I tried, well, it made me realise something.'

They all wait expectantly.

'As I was drawing I was looking at my neighbour's bunch of bananas, I mean they were so much better than mine.' She chortles, 'Frankly, mine looked like a severed hand.'

Kate and Bardy laugh.

'But at the end when I looked at the fifteen drawings I was amazed how different they all were.'

'So comparison *could* be a good thing?' Pia suggests.

'I suppose in the broader sense, it was,' Linda says, thoughtfully.

Pia continues, tentatively, 'I didn't mean to interrupt you, Linda. I can see that the direct comparison with another can certainly make you feel inadequate...'

Is this how Pia feels?

'...but if you stand back you might realise there are many ways to see your...' She looks hesitant. 'Your bananas.'

Kate is pretty sure she's not thinking about fruit.

'I don't really see what bananas have got to do with it all. You *did* say bananas?' Leonard queries, loudly.

Bardy jumps in, 'I don't know if that was art or philosophy, but you're right Pia, everyone sees and appreciates things in their own unique way.'

Bardy is looking directly at Pia now.

Aah.

Bardy looks away and Kate isn't sure what she saw – or even what she thinks – but she finds she is now comparing herself to her very beautiful neighbour.

Bardy stands up. 'Look, before we get into what we might have a go at, why don't we get ourselves some coffee.' He nods towards the kitchen which leads off the training room. 'They've got tea and coffee in there and I brought some milk.' He adds, a little doubtfully, 'There's a packet of biscuits on the side. If I'm honest, I don't know how old they are. Garibaldis.'

'Oh, I think we can do better than some soggy garibaldis,' Linda says, reaching into the large canvas bag resting by her chair. She draws out a cake tin. 'Lemon drizzle.'

At this point the double doors at the end of the room swing open. First through the doors is Tay, shortly followed by Luigi.

It may be Kate's imagination, but Luigi seems to be dragging his feet. On the other hand, he has put on a nice cerise sweater for the occasion.

Chapter 8

Bardy

I hope good luck lies in odd numbers

He can't believe Tay got Lou to come. *Or* that she came. When the doors opened and he saw who it was he experienced a wave of rich berry. Or maybe that was Lou's new jumper. It's rare these days that experiences bring a colour – just people – but this was special. He was cheese-grinningly pleased to see them. Ridiculous really. Five was okay. And he likes odd numbers in a group. But seven is better. He can't wait to hear what Lou is going to do.

    He is now closeted with them in the kitchen, bringing them up to speed with what he's covered so far. Which isn't much. The others are enjoying coffee and cake around the table. Most of it had come back to him. The teaching stuff. Only one sticky moment when Pia asked him a question and he ended up talking *at* Kate. But it got easier. And they're all grand, a nice bunch. Interesting what Linda said about the bananas. He hasn't met her before. Of course, Leonard he's known as an acquaintance for years. Worked with him on loads of community projects. During the pandemic Leonard was so busy helping the town that he became known locally as the Lockdown King. But Linda? She's different. And what a truly splendid colour. A pleasure just to be near her.

Lou is moaning as he helps himself to another slice of lemon cake, 'She wouldn't take no for an answer.'

'Not gonna lie, had to be done, Chad. Couldn't let Bardy down.'

'What's with this "Chad" stuff? *Chad* this, *Chad* that… what?' He glares at Bardy, brushing cake crumbs from his cerise jumper. 'What are you laughing about?'

It's Tay who answers. 'Well *Chad*, it is what it is, but thought we'd better come in case no one else did.'

Bardy slaps him on the shoulder, 'It's basketball club all over again.'

Luigi glares from one to the other in confusion and looks like he is about to protest when Pia pops her head around the door. 'I said I would get another slice of cake for Kate,' she says, heading for the counter.

'Yes, yes.' Luigi steps aside to make way, brushing non-existent crumbs from his front.

'Great cake,' Bardy comments, as she cuts a piece.

Is that all he can think of to say?

Pia smiles at them and leaves, Luigi and Bardy watching her retreating back.

Tay looks from one to the other. 'Pia?' she says in wonderment. '*Really?*'

SIX LITTLE WORDS

'What?'
'What?'
A couple of parrots.
Tay laughs. Which Bardy will take. It doesn't happen that often.

'You two are total idiots,' Tay says with obvious relish and heads out to join the others at the table.

Bardy and Luigi exchange a glance. Jon and Lou. Twelve-year-old boys in old men's bodies. 'Nice jumper,' Bardy mutters as they follow Tay.

'It showed what you could do with a bit of organisation. By pulling together...'

Bardy is half listening. He hopes Leonard doesn't know he's zoned out. The man deserves a bit of respect. He turned his electrical company into a hub. Was there for the town. In his element, organising support, making PPE that actually worked.

'How about the logistics?' It's a gift of a question. Least he can do for the Lockdown King.

Leonard is off and Bardy's mind flits between the conversations around the table. Pia and Linda talking beaches. Kate asking Luigi about Tina. Brave? Or just the right thing to do? Tay not talking but Kate's body language including her. Pia joining in with Kate, then talking about Pisa with Lou. Kate, now on Italian food with Linda. He remembers this. A group in free flow chat. So much covered. Tay is up and off to the telescope at the window. Leonard's eye follows her. He seems envious. Anxious. Why *is* Leonard still stuck on lockdown? Most want to forget it.

'No, really Linda! No!'

Bardy's attention shoots back to Leonard. The words had burst from him.

Leonard colours and says more moderately, 'No, no. Not the time or place, dear.'

Linda stares at him in amazement.

'No, sorry for that, folks.' Leonard tries to frown down his bemused wife.

Linda takes a deep breath. Bardy has an image of her cracking her knuckles.

She's deciding: take him on or let it go.

She waits while Kate draws the others' attention to a murmuration of dunlins cascading and careering across the deepening peach sky.

Leonard sees an escape and heads for it. 'Not a murmuration. That term technically only applies to starlings.'

It seems that this decides Linda. 'What was that about Leonard?' she asks, softly. But there's grit mixed in.

Like Kate, Lou and Pia, Bardy's now watching the beach. But ears straining.

'I'm sorry dear. I know with all those years' nursing you are more open than most. But other people...' Leonard's voice fails him.

In the same quiet tone, face close to her husband's, Linda asks, 'What did you think I said to Kate?'

'It's just that you've only just met her...'

'*What* did you think I said?'

'It's personal... not everyone...'

'What?' Just grit this time.

Leonard leans in and whispers something to his wife.

Linda's laugh is explosive and delicious. Bardy thinks it suits her rich, rounded colour. She is still laughing, as shaking her head she grabs hold of Leonard's hand. 'I said "pasta bake" you ridiculous man, not "masturbate".'

A laugh escapes Bardy.

'Quite,' Linda says, catching his eye.

Leonard pulls his hand away, flushing. 'I am not ridiculous.' He sounds hurt.

Linda takes a deep breath and pats his hand. 'I know you're not. But you do need to wear your… hearing aids.'

Bardy can fill in the blank. *Bloody* hearing aids.

He turns and places his hands on the table, making a light patting sound, bringing the attention of the room back to him. Once a teacher, always a teacher. He nods at Tay who re-joins the group. 'Okay, shall we go round the table and talk about what we're thinking of doing for the competition?' Anxiety settles on the circle like a damp sea mist. He knew it would. 'Shall I go first?'

Relief like a Mexican wave.

Every time.

'It won't surprise you to hear, that with a surname like mine, I like to spend my time… painting.' He joins in the laughter. 'No, you're right, it's writing that I have a go at.'

My wife was the artist.

He doesn't want this thought but it does give him purchase. *Dig in, just keep going.*

'I've spent so much time with other people's words. Years of teaching, plus reading pretty much anything I can get my hands on. But I do also write short stories.'

He doesn't mention the poems he composes on his phone. He's not sure what they're all about. Apart from colour. Today's inspired by the distinctive terracotta-red of an old boat sail. The colour of the local RSPB warden, Steve.

'I've never had anything published, and to be honest I gave up trying some years ago. About the same time I knew that even if I never saw a book of mine in print, I would still write.'

Tay says a name. Voice cracking. Like she has a cold. It doesn't matter that he doesn't recognise the name. He knows what it took for her to speak out in front of all these new people. A girl of contrasts: mouthy if she knows you, otherwise shy and monosyllabic. Except, it suddenly occurs to Bardy, in the café. She must be okay at her job too. She's been there well over a year. Still, he can see her nervously flicking her thumbnail against the underside of her finger.

It seems Pia does recognise the name.

'My nephew sent me a link to his music,' she nods, 'he's really good.'

Thank you, Pia.

Tay's voice settles. 'He said he plays because he has to. Making money is just luck.'

The door to the room slams open and a tall woman in a long padded jacket and burgundy suede boots bundles in. She struggles to close the door with one hand, while answering her phone with the other.

Bardy is irrationally angry. Like the woman has shoved Tay.

'I know we said Wednesday, but you are just going to have to change it. Is that so hard to understand!' The woman's braying voice fills the room. And it's a big room. She is now attempting to unzip her jacket with one hand, while holding her phone to her ear with the other. She dumps a bag she is carrying over her arm on the floor. As she dances to shed her coat she glances down at one of her boots, the sole of which is flapping like an open mouth. 'For Christ's sake! Not again!' she cries, waving her foot up and down, making the sole flap some more. 'No! No, I wasn't talking to you,' she barks dismissively before continuing, 'it has to be Thursday so the electrician can be there. Were you not listening to me...' There is a pause and glancing around the circle, Bardy sees all faces are turned towards the woman.

He turns back to the ranting woman and all he sees is acid mustard. It is similar to the colour of the coastal buses. Although he doubts this woman uses public transport. Or is as useful.

'You really don't have a leg to stand on, the project is running late as it is, and quite frankly, what other work you have on is not my problem.' And with this, the woman hangs up.

Her manner changes. A switch. Now among friends. Or perhaps not. Her appraising look sweeps them. Acquaintances. But one up from trade. 'I'm sorry about that,' she proclaims, waving a dismissive hand. She picks up her bag and limps forward, boot sole open-mouthed and flapping. She glances down and gives an exaggerated amused shrug.

'Is this the right place for the MACKL group?'

She's going to mess it up.

He suddenly realises the group are looking to him.

'Yes, this is our first meeting. Were you interested in joining?'

'Yes, I'm an artist. I sculpt. My husband said I should check you out. Thought there was no harm in coming along.'

Bardy can feel the group draw together. Solidarity.

Acid mustard? Really the woman is almost diarrhoea yellow.

He smiles. 'Well take a seat.' He introduces himself and the others. Then pauses.

It takes a while. But she gets there in the end. 'Oh... yes. I'm Tash. What have I missed?'

'We were just going to go round and talk about what we might do for the competition.'

Tash pats the large bag beside her confidently. 'Off you go then.'

Bardy wonders if he could write a short story about a woman who gets eaten by her boot.

Chapter 9

Kate

That which we call a rose
By any other name would smell as sweet

Kate tries to stop herself but she dislikes everything about Tash, right down to the enormous gold tassels on her suede boots. Tash crosses her legs, tassels swinging, boot sole flapping. This does cheer Kate up. She knows how much those boots cost.

She had no idea she could be such a bitch.

Tash waves a finger at them and repeats, 'Well, off you go then.' And Kate wonders if Tash could possibly trip and fall in those boots.

It is Linda who fills the gap.

'Shall I start?'

Most nod, gratefully.

'As I said earlier, I've tried pretty much everything. But I thought I might have a go at writing. Maybe poetry. Shorter than a book. And how hard can it be? These days it doesn't even have to rhyme.'

The group smile along with Linda, who is clearly laughing at herself.

Tash leans forward, 'Oh I think you will find there is a lot more to it than that. Unless of course you're happy producing doggerel.'

'What a good idea.' Linda smiles broadly at her, and Kate knows she is being sarcastic, but wonders if Tash realises this. 'We love our dogs. Thank you, that's a great subject to start with.'

Kate is surprised to catch a mulish look on Leonard's face. He hadn't liked Tash trying to put his wife down.

'Tash, would you like to go next?' Bardy asks.

Tash's phone pings and she shakes her head. Without looking up, she waves her hand at him. 'No, someone else. Got to answer this text.'

'How about you, Leonard?' Bardy suggests.

Leonard nods at Linda and she draws a small, framed picture from her canvas bag and hands it to him. He looks down at it frowning before turning it to show the group. It depicts an estuary at sunset with boats in the foreground. It is clearly an amateurish watercolour, but Kate rather likes it.

'I've done a little bit of painting – watercolours. My brother, now, he's really good. Even sold a couple through a local gallery. I really think I need to give it some proper time. Focus a bit more on it if I'm going to get better. Get as good as him.' He looks around the table. 'You may know of my company Cowland Electrics... although perhaps I should call it by its new name The Cowland Group. I'm no longer involved day to day. Our boys, Ryan and Tim, run it. And well, of course they want to do things differently from their old man, and that's fair enough…'

He seems to lose his thread and Linda, seamlessly picks it up and Kate finds herself wondering if Linda knits, and also, how long this couple have been married. 'With the boys now able to take the load off Leonard, we have more time. We were involved in a big building project but now it's finished we can concentrate on ourselves a bit more.'

Leonard perks up. Baton dropped. New baton safely delivered. 'Yes, we built our own house, just behind the sand dunes near the lighthouse. Wonderful location. Straight out on to the beach. The grandchildren love it. Now that was a project management job—'

'Which builder did you use?' Tash cuts across him, putting her phone down.

Leonard looks taken aback, but names a local firm.

Tash registers a small grimace of disparagement, then turns her attention to his painting. Pursing her lips, she narrows her eyes. Eventually she sighs. 'Have you been to any classes?'

'I'm sorry?' Leonard leans forward.

'*Classes*. Art classes?'

'Well, no. I haven't really had the time.'

Kate's beginning to feel quite sorry for Leonard.

Tash sighs again. 'Where's your focal point?' She doesn't wait for an answer. 'I'm not meaning to be rude…'

Blimey, what's she like if she really tries?

'…but it needs a focus. A focal point. I do think a beginners' art class might help you.'

Bardy coughs and Kate wonders if he is going to say

something to this awful woman. But after looking down at his notes, he glances to his right. 'Lou?'

Kate catches a look pass between them so eloquent of, 'we've got a right one here' that she almost laughs. Then, simultaneously they glance at Tay and in that moment Kate senses they have combined in a common unspoken agreement. She thinks Tash needs to be very careful what she says to Tay.

Luigi, chest and cheeks puffed out, proclaims, 'I've been giving wood turning a bit of a go.'

'*Have you, mate?*' This is clearly news to Bardy. 'Sorry, go on.'

'Yep, well I've set up the gear in the garage and I thought I'd make something rather than just practising with a bit of wood here and there.'

Both men glance at Tash. But she obviously doesn't think Luigi's announcement warrants a comment. Kate sees Luigi relax.

'Tay?' Bardy says, and Kate sees Luigi adjust his position so he has his back to Tay, stomach facing Tash.

Tay raises a hand as if to touch his back, then drops it. But Kate hears a muttered… something… Chad? It might have been 'Thanks'.

Tay then faces Tash. 'Don't know yet. Not decided.' Her head is on one side, eyes boring into Tash's. Kate sees it for what it is – a challenge. Tash looks away first. She doesn't blame her. For all the apparent vulnerability, there is something rock-hard tough about Tay. Kate hears Bardy and Lou exhale.

'So, who's left?' Bardy pushes on, 'Pia?'

Pia speaks with gentle confidence, 'I am not a creative person, but was persuaded to come along by Kate. I have lived in the area for some time but haven't met many people so I thought it would be nice to make some new friends.' She turns to Bardy and smiles.

Kate thinks the man holds up well. But there is no doubt he is melting slightly.

'I thought it was interesting what you, Bardy, said about creativity. I do not think of myself in this way but maybe I concentrate too much on my work and it would be fun to try something new.' She looks around at all of them, 'Or put a new twist on an old family tradition. Our roots are in Denmark and Sweden and the women in our family have always quilted. Nowadays it's all about the "hygge" as you know.' Her smile holds a touch of mischief and Kate thinks this makes this beautiful woman even more attractive. 'It is something I did as a girl and as a young woman. Now as an older woman I thought maybe it would be nice to make my Norfolk version of a Danish quilt.'

'How lovely,' Linda comments.

It seems Bardy can't actually speak.

Kate's heart sinks. Ah, well. It had been a nice daydream.

'Can you actually make a quilt for this competition?' Tash asks, getting out her phone and scrolling through the rules and regulations. 'Seems a bit arts-crafty to me.'

'I think you can pretty much do what you like. What had you in mind, Tash?' Bardy asks.

She puts her phone down and pulls her bag on to her lap. She pauses, self-importantly. 'I'm an artist by training. I guess it's always been in my blood. I started in acrylics but that medium didn't really satisfy me. Not "hands on" or "hands in" enough for me.'

Kate wonders how often she has used this phrase.

'So I turned to sculpture. And it felt like coming home.' With great reverence Tash reveals the bronze sculpture of a dog's head. It is a pug.

Kate thinks it looks mighty pissed off.

There is silence around the room.

'Very lifelike,' Linda starts.

'Yes, a proper work of art,' Leonard says, once again following his wife's lead.

Kate thinks what nice people they are. 'You could get Noy done,' she suggests, turning to Pia.

Pia looks at her with something like horror combined with confusion. She nods slightly.

She doesn't know if I'm joking.

Kate gives the tiniest of winks and she sees Pia's face relax into a grin.

'Um, Tash,' Bardy says, tentatively. 'Do you sell these?'

'Of course. My pugs are very much sought after and I have just had a commission for a Crufts best in breed bulldog.'

'Tash, you do know the MACKL competition is just for novices. People who've never sold any work. It's really for amateurs, mainly beginners.'

'No it's not,' Tash counters.

'Er, it is. I hate to tell you,' Bardy says. He adds, 'I'm really sorry.'

Pia whispers to Kate, 'He does not sound very sorry.'

Kate doesn't answer. She is staring in horror at Tash who is now flicking through her phone. 'Oh for pity's sake!' She stops scrolling and starts reading. 'Could you have made the text any smaller!' She glares at Bardy. 'What a total waste of an evening.' Tash stands up and, covering up her pug, picks up her bag, 'If you had made that clear I would never have come. There are hundreds, and I mean *hundreds* of other things I need to do.' Her bag bangs into Luigi's chair as she turns and strides to the door. All eyes watch her as she struggles back into her coat, muttering, 'Six hundred pounds for a pair of boots and they don't last a bloody month.'

All but one pair of eyes. Kate is staring ahead of her at a spot a few centimetres from her nose. What the hell is she going to do? She hadn't read that part about the competition either. All she had seen was a creative competition that encouraged people.

She didn't realise it was targeting beginners. What is she going to say? To stand up now would be like aligning herself with Tash and that is the last thing she wants. By now Tash is at the door muttering, 'I should have known! Dog poetry, cutesy quilts, wood turning, sunset watercolours...' The last thing they hear as the door slams behind her is, 'It's just so *bloody* amateurish.'

'Well, dear, we all are amateurs. That's rather the point,' Linda comments to the closed door, as relief and laughter sweep around the table. Even Tay smiles.

But Kate isn't laughing. She knows she shouldn't be here either. She should be heading down the stairs after Tash.

For she is certainly no amateur.

She is JoJo Rose.

Chapter 10

Bardy

The mellow plum

Brilliant! Back to the seven of them. This is going to work.

'Kate?' Bardy prompts. He's guessing art. But you never know. Maybe textile art, like her daughter Ellie. If that's what she did at uni. He can't quite remember.

'Kate?' Bardy repeats. The woman seems miles away, looking out to sea.

It *is* the most amazing spot. Moon now out above the water.

'Sorry. I was just…' She looks around at them, frowning.

Something's upset her. Surely she can't have liked Tash? Maybe she's a friend? No. Not a chance.

'Sorry. I was thinking… would it matter… I mean do people ever just come along, but don't enter the competition?'

He would never have expected her to be this nervous. Then a warning blares in his head. Maybe she's not over the cancer?

Does she have more treatment lined up? Or, worse than that… Bardy's insides lurch.

'Kate, you do whatever you want. Just come when you can manage it. If you can't finish whatever it is you're thinking of, it's okay.'

Except it might not be.

She is now looking totally perplexed. 'If I can get started I expect I can finish it. That's not really the…' Light seems to dawn. 'Oh! I see… no, I'm fine. *Really* I am.' She appears keen to reassure them all.

Bardy sees Linda pat Kate's arm and relief sweeps over him. He has an image of Kate chatting to Lou about Tina.

Kate looks around at them. 'The thing is, I've always wanted to have a go at oil painting.' She reaches into her bag and pulls out her tablet. She flips it around to show them. 'This is the view from my cottage. It looks out over the creek, just beyond the quay and I'd really like to paint something of what I see each day.'

He must have walked past her house dozens of times. There is a murmur of approval from around the table. 'Lovely spot,' Lou comments.

Kate sweeps through a series of photos, light changing as it does in Bardy's memory. The bleak muted colours of a marsh in winter. Then, a saltmarsh spring, strokes of sage-green in the distance, yellow gorse in the foreground. Next, summer sun bleaching the sand, below a blue-white expanse of sky. Finally, a sunset marshland at full tide. Land submerged, a huge expanse of water, the merging of pink and orange. Clouds low, floating on the surface, and the creek reaching up to make watermarks in the sky.

Kate returns to her screen saver, another photo of the creek. Early morning light over a mid-tide, the passage of the creek still visible, but broad. Red rowing boat, glint of an oar breaking the surface. In the distance two dots. Seals? Swimmers?

Kate studies this for some moments then smiles even more brightly around at them, eyes glistening, and Bardy wants to… what? Reach out a hand to her?

Linda: 'You'll do it, I'm sure.'

Pia, softly: 'I will quilt and you will paint.'

Their words are an embrace.

How do women know? How do they do this? It's like a secret club.

Lou raises uncomprehending eyebrows at him. Leonard is frowning at his watercolour painting. Probably looking for a focal point. Not even aware of what's happening.

And what *is* going on?

Bardy has absolutely no idea.

Everyone has left and Bardy stands at the apex where the channel leading to the harbour meets the wash towards the beach. Cold wind in his face. The lifeboat station is to his left – a mass of dark slatted wood with sightless glass eyes. The moon above the water has turned his world monochrome. Hana had told him this is how the old masters used to paint. Creating a tonal world before adding the wash of colour. The colour will come with the sunrise, but for now he is standing in a world stripped bare, eyes flicking between the glimmering sea and the blinking lights of the small dredgers and boats moored to the pontoon below him. Were he to turn, he knows the town will be lying in layers against the same sky, sprinkled with softer lights, evoking the warmth of terracotta and cream. A world of cottages, pubs, shops and fishing boats. Living and breathing. For now he wants to stay where the wind talks to the waves of a width and breath of existence that moves with the cycle of the moon and of migration. The expanse of it awes him but at the same time offers the relief that he is just one alone in the wind. And that maybe it is better to enjoy the lift of the air than to imagine that he can make any impression on that huge sky. Better to focus on the small stuff. Rather than to believe he is in control of the whole.

He revisits the evening.

He still has no idea what Tay is going to do. But that will work itself out. Sometimes he thinks she has life plotted so much better than him. Then at other times... He can't shake the feeling he has got something wrong. He is glad Lou was there – the wood turner – stomach out. As un-Chad-like as it is possible to be. Solid. The others were solid too. He feels something has come together, though he isn't sure where the pieces fit yet. Kate? Maybe this would help with what troubles her. It has happened before. Sam, the guitarist, before and after. A different boy. Leonard? Why did he slot in so neatly behind that thought. Troubled too? The Lockdown King without a kingdom. Who didn't like his brother painting better than him. Brothers! He has some experience of that one.

Pasta bake.

Bardy's grunt of laughter emerges to sit for a while with his thoughts, then sinks beneath the sound of waves, wind and the creaking of wood.

Leonard does have Linda on his side. He decides Leonard should be okay. He is a lucky man. No colour floods Bardy's mind when he looks at Leonard. But when he looks at Linda… boy, what a rich and wonderful colour. She had stood by the window looking out towards the beach and even against that immense backdrop her colour had shone, full and rounded.

Occasionally Bardy finds it difficult to define a colour, unable to pin it down with descriptors. This had been particularly so in his inexperienced teens, but as his strange synaesthesia settled into him, he started to read more, look about him more. Visit galleries, take an interest in paints and pigments. What a language they had revealed. And Hana had helped him. She had the natural eye of an artist. But still there are times when even the words he loves fail him.

However, with Linda it's easy. For Bardy, Linda is mellow plum. Just like the fruit. A proper plump purple. He detects the merest hint of an underlying green, a bygone colour from a younger girl. But these days, overlying all of that glorious purple is a bloom, making the colour, dusky, just like the fruit. In the fruit the bloom is a protection against bacteria. Bardy suspects Linda has developed her own protection over the years. He recalls Leonard saying she was a nurse. Maybe she has had to grow a second skin.

Bardy can also see that Linda is a Smiler.

During teacher training, his first head, Mrs Ovenden, had said, 'Look for the Smiler.' She had then added, 'But don't rely on them.' He had no idea at the time what she was talking about. Forty years on, he gets it. And there is no doubt in his mind, Linda would have been a Smiler. That one child in a class who is looking at you with eager anticipation, willing you to get everyone on board. Keen to raise a hand. Mrs Ovenden had warned him, 'Don't always turn to them. They don't represent the measure of what everyone knows. And don't ignore the tricky ones…' The 'Tays' of this world, he thinks. 'That is just what the tricky ones are expecting. They know that no one cares. Are certain that not a soul believes they can do better.'

'What you are trying to do,' Mrs Ovenden had confided, 'is to make *those* children believe they *can* do more.' It was the days of being able to call a student a child. 'And if you are really lucky you will create a few more Smilers along the way. Not a lot, mind you, but a few.'

That wise woman had been right. He had tried not to lean on the Smilers in the class. But on a really bad day, it was sometimes the Smiler that got him through. Willing him to succeed. Ellie Oliver had been a Smiler. Kate's youngest. That girl had no idea how she had helped him.

Was it bad with Hana even back then? That would have been about seven years ago now. A couple of years before she left. Had he been floundering even then? Knowing he was getting so much wrong with Hana, but unsure how to change or even what he was doing that made her turn away from him. Trying to catch a colour within his hands, to grasp it and hold it. When he knew full well it only existed as a gleam in his mind. He thinks on some days Ellie Oliver saved him from going under. Especially when his dad died and he had no idea how to be, how to grieve. Feeling a disappointment as a son in death, as well as in life.

His father had been a bank manager. He had half-imagined

having, *'In the days when being a bank manager meant something'* inscribed on his grave. It had been his mum's favourite refrain until she died of heart failure three years before her husband. During those three years, Bardy had made a point of regularly visiting his dad, along with his brother, Richard. Richard was an accountant, the financial director of a nationwide group of solicitors. If Richard were away skiing or playing golf, Bardy still suggested he visit alone, but his father's inevitable response was:

'Not much point. Wait until Richard's back.'

He remembers when they started fostering, his father had been scathing.

'If you needed more money you should have chosen a different job, trained for a *profession*.' He didn't need to add, 'Like your brother.'

Bardy knew there was no point in saying that he rather thought teaching was a profession, or that they didn't do it for the money, or even that most of the cash was spent on food and the extras they needed. He sometimes thought if they did need more money he could take up driving a cab. He had navigated his way to most places in the county, and beyond, accompanying their foster kids to visit social services; case officers; education services; doctors and hospitals; mental health workers; estranged family members; and occasionally to the police and the courts.

But when his dad died of complications following routine surgery on his knee he had been disorientated by the grief and the sense of never having said what he really wanted to. Any hopes he had that his father's death might bring him and Richard closer were short-lived. His father had made his brother sole executor of his small estate and Richard had left the funeral tea early, dodging what Bardy had known was an awkward attempt at an embrace. Fending him off with a formal handshake, Richard told him he would email him in due course.

During the following weeks Bardy relied on Kate's daughter, Ellie, the Smiler, more than he should have done. Although he is certain she had no idea how her optimism and general 'fuck-it-let's-do-this' attitude had helped him. He hopes he never needs Linda in that way.

And Pia? The woman with no colour.

Oh, how Lou would laugh at him.

The man in the cerise jumper.

This makes him feel better.

Another thought lifts him. But it brings with it an after wash very close to terror.

Before she left tonight, Pia agreed to meet him for coffee.

Chapter 11

Kate

When shall we three meet again

From where she is sitting in the window seat at the front of her cottage, Kate can see her small bit of garden and the path on the right running down to the gate. She eases her position. Today her scar is sore, itchy. Sometimes it will be the wrong choice of clothes rubbing her. Sometimes she just wakes up this way. A reminder of what was and a nudge into the anxiety that at times lies dormant, but never really goes.

Over the wall to the left she can glimpse her neighbour's garden, identical in size and shape to her own, except there is no small patch of lawn, just slate-coloured stones – easy for upkeep. Her neighbours are a young family from Ely and use their cottage for holidays and occasional weekends. She has to admit she likes it this way and is grateful they don't rent their house out very often. Her neighbours are pleasant, friendly people, but she prefers it when she is bordered by an empty house on one side, with fields on the other. It makes her own home seem larger somehow, like it can breathe out.

It's been three days since the meeting at the lifeboat station, and when she hasn't been occupied with the year-end figures for the furniture company, she has been dwelling on a single thought. Should she tell the group that she is JoJo Rose? She had messaged the girls on their WhatsApp group and asked their advice. Jess had said tell the truth – always a painfully honest child. Bella had said no, it was no one's business. The private one. And Ellie had said it was up to her and did Kate know there were penguins in Patagonia. Their responses aligned with what she knew of her daughters and had made her smile, but she was still left wondering what to do.

Her gaze follows the border of blue borage and white comfrey that runs down the side of her garden. Beside it is a small square of grass, left to grow long, with a procession of snowdrops, crocuses, and now primroses and bluebells. She looks beyond the garden to the brick and flint wall at the front and the triangle of path she can spy through the gate. She cannot see much more of the path from where she is sitting but she knows every inch of it. She knows the drop too, beyond it, down onto the creek. She can imagine the lurch in her knees as if she were making the jump – too big to be called a step, too shallow to be a wall to sit upon. She thinks of Pia, living down the coast where the shingle bank sweeps in a broad arc, protecting the lowlands from the sea.

Maybe she could talk to Pia? Explain about JoJo Rose. They are meeting for coffee later. Would she have heard of her though? Was she living here back then or was she still in Denmark? Kate knows she is being ridiculous. She should just come out and say it. Is it because of Alice? She glances down at her tablet on the seat beside her. You can barely make out the two dots in the creek. But it is as if she can feel the chill of the water, goosepimpling her skin. She rarely swims now. She tells herself it is not safe on her own. But she knows it is because she no longer swims with the person who she most loved swimming with, her sister.

The sister who Kate still feels let her down.

She stares once more at the image of the creek. Sky reflecting water.

A mirror.

But didn't she let Alice down too?

Kate opens the door to the art gallery coffee shop. She spots her at a table by the window.

Pia is with Bardy.

Does Bardy look surprised too? She is glad she thought about what to wear. Well she had to, knowing Pia was sure to be dressed in beautiful neutral colours, looking effortlessly stylish – which she is. Kate is also grateful she decided to walk not cycle. No helmet hair. Chocolate-brown trousers, tweed jacket with nipped in waist with kingfisher cuffs. Contrasting purple buttons care of Alice. They both half rise.

To kiss or not to kiss? That is the question.

Pia hugs, no kiss. Bardy does neither.

What is he doing here?

Well, there is certainly no way she is going to talk about JoJo Rose now. She is already feeling at a disadvantage. Smiling like this is all great fun.

As they sort out their orders Kate mentally shakes herself. This *could* be fun. She likes both these people. So, she had a five-minute 'what if' moment with Bardy. No one knows. She hasn't made a fool of herself. She likes the man. Anyway, he is probably still married to the art teacher.

'Bardy suggested meeting for coffee and I thought it would be lovely if you could join us,' Pia says. 'I hope that was okay?' she adds, tentatively.

'Of course,' Kate and Bardy chorus.

Do they both sound too hearty?

Pia turns to Bardy. 'I imagine you know many people in the town. Perhaps you have taught a lot of them?'

'Oh, a fair few,' Bardy agrees.

'Did you already know Leonard?' Kate asks, intrigued.

'The Lockdown King. For sure.'

'What did you call him?' Pia queries, looking up from her cappuccino.

Bardy repeats it. 'Leonard came into his own in lockdown. I knew him before, I mean he's one of the biggest employers around here and so we had kids going there for work experience. And he's always been a supporter of community projects. But he really was amazing when it all kicked off. He organised fundraising, distribution of stuff, checked in on people who were on their own and made PPE in the factory.'

'I imagine he was well paid for that,' Pia suggests, and Kate reminds herself she is a hard-nosed lawyer.

Bardy is silent for a moment, before saying. 'Yeah, he probably was, but I do know he made a massive donation to the town's funds when it was all over.'

'How do you know that?' Pia asks.

'You can't keep much quiet around here. Look. I know it's just gossip, but my mate on the council hinted that Leonard didn't feel he should profit from it all when so many had had a tough time. But he didn't want it generally known.'

'I'm looking at Leonard in a new light,' Kate remarks. She grins.

'What?' Pia and Bardy demand.

'Pasta bake,' Kate replies.

'I didn't know if you'd overheard that too,' Bardy laughs.

'Oh, yes.' Pia and Kate both grin.

'More coffee?' Kate asks.

'Yes please, and they look like they have some nice blueberry flapjacks,' Pia suggests, hopefully.

'Sounds good.' Bardy begins to rise.

'You're okay, I'll get this,' Kate says and goes to place their order.

This is good. Remarkably easy. But she wonders why Pia didn't suggest meeting at Luigi's. Or was it Bardy's idea? But it *is* a nice spot overlooking the park surrounded by art. Maybe that's why they chose it.

When she gets back to the table, Pia is telling Bardy about her work in lockdown. It seems she had been working from home in London.

'You weren't tempted to come here?' Kate asks, as Bardy helps her unload the tray.

'I was with someone back then, and they... well, they were all about London. I didn't spend so much time here.' Pia is back to sounding forlorn. 'But as it was I was often alone. And then, well... then it ended.'

'I was on my own too,' Bardy blurts. He glances at one of the paintings on the wall. A bright golden sunflower. 'My wife was an art teacher. When lockdown came she left and went home to her family in Wales. Well, half her family. She's originally from New Zealand but her mother was widowed when Hana was young and she eventually married a Welsh sheep farmer. As you do.' Bardy tries to smile.

This makes Kate say, 'My husband left me for a woman half his age. He's in California now.' She adds, 'Living it large.' Word is Dougie has recently put on a lot of weight and had a Māori symbol tattooed on his calf. She knows of these details thanks to Bella who is doing a stint as a physio with a women's soccer team in the US. Bella, while loyal to her father in a vague kind of way, feeds Kate titbits she thinks she might enjoy.

Bardy doesn't smile.

Oh, this is not a man who is over his wife.

'I am sorry,' Pia says and touches his hand.

Bardy jumps.

He may not be over his wife, but this man has got it bad.

'Were you teaching during lockdown?' Kate asks to get away from exes.

'I'd just retired. The government wrote to teachers trying to get them to go back to work, but I figured I'd done my bit. But I guess I felt guilty, so I did a lot of volunteering. Collecting prescriptions, doing people's shopping. It's how I got to see what Leonard did.'

'You sound like you quite enjoyed it,' Pia observes, astutely.

'To start with I was a total mess. And Lou and I…'

Kate wonders what it is that he almost said. She glances at him enquiringly. Something to do with lockdown?

But Bardy just coughs self-consciously, and after a pause continues, 'Anyway, my eldest son Tom was in New Zealand, but then Ned my youngest son came back home and it wasn't so bad. He's a great cook. We did a bit of gaming, watched crap TV. Built a shed. And a pond. And a mammoth barbeque. Yeah it wasn't too bad.'

'Did you write?' Kate asks. 'Short stories?'

He glances at her, and Kate thinks he is pleased she remembered.

He shakes his head. 'No. You'd think I would have had loads of time. But I just couldn't seem to get started. I don't know if that was the stress everyone was under, or Hana…' His voice trails off.

Kate wants to say, 'Stress will do that to you.' But she doesn't want to go there.

'What about you, Kate? Were you busy during lockdown?' Pia asks.

A rush of memories threatens to topple her. It seemed during that time she was either cramming in everything: life, treatment and combating her daughters' fears; or she had periods of nothing, just sickness and her own fear. Times when she let the girls take over. Then there were the hours filled with thoughts of Alice. She thinks of that time as cave black. The darkness you experience when there really is no light.

'I was diagnosed with breast cancer…'

Pia reaches out her hand, this time to Kate.

It looks like Bardy is going to do the same, but he starts to fiddle with a paper serviette instead.

'It was... do you know, I think I'd rather not go there.'

Kate glances at them. Both nod. Their lack of embarrassment makes her go on. 'It was the worst time of my life. But my daughters and friends were unbelievable. They got me through. And the NHS was brilliant.' She looks from one to the other. 'But because of COVID there were times when it was very lonely. And frightening. There was one particular hospital visit that no one else was allowed to attend. It was about how the treatment was going.' Kate takes a deep breath. 'The first medication made me really sick and it hadn't done what they wanted it to. The staff were amazing, so in some ways I felt selfish – that I was being looked after. But my daughters were all on their own...'

With an absent, totally shit father. That was when she found it in herself to really hate Doug.

She sees them watching her. 'Anyway, they adapted the meds and though I lost my hair, this time it worked. And today I just feel so lucky and I'm all clear and have been for a few years now, and I think maybe...'

Pia suggests, 'Maybe now is the time?' It is said with a gentle lilt and Kate feels something settle within her.

'I think this could be a good time for all of us. The writer,' Pia nods at Bardy, 'the artist. And the woman who is creative as a stone, but who can quilt.' She looks towards the gallery, then turns back, 'I don't know,' she muses, 'maybe I will think of something else.'

Kate thinks Bardy is going to say something when someone raps loudly on the window beside them.

A middle-aged woman with curly hair, wearing a knitted jacket in purple and pink, is waving at Pia.

'Ah, hello Brenda,' Pia mouths, giving her a small wave.

'There's Noy,' Kate spots.

'Yes, Brenda's my neighbour. She's very good about having him.' Pia looks around. 'I wasn't sure if they let dogs in here, especially with it being school holidays, and busy.'

The woman outside the window is giving Pia a thumbs up sign. 'All's well with Noy Boy. We've been for a lovely walk,' she shouts.

'Thanks a lot, Brenda,' Pia mouths back.

Brenda lurches forward and picks up the whippet, who looks bored but resigned. Brenda has him around the stomach and is waving his legs in the air. Noy appears to have them locked forward like a dog skating on ice. 'Say hello to Mummy,' Brenda booms.

A few people in the café turn to look.

Pia starts to get up. 'Brenda, shall I take him now?'

'No, no. Noy Boy and I are having fun. You have your coffee.'

Brenda grabs one of Noy's paws trying to wave it, still straight legged, at Pia, 'Wave to Mummy!'

Bardy says in Kate's ear. 'Does that look like a fascist salute to you?'

Brenda has now put Noy back on the ground. 'See you at my house later,' she calls and turning she starts to bound across the park, Noy now happily running by her side.

Pia sinks into her chair. 'Brenda is very good.' She looks pained, 'But she is…'

Pia can't seem to finish.

'A Nazi?' Bardy suggests.

Kate nearly spits out her coffee.

Chapter 12

Bardy

Thou shouldst not have been old till thou hadst been wise

Why does he feel like he's in a Shakespearean play?

Coffee had been good. He hadn't expected Kate. At first he was thrown. Hoping to get close to Pia? Yeah, the woman he could barely talk to. But actually, having Kate there had worked. God, what a shit time she'd had. Brave woman.

Still, in the end, being together had worked.

Then why does he keep coming back to the three of them and thinking it is like something he's taught?

He is now on his way to see Lou. Had suggested they meet at his house as it's Lou's day off. They would normally go to the pub or for a walk. Or both. But Bardy wants to see Lou's garage. Can't help feeling his mate has been holding out on him. Lou the wood turner.

Lou answers the door wearing a pink spotty pinny. One of Tina's. But no cerise jumper. Normal checked shirt. His hands are black. He catches Bardy looking at them. 'I've been having a go at the silver,' he explains, leading the way down the hall to the kitchen. Theirs is an Edwardian house, long and thin. Enough bedrooms for their two kids, Gina and Mark. Long gone now, Paris and London. Bardy wonders if Lou will ever sell. Maybe buy a box like him. No. He won't change a thing. Just like the café.

The silverware is laid out on the kitchen table. Photo frames, vases, platters. Mainly family gifts for their silver wedding anniversary. Lou stands looking down at them. '*Oh, fuck it!* That will have to do.'

Bardy isn't fooled into thinking he is swearing because of the cleaning.

Nearly five years since Tina died. Six months before Hana left. They hadn't been close, the two women, but maybe her dying had made Hana think. You only get one shot at this.

'Coffee?' Lou asks from beside the kettle, ready to fill the coffee pot on the stove. Bardy can hear Lou's dad saying, 'Always use boiling water.' Long dead now. But Lou and Bardy still following his instructions. Well, he was Mafia, wasn't he. Bardy smiles.

'What you grinning at?' Lou demands.

'Thinking about your old man.'

Lou nods. 'He was okay, my dad.'

'For someone in the Mafia.'

Lou snorts. 'Can't believe you bought that one.'

'We all did. You were a scary bugger even back then.'

'Yeah, right.' Lou – big stomach, nearly bald, in a pink pinny – scoffs.

But Bardy thinks his friend carries it well. Like... what was his name... Clemenza in *The Godfather*.

They don't ever really talk about Bardy's dad. Only the once, Lou had said – not looking at him – 'Hard man, your dad.' Bardy's not sure he even replied. Grunted probably. But it was enough. An acknowledgement from the Mafia that Bardy hadn't had it easy. No abuse. Nothing like that. But maybe that's why he took to the oddballs that he taught and fostered. Knowing you don't always fit.

'Come on then, let's see this garage of yours,' Bardy demands.

Ten minutes later they are sitting on plastic-latticed beach chairs surrounded by shavings and old bits of wood, finishing their coffee. Lou has shown Bardy his lathe, his band saw and the work bench, and explained the range of gouges he has suspended on the walls in order of size. Bardy is impressed and something else. Lou kept mentioning the guys down the wood mill, Tony and Jakub, who were helping him. Is he jealous? Does he feel left out? But then hadn't he been a bit of a misery lately? Staying in, feeling sorry for himself?

'Fancy a beer?' Lou asks, nodding at the ancient fridge in the corner.

'Does Dolly Parton sleep on her back?' is Bardy's instant response. Always makes Lou laugh. Good to share a drink and laugh with your best mate. Bet Lou doesn't do that with Tony and Jakub.

His chair creaks as Lou sits back down, handing Bardy a cold bottle.

They sit for a while in silence glugging their beers.

'I had coffee with Pia and Kate today,' Bardy says, suddenly glad Kate was there too. Less likely Lou would take the mick.

'Was Tay okay?'

Ah, how to say this... 'Oh, we went to the gallery by the park.'

'Oh.'

'Pia's idea.'

Why is he lying? He hadn't wanted to go to Luigi's. Had forgotten it was Lou's day off. Didn't want to be watched by the man who sucked his stomach in for the beautiful Dane.

A pause.

'Not true.' Bardy shifts in his seat. God, is this thing going to collapse? 'Thought you'd take the piss.'

Bardy can feel his friend relax as Lou laughs. Maybe Tony and Jakub aren't that bad. Might be good to meet them.

'What did you talk about?' Lou asks.

'Lots of stuff. Lockdown, funnily enough.'

'Can't see those two as rule breakers. As rebels,' Lou observes. He hurries on, looking worried. 'You didn't tell them though? About...'

Bardy shakes his head. 'Code of omertà, mate.'

Lou puffs out a breath, 'Not so bad now when you think about it. After what all those bastards did. Partying and the like.'

'Kate had to go through chemo around then.'

'She okay?'

'Seems to be.'

'That's good.' Lou nods. He has a tear in his eye, which Bardy ignores. 'That's good,' Lou repeats.

'What we did wasn't so bad,' Bardy tells him.

'No. But best not say,' Lou says, firmly.

The plastic beach chairs creak beneath them. The same chairs they took down to the riverbank at 4am some mornings during lockdown, to share a few beers and chat. Somewhere no one could see them. Two lonely, broken-hearted rebels.

'You know she's out of our league, mate?' Lou sighs.

'Who? Pia?' Bardy returns to the present.

'Yeah, you and I are idiots, we wouldn't get a look in. She'll be with some tall, good-looking type. Property developer or banker.'

'She's not...' What's he trying to say? Not pretentious. Gentle. Very direct sometimes. A funny mix. Was that her being Danish? He has no idea.

'She's not what?' Lou prompts.

'Not Hana.'

Where did that come from?

A longer pause. More beer slugging.

Lou talks at his bottle. 'Thought you were getting better. But recently... I don't know mate.'

Nor does Bardy.

'You going to tell me? Or just keep acting the bollox.'

Bardy remembers sitting in Lou's café wondering *what's the point*. That certainly hadn't got him anywhere. So he says it.

'Hana's moving to New Zealand.'

He relives the shock and hopelessness he felt when he'd read those text messages. Hana had been living in Wales for some time now, but she always came back a few times a year, to see their old foster kids, and he hopes, to check up on him.

'Oh mate.'

They sit in silence. Then Lou prises himself from the chair and gets a couple more beers from the fridge. Eventually Lou asks, 'And Ned?'

'Going to stay there. Met this woman. Friend of Tom's.'

'Serious then?'

'Seems so.'

'I always thought you might...'

'Yeah. Me too. Was looking at a place...'

'They living near each other? Tom and Ned?'

'Same town. Just outside of Auckland.'

'And was the place you were looking at...'

'Yep, nearby.'

'And the lads knew?'

'No, hadn't really told them, well not, *told them, told them*. Just talked vaguely. Wanted to get a few things sorted.' Bardy had thought they had got the drift. He'd always been solid with his sons, even after the split. But now he wonders if they had any idea of what he'd been hinting at.

'And Hana?'

'Yeah. Same area. Look, I get it. It's where she grew up. Wants to be near the boys.'

'Couldn't you still go?' Lou answers his own question. 'Nah, that's not going to work.'

'Maybe for a visit. Yes, definitely for a visit. But living next door to Hana? Always bumping into her? Not a hope. And what would she think? Me following her to New Zealand? Nope. Best move on. About time.'

Lou nods consolingly.

'It's her home, not mine,' Bardy declares, 'I'd be like a bloody cuckoo.'

'Don't you mean kookaburra?'

Bardy snorts. 'You're thinking of a kiwi, mate.'

He can sense rather than see Lou's grin.

'No, gotta move on,' Bardy repeats, wondering who he is trying to convince.

'And you thought maybe, Pia?'

Bardy thinks it's good of Lou to pretend he stands a chance.

'What d'you think?' Bardy replies.

They look at each other and start to laugh. Ten-year-old boys, cracking up at a joke. Not two old men in danger of putting their arses through plastic beach chairs.

They have moved on from the beers and decided to get something to eat. Indian or Thai, maybe fish and chips. Lou says, anything except Italian.

As they walk into town, Lou remarks, 'Not sure everything's okay with Tay.'

'What do you mean?' Bardy, anxious.

'The women who she works with.'

'At the call centre?'

'It's a bit more than that mate. She's doing well. Been promoted to a team away from the phones.'

Why doesn't he know this? He really has been self-obsessed. Perhaps it's a good thing Tay set up the creative group for him. Now he feels even worse. She has been looking out for him, and he has been letting her down.

'What about the women?' Bardy asks, as they turn into the High Street.

Lou pauses in front of a Thai restaurant, and Bardy nods his assent. Lou opens the door and they wait behind some other couples looking for tables. Lou continues, 'They're all a lot older than her. Middle-aged and I think they treat her like she's one of their kids.'

'She won't like that.'

Lou looks thoughtful. 'Do you know what, I think to start with she did like it. They made a fuss of her.'

Why did it work so well with Hana then? Not a fuss maker. But interested in Tay. And all the others. Gave them space, just to be. Is that what Hana had needed? More space? Bardy realises Lou is waiting. Needs a prompt.

'But now?'

'I guess she's finding out what it can be like to be one of their kids. Bossing her a bit. Not really listening...'

Bardy consoles himself: he does listen.

'Are you listening mate? You seem miles away.'

Bardy turns a laugh into a cough. 'And...?'

'I don't know if there's much more to say. I just think maybe she's upset about something.'

'Oh.'

Bardy doesn't know what to do with this. He should have known, shouldn't he? But it's not too late. Hana may be off to the other side of the world, but he can still be there for her. Try and get to the bottom of what is bothering Tay. And he's not alone. He has Lou the wood turner by his side. An odd couple for sure.

SIX LITTLE WORDS

A waiter joins them. 'Table for two?' he asks.
They nod.
'Shall I take your coats?'
They nod again.
'And would sir like me to take his apron?'

Chapter 13

Kate

Presume not that I am the thing I was

Kate had got up early and driven down the coast road to the National Trust car park that borders the nature reserve. From there she ran, past the old windmill, following the ancient sea wall, zigzagging between dog walkers and bird watchers, until she found what she was looking for; a little known path through the reedbeds.

Now she is sitting on a grass bank looking out over this feathery world. The sky is a pale watery blue above her, clouds stretched by a stiff spring breeze. The long line of reeds in front of her is a band of gilded grey, striped green at the bottom near the water. This line snakes away from her like a river and the sound of the wind through the reeds reminds her of the rush of water. At first she had been conscious of this, and of the calls of the warblers and larks, until she became so submerged in thought, that all she is now aware of is the undulating ribbon in front of her and the slow stately progress of two egrets delicately picking their way through the shallows. Bodies strutting, question-mark-heads bobbing.

She has reached a decision. There is no need to mention JoJo Rose. That is all in the past, and she has no desire to go back to that time.

She had been at art college for two years. Had been amazed this was even an option. Her teachers at school had asked her what she wanted to do. She had replied, 'Maths, I suppose.' She was good at it. It was a sensible choice and her parents approved.

'You can't go wrong with a degree in maths,' her father had told anyone who would listen. He was a fitter, a manual worker, but he understood the importance of numbers.

Only one teacher heard the, *'I suppose.'* Her art teacher, Mr Morris, had said, 'You do know there is such a thing as art college.' She couldn't believe that she could actually go to college and do the thing she loved most – not really work – but more like playing. 'Oh, yes,' he had said, like he was letting her in on his favourite secret.

So, with his help she had explored what was possible, she had applied and got in. Moving from Reading to London. Her dad had stopped talking about sensible choices and started talking about the danger of drugs. Her mum pointed out someone with a maths degrees working in the City could afford far more drugs than a struggling artist. Then her mum told Kate that art college is what she would have chosen. On one of her infrequent visits Alice had swept in wearing one of the jewel-coloured peasant skirts she made and sold, and hugged her sister and told her she was proud of her. That was enough for Kate.

Art college hadn't been quite what she was expecting. She had thought she would be taught how to draw and paint. But the tutors were much more interested in free expression, although she did get a good grounding in art history and critical appreciation. She found her way with different media. Loved collage, acrylics, charcoal and textiles but not so much watercolours. She wanted to know more about oils, pushed for help, but her tutor eventually confessed they didn't have anyone on the faculty that really knew what they were doing with oils. So it remained out of reach – a mystery.

Then, after two years at college her mum had died of a sudden brain bleed. One minute she was seeing her husband out of a parking space in Sainsbury's, the next they were standing around in her parents' front room eating sandwiches Kate and Alice had made for the funeral guests, and serving tea from her grandmother's tea set.

If she had known then, what she knows now.

Kate had expected Alice to stop her life of travelling and come home and look after their dad. At least for a while. Kate was twenty, her sister had just turned thirty. She thought their dad needed them. He told everyone that he was okay yet was unable to make the simplest decision. He talked about going on a cruise but couldn't even find his way to the shops.

'Oh, he'll be alright,' Alice had told her after the funeral, repacking her bag to head back to Turkey.

Alice had always been Kate's beacon of warmth and light, a luminous dragonfly who flitted into her orbit hinting at what might be. *You are my sister. You might fly away like me.* But Kate's daughter, Ellie, was more like Alice than Kate was.

Was Alice the reason Kate liked Ellie to travel? She missed her but wanted her to be who she wanted to be. Thought if she travelled her aunt Alice was somehow with her?

Perhaps she had been mad to expect Alice to return home, but it hadn't stopped her resenting her when she gave up college and moved back home to cook ready meals for the man who couldn't work the oven.

It was the only time they had had a real fight. Alice appearing one day – she had started working for an environmental group in London. Kate couldn't understand why she wouldn't help her. Alice had shouted at her. Told her she was a fool. Kate had said to think about what Mum would have wanted.

Alice had screamed, 'You think Mum would have wanted you doing *this!* She should have done more with her life. For fuck's sake Katie, don't make the same mistake she did.' Kate can't remember what she shouted back. Just that Alice had told her that her dad didn't need her. That he would be okay, which just made her think everything was a mistake. Her mum dying. Her sister not being there for her. Her giving up the life she loved.

And sometimes she thinks what she still hasn't forgiven Alice for, is that her sister was right.

Four months later, about the same time Sainsbury's moved out of town, her dad was dating Maureen from the newsagent on the corner. By the spring they were married. Her mother's cherry Cornishware china was relegated to the attic and her grandmother's tea set sat gathering dust in the sideboard that nobody ever opened. Maureen took charge of the ready meals and they started eating on their laps in the lounge watched over by Maureen's collection of Lladró figurines.

Kate moved out and got a job at a local firm in the accounts department. After all, you can't go wrong if you're good with numbers. She had reconnected with some old school friends and through them met Doug, who for a while seemed to be the answer she was looking for.

Then her dad died of a heart attack.

Doug had been kind. *Really* kind, and she would never forget that. It was perhaps the bedrock on which they built their family. And Alice had come back. There was a reconciliation of sorts but without the words that needed to be said.

The sisters soon discovered that their father had made a will in their stepmother's favour and they were not to receive a single thing. They had not expected much. Not bricks and mortar, but there was their mother's jewellery and the beautiful rose tea set that had belonged to their grandmother – their mum's mother.

Alice had shrugged and returned to her life in London, now working for a political campaigner. Kate had gone to see Maureen to ask if she might have the cherry Cornishware from the attic and her grandmother's tea set. Maureen gave her a cup of coffee and a slice of angel cake, served on sludge-coloured Denby china.

Then she said no.

The Cornishware had gone to the tip and her husband had wanted Maureen's girls to have the tea set one day. It seemed it might be valuable.

Kate dropped her Denby teacup, saucer and plate on the flagstone floor along with the untouched angel cake and left. As soon as she got home she got out her paints. And that is how she became JoJo Rose.

Using gouache, which she knew from her days at college would produce beautiful pastel shades, she created a series of paintings of individual teacups. Like her grandmother's set they were overly pretty. But they meant something to her and they were a connection to the mum she missed so much. She signed the paintings boldly with her mother's name, JoJo Rose.

At first she gave them away to friends who spotted them in her flat. Then eventually local shops wanted them. Until there wasn't a gift shop in the county that wasn't selling her paintings of china. From there, came the prints, coasters, mugs, bags and aprons. It was a fashion phase, that didn't last anywhere near as long as Cath Kidston, but it gave Kate a nest egg and the money to buy her cottage. It also saw Doug in his element organising the business side. But best of all it brought Alice back into her life. She might not want Kate's china paintings on her walls but she loved the wit of this revenge, and Kate made sure she received a share of her earnings from the paintings. Something Doug could never understand. But Kate saw it as Alice's inheritance too. Together they drank wine and chatted as Alice embroidered a rose teacup on the cuff of Kate's denim jacket. And they laughed at the thought of Maureen seeing images of the china wherever she went. Signed with the name of her husband's first wife.

Then it simply went out of fashion. Doug tried to breathe new life into it with overseas sales, but Kate knew it for what it was. A thing that was never going to live that long. Born out of the wrong stuff. As Alice said, 'It was a joke, Katie. A bloody good one, but you don't want to keep on telling the same old joke.'

But now there is no Alice. No laughing at the things that only they could share.

One of the last things Alice had said to her before she died at the age of fifty-eight – when they were sisters again, laughing and swimming together, and finally finding the words that needed to be said – was: 'You need to paint again Katie. But paint something that really means something to you. Show people how you see the world.'

The eight years that have passed feel more like four, concertinaed by her own illness and the pandemic, but Kate knows that Alice was right. But with her sister gone, she's not sure she knows how to do this. Or even how it is that she sees the world.

WEEK 2

On the freshwater lagoons the black-tailed godwits are the inbetweeners, their eclipse plumage neither winter nor summer. Copper breasts bursting from leopard skin coats. The shelduck bustles her ducklings away. A lone Egyptian goose – a handsome fellow – forages on, unconcerned. An exotic migrant who stayed on to make this place his home.

Chapter 14

Bardy

He thinks too much: such men are dangerous

Bardy thought the least he could do after the betrayal of the art gallery was to hold the second meeting at Lou's.

Anyway, everywhere else is booked.

Still, he thinks Lou makes a great host. At his best. He has the long table piled with pastries and florentines. The coffee machine is cranking up in the background and two bottles of wine are open, glasses ready. Lou has even plumped the cushions on the long bench – a Tina touch.

No jumper. Good shout. Clemenza would never have worn cerise.

'All set?' Bardy asks, drawing up a chair.

Lou does a quick professional scan of the room, turns one central light off and flicks on the fairy lights that hang above the row of espresso cups. He absentmindedly touches the nearest cup.

Lou turns back to Bardy, 'Wine?' he asks pulling up a chair at the head of the table.

The Godfather.

Bardy nods and throws another nod at the wrapped package on the counter. 'Going to show me what you've made?'

The wine glugs into glasses. Good sized glasses. Thin glass. Lou said it made a difference. Bardy thinks he could be right.

'Going to have to wait, mate. I want to see how the others are getting on first.'

Leonard and Linda arrive, followed shortly by Tay who disappears behind the counter and starts making herself a coffee. Bardy thinks she looks tired. But tricky to tell with so much black around her eyes.

Lou, Linda and Leonard are chatting over wine, when Pia and Kate arrive together.

'No Tash? That's a shame,' Pia says, and it takes a split second for the laughter. No one had expected the joke. Well, not from Pia.

'Whoa, he's a beauty.' Bardy has just spotted Noy at Pia's heels. Not sure about the sheepskin coat. Dogs and coats? But stylish, definitely that. And if he were that thin he'd probably feel the cold.

Noy moves with Pia, as if velcroed to her legs until they reach the table, and he makes a beeline for Linda. Bardy wonders if dogs see people in colour too.

'Luigi... or may I call you, Lou? You do not mind me bringing Noy?'

Pia smiles at The Godfather.

'Yes, happy. Very. Whatever you like,' Lou says, somewhat incoherently.

Now they'll all be calling him Lou. Tony and Jakub come to mind. Bardy tells himself to get over himself. 'Right, Lou, d'you want to go first.' Bardy smiles blandly at his best mate.

Lou gives a small open-palmed shrug – very mafioso. *Why me?*

Tay comes from behind the counter and hands him the wrapped package. 'There you go, Lou.'

God, they *are* all calling him Lou. It was Jon and Lou.

Tay and Lou?

Not so bad.

Tay heads towards Bardy, but not before she has detoured to stroke Noy's head. Small delicate hand caressing his ears. The look on her face surprises him, soft, a little wistful. Between a child and an adult. He is taken back to teaching To Kill a Mockingbird – that poignant coming of age story. She joins him at his end of the table and twists her chair slightly towards the door. Phone in her lap. Noy settles between Pia and Linda who are sitting on the bench. Head on Pia's lap, back arched for Linda to pat. Smart dog. He heard somewhere that whippets are emotionally intelligent. Gentle dogs. Read you should never shout at a whippet.

Lou coughs self-consciously, as he unwraps his package, exposing a wooden bowl. It seems perfectly round and smooth to Bardy, but when Lou tilts it to the light, he can see ridges in the interior. 'This is a first attempt. Nowhere near perfect.' Lou runs a big finger over the ridges. 'But I thought, well, it's a start.'

'Nice bit of wood. May I?' Leonard asks, holding out a hand.

He runs his palm over the outer curve. 'Very nice. What would that be? Ash?'

Lou holds his head higher and nods. He looks around at them all. 'Look I know this isn't the sort of stuff that's going to win anything. May not even enter, but I've got seven weeks to get better.'

'Oh, you have to aim for something. And you can use this now. Put a nice green salad in it and no one will ever see the inside.' Linda. Kind. Mellow plum.

Noy sees his chance and takes it. One swift movement. Forepaws on the table. Pastry gone.

'Noy!' Pia cries. Although to be fair it sounds more like 'Nooahaii'.

Most are laughing. Except Noy who is gulping down the pastry as fast as he possibly can. He then puts his head under the table, bottom in the air.

Even Pia is reluctantly laughing now. 'He thinks we can't see him.'

Noy certainly looks surprised when Pia hauls him out from under the table. Both ears are lying back. Pia looks at him with such adoration that Bardy wishes he was a dog. 'They tell me that you are clever, but you give yourself away every time.' She runs a hand over his head and he nuzzles into her. She looks up, 'When his ears are back it is a sure sign he has stolen something.' She looks down again, 'And you think you're so smart.' Noy gives a small bark, circles twice in the tiny space between Pia and Linda and settles, curled at Pia's feet. Pia turns to Lou. 'I am so sorry about that. And I am sure it will have had the most expensive ingredients, that pastry that he stole.'

Lou gives his head a small twist, lips pursed. Impressed. 'It did.'

The man really could be an extra if they ever got round to making *Godfather IV.*

Bardy wonders for a moment why this man, his best friend, has no colour. He thinks Lou should be a rich claret red. Still he reflects, with a mental shake of the head, he really gets no say in it. Only in the poems he writes about colour.

'Who's next?' he asks.

Before the words are out Leonard is pulling a canvas from his bag.

Proud? Or wants to get it over with?

'I decided to have a go at acrylics. Spoke to my friend Stan who goes to the u3a art group. He gave me some tips.'

'U3a?' Tay asks, looking up from where she has been surreptitiously flicking through her phone.

Something's up. Or maybe she's bored being here. Good of her to come really.

'University of the third age,' Kate explains.

'They cover most subjects. It's really for people who've retired. You'd be amazed what you can study,' Linda adds.

Tay: 'Real.' Her version of Lou's head-twist of approval.

Leonard turns the canvas around. This time a brighter sunset scene. Countryside and trees in the background. Only one boat on the water. Dead centre. Flag flying.

'I see you've got your focal point,' Bardy says, suppressing a grin. He thinks the watercolour was heaps better. He glances around and the rest are nodding at the painting – except Tay who is looking at but not touching her phone. Expecting something? He sees her knee is bouncing – a sure sign she is nervous.

'That definitely leads your eye into the picture,' Kate says. Smiling. But not unkindly.

It dawns on Bardy that Kate has no colour. She is definitely a woman who should have a colour.

Leonard doesn't even glance at Kate. Bardy wonders if he has heard her. No sign of the (bloody) hearing aids.

Leonard ploughs on, 'I spoke to Stan about different media and I've now *thoroughly* researched focal points…'

Then Leonard talks at length about what he has read. Which is a lot.

'You don't think maybe you're over thinking this, mate?' Gentle but firm, from the Godfather. 'I liked your watercolour. Sort of thing I'd buy.'

Bardy rows in behind. 'Focal points aren't the be all and end all.'

What does he know? But he does agree with Lou.

'It's all he's talked about all week,' Linda complains. 'Made me walk around our house assessing all of our paintings.'

'That *is* quite a good idea,' Kate comments.

'Yes it would be Kate if it had taken ten minutes. Half an hour, maybe. *Two* hours later and we are still on the ground floor. If I ever see that Tash woman again, I will rip the sole off her other boot.'

'Really Linda, I don't think there's—'

Bardy jumps in, 'So, how's the poetry going, Linda?'

Linda laughs, patting her husband's hand, effectively shushing him. 'I don't think poetry's going to be my thing.' She pauses. 'I'm thinking I might have a go at a pen and wash drawing. I saw some nice pictures in a teashop this week. *Lots* of focal points,' she says, mischievously. 'I mean, how hard can it be?'

'Did you manage to write anything? I have always thought poetry might be quite hard,' Pia confesses.

Linda chuckles. 'Well, I did but it wasn't up to much.' She sips her wine, adding, 'Do you want to hear it?'

There is a loud chorus of assent from around the table. Even Tay stops looking at her phone.

Linda draws a sheet of paper from her bag. 'Last year Leonard made me go camping.' She shakes her head as if in disbelief. 'I am not built for camping. And at our age...'

Leonard leans forward, 'But such a good cause.'

Linda continues, 'It was part of a fundraising event for the local hospital. A jamboree of some sort he'd organised.'

'Such heroes,' Leonard interjects.

'No one is arguing with that Leonard, I was a nurse for over forty years, I know how hard everyone works. But *camping*?!' Linda carries on quickly before Leonard can say more. 'Anyway, he's been on at me to sign up again for this year and it inspired me to write a poem about last year's experience – which if you like I will share with you.'

More noises of assent. Leonard looks pained.

Linda starts to read.

'We're out in a tent,
My back is all bent.
Oh, I wish I was in my own bed.

The rain it is falling,

The damp is appalling.
Oh, I wish I was in my own bed.

It's just gone three,
I'm bursting to pee.
Oh, I wish I was in my own bed.

It's four in the morning,
My husband is snoring.
Oh, I wish I was in my own bed.

Can't straighten my leg,
The tent smells of egg.
Oh, I wish I was in my own bed.

This morning I woke,
I think I'm all broke.
Oh, I wish I was in my own bed.

But I'd do it once more,
Though my arse is still sore.
To raise funds for a hospital bed.'

There is a loud round of applause. Above which Leonard can be heard, 'You will? You'll do it again?'

'Yes,' Linda says, resignedly clinking her wine glass with her husband's, 'I will go camping.'

Bardy thinks Leonard may be blushing. Or crying.

'Solid. I like it.' Tay is on her feet, nodding at her phone. 'Got to go.'

'Oh.' Bardy's not sure what to say. He tries, 'Did you do anything for…'

'Nope. Didn't have time.'

'Do you want to do anything?' Maybe she just set this up for him? Doesn't want to get involved.

'Yep. I want to draw something. '

'*Really?*'

'Yes, *REALLY*. You said you could get teachers in?'

Bardy nods, wondering what's coming next.

'Could you set up a life class?'

'Oh, that would be fun!' Linda approves. The others join in. Maybe not Lou.

'Okay.' Bardy nods at Tay who is now at the open door.

'And don't give me grief, Bardy. Have you written anything?'

He hasn't – apart from a poem about the colour of teasels, brought on by a memory of his father. Filled with nasty spikes, a teasel.

But, he says, 'Yes.'

Tay pauses, silently demanding more.

'It's a short story called… "The girl who surprises the world".'

A different type of Tay grunt as she slams the door after her.

So Leonard is crying. And Tay is laughing.

Not bad and they're only halfway through the evening.

Chapter 15

Kate

Tell truth and shame the devil

'It is nice to have young people around,' Linda comments, after the door closes. 'Very good of her to come along. Have you known her long?' she asks Bardy.

'My wife and I fostered her mum for a while. Tay hasn't had the easiest start. I guess I feel a bit like a surrogate granddad.'

More like dad, Kate thinks.

'She works in customer service.' He adds, 'She's recently got a promotion.'

'Has she? Who told you that?' Is Lou laughing at Bardy?

'Is she also at college?' Pia asks.

'No. Although she's very bright,' Bardy says, and Kate thinks he sounds defensive.

'You can see that,' she remarks and Bardy smiles at her.

'She does go to college two afternoons a week,' Lou intervenes, and now Bardy looks put out. Kate thinks he is going to say something, but then he turns to Pia. 'So have you had any more ideas? You mentioned you might be having second thoughts about quilting.'

Pia pulls what looks like an overnight bag towards her. 'I did try and think of something else, but I'm afraid that is not the way my brain works. If I were able to draw, it would be simple, I would do that. It would be logical.'

'You are musical,' Kate suggests, 'you said you played the piano.'

'Ah, but my family are *so* much better than I am. Everyone is so accomplished.' Her amber eyes twinkle. 'I find I do not like to be second best. No, I like to be good at things.' She shrugs, 'Maybe that is why I am finding this so hard.' She unzips her bag. 'So I decided to go back to my first idea and look at one of the quilts I made in the past.'

She pulls from the bag a pale cream quilt. Very plain, but covered with delicate stitches. There is no other colour. 'I, rather like you, Leonard, have been doing my research.' She smiles warmly at him. 'This type of quilt is what I believe you would call a Durham quilt.'

Linda is now stroking the edge of it, 'Yes, that's right. I remember these from my grandmother. Is this machine or hand sewn?'

'We use a combination of both. It is really about the layering, building up the fabrics that will create the greatest warmth and softness.'

'It is *beautifully* soft,' Linda comments.

'I told you it was all about the "hygge".' More twinkling. 'The only thought I have had is perhaps the stitching could tell a story. I once read a phrase which talked of the shadows cast by the stiches.'

'Now that is poetic,' Linda comments, 'I wish I'd written that.'

'So for now,' Pia continues apologetically, 'this is all I have to share with you.' She turns to Bardy. 'But you think it will be good enough? This idea.'

'Oh yes,' they all agree. Especially Bardy.

Kate looks at him and sighs inwardly. Just one of those things.

'So what about you, Kate?' Bardy is now focused on her.

Like Leonard, she pulls a canvas from her bag, but gingerly; her oil paints are still wet. It strikes her that it feels natural to talk to these people about this – even if she doesn't go into how painting felt like coming home, like Tash had said when she burst into the last meeting. But it *was* like rediscovering a part of herself. Even if she found the oils tricky to work with in many ways.

Kate turns the painting around.

'Oh what fun!' Linda cries.

Despite her best efforts Kate starts to laugh.

'What?' There are confused exclamations. Pia and Lou combine in protesting, 'But it's really good!'

'I'm sorry,' Kate manages, grinning at Linda. 'It's just I used to paint with someone who would always try and put you down.' She holds her hand out towards Linda. 'I'm not for a moment saying that's you. This woman was... well she was more like Tash. Looked down on us all and her favourite putdown was to pretend she couldn't tell what you had painted. So, she might ask if something was, say, a sheep. And when you said, it was a hedge, she would cry, "Oh *what* fun!"'

Linda is laughing, 'Well, I can see for certain that *that* is a mackerel.'

'Anyone could, Kate. It's really good,' Bardy says.

'Why a mackerel?' Pia asks.

Kate props the painting on the ledge beside her, careful not to get paint on Lou's walls. 'It was the strangest thing. I haven't been able to paint or draw for ages. I just couldn't seem to get started. But after last week's meeting I woke up one morning and thought – I want to paint a mackerel. Weird.'

Had dwelling on the past and thinking about Alice unlocked something in her?

She doesn't tell them this, but she does share, 'Maybe it was because I'd seen a mackerel cloud the evening before down on the beach.'

'Ah, a mackerel sky!' Leonard proclaims, 'Cirrocumulus at their best.'

Kate smiles, 'No, not so much a sky with those lovely mackerel patterns, but an actual cloud that, well, looked like a mackerel. Bones and all.' This makes her think of Alice saying, 'Paint how you see the world'. She knows Alice would have laughed at a glorious fish cloud swimming in a bright blue sky. She remembers once, after one of Alice's flying visits, pulling on an old navy blazer and finding an embroidered goldfish swimming out of the inside breast pocket.

Bardy is leaning in, looking at the painting. 'This is great Kate. Did you study art?'

Suddenly she knows she's on tricky ground. She says carefully, 'I did for two years but dropped out when my mum died.'

The murmur of sympathy makes her feel like a fraud. She

can't bring herself to add – *I went home to look after my dad*. All she can think of is Alice.

'I thought you wanted to paint the view from your cottage?' Pia queries, and Kate is thankful for the diversion. 'I do. This is more of a practice piece.'

Bardy is not so easily distracted. 'You could sell this, Kate. It's great.' He presses, 'Have you never sold any of your art?'

She looks around at their faces. She likes them so much. Wants to keep coming to the group. Everything will change if she tells them the truth. Even if they let her stay they would feel awkward with a 'professional' in the room. Leonard would hate it. Or he would never leave her alone. Also, isn't it a bit arrogant to presume JoJo Rose was – is – such a big thing? And, worse, she would have to explain all about her mum and dad and Alice.

'No. I've never sold anything.'

The briefest of silences follows. A breath. It is an infinitesimal gap. But to Kate it seems a chasm. She cannot possibly take the step over and keep lying. She needs to laugh now and confess. These people don't deserve to be lied to. She opens her mouth to speak.

The door handle to the café starts rattling furiously, and all turn, to see a couple, their noses pressed against the glass.

'It's open. Just give it a shove,' Lou calls to them.

The door swings open and a woman stumbles in. Youngish. Maybe not yet forty. She is followed by a man about the same age. He all put pushes her into the room.

'This is the place, Satya.' He nods at Bardy. 'Hi Bardy, Satya is interested in doing more photography. Told her she should come along.'

Kate forgets what she might have said. She just wants to laugh. Satya looks like she has been dragged along. Not exactly unwilling but certainly flustered.

'Got to go!' He kisses Satya on the cheek. 'Love you. See you later.'

Just before he heads for the door, he grabs Bardy's arm and furiously whispers something to him that Kate can't hear. She hears Bardy's stifled bark of laughter.

His last cry at the door, to Satya, who is now taking off her coat and sitting down beside Kate is, 'Have fun!'

Chapter 16

Bardy

It's a wise father that knows its own child

Bardy turns and introduces Satya to the group. Their faces are a picture. Not at all sure they want a newcomer.

Except this is no Tash. No acid mustard. He has known Satya's husband, Jack, forever. One of Tom's best friends from school. And Satya nearly as long. The couple met as lanky fourteen-year-olds in the school grounds. He had to keep turfing them out of the cupboard off the sports hall for snogging. He stifles a laugh, thinking of what Jack had whispered to him. Well, begged him.

'Just keep her here. Had to get her out the house. Think the boys were going to kill her.'

How old were they now? Three boys somewhere between two and seven. Which probably means between seven and twelve. Always surprises him.

Jack had added, 'And if they don't kill her, I will.'

Satya is now smiling around at everyone. She has no idea

they worry she is the new Tash. That the group are thinking they like it the way it is. Even Lou looks cautious. What you need in this situation – he has been here before when a latecomer arrives – what you really need is...

And there she is: the Smiler.

Linda: 'Can I pour you a glass of wine, Satya? And you're going to have a go at photography, you say? How interesting.'

Satya smiles back gratefully and Bardy sees the group relax. Not a lot. But a little. Room enough for Satya to wriggle in. Which he is sure she can do – she's a nice woman, after all.

Who her boys want to kill. He allows himself a proper smile as he passes Satya the glass that Linda is holding out.

'Yes, I used to do quite a lot of photography, and then just kind of stopped. But a few years ago I went to an evening class, but then didn't really stick at it because of work and the kids. You know how it is.' She looks around, and Kate and Linda nod encouragingly.

Looks like Kate is moving on side too.

'Jack bought me a new camera for my birthday and as you can see...' She laughs. 'He thought it would be a good idea for me to come to this group, and maybe enter something for the competition.' She sips her wine. 'I'm afraid I'm a bit of a workaholic and find it hard to stop.'

'What do you do?' Pia asks.

'I run an online beauty and wellness company, mainly make-up and skincare, but we're expanding into supplements as well.' She then names a brand that even Bardy has heard of. And not just because he knows Satya and Jack.

'Your skin concentrate serum is *very* good,' Pia comments.

One more in.

'Can I pass you a pastry Katya?' from Leonard.

Ah well, Linda will sort that out later.

'Oh these are delicious,' Satya exclaims, taking a bite. 'Did you make them, Luigi?'

'Oh, please call me Lou,' says the wood turner and baker.

Bardy sits back. Full house.

Apart from Tay. But surely Tay is going to be interested in a woman who has built her own company from scratch.

'Have I missed much?' Satya asks.

The remaining time in the group is spent discussing what they are all going to have a go at for the competition. Satya asking interested questions.

It always frustrates Bardy how people relegate creative projects in their lives. Satya talking about never having the time. She clearly loves the idea of getting back into photography but confesses to Linda that it is always at the bottom of her list. Linda, who never seems to give anything the time it needs to improve. Bardy hears her laughingly telling Satya, 'The thing is I really think I'm going to be good at them straight away. It's a bit of a shock.'

Pia and Leonard are talking painting and music. He has seen this before too – how a family can influence what you do, or rather don't do. Pia is describing her super-musical family, and confesses that she never feels quite good enough to play. Leonard tells her about the brother who paints so much better than him, and his father who told him – you are the scientist, your brother's the artist. It turns out Leonard plays the piano too. He talks of the joy of a Bach fugue, the initial theme stated and then restated and entwined until it becomes a triumphant resolution. He'd like to play more but...

Lou is telling Kate more about Tina, and asking about her own chemo. Kate confessing how the stress of the past four years, and perhaps even earlier has stopped her going out and sketching. Lou talking about not having the space before. He had always fancied working with wood. *Who knew*. But didn't really have the place for it. He would really like to create something that is just a beautiful shape. But this seems wasteful. So he's going to have a go at making something useful, like bowls and platters.

Bardy has heard much of this before. How a comment as a child could stop a fledgling talent dead in its tracks. Or prohibit the simple enjoyment of something creative.

'Oh, you have to be really good at art to get anywhere.'

'Do you know how many books come out that only ever sell one copy?'

Hana told Bardy that husbands were often the worst for the women she taught. A laugh and a throwaway, 'Call that art!' had stopped one woman picking up her brushes for ten years. And so many people felt they could only do something if they were good at it – not thinking that it might just be enjoyable or therapeutic. Or that with time they would get better.

Hana changed how he thought, and he is grateful for that. She once told him, 'I used to feel like I had to justify why I painted. Now I just paint. It is who I am. It makes me happy.'

Simple really.

Does his writing still make him happy? Yes, mainly. But he gets where Kate is coming from. Stress can be a killer. Not being in the right frame of mind. Still, he does always write his phone poems on colour. His version of temazepam. Or beer. Today's was called 'Dutch Corner', based on the bank of orange created by Netherlands supporters who gather on a particular section of the Tour de France. He had seen it once, and as orange smoke from flairs had drifted across a sea of orange had experienced the pure rush of joyous colour.

'We're doing life drawing next week,' he hears Linda tell Satya. It brings him back from his detour into his hobbyhorse. *Maybe he could write a poem called Hobbyhorse Grey?*

'Is that just for the artists?' Satya asks.

'No, we all do it,' Bardy assures her. 'I think it's good to try different things. It can end up influencing what you do. Even if it's about form and shape and the whole process of really looking.'

Leonard now looks uncomfortable. 'Will it be a female or a male model?'

'Oh, I think male, don't you Bardy?' Linda is smiling at him. So is Kate.

Quite frankly he has no idea. He knows his mate Colin, an ex-art teacher, will help him with the class. But he has no idea where he will find a model. One thing he is sure of though. He won't be volunteering.

Bardy decides to walk the long way home, past the fishing quay. The tide is in and the water is flat calm. Lights reflected from the buildings form luminous drips running into the inky depths. The town is quiet, despite it being the Easter school holidays. The air is cold and it is late on a Monday night. The only human sound coming from a few couples hurrying past and the occasional opening and shutting of the fish and chip shop door, the volume of conversation from within ebbing and flowing on the ring of a bell. Bardy sits on the harbour wall next to a tetris of lobster pots and pulls his jacket closer around him. Out in the channel an iron sculpture of a man stands, arms outstretched like a wind turbine. Only arms and a head currently visible, dark outlines against the water. Perhaps he could get their model to stand like that? That would freak out Leonard. And Lou. Bardy smiles. Closer in a tall ship, painted black and white, creaks on its moorings, as the smaller work-a-day fishing boats beside it shift in the wash from some movement unseen in the channel beyond.

Bardy reviews this evening's session. It was good to see Jack. Even briefly. There were times when it seemed like Jack had taken root in their house. His parents hadn't seemed to mind. Well, they wouldn't. He was using Bardy and Hana's fridge like his personal larder. Probably saved them enough to send him to uni. He knew Jack and Tom still stayed in touch. He really should get his shit together and visit. Not live. Not a kookaburra. Bardy digs his hands deeper into his pockets. He must set up a video call. The time difference was a bugger. The boys always ahead of him. Nothing new there then. He had long ago given up trying to keep up with everything his boys were into: the manga... the sci-fi... the bands. Now, Tom's job in interconnected tech environments and Ned into designing low emission co-working pods. Yep, beyond him. But boy, he misses them.

Still, good to see Jack. A blast from the past. And it was fun having Satya in the group. Maybe she would talk to Tay? Or is that interfering? But is all well with Satya and Jack? Bardy doesn't know what to do with this thought. Relationships? He was the man who had no idea his wife was so unhappy.

Blue and green should never be seen.
One of his mum's sayings.

Satya: lapis lazuli blue. A blue you can't ignore. A hard stone? No. Something comes back. Ned studied geology, before he got into the pod start-up. Diamond was the toughest, talc the softest. Wasn't lapis somewhere in the middle? He's overthinking it. It is just about the colour that shines from the woman. The most beautiful, iridescent blue.

And Jack was the green of toy soldiers. Is that because he still sees the boy in him? Always easy company was Jack. No trouble, despite the gargantuan appetite. Why does he think now of toy soldiers and a flat matt green? Difficult to see what is going on under the surface.

Bardy gets up, easing shoulder blades cramped from the cold, and heads for home. He is taking this too literally – his weird colour thing. Just because blue and green aren't complementary colours. It doesn't mean anything. The colour wheel doesn't hold all the answers.

Invented by Sir Isaac Newton.

And what did he know?

Chapter 17

Kate

Whether you will or no

Kate has cleaned her cottage and cleared the clutter. Pia is coming for coffee – the main reason for the decluttering – and later Linda is coming over for a pen and wash lesson. Guilt about not confessing to being JoJo Rose made her offer. Although she might have suggested it anyway. She thinks it will be nice to hang out with Linda.

She likes her cottage, her biggest investment from when she was making money through the JoJo Rose range. But she hadn't wanted any of her china paintings on the walls, too much of a reminder of her parents' deaths. This was also the reason she never gave interviews about being the creator of the range.

Since her girls left home she has rearranged the accommodation to suit herself, and redecorated. Mainly blues and greens, but not a 'seaside' theme. She has avoided that, seeing too much of it in the second homes that proliferate along the coast. She is unsure how she feels about the second-home owners. She likes her neighbours and appreciates that this area should be shared, plus she realises that tourism is an important industry. But she is pleased that the council are looking to make sure newbuilds have to be primary residences. She worries about the young people trying to stay in the area, who now can't afford houses. She knows the fire station and the RNLI struggle, as crew members need to live near and be on call but sometimes can't afford the housing.

But important as this is, she now has other things on her mind. How to make her home acceptable to a supremely stylish Scandinavian. She throws a few more things into cupboards. She imagines Pia's home is effortlessly minimalist. She places Ellie's sewing machine ready in the hallway. She hopes Pia might find it useful.

Pia arrives with Noy (smart green quilted coat on today) and a plate of what she says is brunsviger – small squares of cake marbled with caramelised butter. 'It's what I always have with my sisters when we meet for coffee.'

Kate bites into the gooey, crispy caramel top. The cake beneath is light and fluffy and absolutely delicious.

'These are fantastic,' Kate declares, appreciatively.

Pia murmurs modestly, but Kate can tell she is pleased.

They are settled in chairs in the kitchen, a raised brick and wood extension that has views out over the creek. The day is calm and the water is flowing fast, the creek now a broad channel of water. Across it the sea blight and sea purslane are becoming submerged. To Kate it always feels like the landscape is sinking beneath the water, not being flooded by it. She feels if she were to walk on the furthest shore now she would no longer find any land, or her feet would punch holes in it. In an hour or so, all will be water. On the far shore three children are slipping and sliding into the creek, their laughter mixing with the sound of gulls. They are local children and Kate has no fear they will become stranded by the tide. They have their small rowboat within easy reach.

She misses her girls with a sudden longing and sends them a quick photo of the view. Tempting them back? She really must chase up her boat-building friend who is giving *The Rose* an overhaul. It would be good to see her moored by the edge of the creek. Waiting. Like her. A sign of hope that one day they might all squeeze aboard once more. She will try and organise a group FaceTime at the weekend. Timings can be difficult: Bella working with her women's soccer team in Texas; Ellie in Patagonia, for the time being at least; and Jess teaching maths in Edinburgh. Or should she just call Jess? Still no baby news. But she doesn't want to be one of those mothers that keep asking.

As Kate pours coffee, Pia tells her about her own family and growing up on a promontory surrounded by water. She knows this type of joy and understands the ebb and flow, the change of landscape from a creek that meanders, carving a path in mud and sand to being surrounded by a breadth of water that brings the ocean within touching distance. She describes her parents' current home on an island. Both her parents had been dentists. Her mother a dental surgeon. She worries a little about their isolation now they are older. 'But that is the way they like it,' she tells Kate.

'What do you miss about Denmark?' Kate asks.

'Apart from my family, I suppose it is the little things,' Pia says, thoughtfully. 'I don't often say, as I would not like people to think that I don't like living here in England. And I do, I really do.' She smiles suddenly. 'It has been wonderful to be part of this group. It does make me feel much more part of the community.' She nibbles on a piece of brunsviger. 'I think it is not so much what I miss, but sometimes the things I don't understand.'

'Such as?' Kate is intrigued.

'Why do you buy horrible sandwiches from garages?'

Kate grins, 'Well I don't. Or not that often.'

'We would never do that. Lunch is an important part of the day. Something you savour. And when we have friends over…' Pia leans forward, warming to her theme. 'We would buy the best ingredients to make a meal, but would not create a feast as the English sometimes do, with tables groaning with food. We would offer our guests the most special thing we can afford, but it might be something small.' She shakes her head, 'And Danish bacon. You all think we eat this stuff! We do not cook bacon for breakfast. Ham, yes, beautiful ham, but hot bacon! No, I thank you.'

'Anything else?' Kate is enjoying seeing Pia open up.

'Yes! Conversations. In our London office, each morning people greet each other and ask the same thing of everyone they meet. Then the next day they do it all over again.'

Kate is laughing now.

This brings Pia up short, she looks perplexed. 'But I do wish I understood your humour more. After all the years of living here I do not always know when people are joking. Your humour is very dry.'

'You made that joke about Tash,' Kate reassures her.

'Yes, but I thought about what I was going to say before I arrived.'

Kate thinks this is rather sweet.

'When you mentioned Tash making a model of Noy,' Pia grins, 'I thought you might be serious. It is just the sort of thing Brenda would like.' She stops, looking stricken and Kate can't help but laugh as she remembers Pia's dog walker waving Noy's paw at them through the café window.

'I should not have said that. Brenda is really very good,' Pia sighs.

'She certainly seems to like looking after Noy.'

'She really spoils him,' Pia says stroking Noy, who is looking lovingly up at her. 'In her house she has a special bed for him and toys. She has even knitted him his own blanket with his name on.'

'Do you mind?' Kate asks, wondering about the slight frown on Pia's face.

'No, not really. How can I when she makes my life so much easier for me? It's just that... I wish she wouldn't call him Noy Boy. And she does feed him too many treats. I worry he will get fat.'

Kate suddenly has an image of Kate Moss with a pot belly. She decides to ask something else. 'Do you spend much time in London these days?'

Pia shrugs. 'I try not to. I did spend most of my time there. I was in a relationship for a long time. I guess I am finding it hard to adjust. But I can't say I miss London.'

'It can be tough,' Kate sympathises. But what does she know?

Since Doug left she has hardly dated. Her attempts at online dating being, at best, funny anecdotes that her friends enjoyed. She gave up in the end, deciding she didn't want her love life to be the butt of any joke. Still, she knows quite a few people it has worked for. 'Have you thought about getting out there again?'

Pia smiles mischievously at her. 'Let's say it has crossed my mind.'

Kate takes this and her thoughts to the stove to make more coffee. When she is back Pia is looking around her. 'This is a lovely cottage. Very you.'

'I am imagining your house is very simple and stylish.'

'Such a stereotype, Kate,' she chides. Then laughs. 'But absolutely right. I don't know if you've seen it but I live in the wooden house set back from the road, along from the green with that great deli.'

'I know it! Wow, that is a lovely house.'

'You must come over sometime and I will cook for you.'

'I'd love that.' Kate chooses her next words carefully. She wants to approach this sensitively. 'What did your ex-partner do? Were *they* a lawyer too?'

Pia glances at her consideringly. The emphasis had been very slight. A brushstroke of enquiry.

'She was in the police. She was in silver command. Dealing with potential riot situations. A huge amount of responsibility.'

'Do you mind me asking why it ended?'

Pia stares out of the window for a while, watching a flock of geese spanning the sky. 'We were both wrapped up in our work, of course we were. It is very much what drew us together in the first place. But I think in the end Grace wanted different things. She is much more of a party person than I am, and I think she had a thing with a woman at work. She says not, but I don't know...' She looks back at Kate. 'We weren't very kind to each other at the end. I regret that.'

'I'm sorry,' Kate says, thinking of some of the things she said to Doug. 'I know it's a cliché, but time can help with that.'

'The thing is, I worry she was right about me.'

'In what way?'

'She said that I struggle to share myself with people. That I wouldn't put myself out for other people and was selfish and didn't have any real friends. And that a whippet didn't count.' Pia tries to smile.

'Well, you have friends now,' Kate assures her, remembering Pia's comments about comparing herself to someone. Perhaps Grace was someone who made friends easily and Pia felt at a disadvantage? Had she sometimes felt lonely when Doug filled their home with his yachty friends? For a moment she wonders if Bardy is lonely. He had mentioned two sons, but they must be well and truly grown up now. And Tay? How much did they rely on each other?

Pia interrupts her thoughts. 'And you? I know you said you were divorced. Have you...'

'Not really. I was bringing up my teenage girls on my own, so didn't have time. And then my sister got sick. Then I got sick. Not ideal for romance really.'

'I'm sorry. And now?'

Kate smiles a little sadly. 'There is someone I like, but I'm afraid he's got his eye on someone else.'

Pia stands up. 'Would you show me round your cottage, and maybe then we could take Noy for a walk?'

Her confidences seem to be at an end.

As it is high tide, they take the path which overlooks what is now a broad bay of water. The path is edged on one side by a bank of statuesque lime-green angelica hemmed with short, purple muscari; on the other is a hawthorn hedge, separating them from a field of pungent yellow oil seed rape. But overlaying it all is the scent of the sea and the sound of birds. Noy either walks contentedly sandwiched between the two of them or shoots off at speed, like a greyhound over the flat. He runs with a fluidity that Kate thinks is joyous to watch. When he suddenly stops to snap at a cabbage white butterfly and then dig at something in the bank, he is transformed from an elegant, rippling wave of muscle to an excitable, scrabbling thing, all ears and paws. Kate begins to understand why Pia likes him so much. When Pia spots some walkers ahead she calls Noy to heel and puts him on the lead. 'I love to see him run, but I know some birdwatchers are not always keen to have dogs around.'

They chat about art, music, times in London and places they have visited in Norfolk. Nothing more is said about relationships until they have returned to the cottage and Pia is getting into her car. She looks up at Kate from the driver's seat and smiles.

'You've never thought about, maybe...' Pia doesn't finish, but she doesn't have to.

'No. It's always been men for me. Which when you think what idiots most men are is madness.'

Pia grins, 'True. You have no idea what you are missing.'

Kate waves her off and thinks she is probably right.

How does she feel? Flattered? Yes. Surprised? A little. Not so much by Pia's sexuality, but by the fact that it is clear that she likes Kate.

Poor Bardy.

But appropriate somehow.

Which play was it? *Twelfth Night?*

A traditional Shakespearean love triangle.

Chapter 18

Bardy

This was the most unkindest cut of all

The first thing he notices is the angry slice across Lou's cheek. He was going to head straight for the bar and order a pint. Lou is already at their favourite table in the Angry Beaver. They have been drinking in the pub for so long he finds he is surprised when people laugh at the name. He makes a detour to the table.

'What have you done to your face?'

Lou touches it gingerly. 'A nasty catch.'

'A what?'

'A catch. It's when the wood splits and bits fly off when the lathe's spinning.'

'God, that could have been your eye.'

Lou says gruffly, 'I'm not a complete idiot. I do wear safety goggles.' He adds, more sheepishly, 'Got a full-face visor coming from Amazon.'

'You be careful mate. Want another pint?'

'No, you're alright, got over half of this one to go.'

Once back at the table, they chat about the local football team (who are likely to go up a league) until Lou says, 'You know who I keep thinking about?'

Apart from Tina?

'You're going to have to give me more of a clue.'

'Mr On-there-like-that. Remember him?'

'Blimey, yes. Woodwork teacher.'

They are off. Adopting broad Norfolk accents.

Lou: 'Boys you want to put that bit of wood *on-there-like that.*'

Bardy: 'Get that screw in boys, *on-there-like-that.*'

Lou: 'Now hold the saw and move it down *on-there-like-that.*'

They laugh but exchange a look. Definitely old men now. Not the boys they once were. They both look uncomfortable.

'We gave him such a hard time,' Bardy voices their thoughts. They had been given woodwork, because that was just the way their timetables had worked that year. They had resented being there. The class for dummies. If you were a boy and not good at anything you got woodwork. If you were a girl, it was childcare. Bardy sighs. Nice to know the future of children and practical, creative skills were so valued. 'What about Mr On-there-like-that?'

Lou glances at him, checking.

Bardy knows that look. Has used it himself.

Are you going to take the mick?

'Go on,' Bardy tells the man who has been his best friend for fifty-six years.

'I'm really enjoying this stuff,' Lou says, 'despite the…' He gestures to his cheek. 'I think back to how we wouldn't listen.

Made his life a misery.' He checks Bardy's face, who holds his look. Lou takes a deep breath, 'So, now every time I start my lathe up and pick up a new bit of wood, I say, out loud. "I'm sorry Mr On-there-like-that."'

Bardy nods. 'He'd like that.' Any teacher would. It just showed you could make a difference. Sometimes years on. Bardy takes a drag from his pint. 'You know he won the lottery?'

'No!' Lou sounds incredulous, but is there a bit of hope in there too? The possibility of redemption. Scales balanced.

'Yep, heard that from his daughter who I taught... Meghan. He and his wife went on a trip to Canada.'

'I always fancied that. Tina and I talked about a train trip across the...' Lou's voice fades.

Bardy continues, 'They gave all their kids some money and then they moved to the Cotswolds. Big house.'

'Ah, that's good. Glad he got a bit of luck.'

'Meghan said he bought himself a Range Rover, said he'd always fancied one.'

They are back to broad Norfolk.

'Expect he's still got the caravan hitched... *on-there-like-that*.' Lou snorts.

'With a big house, there'd be plenty of room to park... *on-there-like-that*.' Bardy responds.

Some things change but some things don't.

'Your bowl was pretty good,' Bardy tells him. 'Mr On-there-like-that would have given you a B+ I reckon.'

'The inside was pretty rubbish.'

'That won't matter once you fill it with a nice green salad,' Bardy tells carb-loving Clemenza and they start to laugh.

'Nice woman though,' Lou says after a while.

'I think they're all pretty good.'

'I can't seem to speak when Pia looks at me, mate. Total tosser.' Lou shakes his head.

'Me too. But it's getting easier.'

Why does he keep thinking back to coffee with Kate and Pia and thinking of… that's it… *Twelfth Night!* What is that all about?

'You know Satya?' Lou asks.

'Yep. Jack used to hang out with Tom. Was pretty cool back then. Played guitar in a local band. But once he met Satya that was it.'

'What? He didn't play anymore?'

'No,' Bardy says slowly. 'He kept that going for quite a while. Just that they fell for each other. Like you and Tina.'

But now? Hadn't Jack put a lot on hold for Satya? Well, that's what Tom said. He did the bulk of the childcare. Bardy certainly doesn't see anything wrong with that. So often the other way round. Then why is he vaguely worried?

Blue and green should never be seen.

'Does he play now?' Lou asks.

'I have no idea,' Bardy replies. But somehow he doubts it.

'You going to come to the life class?' Bardy asks him.

Lou blows out a long breath. 'I guess so. Would look a bit obvious if I said I was busy.'

'It's not how you think it will be.'

'And how's that?' Lou demands.

'All breasts or cocks.'

Lou laughs. 'I was hoping more for the breasts.'

'No, seriously mate, you're so busy looking…' He casts Lou a reproving look for the guffaw. 'No you'd be amazed. You're looking at the shape and proportion, and how the muscles sit. And if you've never drawn from life before, it really shows you, how you have to trust your eye. Not what your mind tells you is there.'

Why does this make him think back to coffee with Pia and Kate? What had his eye seen that his mind is missing?

Chapter 19

Kate

Yet die we must

Kate and Linda are at Kate's kitchen table, pens and watercolours out. A scattering of experimental drawings in front of them. Pictures of imaginary shop fronts – a florists and a bookshop – and kitchen dressers dotted with china. This wasn't Kate's choice and she had stuck to cherry Cornishware for her dresser. Kate thinks Linda is doing well. Linda was amazed to find out about the vanishing point – that spot in your drawing where your eye would be looking – and how you can use this in one dimensional perspective. 'I can't believe no one told me that before!'

Kate had replied, 'It's really easy. Once you have found that point, all lines run to it so you will get your perspective angles right.'

However, Kate can see that Linda has a low boredom threshold and that she wants to move on quickly to the next thing before really finishing what she is working on.

Kate asked about her family and Linda is now telling Kate how she and Leonard met. He had come into hospital with a friend who had fallen off a ladder. And that was that.

'How long have you been married?'

'Too long,' Linda laughs. 'No, I'm joking. It's just sometimes…'

Kate thinks back to showing her around the cottage earlier. She had worried much less about the clutter but had apologised for the stuff left on the stairs. 'Oh, don't you worry. I'm always leaving things on the stairs ready to take up and Leonard is *always* having a go at me.' Linda then muttered, 'Sometimes I think, maybe I'll leave the pile at the top of the stairs. Then just one trip, one little push, and off you go Leonard.' She had laughed but there was a certain weariness in her voice.

Kate doesn't know what to say or ask in response to Linda's unfinished, 'just sometimes'. In the end she just murmurs, 'pasta bake'.

Linda laughs out loud. 'That is *it*, that is just it. Why won't men wear their bloody hearing aids. The doctors have told him that if he doesn't his hearing is going to get worse. The boys have tried. I have tried. But all he will say is they are uncomfortable and that he's not an old man. He's nearly eighty for God's sake. We *are* old!'

'It must be hard,' Kate sympathises.

'Do you know what, Kate. It's lonely. He doesn't seem to realise he is living in his own little world. And he talks *at* people, especially if we're out and he can't handle the background noise.' Linda slowly flicks her paintbrush back and forward over the yellow paint. 'I know Leonard is… oh, maybe he's not the most exciting man. But he is a good man. And he's my man.

Now there are times when I think I am going to be spending the rest of my days with a boring, selfish old fart.'

Linda looks up and Kate sees tears in her eyes. Before she can say anything, Linda puts her paintbrush down and fixes Kate with her eyes. 'There is something I need to tell you Kate.'

She knows I'm JoJo Rose.

Is she ashamed or would it be a relief?

'I knew your sister Alice.'

Kate's breath leaves her body in a rush. She had not been expecting this.

'I was a palliative care nurse for over thirty years. It was the best job I ever had.' She smiles a little sadly at Kate. 'I know in the last few weeks of her life Alice was nursed in the hospice here. That she was moved from London. You and I never met because I was working nights at that time. But I recognised you, well, from Alice. I know you don't look alike, and have different surnames, but there is something in your expressions.'

Kate's hand flies to her mouth and tears start in her eyes. Everyone had always commented on the differences between them. To have someone tell her she was like her sister in any small way is like being given the most precious gift. She shakes her head and cannot speak as the tears fall.

Linda reaches out and takes her other hand, patting it. 'I don't normally say anything when I meet people I have nursed – the lucky ones. Or the families of those that have died. So many people want to forget that time. And they don't want to be reminded of it when they bump into a nurse in Waitrose. But Alice, well, she was special.'

Kate grips Linda's hand tight and forces the words out. 'I

miss her so much. She was a bit older than me but she was so…' She cannot finish.

'Kate it was so easy to see, even at that stage, what a wonderful woman she was. She was bright, luminous.'

Dragonfly bright.

'She was one of the last people I nursed before I retired, and I will never forget her. We did laugh, Kate, I mean *really* laugh. She talked about her nieces; I presume your daughters?'

Kate nods.

'They clearly meant the world to her, and that did make her sad, the thought of not seeing them grow older. But she did tell me Kate, that they had the best mum. I think she had seen what you had done for them…'

Kate goes to interrupt, but Linda holds up her hand, smiling. 'She said, you didn't see it yourself. Just got on with things.' Linda frowns, 'I think there was a time she felt she had let you down, Kate. She didn't tell me what it was. But I hope that in a small way I reassured her. Oh, it was so easy to see this was a woman who had brought a lot of love into people's lives. And laughter.'

Kate nods and looking at Linda, she realises Linda is crying too. This means so much to her. That her sister, years on, could have made an impression on this woman, who will have seen so much. However, the thought that Alice was worrying about the time when their dad died hits her hard. They had talked about a lot towards the end, she thought she had reassured Alice – but maybe not. Somehow, she is sure Linda will have said the right thing. This does help her.

It strikes her for the first time, that maybe her lingering sense of Alice letting her down has nothing to do with that time with their dad. It is simply that the loss of her is so great she feels bereft without her. Alice had left her. Now with Linda beside her something eases. She wishes she could tell Linda how she feels but she cannot speak for crying.

'And how are you, Kate?' Linda asks, looking down at Kate's hand in hers, knuckles gnarled as a side effect of the drugs she has been taking to suppress the oestrogen in her body. A way to combat the possible return of cancer. 'Look, don't answer that yet. I'm going to get you a tissue and if you don't mind me rummaging in your kitchen, I'm going to make us some more tea.'

Kate nods at the woman who is now standing beside her. So grateful that this wonderful woman nursed her sister. Knowing she made Alice laugh is a solace that reaches into the heart of her and Kate leans back and lets the tears fall.

Ten minutes later they are sitting on Kate's sofa with their feet up on the large wooden chest in front of them, nursing mugs of tea in their laps. Kate feels shaky, like she is recovering from an illness. She has explained to Linda that her prognosis is good. Linda had asked detailed medical questions, which Kate was able to answer to her satisfaction. There is one thing more she wants to say to Linda. Well probably two. But she doesn't know if she can voice the second one. The first will do. Both are about guilt.

'I think about how unfair it all was. Sometimes if I say that people think I am talking about me getting cancer. But that's not it. I mean why shouldn't I get cancer? So many people do.'

Kate shrugs. 'The thing I am struggling with the most is that I have survived cancer and Alice didn't. *That* seems so unfair. If she had died of anything but cancer I think I would be able to cope better. But...'

'You keep thinking why Alice and why not me?' Linda finishes.

'Yes, exactly.'

'That is a hard one. Maybe you already know that—'

'—there is no answer.' This time Kate finishes.

Linda takes a sip of tea. 'No, that wasn't what I was going to say.'

Kate studies her.

'I was actually going to say, that that *isn't* a question. Well, not one that makes sense. Knowing what I know about illness and death. It's like asking... I don't know... why isn't the sun the moon? It just isn't, that's all. Having nursed the dying for over thirty years I honestly believe there is no reason why Alice died, and you lived. That is just the way it was.'

Linda sighs, 'I don't know if that is any help at all. Working with death does make you less frightened of it and yet you also realise the inevitability of it. It was probably Shakespeare who said, *die we must*. He certainly said most things.' She continues, 'Kate, there is no point in trying to make sense out of, why Alice, and why not me. It's a question that honestly has no place in reality.'

Maybe she should listen to this woman who has seen so much of death.

'The very little I knew of Alice, I would say, she would want you to be making the most of your life. Asking the right questions.'

'Which are?' Kate gives a watery smile.

'Well, one to start with is why is Bardy making such a fool of himself over Pia when it is quite clear the woman likes you.'

Kate chokes on a laugh, and Linda joins in.

Does Linda know that I like him? She is not ready to ask, so just enjoys laughing with the woman who has been dreaming of pushing her husband down the stairs.

As they sit companionably on the sofa, feet up, sipping tea, Kate wonders if they are both thinking of another woman who liked to laugh: Alice Rose. Her dragonfly-bright sister.

Kate leans in closer to Linda.

'If you ever need someone to sit on Leonard and hold him down while you put his hearing aids in, you know you only have to ask.'

And you never know, she might be helping to save Leonard's life.

WEEK 3

You hear the curlews before you see them. Sometimes you can feel their call. They will be there in the pools and marshes hidden in plain sight. Of the earth and apart from it. The sailors used to say: I take my gladness in the sound of the curlew instead of the laughter of men.

Chapter 20

Bardy

What hast thou done

'Good God Lou, what have you done to your ear?!'

Lou now not only has a graze on his cheek – admittedly healing nicely – but a bulbous plaster adorning his right ear.

Lou winces as he touches the plaster. 'Tricky catch, shot off like a bullet. Half the bowl I was making split away.'

'What about the new visor?'

'Well, obviously it doesn't cover my ears,' Lou replies testily. He continues huffily, 'I've got some ear defenders coming from Amazon.'

They are in the art gallery, laying out chairs for this evening's group. The gallery is closed, but the manager, Nathan, said Bardy could use the area that acts as both a classroom and a spare exhibition space. 'And if you could spread the word, Mr Shakespeare… er… Bardy… we need to make the gallery work harder for us.'

'Funding?' Bardy had replied, feeling guilty that Nathan was letting him use the space for free. On the other hand, he reflected, he had got the lad through his GCSEs, then persuaded him to take A levels and go to university.

Sometimes praise worked with these lads. And Nathan had certainly been one of 'these lads'. But Bardy knew direct praise rarely worked. Nathan's mates would have taken the piss. So, you approached it differently, just dropped it into conversation: 'when you're at university…'

'*I ain't going to no university.*'

'Oh, aren't you?' Vague like you're not really interested. 'Why wouldn't you want to do that?' Then move on. Not expecting or even wanting a reply. Just planting a seed.

Nathan had gone on to get a degree in archaeology and museum studies.

Sometimes they still had the power to surprise you.

'Where do you want these chairs?' Lou is asking.

'Those are fine in a circle and then we'll arrange a couple on that raised bit for the model.'

'Who've you got coming?' Lou asks uneasily.

'Not sure. Some bloke Colin knows. Colin's going to come about half an hour after the others arrive, so we can have a catch-up first.'

Leonard, Linda, Pia and Kate all arrive together. Linda and Kate are deep in conversation. Linda hands a cake tin to Bardy. 'Ginger and spiced orange loaf.'

'Thanks Linda.' Bardy looks around, lost. He had remembered drawing boards, art pads, pencils and rubbers, but he hadn't really thought about refreshments. Lou takes the tin from him. 'Come on Linda, there must be a kitchen round here somewhere.' As they wander off together, Bardy can hear Lou asking, 'Now, do you spice your own oranges?'

'This is a lovely space.' Pia is walking down one side of the room, looking at a small exhibition of watercolours that is hanging there. Against a backdrop of coastal images, Bardy once more thinks of a curlew. Bright eyed. Beautiful. Hidden.

'Leonard, you should look at these, some of them remind me of your first painting,' Pia suggests.

Kate is on the other side of the room at a long line of windows that look over the park. A few people are there strolling and walking dogs. It is mid-April and the weather has turned warmer. She glances back to the dais set up for the model. 'Shall I close the blinds on the first few windows so they won't be seen from the park?' she asks.

'Good idea.'

Linda and Lou are back carrying trays loaded with mugs and slices of cake. Lou's plaster looks considerably neater. Nurse Linda has been doing her stuff.

Bardy glances at the door. Will Tay come? It was her idea. But you never knew. He hasn't seen her since last week and she hasn't replied to any of his texts. That isn't that unusual. Then why is he worried that something is wrong between them? That he is missing something. Lou said that work isn't going so well. Is that it?

It is only as they are settled in a circle, drinking coffee and complimenting Linda on her cake that the door opens and Satya rushes in. 'Am I late?'

He had completely forgotten about Satya.

She is met by calls of welcome and she takes the empty chair next to Kate. They are all so busy offering her coffee and cake that it is a moment before Bardy realises that the door has opened again and Tay is pulling up a chair beside him.

'You came!'

'No. This is my twin sister.'

The group turn their focus on Tay and he can feel her stiffen beside him, uncomfortable with all the attention. However, she does take a slice of cake from Linda. She also draws a well-used art pad from her bag.

So the girl means business.

'Right,' Bardy starts, 'my friend Colin, who used to teach art, is coming along in—' he glances at his phone '—about fifteen minutes to guide us through this drawing session. But to begin with, why don't we go round and say how we've been getting on since we last met. Who wants to start?'

'I will,' Pia volunteers. 'Mainly,' she says, 'because I have so little to say. It is very frustrating.' Bardy thinks she sounds angry with herself. 'I have been quilting... but...'

Kate prompts, 'Don't you like it?'

Pia makes a sharp 'ttching' sound. 'It is a quilt. Or the beginnings of one. But it is no more than that. It certainly isn't art.' Now she definitely sounds cross.

'Kate?' Bardy asks.

'I know how Pia is feeling. I think I have watched every single YouTube video on oil painting, but it's so... oh I don't know... I just don't seem able to crack it. Everything from the blending to the colour palette isn't really working.'

'Tell me about it,' Linda joins in. 'Pen and wash. It's more like pen and awash. The paper is curling up and the colours are running everywhere. I tried to paint a bookshop and it just looks like they've had a flood. I'm not sure pen and wash is my thing.'

'How about you, Satya?'

Satya pulls some images from her bag, black and white shots taken in the kitchen of Jack and three boys, aged somewhere between eight and twelve. 'I printed these out so I could really study them. I mean they're not awful, but they don't really tell a story. Apart from the fact all the boys like to eat a lot.'

Like father, like son, Bardy reflects.

As she hands around the images they make encouraging noises.

Bardy thinks the photos are nicely composed – he likes the one of all four figures in front of an open fridge; maybe it reminds him of all the times Jack was staying. But Satya is right, they are missing something.

'I like the one by the fridge,' Kate comments. 'I remember what it was like when my girls' boyfriends came to stay.'

'Eat you out of house and home,' Satya laughs, 'and the mess! And will they ever keep anything tidy? Or realise things need to get done on time? The four of them are a nightmare.'

'Jack…' Kate starts.

'He's the absolute worst,' Satya exclaims.

Blue and green should never be seen. He hears his mother's voice in his head again. Followed by – *the boys are going to kill her. And if they don't, I will.* Bardy shifts uneasily in his chair.

'Leonard, are you still painting in acrylic?' Pia asks, glancing at the paintings on the walls.

Leonard shakes his head. 'Not going well, I'm afraid. I'm not sure I like acrylics. I think I might go back to watercolours.' He looks towards the paintings on the wall, 'Or maybe I will just give up. Perhaps one artist in the family is enough.'

'How about you, Lou?' Kate asks.

Lou shrugs and points at his plaster. 'Not so good *ear* either.'

They all laugh, apart from Leonard who demands of Linda, '*What* did he say?'

Linda sighs.

This is not going well. Even his Smiler has stopped smiling.

'Tay?' he asks in desperation.

'Nah. Too much going on. What about you, Bardy?' she demands back.

What can he say? That he's struggling to write stories? That he's not ready – if he ever will be – to share his colour poems. Like the colours that flood his mind, the poems just seem to come to him.

In an attempt to calm himself he lets the red ochre wash over him.

At least she came. He'll take that as a win.

But is the red ochre fading slightly? Is something seeping away?

'Well?' Tay says, and he realises they are all looking at him.

More than anything he doesn't want to let Tay down. So he says, 'I've written a short story.'

'What's it about?' Linda asks. A bit of a smile.

He is lying, of course. But the slight smile makes him keep going.

'It's about a baker,' he replies, looking at his best friend.

'Go on,' Lou, the wood turning baker says warily.

Bardy sits back in his chair and crosses his legs at the ankles. He looks up at the ceiling for inspiration. 'It is the story of a baker who made the most wonderful cakes and pastries. His madeleines were so light that people compared them to clouds, his florentines were exactly the right combination of chewy and crispy. And as for his fruit tarts. Well, they were famous all over the kingdom.'

'Ah, a fairy story,' Kate murmurs.

Maybe it will be. He's winging it here.

He looks around at them all. 'The king heard of the baker's great skill and he called him to the palace. The baker travelled three days across the kingdom to meet him, and the king said, come and cook for me. But the baker replied, thank you your majesty, but I like my little shop…'

Bardy pauses.

'I like where I live. I don't really want to travel.'

Bardy sees Lou watching him. He wonders if he sees what he has just seen. Hana had always wanted to travel. She was a golden yellow wanderer. Bardy was not. They may have met teaching in Botswana but at heart he is a home bird. Had that initial meeting fooled her into thinking he wanted more? He does not ache with the rhythm of migration, he wants to stay among the creeks and marshes, and the breath-taking ever-changing skies. How could he have thought he would ever move to New Zealand? But Hana would.

It was her home.

How could he not have seen this?

He had thought she was talking about more exotic holidays.

She was telling him how she wanted to live the rest of her life.

The thought stuns him and robs him of words.

'So what did the king do?' The Smiler is back, encouraging him. He glances from Linda to Kate and wishes he could tell her how her daughter, Ellie, had helped him. Wishes he could tell Linda how glad he is to have a Smiler with him now. He lets his mind flood with mellow plum and takes a deep breath.

'He did what any king would do. He offered the baker great riches and jewels to become his personal baker and to move to the palace where he created the most glorious kitchen for him.'

'I wish,' mutters the baker.

'He had mixing bowls made from the finest copper and spoons whittled from wood chopped from the royal forest. The ovens were so big that the kitchen boy could stand in them without bending down. The village came out to wave him off and although they were sad to say goodbye, they were proud that their baker was to become so famous.'

Lou sits a little straighter in his seat.

'So the baker started to cook and the king and his court waited for these wonderful cakes, of which they had heard so much.'

'And?' Satya asks.

Bardy knows he struggled with some of the children they fostered. Anyone would. But none of them had ever complained about his bedtime stories.

'And,' Bardy continues, 'the cakes were an enormous and breath-taking disappointment.'

Pia lets out a small, 'Oh.'

'His once tasty offerings were bland and unappetising. His cakes were soggy and his biscuits that once were crisp and delicious were so chewy they had to call for the royal dentist. The baker did not know what to do. He re-read his recipes. He came up with new more exciting recipes. But nothing worked. Now the king had a dog... er... a whippet.'

This time Pia lets out a small happy, 'Oh.'

'...of which he was very proud as he was a most expensive dog. This hound could always nose out the most succulent truffles, and if he were to steal something from the kitchen, which I am afraid to say he did on more than one occasion, the baker had noticed that he always found the best, the most expensive ingredients to snaffle. The baker liked and respected this dog and the dog liked the baker in return. So the baker started to take the dog out with him when he went to the market, and with his help ensured that he brought back to the palace kitchens only the most succulent and tasty of ingredients.'

'And?' Linda asks.

'And still the cakes and pastries were a disaster.'

If he keeps talking he won't have to think about Hana.

'There were whisperings in the privy council about the duplicity of the baker and the king began to listen. Maybe he should be thrown into the dungeon and that would be the end of that.'

He catches Tay watching him. He cannot read her expression.

'Around this time his great friend from the village came to visit him. He had stopped receiving letters from the baker and he was worried. He travelled the great distance to the palace and eventually after many mishaps found the baker sitting on a stool in the kitchen all on his own. Except for the whippet who was by his side, with his head resting in his lap.

'The baker was overjoyed to see his friend, and over wine and soggy cakes told him his sad tale. Now his friend...' Bardy catches Leonard's eye '...was... ah... he was an engineer. But he had the soul of a poet. Which is an unusual and wonderful combination. He looked around the kitchen at the expensive equipment, he stroked the dog – he was a man who liked dogs – and he made a discovery. And this is what he said to the baker.

'"Your oven is too big," his friend proclaimed. And like a blinding light the baker saw what his friend the engineer had seen at once. That with an oven that big, he needed to give his recipes much more time to cook.'

Bardy now knows what he wants to say.

'What the baker realised is that sometimes to achieve the best results you have to give it time. What you really want cannot be achieved in the blink of an eye. It needs time and yes,' he glances at Linda, 'patience, to get to where you want to.'

'So what happened to the baker?' Linda asks, still smiling, but with a good deal of understanding in the gleam of her eye.

He looks around at the others watching him. *Will this help them?*

'He did the obvious thing,' Bardy tells her.

'Which was?' Tay asks. And he is reminded of the little girl who used to sit on the sofa listening to his stories. In the days when he sat in a chair on the other side of the room.

'He baked the king the most wonderful cakes, the likes of which had never before been seen or tasted in the palace. He piled them high on the king's golden table that stood in the privy council chamber. Then he hung up his apron, left a polite note on the kitchen table and returned to his village with his friend, to live where he was happiest.'

Was that it? After all this time.

This was his home. It was never Hana's.

'And the dog?' Pia asks.

'Ah…' Bardy pauses, momentarily caught.

But Bardy's stories always had happy endings. It was what his listeners had wanted. Hope that it could be better. Or somewhere where they could hide. 'The baker took the dog with him. The king had never really loved the dog, he just prized him because he was expensive. He did not realise how special he was – a good and loyal friend, there for him when things were bad.'

A very gentle 'ah', from Pia.

Lou wipes something from his eye. Wood dust probably.

A round of applause from the others.

Bardy wants to walk out of the room and keep walking. To be alone with his thoughts. He is saved by an alert sounding on his phone.

Chapter 21

Kate

Our doubts are our traitors

Colin cannot make it and Bardy is clearly thrown. Or has something else upset him? It was a strange story to tell them. Sweet and completely unexpected. She got what he was telling them all, and of course, he was right. These things took time. She will just keep going with her painting, perhaps she will look at how other artists approached oils.

'He's really sorry to let us down, but his mother has had a fall,' Bardy explains.

'Nothing he can do about that. Your mum's your mum. Got to come first.' Lou nods. 'What about the model?'

'Am I in the right place?' a voice booms from the door. Very Welsh. A large man wearing camouflage trousers and a neon-orange jacket. 'Colin said this was the spot. Which one of you is Bardy?'

Bardy rises to greet the man. 'I'm sorry, that's me. I'm afraid Colin can't make it, His mum…'

'Enid? Has something happened to her?'

'She's had a fall. They are on the way to the hospital now.'

'Best place,' the Welshman says philosophically.

'So you see—' Bardy starts.

'Could I help, Bardy,' Kate cuts in. 'I've done a few life drawing classes in the past. Would you like me to organise this?'

The look he throws her confirms what Kate is thinking. For some reason or another Bardy is barely hanging on.

Kate turns to the model. 'Come and meet everyone…'

'And let's get you a coffee and some cake,' Linda finishes.

A few minutes later 'Bazza' and Kate are on the dais, talking about the arrangement of chairs and the pose. Bazza has taken off his jacket but still has his trousers on and a black Bruce Springsteen T-shirt that has seen better days. 'Eighteen concerts. No one comes close to the Boss,' he tells Kate.

Chairs arranged, Kate suggests, 'Would you like to go behind the screen to undress? We are ready whenever you are.' Kate returns to the chairs that have now been lined up facing the dais. Everyone has a board and art pad – it seems Bardy has bought in bulk – and a selection of pencils. Kate has kept hold of all the rubbers. Her first art teacher had said you need to look and have confidence in what you draw. Even if you get it wrong. Kate glances along the row. All are looking nervous. Bardy is doodling something on the page in front of him.

Bazza comes out from behind the screen naked as the day he was born. Kate knows that it is a huge advantage if the model is professional and confident. It puts inexperienced artists at their ease. Bazza exudes a world-beating-awe-inspiring-jaw-dropping confidence. He stands, hands on hips, legs apart. 'Well, now,' he booms, 'let's get this show on the road.'

He settles on the chair and shuffles like a hen about to lay, legs still akimbo, then he leans back into the pose that Kate and he had decided upon. The group are quiet and respectful, although Kate can sense they are like children in church trying not to laugh.

'Thank you, Bazza,' Kate calls. 'Now let's get started. And forget what your mind is telling you. Just draw what you can see.'

'I think I need my glasses,' Linda murmurs from beside her.

Kate pushes the laughter down inside her. She can't say she has a huge amount of experience of different penises, but there is no doubt that Bazza's member is by far the smallest she has ever seen. She didn't actually know they came that small. Which makes his overwhelming confidence even more admirable. She glances along the line. Lou and Leonard are sitting that bit taller. Bardy is drawing, concentrating. There is a grim look on his face which she thinks has nothing to do with whatever he thinks of Bazza's body. He is miles away.

'Okay for this first pose we will give it ten minutes. Just try and get down a basic outline, a sketch. You are looking at the overall proportions of the body. It doesn't have to be perfect. This is about warming up and getting your hand and eye in.'

There is complete silence apart from a gentle humming from Bazza – 'Born to Run', very melodic – and the soft scrape of pencils over paper. Kate quickly gets down the form and pose. This she can do. It is oil painting that is sapping her confidence. She loves this looking and absorbing shape and form. She now sees that the man in front of her is a joy to behold. Mountains of stomach rounded and rather magnificent. Powerful thighs and graceful, curving calves. Beautiful neat ankles. Feet are a problem to draw. She knows one artist who always starts there – says, if you can get the feet right, the rest is a walk in the park. She looks up to check the blinds are shielding Bazza from the gaze of those enjoying a late evening walk. Not that she thinks the man would care in the least.

Leaving her drawing on her chair, she walks along the line, checking how everyone is getting on. Most are holding their pencils way too tight and, as she suspected, are concentrating nervously on the detail, going over the same part again and again. She knows if they had rubbers there would be more eraser marks than pencil marks on the paper. She makes some gentle suggestions and moves on along the line.

Tay is really good. Confident. She's having trouble with the feet too.

Pia's effort is not at all bad. Although she is scowling at her paper.

Leonard's proportions are good but his perspective is way out. She wonders if he once worked with technical drawings.

'I just don't want to make a mess of it,' Satya says, turning her pad this way and that.

This gives Kate an idea. She knows doubt and nerves make people tentative when they draw. They worry about spoiling what they've put down, or even ruining the book they are drawing in.

'Okay, thank you Bazza, you can relax that pose.'

Kate flips through her art pad to the last few pages and pulls these out. She then tears each page very roughly into four. She then gives each person four pieces. 'Right we are now going to do a series of four quick sketches on rough paper. These can be thrown away, they are just for practice. Two minutes each.' She looks at Bazza who nods back. A professional. 'Bazza will choose each pose. You can draw a quick sketch of the whole pose or look at one part and get that down. My advice is don't think too much about it. Off we go then.'

The atmosphere changes completely. People start to chat – and, Kate suspects, breathe normally. After eight minutes, the group ask for four more poses. Some pieces of paper are discarded but she can see one or two of the small swift sketches are being held on to. Leonard's outline of Bazza's head. Lou's drawing of his whole outline. Pia seems fascinated by the big man's hands. Only Bardy seems to just be going through the motions. Although what he is producing is competent. Then again, he was married to an artist. Has something happened to Hana? Only once this evening has Kate caught him looking at Pia and that was when she and Pia had their heads together talking about perspective.

'Okay, Bazza, do you need a break?' Kate asks.

'A coffee and another slice of that orange cake would go down a treat.' He takes a small towel from his backpack and wraps this around to (almost) cover his modesty and joins the group.

Kate goes with Linda to the kitchen to replenish the coffee and cut more cake. When they return, the group are gathered around the semi-naked Welshman.

'I'm sure I know you from somewhere, Barry,' Leonard is saying.

'Well, I ran the post office out by the dyke road for many

a year. But I had to give up when all that nonsense happened with the computers. Terrible it was.'

Despite his near nakedness Kate can sense the group draw closer in sympathy.

'So were you one of the sub-postmasters caught up in it?' Pia asks.

'Not personally but friends of mine were and I could see they were getting stitched up right, left and centre. Decided to throw in the towel, so to speak.' He tucks his towel more securely around him. 'Now I'm a delivery driver.'

'Amazon!' Bardy has come out of his preoccupied fug.

'That's right.'

There is a collective 'Aah,' and Kate thinks they are all mentally reviewing everything they have ever ordered from Amazon.

'That is an interesting ring you're wearing,' Pia comments, pointing to a large metal band on Bazza's left hand. It has a small ball of metal at the top of the band with a small metal ring suspended from it.

'Ah now that,' Bazza informs them proudly, 'signifies that I am a dom. If it was on my right hand I would be a sub.'

'I'm sorry?' Pia queries.

'I'm president of the East Anglian Sado-Masochistic Society. We meet every other Tuesday. New members are always welcome.' He beams around at them.

Kate can't help the laugh. Nor can others.

Bazza continues to smile at them. Kate thinks he must be used to this. Kate sees Bardy cast Tay an anxious glance and in return, she widens her eyes at him. It is a look that is youthful but also says, *for goodness' sake, I'm not a child*.

As if aware of this, Bazza continues, 'It is all consenting adults. We are very strict about that. We sometimes have to exclude the goths who think the ring is a fashion accessory, but for us it is a way of communicating to other like-minded enthusiasts. I used to laugh with fellow members from the post office. Other sub-postmasters. We would say, "Sub by day. Dom by night." Oh, how we laughed.'

They are all laughing now.

'You are remarkably open about this,' Linda observes.

'Nothing to be ashamed of, dear lady. As long as the safe words are in place and we ensure it is all age appropriate. Why shouldn't we be with people who have a similar sexual preference?'

'No reason whatsoever,' Pia agrees, and she gives Kate the smallest of winks.

'Now back to work,' Bazza says flicking off his towel and striding back to the dais. Ever the professional. Kate wonders if she will ever order anything from Amazon ever again.

The last ten minutes are spent on one pose. There is some conversation but an air of concentration fills the room. It is Bardy who now patrols the line of artists. He seems to have overcome whatever was bothering him. When he comes to Kate he leans forward. 'Thanks for all that,' and he touches her lightly on the shoulder. He pulls his hand away as if burnt. Kate wants to say, it's okay. She knew it for what it was, a friendly gesture. She knows she *really* likes the man, but friendship would be good too. Knowing Pia is gay and that Bardy has no chance with her makes very little difference to what she hopes for. Pia had said, when talking about her musical family, that she didn't like to be second best. Neither does Kate.

Bardy addresses them all. 'I really want to thank Kate for stepping in for Colin.' There is a round of applause.

Satya looks down at her current drawing. 'I know it's not brilliant, but I'm quite proud of this.' She looks up. 'And I think it is going to influence how I photograph people.'

An image flashes into Kate's mind of Satya presiding over an exhibition of arty black and white sado-masochistic imagery.

'I still feel like a fraud though,' Pia admits, though Kate can tell by her voice that she is secretly pleased with what she has drawn.

'You have to fake it to make it,' Tay says, packing up her bag. She glances at Bardy. 'It's what someone we know used to say.'

Hana.

'Yeah, my wife was an artist. She said you had to start somewhere. No one is born an artist.'

'Well, they are,' Tay challenges him.

Kate has a sense of what is coming next. What an interesting girl Tay is.

'Picasso said all children are artists,' Tay finishes.

It is Satya who follows this. 'Our boys were like that. They would just go for it, they came up with the most amazing ideas and then they seemed to lose confidence.'

'School,' Bardy mutters sadly.

'After that they would always try and copy each other, wanting to be sure they were getting it right, worried if someone was doing better... and now...'

'Now?' Leonard says.

Kate isn't sure if he is asking a question or querying if he has heard right.

Satya quickly packs her own bag. Head down. 'I don't know.

Jack does all of that sort of stuff.' She mutters, 'Why does everything have to be money making and fame making. It's not fun anymore.'

Kate doesn't think Satya expects an answer, but she does wonder if Satya is talking about art, business or life.

Kate lies in bed that night, curtains and window partly open so she can smell what she thinks of as the eau-de-nil scent of blue saltwater mixed with vegetation, turned greeny-grey by the night. She listens to the gentle wash of the tide and thinks about Bardy. What had upset him earlier? Tay? No, he and Tay seem argumentative but close.

She's an interesting girl. A child still but sometimes so much older than her years. A quicksilver mix of anxious and confident. Strong though. And Satya? Why does thinking about children and Tay make her think of Satya and her photographs? She reviews the images in her mind and thinks of how Satya spoke of her family. Then it comes to her.

Her boys.

Was Jack just one of her boys?

Loved, for sure, but often irritating, just one of the pack to keep in line?

Chapter 22

Bardy

More sinned against than sinning

It is 3.16am and he can't sleep. Nothing makes sense. Or maybe too much now makes sense. How could he not have realised that about Hana? Had he just heard what he wanted to hear? Wanted to believe she was happy with him? That this was home. How can he ever have thought that he would move halfway around the world? However much he loves his boys.

He remembers the months, stretching into years of Hana finding fault with things – and how he'd somehow felt responsible. But now looking back, was it aimed at him? Maybe he just took it that way, wedded as he is to this place.

The people were too narrow minded.

The weather too this or that.

The landscape too flat.

Never the right light.

That glorious light that is as vital to Bardy as breathing.

He thought she was talking about the light for her painting. Increasingly she spoke of wanting to get away.

He worried about the holidays they couldn't afford.

Now his world has been flipped. Reflected to reveal what Hana was really telling him. This was not a criticism of his home, the place Hana had ended up. She was showing him she wanted to be with her people, with the weather she knew, the landscape she loved. She wanted a world with a different light.

Why hadn't she just come out and said it?

Was it because she knew him for what he is – a home bird of the marshes? She knew there really was no solution. So she became closed down, knotted tighter and tighter in her discontent. Increasingly distant from him.

And now out of the blue Hana has contacted him. Sent a text. Wants to meet. Not the normal periodic popping in to visit the area. This had been more pointed. What is that all about?

And Kate! That had freaked him out. Not the Pia thing. He'd seen the wink. Understood. Felt a fool. But then he was used to that.

Curlew. Amber bright. In plain sight.

He's *such* an idiot. That is what Tay had said to him and Lou. Did she know?

Bazza. Nice bloke. Sub by day, dom by night. Bardy's not going to order anything from Amazon any time soon. Couldn't look him in the face. But was Bazza's group so very different from this group? People with a shared interest getting together, making friends – just Bardy's group used fewer whips and chains.

But Kate!

The moment he touched her shoulder. A glimpse like the flash of a fish tail breaking the surface. Gleaming. Pure shimmering silver. Then he snatched his hand away and it was gone. That has never happened to him before. Was it a colour or just light? He has no idea. Didn't dare put his hand back on her shoulder. However much he'd wanted to.

What the hell is going on?

Bardy does the only thing he can think of.

Bardy and Lou lower themselves into the plastic-latticed beach chairs. They are hidden by the reeds from the path. Not that anyone is going to be here this early. It is 4.23am. In front of them is a pool of water, a film of mist lying low, from which emerge clumps of reedmace. They look like islands hovering above the water. The moon is part obscured by cloud adding to the other-worldliness of the scene. Above the creaking of the beach chairs there is the shriek of a solitary barn owl.

'Tea or beer?' Lou asks.

'Start with tea,' Bardy wraps the spare blanket Lou has brought over his knees. He wonders if the blankets have been used since their days as lockdown rebels. Rebels with comfy fleecy blankets.

'Do you know what Hana wants?' Lou asks, passing him a steaming thermos cup.

'No and I didn't like to ask.'

'Maybe she just wants to say goodbye. Ask if you want her to take anything to the boys.'

'Maybe.' But Bardy has a feeling it is more than that. Or is it that he wants to say something to her?

'Did you think Hana and I were suited?'

Not their normal chat. But needs must.

'Oh, mate…' is Lou's helpless response.

'What did Tina think?' Bardy tries. 'I know they weren't close but did she ever say anything?'

The silence tells Bardy that she did and that he's not going to want to hear it.

There is a rustle in the grass just below them.

'Water vole?' Lou suggests.

'Maybe an otter,' Bardy responds.

They both know they are buying some time.

And that it is probably a rat.

Two romantics at heart.

Lou gives a deep sigh. More creaks from the chair. 'She did think Hana wasn't so happy living here.' He holds up a hand. 'I know she threw herself into everything, her work, after school clubs, painting, fostering, French classes. But Tina, well, she said nobody needed to be that busy.'

Was life with him that bad?

'And Hana and me?'

'Ah, sorry mate. Look Hana was… is… amazing.'

Yep, too good for me.

'But Tina thought you could do better.'

'*What?!*'

'Look don't shoot the messenger. And Tina…'

Is already dead.

It's Bardy's turn to say, 'Ah, sorry mate.'

They sit in silence for some time.

'She really thought that?' Bardy follows up quickly with, 'She was wrong.'

Lou holds up both hands now, placating – spilling his tea in the process. 'You asked.'

Bardy had known Tina and Hana hadn't been particularly friendly. Was that it? Tina just not liking Hana. But then Tina was great. And what a colour.

'Did she say why?'

'Just that you were a big softy and that Hana was kind of hard.'

'She's not,' Bardy fires back. 'My God, all those kids, and our boys, they love her.' He thinks of Tay walking into Hana's embrace. Red ochre merging with golden yellow.

'Beer?' Lou asks. A diversion.

'Yeah, go on then.'

It may only be 5.04am but Bardy feels like he needs one.

Bardy has never been in so much demand. Hana is travelling back from Wales and has asked that they get together for something to eat at the pub. Linda has set up a WhatsApp group for the eight of them and has invited them all for supper at their house. And now Tay has messaged him. Wants to meet him.

All other thoughts are banished.

They meet in a coffee shop that looks out over the harbour. The sign on the door reads, *Barista is RNLI crew so please be patient if he is missing.* No argument from anyone around here. Bardy is good enough with a boat but knows his limitations and sticks to that. Most people know someone who has got into trouble. So he does what he can for the RNLI. Once persuaded Lou to be Santa, arriving in the town on a lifeboat.

Tay is waiting for him at a table by the window, she already has her usual flat white in front of her. He nods at her from the counter – Finn is there, no callout today – and mouths, *cake?* She shakes her head.

He budges on to the bench seat opposite. 'Okay?' he asks.

'Yeah.'

It doesn't carry much conviction.

'Work?' he asks, remembering what Lou had told him.

'Yeah.' This time she sounds surprised. Good he's got something right.

'Want to tell me about it?'

'Yeah.' This time with an eye roll: *why do you think I messaged you.*

Bardy waits.

Tay picks at the skin around her thumbnail. 'I've got to go to this stupid disciplinary meeting at work. I mean I could just leave but then *she* will have won. And it's not so bad there. The pay's shit but I like dealing with the people who come to me with problems.'

Before Bardy gets to who *she* is, he thinks he'd better find out exactly what Tay does. Wishes he'd asked before.

It transpires that in the customer service department of the insurance company where she works, she is now off the phones and deals with more complicated complaints and queries. Mainly by email but some phone work and the occasional visit. She is the newest member of a team of twelve women, and although she is not directly accountable to other members of the team – all of whom are much older than her – it seems they treat her like she is. 'And I understand the CRM system way better than they do, some of them can't even work their way round a basic spreadsheet.'

'CRM?'

She widens her eyes at him, 'Customer relationship management.'

'Who is your boss?' he wonders – if these women aren't.

'A woman called Jan, but she's often in London. She's kind of doing two jobs at the moment as someone is off sick.'

'And who is the "*she*"?'

'Karen. She's a right bitch,' Tay says, cutting to the chase. 'To start with you think she's okay, she comes over all friendly. Then you realise what she's really like. They're all scared of her. She's got these ratty little eyes, in fact she reminds me of a rat, small with scraggy hair – except I quite like rats. Anyway, what Karen says goes and if you stand up to her well… then she starts.'

'What happened?'

'She just kept pushing my buttons.'

'And?'

'I told her to piss off.'

'Aah.'

'But she had just said that I was a piece of shit like my mum and wouldn't ever get anywhere. She was at school with Toni for a while. But no one heard that and of course now she says she didn't say it. And she said that it's not fair I get time off for college. But that's a law thing because of my age, it's nothing to do with me, or *her*.'

Bardy's distracted. 'What are you studying?'

'Project management. Which is okay.'

'Sorry, so what has this Karen done?'

'She made a complaint and HR had to investigate and the bloke we have to deal with, Jonathan, is *useless*. He just goes on and on and no one has a clue what he's talking about. He's scared of Karen too.'

'But surely she must do this to other people?' That was one thing Bardy knew about bullies. 'It will all come out.'

Tay looks at him like he's stupid. 'Of course she's been getting them all on side. She's been going on about how it's unfair me going to college and that I'm just taking time out. Taking the piss. And she's even got them all listening in to my conversations, saying my work needs checking. And I don't know how she did it but *she's* now looking after Mrs Willis.'

'Who's Mrs Willis?'

But Tay hasn't finished. 'She said something about her not being happy. Which I don't believe. But she says I can't ring her because of bloody GDPR. I asked Jonathan if that was balls and he just said that Karen was probably right.'

'He does sound useless,' Bardy comments.

'I told you.'

'And Mrs Willis?'

'She's done it because I like Mrs Willis. Her dogs are minging, but she's not so bad and I was helping her. We got on. And I don't need *her* telling me what to do and checking my work like I'm thick…'

Bardy lets her speak. It seems Tay has a lot to get off her chest.

Eventually he asks, 'How long has this been going on, Tay?'

He thinks back to how preoccupied she has been.

She frowns. 'Forever... well, months. To start with she just threatened to make a complaint about me, went on and on about it. Then I said I didn't care. Told her to piss off. Again. And then she did it and HR stuck their noses in and there's some sort of process and... I don't know. Maybe I should just leave.'

'No, don't do that. What's this disciplinary meeting?'

'That's when they tell me about the investigation and rip into me about it all, well, that's what Uzma said.'

'Whose Uzma?'

He doesn't think he's ever taught an Uzma.

'She's my mate. She's okay. She said just suck it up, pretend I don't care. Everyone knows she's a total bitch.'

Perhaps that is who she has been texting. He'd like to meet Uzma.

'Do you want to leave?'

'Yeah, *obviously*. But not like this. And if I leave now they'll give me a shit reference. It will be on my record. I won't get to finish college. And anyway, I was thinking maybe I could move to one of their other offices. Uzma's from Leeds, she says that's quite cool. Maybe we could get a flat. Not that I could leave Toni. Like she's so *utterly* useless and shit.'

A razor wire of rust for the woman she stopped calling 'mum' some years ago. But Bardy knows whatever Tay may say to him, she will never repeat this stuff to Toni's face. She is too worried it would break her.

He can see tears starting in Tay's eyes.

She never cries.

'You can't live all your life looking after Toni,' Bardy tells her.

'Yeah, and what happens when she's so drunk she falls down the stairs and isn't found for months and her head's cracked open and there are maggots and flies and slime?'

Bardy has always thought Toni let Tay watch *CSI* way too young.

He picks his words carefully. 'I know this is frightening, but you cannot be Toni's full-time nurse and bodyguard. You have your own life. And something could be worked out, Tay.'

A tear trickles down her face. She does not wipe it away.

'Look, we could set up a system. I could check on her once a week and let you know.'

'*But you won't be here!*' she hurls at him.

Her hurt soaked rage forces him back into the seat. 'What do you mean?'

'You're leaving! You're going to New Zealand. I saw the house details in your flat when I came over once.'

He instinctively reaches for her hands. She pulls them away, now scrubbing furiously at her face, grubby with mascara and tears. 'I thought if you did this group thing you might remember you liked it here. And when you told that story and how the baker…' She fights a sob. 'He liked his home… and didn't want to go. I thought… maybe…' The sob wins and Bardy wants to rip his heart from his chest. 'But I get it. They win. They're family. We're not.'

Bardy's insides twist with the anguish of her pain and his guilt. How can he have been so stupid? He knew something was wrong – but not this. He holds out one of his hands, palm upwards. 'I am *not* going to New Zealand.'

She stops stock still. Her hand inches towards his. 'You're not?'

'Look, I did think about it. I won't deny that. But things change.' He is fighting his own tears now. 'I am so sorry Tay.'

She tentatively puts her fingertips near his. Not touching. But close.

'I am *so* sorry. I am going to be staying right here.' He stifles a gulp. 'Anyway what would Lou do without me?' He says this to make her smile – which works. But he is flooded with another wave of guilt. He can't believe he talked so blithely about leaving to his best mate. That wonderful man had not shown him an ounce of the hurt he must have been feeling. Bardy is rocked by his shame.

'Yeah, he would be pretty lost without you.' Tay gives a watery sniff. 'Two *total* idiots.'

'Pia?' Bardy asks.

'Couldn't you see it? It was so obvious Kate stood more chance than you two did.'

Good call. Silver bright Kate.

'Are you gay?' he asks conversationally. It couldn't matter less.

'Oh, Bardy we don't think like that. You're into who you're into.'

Fair enough.

'So are we good?' he asks her.

She nods.

'Anything I can do?'

'Yeah, this disciplinary meeting...'
God, he'd forgotten about that.
'...I can take someone. Will you come with me?'
'Of course I will, Tay. *Of course* I will.'

Chapter 23

Kate

O let me teach you how to knit again

Ellie's sewing machine is set up on a dark wooden table set at right angles to a huge window. The cream quilt is stretched out over the table, a landscape of soft undulating hillocks of fabric. Pia throws her arm wide to the view beyond the window. 'I seem to be sewing a pocket of English countryside... I don't know... something neat and contained. And just look at that.'

Kate does look. The view is vast. It would be impossible to take in the sky within a simple glance. She turns her head to the left and to the right to take in the whole. Today the sky is an ethereal, watery blue. It looks as if clouds have been spilt across it, streaking it white. In some places, larger patches of white have pooled. At the horizon the clouds seem to drift until they butt up against a solid, luminous line of sand. Between this and Pia's house sit wetland meadows and marshland: layers of green, rust and ochre, dissected in places by the line of a dyke or a fence-like band of reeds.

No. The quilt does not capture this. Kate thinks of her attempts at painting and wonders if anything ever could. The quilt is cosy middle-England. This landscape is something else altogether.

'Are you enjoying it though?' Kate asks.

Pia has moved across the large open-plan room to the kitchen area where she is now preparing coffee and retrieving something from inside the black Aga. 'I do quite enjoy it,' she admits, 'especially the hand sewing. I think there is something soothing about the repetition of pulling a needle through fabric.' Pia places the coffee on the low table by the three grey sofas that form a horseshoe, looking at the view. 'Wienerbrød?' Pia asks, nodding at the plate of pastries.

Kate has never heard of wienerbrød, but it looks delicious. When she bites into the flaky layers of pastry her taste buds are flooded with a glorious mixture of blueberry, lemon and almond. Pia certainly can bake.

Kate gazes around her at the beautiful living space. 'Pia, how can you say you're not creative when you cook like this, and can create a space like this?'

Pia nods dismissively at the wienerbrød, but she studies the room more seriously. 'I don't really know. It just happens.'

'But how does it happen?' Kate is intrigued.

'Well, I guess I always look at magazines and books on design. I remember places I have been. Then I just let it sit. It's like…' She says something in Danish. Then tries to explain, 'Like a meditation that is more like drifting. And from there ideas emerge.'

Kate shakes her head. 'And you say you're not creative.' She grins. 'That's just how it is with me and painting. It's not about chasing ideas, I have to give myself time and relax into the things and experiences that inspire me.'

'Like a mackerel cloud swimming in the sky.'

'Exactly.'

'Kate, I still may not be doing so well with my quilt, but thank you for asking me to join this group with you. It *is* a good thing to be part of.'

'Tay is an interesting girl,' Kate comments.

Pia nods, stirring her coffee. 'I think she has had quite a tough time. I get the impression she doesn't have much of a family.'

'She has Bardy.' Kate wonders why she feels defensive.

'Ah Bardy,' Pia grins at her.

'What?' Kate feels herself colouring.

'You don't think you and…'

Kate moves some crumbs around the plate with her finger. 'You once told me that you didn't like to be second best.'

'Did I?'

'Music, and your family?'

'Ah, yes. When you are surrounded by people that good it…' Pia shrugs.

Kate suddenly wonders about the other kids at school. She was always 'Kate, the one who can draw'. Did that make other children feel like they had very little to offer?

'And?' Pia prompts.

'Oh, just that I find I don't like being second best either.'

'Ah,' Pia says, with understanding. 'There could never be anything between me and Bardy,' she insists.

'I know that, but you can't deny he has got a bit of a thing for you.'

'Has he?' Pia says vaguely. Disinterested.

Kate wonders if this is what Bardy would say if someone were to tell him Kate had 'a bit of a thing' for him. She knows he likes her, but nothing more. He certainly doesn't look at her like he looks at Pia.

'How's your painting going?' Pia asks.

Kate perks up. 'Better, definitely better.' Then she laughs, pointing at the view, 'But when I look at this, it kind of makes me want to give up. It's not just the light, but the colours I'm struggling with. This feels like... well... like a whole world. I feel like sometimes I'm getting somewhere with the sky, and sometimes I'm really painting the land and water in the way I want to. But it doesn't seem to come together.'

'And it is always better to come together,' Pia says with a twinkle.

Kate grins. 'Sure is.' She changes the subject. 'Are you going to Leonard and Linda's tomorrow for supper?'

'Definitely.'

'I do like them,' Kate says, 'although I wish Leonard would wear his hearing aids. Did I tell you Linda nursed my sister, Alice, when she was dying?'

Pia leans forward. 'I'm so sorry, Kate.'

'It was oh, eight years ago now. But I can't tell you how good it is to know she was looked after by Linda.'

'Tell me about Alice,' Pia says simply.

So Kate does. All except how Alice laughed when Kate

painted as JoJo Rose. And also about the secret guilt that still sits deep in the heart of her, of the time she let her sister down. In turn Pia tells Kate about her sisters.

They are on their third coffee when Noy bounds into the room. They can hear Brenda behind him, lumbering up the stairs to the first-floor living space, 'Lovely walk. Thank you for letting me take Noy Boy out.'

She reaches the doorway and pops her head around. 'We had such fun didn't we boy.'

But neither of the women is looking at her. They are staring at Noy, who is now investigating the empty plate of wienerbrød.

Having made sure there are no crumbs left he sits at Pia's feet looking up at her, a slightly quizzical look on his face.

Kate thinks he might well be puzzled. So is she.

Having caught her breath, Brenda bustles into the room. 'Doesn't he look smart! I do so love to knit and now the grandchildren are all grown and into their designer brands, well, I have all that wool just sitting there and Noy Boy hates the cold, don't you boy.'

Noy is sitting in front of Pia wearing a smart new jumper in cerise wool – not unlike the colour of Lou's jumper. It is edged in orange. He also has a matching hat with orange stripes. At the back of which is a large purple tassel.

Brenda is beaming.

Noy looks perplexed and it may be Kate's imagination, but he seems to be looking at them, brows drawn together and a 'why me?' expression in his eyes.

However, Kate thinks Pia's expression is the one she likes

most. The immaculate, elegant Dane looks like someone has just hit her in the face with a very smelly fish.

And Kate finds once she starts to laugh she can't stop.

Kate is still smiling at the memory of this moment when the taxi drops her off outside Leonard and Linda's house the following evening. She had suggested sharing a lift with Pia but Pia is coming directly from a meeting in London. Pia had not been angry with Brenda – or certainly had not shown it. But she had been firm in insisting that she did not wish for Noy to be dressed like this. Kate had heard the steel in Pia's voice, but she is not sure Brenda did. She just kept saying, 'Of course, of course. He's your Noy Boy,' while smiling and patting the whippet. Kate might not like Brenda's choice of knitwear, but you can't deny she loves Noy.

Kate gets out of the taxi and pays the driver. The house in front of her is a mix of flint brickwork, wood and glass. It is far more modern than she had been expecting, even though she had remembered Leonard and Linda saying it was a newbuild. She realises she has made the mistake of presuming, because they are older, they would want something more traditional. She thinks it is a spectacular house, and what a position – tucked into a large bowl between sweeping sand dunes. It must be barely a minute's walk down onto the beach.

Linda emerges from the broad, wooden front door. 'Come on in. You're the first.'

A few minutes later Kate is inside being given a guided tour by Linda. They start in the kitchen, a vast airy room, with a long modern table that looks like it could sit twenty. There is a broad ash wood shelf running the length of the room, displaying numerous photos of their sons and families – mostly taken by the sea. Large glass doors look out over a garden planted with different types of grasses intersected with pale stone paths. Kate thinks it is the perfect complement to the backdrop of sand dunes.

'So, this leads to the hallway, bathroom on your right...' Linda looks over her shoulder. 'When you get to my age, that is always the first thing you need to know.' She moves on, arms sweeping left and right. 'Sitting room off to your left, and Leonard has a study to the right, with his piano.'

Kate peers into a huge square room filled with long low sofas and chairs all in different shades of blue. There is an enormous fireplace and on the walls modern seascapes – one which she recognises, by a famous local artist. 'It is wonderful, Linda.'

'Come on, down here, this is the fun bit.' Over her shoulder she adds, 'I must admit when Leonard suggested this next bit I thought he was going too far, but the family and kids just adore it.'

The broad corridor opens up and to the left of Kate is an area the size of a small sitting room. Linda flicks a switch and lights come on behind a wall of glass shelves.

'I love it!' Kate exclaims.

They are standing in a small bar. Shelves gleam with bottles, there is a counter with bar stools and lower tables with small cube-like chairs around them. The walls are covered in family photographs. A pink neon sign above the bar reads *Leonard's* in swirly script. Linda raises her eyes to heaven. 'The boys gave it to him. He loves it, of course.'

'Go on, Linda, you love it too,' Kate teases.

'Of course I do,' Linda admits, 'just don't tell Leonard.'

The doorbell sounds just as Leonard enters the room, accompanied by two Labradors. 'Leonard, you get Kate a drink. I'll get the door.' She peers through the long thin window beside her.

'Ah, looks like it's Bardy.'

Kate's stomach lurches.

Chapter 24

Bardy

My library was dukedom large enough

Silver bright Kate is standing with a cocktail in her hand. Bardy is trying to take it all in. The bar. The sign. Silver Kate. Pia who arrived just as he and Tay did. For some reason he thinks about when he gave up smoking. It's a struggle for many, he knows, but one day he wanted to smoke – the next day he didn't. Pia is beautiful, no doubt about that but, oh, Kate. How did he not see what is staring him in the face? Well, punching him in the face. He is grateful Tay is with him. It will steady him. He turns to the Smiler who is now offering him a canapé, Lou and Satya at her shoulder. They have just arrived.

He sits on a cube.

He breathes.

The Lockdown King passes him a beer.

He looks around.

Tay with an apple juice listening to Linda. Leonard back

behind the bar. Very un-Leonard. Quite cool really. Silver Kate now with a glass of fizz, laughing with Pia (red wine) and Lou (cocktail). Blimey.

Careful, Clemenza.

Satya listening. Looking kind of lost.

Bardy struggles up from the squishy cube and heads for Satya. 'This is a bit different.'

'Hmm.'

The woman is in her own world. Maybe their home is like this? Hadn't she won some award recently? British entrepreneur? Iconic export brand? He is about to ask, when the words, 'Is everything okay with you and Jack?' pop out of his mouth.

Her head snaps towards him. 'Why do you ask?'

He has absolutely no idea, so says nothing.

'We had a fight before I came out.'

He didn't know lapis lazuli could be so dark it is almost black.

'It's just so…'

He waits. Listens. When you don't know what to say it is all you have.

'It's like we are out of step and when I try to make it better I get it wrong. He seems to think what I do is easy. He can't see that he and the boys could help more.' She makes a frustrated movement with her hand. 'He says that all I do is nag. That he's not one of my employees… we call them colleagues anyway. Doesn't he listen? And he says I can't relax. But how can I when I come back to the house looking like that? And they think they're oh so funny. And I'm always the one in the wrong. It's just not fair.'

Bardy had been thinking of asking Satya about the Tay situation. He rethinks. 'Could the two of you get some time just on your own?'

He doesn't think it's his stupidest suggestion ever, but Satya looks at him like he is mad. 'We don't shout in front of the boys. Put Jack and me in a room on our own at the moment and I think I'd kill him.'

Bardy had known Jack was joking when he'd said, *'If the boys don't kill her, I will.'* He's not so sure about Satya.

Linda is at the entrance to the bar, 'Do you all want to come through to the kitchen. Bring your drinks.'

The meal had been all he had expected from Mellow Plum. Warming and delicious. Bardy had even suggested to Linda that this is where her creativity lay, but she just laughed and shrugged. 'I cook what is easy. I want you all to have a nice meal, but I'm no foodie.' Bardy might disagree, but he can see what Linda enjoys most is being with her guests.

There had only been one hiccough. Well two.

First, a text from Hana confirming their meeting early next week. He showed Tay who just said, 'I know. I'm seeing her the night before.' He could read little into this, except he hoped Hana would give Tay some advice before her disciplinary meeting.

The second had been when Lou had been teasing Kate who said she wanted paints that had the sheen of oils but would dry like acrylics. Lou had declared, 'So you want to have your cake and eat it.'

Leonard had leant in, saying loudly, 'Who's Edith, do I know her?'

They had all turned to him.

'Kate and Edith. Friend of yours?' he asked.

Linda had said, slowly and loudly, 'Lou said, "have your cake and eat it".'

Most laughed, Pia had said quietly, 'Have your Kate and Edith, now there's an idea', but Bardy noticed that Linda just looked tired.

Now they are split into little groups around the long table. He has got into the configuration he hoped for, sitting with Pia and Tay. Pia is asking Tay about her work. Bardy makes a tentative suggestion, 'Why don't you tell Pia about your situation?'

He had expected a rebuke, but Tay just nods, 'Okay.'

Before Tay starts he asks Pia, 'What sort of lawyer are you?'

'Mainly employment with a bit of human rights, where it relates to employment law, particularly in relation to refugees.'

'There you go then,' Bardy says encouragingly to Tay.

She tells her story. Pretty succinctly. Not too much swearing.

They both sit watching Pia's face.

Pia then fires a number of questions at Tay: how long has this gone on; the exact wording for the disciplinary; Karen's track record; her relationship with others in the team; Jan, her boss's actual role; and a bit about Jonathan in HR, and her client, Mrs Willis. Finally she asks about Tay's contract and her pay. Listening to Tay's response, Pia's eyes suddenly flash – 'Oh that old one! "We cannot give you more money, but we *can* give you more responsibility." Basically, you do a great deal more work which you are not paid for.'

Bardy has a sudden idea, 'Could you go in with Tay?'

She shakes her head, 'No. I'm really surprised you're

allowed to go. Usually it's someone from the company. It may be because of your age, Tay, they're letting you have someone closer to you, more like a guardian.' She turns to him, 'And when you're in there Bardy you can't really say that much. This has to come from Tay.'

She looks at their faces and seems to register their disappointment. 'Look, this is just reporting back on the investigation Jonathan must have done into the complaint and they will feedback their findings and a "what next". It will probably be a representative from HR, presumably Jonathan, and Tay's line manager Jan.'

'Karen won't be there?' Tay asks.

'No. She will have been interviewed as will other relevant people, but they won't be in the room. You can also present your own evidence.'

Tay picks furiously at her thumbnail. 'No one will say what she's really like. They're just going to say whatever Karen tells them to. Should I call Mrs Willis?'

Pia shakes her head. 'Absolutely not. That would get you in real trouble. You could suggest Jonathan speaks to her though if you think Karen really has interfered.'

'Is there nothing we can do?' Bardy asks helplessly. Secretly he had hoped for the legal equivalent of the cavalry.

'Look this is just reporting back. We can definitely talk more when you know the full picture.' Pia looks upset. 'It's really best to follow the process. I can't push my way in and I don't want to offer you false hope. But…'

They wait.

'There are some areas of concern.'

'Such as?' Bardy asks.

'How long this process has taken. And also Tay's age and the relationships within the team.' Pia pauses. 'Keep talking to me about it and I will give it some more thought. I promise. And if you can get someone at work to say anything about how Karen behaves, that would help.'

Tay casts Bardy a helpless look.

He looks up and realises the others have left the kitchen. From nearby there is the sound of a piano. By unspoken agreement, they get up and follow the music. All the others are gathered in Leonard's study, which to Bardy looks more like a largeish library. He is playing a Frank Sinatra song and Linda is pouring coffee. Leonard really is good. When he finishes he receives a round of applause. Flushed, Leonard beams at them. He turns to Kate and says a little self-consciously. 'Sorry about earlier Kate. I do find it hard when everyone is talking at once.' He glances at Linda. 'I have been wearing my hearing aids more,' he declares, defiantly. 'When I'm out and about. No need when I'm home of course.'

Bardy sees Kate glance at Linda, a look of concern on her face.

Maybe if he passed Kate a coffee he might touch her hand by accident.

He goes to rise, but Satya is there before him, helping Linda, holding cups out to Pia and Kate. It strikes him that Satya looks tired. She says a little too heartily, 'That was very good Leonard.'

'Have you been doing more photography?' Linda asks.

'Not so much.' Satya brightens slightly. 'I did do a bit more drawing after…' She pauses.

'*Bazza*,' they reply in unison and laugh.

'Seriously though, I spent three hours drawing. I can't believe how the time flew.'

'It will,' Kate agrees.

Is it his imagination or is Kate avoiding catching his eye?

'I didn't know doing nothing could feel so good,' Satya concludes.

But you weren't *doing nothing!* Bardy wants to shout. But he realises he is too tired to shout. Not that he shouts anyway. He suddenly feels despondent.

'Let me show you around.' The Lockdown King is at his elbow.

'Sure, Leonard,' Bardy gets up from the desk where he has been perching.

There follows a detailed description of how Leonard catalogues his books. By subject and then by category, then by author. He finishes by saying, 'So you see I have everything I need right here in my library. A quiet evening on my own with my books is all I ever want.'

Out of the corner of his eye Bardy sees Linda turn abruptly away.

When he can, he escapes Leonard and goes in search of her. He bumps into Kate in the doorway.

'Whoa! Sorry!' He knows he shouldn't, but he holds her briefly at the top of her arms, as if steadying himself.

'You okay, Bardy?'

He steps away, dazed. Washed in a wave of silver, threaded with light or was it colour? His mind chases it, but it has gone.

If touching her is like this, what would kissing her be like?

'You okay?' she repeats, laughter in her voice.

'Yeah. Yes. No. Yes. Have you seen Linda?'

Kate is really laughing now.

Perhaps she thinks he's drunk?

'Maybe try the kitchen,' she suggests, heading back into the library.

Bardy spots Linda through the glass doors at the end of the kitchen. She is walking in the small garden. Running the heads of the grasses through her hands. He is debating whether to join her when Pia appears beside him.

'I'm sorry I can't do more for Tay. But she is right to take this seriously. She doesn't want this on her record if she can help it. And Bardy…' She touches his arm gently. No colour. Just calm. Which is good. 'You have to let her do this. I know it's hard, but it *will* make her stronger.'

He can't help feeling disappointed in her response. A feeling that is tinged with something like despair. How can he tell her that Tay has experienced enough to make her as strong as anyone would ever want to be? And that sometimes things just break you.

WEEK 4

The lapwings are rising, zigzagging crazily, black and white against the sky, with a glint of jade that flashes as fast as the birds fly. Far below a marsh harrier skims the reedbeds, wings wide, back-as-if arched, searching for prey. At this time of year young birds are always the most vulnerable.

Chapter 25

Kate

***Dost thou think because thou art virtuous
there shall be no more cakes...***

Kate is running in the sweet spot where the shoreline is packed hard, no slurpy sand sucking at her feet or soft undulations pulling at her pace. She is in rhythm: legs and body and breath. The wind is her face, the last of the sun's rays on her back. If she keeps running – and painting like she has today – maybe she will catch up with the happiness that has been eluding her. She also had a good video call with the girls. All seemed well, with much the same squabbling and laughter. They had all been pleased when she told them she was painting again and trying oils.

She settles into the rhythm of her run, her senses flooded with the scent of the sea and the call of the birds. Anything seems possible.

Bardy?

Well. Maybe not.

But Simon?

That was a surprise. She picks up her pace.

Simon was an old friend and colleague of Doug's. A man she had well... nothing really to beat herself up about, but a memory. She had thought he was in Dubai. But it seems Simon is back and texting her. That was a shock. A blast from the past. She didn't even know he had her number.

This thought creates a final spurt of speed and she pulls up gasping in front of the lifeboat station. She is hot and sweaty. This week's meeting will start in ten minutes. Not enough time to go home and change. But Bardy isn't the only one who knows someone in the RNLI; Kate has the combination to the locker room and permission to use their showers.

'I couldn't decide which to make, so I made both. A banana loaf and some apricot flapjacks.' Linda is unloading cake tins on to the long table.

Leonard is at the telescope, while Kate, Pia, Satya and Bardy are gathering around Linda. The door opens and Lou walks in. His hand is heavily bandaged.

'Mate!' Bardy cries. Kate thinks his obvious distress says it all.

Leonard comes to join them and Linda pulls out a chair for Lou next to her. 'My goodness, what have you been up to? I had no idea wood turning was so dangerous.'

'Not turning. Polishing. Got my rag caught in the lathe and it pulled my hand in.'

'You could have lost a finger,' Satya exclaims.

'I know! Don't mind admitting it gave me a fright.'

'Have you had it looked at?' Nurse Linda asks.

'Yep. Four stitches. Couldn't have been kinder. Trouble is I can't really use the gouges with my hand the way it is.'

'Maybe try a bit of poetry,' Bardy suggests and Lou laughs.

'Okay shall we get started?' Bardy proposes. 'Go round in turn?'

'No Tay this week?' Kate queries, looking at Bardy.

'No, she's got a lot going on at the moment.' He exchanges a glance with Pia. Does she know something about this?

'I don't mind starting,' Kate says, her confidence still buoyed by the endorphins.

'I've gone back to watercolours,' Leonard declares.

Kate hears a subdued, '*Oh, Leonard,*' from Linda.

Kate glances at her and shakes her head slightly – not a problem.

So much for Leonard claiming he wore his hearing aids more often.

'I thought I would give watercolours one last shot. Maybe try some new techniques with the paints.'

Kate thinks it is odd to hear someone sound so bullish and at the same time so despondent.

'Kate, you were saying?' Bardy interjects.

'It wasn't much. Just to say I am getting the feel of the oils but still struggling a bit with my colour mixing.' She doesn't add that it was much the same when she was getting the hang of the gouache paints that she used for her JoJo Rose paintings.

Bardy looks at her. Why does it feel like too long? Does she look red and blotchy from the run? He can't possibly have guessed she was thinking about JoJo Rose.

'I could try and get someone in to talk to us about colour. I'm not sure if... well... if she's going to be here long. But she *is* amazing on colour.'

Kate and the others make vaguely positive noises. Kate suspects no one really knows what Bardy is getting at. Still, Bazza turned out to be fun, and useful too.

'Okay leave that with me,' Bardy says. 'Pia?'

'Well my quilt is certainly getting bigger.' She smiles. 'I keep going, thinking that if this is a Norfolk quilt it needs to be a big expanse. But then I think I am just going to end up with a carpet,' she laughs.

It strikes Kate that even though it doesn't seem to be going well, Pia must be getting something out of this. She seems far less worried about not being good enough.

'Satya?' Bardy says.

Satya looks at Bardy and grimaces. 'Do you know what, I probably shouldn't even have come. I haven't done anything on my photography, I've just got so much work to do.' She groans. 'I'm so tired and I skipped supper. I tell you what, I could really do with a piece of Linda's cake and a coffee. It's been a pig of a week.' She looks around helplessly.

'You've got it.' Linda and Lou are on their feet heading for the kitchen. After a moment Satya goes to join them.

Kate watches their retreating figures and thinks how much she likes these people. Thinks how much Alice would have liked them. Especially Tay. She always had a soft spot for the young, the vulnerable.

'Is Tay okay?' she asks Bardy.

Once again, Bardy looks fleetingly at Pia. 'She's having a

tough time at work. Got a meeting she's not looking forward to.'

This doesn't look like it's news to Pia.

Leonard surprises Kate by saying, 'I know the company she works for. Middle sized but not a bad reputation. She was telling me about them over supper. My friend Ray runs it, or he certainly used to. You say she's having problems?'

Linda, Lou and Satya are back, trays loaded with refreshments. 'What's this?' Linda asks.

'Tay. She's having a tough time at work,' Leonard informs her. 'Nice girl, when you take the time to talk to her.'

Linda looks at him but says nothing.

'Are you involved with this?' Kate asks Pia.

'Not really. It's just that Tay told me about it. A problem.' She hesitates. 'It's not anything I could get involved with.'

She appears reluctant to continue. Kate recalls Pia saying her partner Grace had claimed she didn't put herself out for people. Was Grace right? This thought prompts Kate to ask, 'I remember you said employment law was your area. Could Tay do with your advice?'

'She doesn't need a lawyer,' Pia fires back.

Defensive.

'That cake looks delicious, Linda,' Pia adds and Kate wonders why she is so keen to change the subject.

Leonard is not so easily diverted. 'If she's got some issues I could give Ray a call. Nice girl Tay. Really very surprising.'

'*Really?*' Linda's tone is weary with exasperation, 'Would that be surprising because she has a pierced nose and eyebrow? Or because her father doesn't play golf?'

'No. No, not at all.' Leonard sounds flustered. 'If she needs help, I will give Ray a ring, that's all.'

Pia intervenes, 'Leonard, it really is nothing, it's not that important.'

Kate can't read the expression on Bardy's face.

'It wouldn't be appropriate for your friend to get involved. Tay is dealing with this through the proper channels,' Pia insists.

'Leonard, you don't know anything about this, and it sounds like Pia is giving Tay the advice she needs,' Linda says, firmly.

'Don't give it a thought. Happy to ring Ray,' Leonard exclaims. 'Best go straight to the top man.' He smiles around at them.

He doesn't seem to notice that nobody is smiling back.

'Satya, why's your week been so bad?' Kate asks, hoping to defuse the situation.

Bardy seems to come to life, 'Yeah, Satya. Anything we can help with?'

Satya glances at Leonard, and Kate's certain she's not going to want Leonard's *talk to the man at the top* approach. She picks at the crumbs on her plate. 'We've had consultants in all week working on our mission statement and brand values. It's taken a long time but I think we're getting somewhere. Their main push is towards how our organic growth is rooted in the heart of the brand's kernel and our essence of positivity leads from the middle.'

Kate's not surprised she's had a shit week.

Linda leans forward, 'Do you mind me asking, Satya, what does that actually mean?'

Kate thinks Satya might cry.

But Satya is made of tougher stuff – it is no coincidence that she built her company from scratch. Satya talks to them of the brand essence and customer focus. She expands on product positivity and the analoguesque, decentralised customer journey, until everyone around her is nodding, Kate thinks more in the hope she will stop rather than because they understand a word of what she is saying.

Eventually Bardy cuts in, and says, with some sympathy, 'That would get anybody down. Quite get that you haven't had time for photography.' He pauses. 'So, Linda, how about your... actually I can't remember what you are doing. Pen and wash? Or have you moved on from that?'

Linda looks at her husband then back at Bardy. 'Yes,' she says. 'I have decided to write a short story.'

'Oh!' Bardy sounds surprised. 'What's it going to be about?'

'It is the story of a deaf man who gets run over by his wife.'

Kate thinks she should want to laugh, but it's all too sad. This evening is going from bad to worse.

'And how's your story writing going, Bardy?' Linda asks, a mulish look on her face.

Bardy takes a while to respond. 'Still working on the baker's story,' he says, glancing at Lou. 'I've been thinking about him, and the baker's friend. Maybe his friend owes the baker an apology.'

Kate is really struggling. No one seems to be making any sense this evening.

For the first time, at the end of the evening, Kate is glad to leave. Things seem out of kilter. Pia, Bardy, Satya, Linda and

Leonard. Even Lou looks like he might end up killing himself with his wood turning. And no Tay.

At the door, Bardy breaks away from talking to Satya to intercept Kate. He holds out a hand as if to touch her arm but leaves it hanging mid-air. He looks like a man who has just remembered something. Or maybe a man who has had a shock.

'Yes, Bardy?'

'*Twelfth Night*... and *A Midsummer Night's Dream*.'

What is the man on about?

'Kate, would you like to come and have something to eat with me sometime. Not me cooking because that wouldn't be great. But something else. Out out. You know a restaurant. Out. Or a pub if you prefer? Out.'

It is delivered so disjointedly that Kate wonders if he even meant to say it. It doesn't make any sense – why those plays? And why now?

She is suddenly weary, unable to read the man in front of her. Wanting to reach out and touch his face. It is such a nice face. She wants to step towards him. Lean into him.

He stands wavering. Anxious. And as he wavers, so does she.

She wants to say 'yes'. Just sit with Bardy and chat about the group and other things – the things that are bothering her. It has been so long since she has had that sort of support – well, from a man in her life. But she instinctively knows if she lets her guard down, lets Bardy in, she won't be able to pick everything up again. She has spent so many years on her own shouldering it all. And really, she has no idea what he is actually asking her. All of this goes through her mind in the blink of a second.

'Kate?' he says, tentatively.

Part of her thinks – just go, it's only a meal. The other part tells her not to risk it. Then she catches sight of Pia's coat hanging by the door. Oh, so stylish.

'Shall we leave it Bardy. I appreciate you asking but probably best to keep it like this. Friends?'

No one wants to be the consolation prize, Bardy.

'Yeah, fine. Of course.' Fired out quickly.

Relieved or upset?

But as he turns away, Kate wishes he had listened. Really listened.

She hadn't said. 'Friends.'

She had said, 'Friends?'

It was a question.

Chapter 26

Bardy

What's done cannot be undone

His namesake has never let him down before. It had come to him. *Twelfth Night*. It had sounded like a klaxon in his head. Love triangle, he had thought. A common enough theme in Shakespeare. *A Midsummer Night's Dream* was another. He had joined the dots.

I liked Pia.
Pia likes Kate.
Which means... Kate likes...

So he'd spewed out that invitation. How many 'Outs' had he peppered her with? Tried to make a triangle. Except he was no Pythagoras – never really got maths – and she'd said no. Thanks but no thanks.

Bardy struggles up the shingle bank. Good word, 'shingle'. Just like the sound his feet are making now. He is early for his meeting with Hana, has walked the seven miles out of town along the coastal path. Made good time. He detoured onto the shingle before heading to the pub on the green. When he is at the top of the bank, he turns and looks out to sea. It looks cold and grey. Miserable. Bit like his mood.

Aah. He breathes out.

A seal is swimming parallel to the beach watching him. He never tires of spotting seals. This one looks smart, perky. Intelligent eyes. This seal wouldn't have mistaken friendship for a love triangle. Bet his wife didn't just swim off one day and he was left paddling around in circles in the grey ocean wondering what had happened.

Now Hana has paddled back to see him.

What *does* she want? Well, only one way to find out.

Bardy makes his way down the puddled path to the road. It has been a subdued day of drizzle and showers. Impossible to believe it is nearly May. Although this is North Norfolk – at times, with weather all of its own. Despite the dreary day, it comes to him – how could he ever have thought he would leave this? The path he is on crosses over a dyke and his eye follows the line cutting between the reeds. In the water is the reflection of troubled sky mixed in with terracotta. He spots some scurvy grass growing in clumps. On one trip away to Birmingham, he can't recall what he was doing, but on the central reservation of the motorway he had seen scurvy grass. Later he had googled it. It grew there because of the salt they spread on the roads in the winter. He remembers finding it comforting, like a piece of home.

And you thought you could leave all this?

Hana is waiting at a table, a glass of white wine in front of her. The flood of colour threatens to wash him out the door.

And yet there is comfort in the familiarity, mixed in with the pain. But there is a change too. A deeper yellow. More of the earth about it. They kiss. On the cheek. How strange that feels. She looks well. Tanned. Clear eyed. A new tattoo snaking down the finger where his ring had once been.

'Hi Bardy. You look well.'

He's sure he doesn't.

Better than Lou though, with his bandaged hand and patched face. This brings immeasurable comfort. Not his accident-prone friend's discomfort but the thought of them sitting on ancient beach chairs by a pool listening to a rat that they want to be an otter.

Tina thought I could do better.

He looks at his ex-wife and thinks Tina must have been mad.

'How are things? You off soon?' he asks.

Is he trying to get rid of her already?

'You trying to get rid of me already?' She smiles.

Thirty years of marriage will make its mark.

'No, of course not.' He returns her smile. 'I'll get some menus and then we can talk as we decide what to eat.'

When he returns with a pint and the menus she says quietly, 'This is harder than I thought.'

For a moment he thinks she's going to deliver some news, like – I'm getting re-married. But this just flits through. It doesn't stop. The next thought does. Meeting up after so long – so long together and now, so long apart – was never going to be easy. He sits down. 'Were you always unhappy living here? Living with me?' His words surprise him. Then he wonders why. Isn't it pretty much all he has been thinking of?

'Oh, Bardy. No of course not. I really loved you...'

You don't have to be an English teacher to recognise the past tense.

'...and this place is beautiful. Coming here with you, bringing up the boys in such an amazing spot, oh, and so much more. But then yes, Bardy, I did want more.'

'Did you tell me? Wasn't I listening? I would have changed.'

Hana doesn't have to answer his rapid-fire questions.

Yes. No. And no you wouldn't.

He is relieved when the waitress comes for their orders.

'Have you lost weight?' Hana says, studying him. She flicks her hair back off her shoulder. The gesture is so familiar that even after all this time apart, the divorce, the realisation that they are different people wanting different things – he still wants to wake up and find this has all been a bad dream. He thinks of Tay to try and refocus.

Mistake. Worry is heaped on his distress.

'Has Tay told you about her work stuff?' he asks. Maybe Hana will have some ideas. They were always a good double act when it came to the kids.

Hana nods.

Of course she has. He thinks of Tay walking towards Hana. Hana's arms held wide. Tay walking into that hug. It isn't jealousy he feels, just the weariness of always finding it so hard. The weight of the worry.

'Tay's going to be fine. She's tougher than you think...'

'I doubt that.'

'What do you mean? That she's not tough? Or that she

couldn't be any tougher?' Hana had always liked to get to the bottom of things.

He wants to say 'both', but dismisses this with a slight shake of the head – a 'move on' gesture.

'Well, it's not like she's going to end her days working in insurance. I'm still amazed she took the job. It's not really her, is it?'

'She's doing well though,' Bardy insists – and what options had there been for a sixteen-year-old carer, with few qualifications.

Hana says, derisively, 'Yeah working with a bunch of bitchy middle-aged women.'

Bardy wonders if Hana didn't have girlfriends because she was always so busy. Or was that another legacy of living your life in the wrong place?

Or maybe Tina had been right.

He wants to look at Hana and feel like a man moved on. He can't even see an outline of a door. No exit sign. No way out.

So instead he asks about her family, and then they talk about the boys. Safe ground. A place to meet.

The meal is drawing to a close and Bardy has been telling her about the creative group. His description of Bazza brought easy laughter that felt good.

'I think I remember him from the post office,' Hana says, grinning.

He is just embarking on Kate's struggles with colour and Hana is leaning forward, interested, nodding, when it dawns on Bardy that he doesn't know why she wanted to see him. So he asks.

'I think I wanted to say goodbye. To just check—'

'Can I get you two coffees?' a waitress is back.

They head down the alleyway of cafetières and would they like something with that. All the time Bardy is wondering – check what?

'You said check,' he queries as soon as the waitress has cleared the pudding bowls and disappeared back to the kitchen. It took a lot of time. It didn't help that he had taught the waitress.

He is not really surprised when Hana says, 'Did I? I can't remember what I was going to say.'

She was never a very good liar. Hid stuff – he now knows – but not a liar.

He leaves it.

'I wanted to see you before I left for New Zealand. Say goodbye properly.'

It flashes into his head that maybe she will sleep with him one more time. Nonsense of course. And it would finish him off. He thinks he's been holding up okay, not looking a total loser without her. Able to talk about the creative group like he's got his shit together. He is so glad he is going with Tay to her meeting tomorrow afternoon. Some payback.

'How long are you around for?'

'Not sure.'

'I wondered, if you're going to be here, whether you would come to the group and do one of your sessions on colour, like you used to do at the college?'

Hana hesitates. 'I'm not sure, Bardy.' She looks at him. 'Look, if it would help I could meet this Kate of yours for a coffee, chat some stuff through with her.'

Kate of yours. Got that wrong, but he nods.

They leave it there and as they move outside they manage a hug that is okay. At least he pulls away before he has fastened himself onto her like a limpet.

He stands on the edge of the car park, long after Hana's taxi has gone.

He is roused by his text alert. Leonard is on the group chat.

Good luck tomorrow Tay. I'm sure it will go well. I did try to call Ray but sadly he passed away six months ago. Pancreatic cancer. Very sad.

Bardy wonders how he knows about the timing of the meeting. Maybe Leonard contacted Tay? He looks at his phone and waits. No one else responds. He thinks of Pia who is seeing Tay tonight to talk through her meeting. It had made him feel warmer towards her. Guilty because he had thought she wasn't taking it seriously. Couldn't be bothered.

He wonders what Linda thought of Leonard trying to get in touch with Ray. Bloody irritated he suspects. But you can't deny the man has his heart in the right place.

You've got this, Tay.
To your own self be true.

A text from Kate.
Nice. The Bard. He didn't often let you down.
Good luck texts come thick and fast from the others.
No response from Tay, but he hopes she sees them.

His phone sounds again.
A text just for him from Lou.

Leonard! Bloody hell, doesn't the man ever listen?!!

There follows a gif of a man with a trumpet hearing device saying – *what? what? what?*
Before Bardy can reply, Lou types some more.

We should take him out for a drink try and give the poor bugger some pointers before Linda really does run him over.

Bardy sends a thumbs up emoji.
He thinks Leonard isn't the only one with his heart in the right place.

Chapter 27

Kate

Once he kissed me

Kate has agreed to meet Hana mainly out of curiosity. Still, she takes care over dressing, even more than she does when she is meeting Pia. As she stands in front of her mirror she laughs. She seems to be channelling her inner Scandinavian. All creams and greys. Simple layers. She is definitely not going in on her bike today.

She arrives early, so walks through the gallery before heading to the coffee shop. She spots a poster, *Save our Gallery*, at the same time as she spots Nathan, a friend of Bella's from school. She reflects, that Bella always did have a soft spot for a bad boy. But look how Nate has turned out, managing this gallery. Not so very bad. But then he never really was.

'Nate, how are you?'

'Hi Mrs O. Good to see you. Okay I guess.' He nods towards the sign, 'This is keeping me busy.'

'What's the problem? Are you really in danger of closing?'

He nods, his face grim. 'We've lost a lot of our central funding.' He shrugs, 'Everyone's under pressure, and some people feel supporting health and care projects should take priority.'

'But you do a lot of educational stuff – I'm always seeing your posters around.'

'You'd think it might make a difference, wouldn't you?' He tugs at one side of his hair. A habit she knows started around the time his dad had left. Bella had scooped him up and brought him home for suppers, barbeques and just hanging out by and in the creek.

He brightens a little, 'I've been in talks though with other galleries and I think we're going to put on a small display of Constables. Paintings of the area. It won't be a full exhibition, but it might get the press along and we can talk about what we need.'

'And what is it you need?'

'Some of it is funding but the main thing is this building, we might lose it.'

'But this is part of the town. I'd always thought it was owned by the council or something.'

'No, we had it on a long lease from a local woman. Bit of a local do-gooder. But she died and her son wants to sell it off for flats.'

'No! Surely he can't do that?'

'He won't care. Just wants the money.' Nathan looks thoughtful, 'The only thing I did think when I met him was that he didn't like the idea of bad publicity. He's got a company he's trying to float. Or something like that. That's why I thought getting the Constables in might bring the press.'

'I think it's a great idea. I'll spread the word.'

'Thanks Mrs O. How's Bella?'

'Having a great time. She's travelling all over the US with a soccer team. She was in Florida last week.'

'That's the life. Say hi when you next speak to her.'

As a result of this conversation Kate is a few minutes late meeting Hana. Hana is already sitting at a table with a coffee. She is wearing a denim jumpsuit, hair loosely tied back with a black and white scarf. Kate approaches the table wondering if Hana will be surprised that she already knows what she looks like. As it turns out it is Hana who's surprised: 'But you're Jess's mum!'

They shake hands and Kate sits down. 'How do you know Jess?'

'Ned, our youngest had a thing for her for ages. He thought because he was a couple of years older he had a chance. And I know I'm his mum but he *was* pretty cool. But she wouldn't go out with him. She came over quite a few times with a crowd of others. But she was always with this guy... oh I can't remember his name. Big, rugby player type.'

'Matt. They're married now, living in Edinburgh,' *And may be having a baby*. Or maybe not. No news on their last phone call. 'What's Ned up to now?' She never met him, but thinks Jess may have mentioned a 'Ned'.

'He and Tom, that's his older brother, are both settled in New Zealand.'

Oh poor Bardy.

'That's where you're from?'

The slight lilt still a giveaway.

'Yes, and I'm heading back there soon.'

'To live?'

'Yeah, I think so. But I think I've also got a lot more travelling I want to do.' Hana sips her coffee. 'So tell me about your painting.'

Kate explains about her early attempts and shows how her work is progressing through photos on her phone. Hana laughs when she sees the mackerel. Kate can't help liking this woman. How could she not when she reminds her of Alice? Another free spirit. Also, she has a way of appearing intensely interested in what Kate is saying. She corrects herself. She believes that Hana *is* genuinely interested.

They talk for some time about colour palettes and then Hana asks, 'Do you mix your own colours?'

'Not always. I do always mix my greens from scratch. I've found the tubes of green never capture the colours you see in nature.'

Hana nods. 'Look, what I suggest you do is just start with primary colours – blue, yellow and red. Oh and white. Mix everything from those on your palette, create like a caterpillar of colour. Different shades. And mix plenty of paint so you have them ready. Then everything on your painting should pull together.'

'That's the biggest problem I've had,' Kate confesses, showing Hana one of her landscapes. 'The sky feels like a different painting to the land and water.'

'This will definitely help. You will be using colours that come from the same roots in both. The sky will speak to the land.' Hana pulls up some images on her own phone. 'These are from a recent trip I took to Costa Rica.'

Kate thinks the images are stunning. There is no doubt Hana is an accomplished artist.

'If your colours come from the same roots it will become a whole.' Hana smiles, 'In a landscape everything reflects everything.'

Kate can see what she means from Hana's own paintings – the luminous skies talking to the sparkling water in the foreground.

'What particular colours do you start with?' Kate asks.

'I'll be using different ones to you I suspect, I will choose the base colours based on the light where I'm painting. So thinking of blue, an ultramarine is a great blue as a starting point for mixing a British sky. In Costa Rica I started with a cobalt blue or even cerulean blue. You can experiment and play games – perhaps bring a bit of a Costa Rica colour to Norfolk. It isn't always about painting what you see, but what you feel, and what you want to say.'

Kate thinks of Alice saying, 'Show people how you see the world.'

'And don't ever use a shop-bought black, mix your own...'

Kate shakes her head. She doesn't. She knows how the ready mixed blacks can often kill a painting.

'...and if you need to tone down part of your painting, use a colour from the opposite side of the colour wheel.'

'This is really helpful, thank you.' Something prompts her to continue, 'My sister said I needed to think about what it is I wanted to express in my paintings.'

'Your sister is right.'

Kate doesn't correct the tense. Something about Hana's intense interest in her makes her continue. 'Years ago we went to the cinema to see *Life of Pi*. Afterwards Alice, said, "The thing with you Katie is you want to see the story of the tiger and a boy. You won't look at the pain."'

'And Alice?'

'Oh, she searched out the pain and did what she could to help. She was fearless,' Kate says proudly.

Hana doesn't seem to notice the change of tense.

Kate wonders what it is she wants to say through her painting. Is it just a story? Is it really possible to ignore the pain? She thinks of when she was diagnosed, and of the cave-black days. She doesn't want to express that. But the cancer has changed her. More than just a scar running under her breast. She will never lose the memory of all she has been through. She is coming to terms with the randomness of her luck, to believe in her new life. But there is a lurking fear that walks beside her. She suspects it always will.

Kate changes tack. 'Are you still teaching art?'

'A little bit now and again. Adult education, mainly.'

'Is it very different teaching adults rather than kids?'

'Well, it's less about crowd control which is good, and it's great to see people getting so much pleasure out of something they had forgotten about or had never allowed themselves to have a go at.'

'But?' Kate feels there is more.

'Kids may be rowdy but at least they have boundless imagination and are less likely to get into a flat spin about what other people think. And they do assume you know what you're talking about. Some adults just think they know better, so will argue when you offer advice.'

'Who are the worst?'

Hana laughs. 'I call them all-the-gear-but-no-idea.'
'Men?'
'Mainly, but not always.' Hana grins.

Kate is interrupted from what she is about to say by a hand on her shoulder, she looks up.

'Simon!'

He stands beside her, well over six foot tall. Blond with more grey now, face crinkly, but he is still a good-looking man. It must be more than fifteen years since she has seen him. Her hand goes to touch her bristle-brush hair, but she manages to stop herself. She starts to rise.

'Don't. I'm disturbing you,' he says, smiling at Hana.

She has a flashback of Simon at a work barbeque, showing her the rose garden of the house they had been invited to. He had kissed her. And she can't deny it, she had kissed him back. But that was all. A laugh, an apologetic, where did that come from dance, and they had returned to the others. But she has thought about that never- repeated kiss over the years. She wonders if this is in his mind too as he continues, 'I just wanted to say hi, since I'd spotted you. I'll text you. Maybe we could catch up over supper sometime?' He gives Hana a final smiling nod and moves on.

'Looks like you've got yourself a date,' Hana says, grinning.

Kate registers this with a kind of shock. She blinks. 'Yes, looks that way.'

Then why is she thinking of Bardy?

Chapter 28

Bardy

And though she be but little, she is fierce

Tay is waiting for him in reception. She looks smart. Black trousers, white shirt. Bit like the café uniform, but there she wore them baggier with a loosely tied apron, more in her normal style. They don't hug. Just nod at each other. He looks over his shoulder. 'Pia's outside, she said we could text her if you get any tricky questions. She'll meet us later.'

Tay nods again.

'Was she helpful, yesterday?'

'Yeah, kind of. I've got this stuff she's put together for me.' Tay holds up a folder. 'Okay, I guess I'd better sign you in.'

Tay signing him in to the office where she works.

It gives him hope. It's a long way from basketball club. Or the police station.

He checks: a little muted maybe, but still red ochre.

Tay leads him to a meeting room on the ground floor,

knocks and enters. There are two other people in the room. Introductions are made.

Jonathan is a man in his late forties, suit slightly shiny, nondescript tie and a moist, limp handshake. He has black glasses with overlarge frames that makes Bardy wonder if he works with a team of younger people and is worrying about his age. He's seen it in some teachers, very-latest trainers, hoodies. One guy traded in his Vauxhall Vectra for a Harley-Davidson.

Jan is more impressive. A tall woman with glasses that suit her look and her face. If Jonathan's glasses say sad man walking in inappropriate shoes (Bardy glances down – yep), Jan's say a woman on the up, a woman who means business. He can't decide if this will ensure Tay gets a fair hearing or not. She does keep glancing at her phone and that worries him. More important things to do? Short of time?

Jan is also nettle green. He can't decide if this is a good thing or not either.

Jan starts. 'Tay, I am sorry that it has come to this. Mr Shakespeare, thank you, for coming along this afternoon. My aim is that we hear the results of the investigation into Mrs Noble's complaint and my hope is we can find a positive way forward.'

Tay just stares at Jan.

'Right, Jonathan over to you.'

Jonathan flicks open the file in front of him and also adjusts his laptop screen. He makes a nervous beginning, stumbling over some words, but then gets into his stride, even sitting back in his chair, and bouncing slightly. The more he talks the more Bardy hopes it will tip over backwards. Bardy glances down at the phone he has discreetly in his lap. Nothing to report to Pia yet.

The case as told by Jonathan seems to be that Mrs Noble claimed Tay told her to 'Piss off'. Twice. And that this was heard by two other members of staff who also made statements. Mrs Noble claimed Tay was surly and uncooperative, not fitting in with the team. There are also notes about Tay's work. Her record is undeniably good, but her team expressed concerns about her manner on the phone, which Mrs Noble described as too casual and unprofessional. There did not appear to be other witnesses to this. At the end, Jonathan shakes his head as if disappointed with an unruly child.

During this recital, Jan makes notes but also glances at her phone. She now asks, 'Tay is there anything you would like to say to this? Or any questions you have?'

Bardy's hands are clenched tight. He wishes he could stop this. Have these people any idea of what this girl's life has been like? Is like?

Bardy can see Tay's knee bouncing under the table, but her voice is steady. A little squeaky, but her words are clear. 'I have a statement and some questions.'

Bardy sees a look of surprise on Jan's face. She stops looking at her phone. Jonathan is picking at something on the sleeve of his jacket and doesn't look up. Tay's knuckles are white where she is holding tight to the page that Pia has prepared for her. She starts to read.

'I don't deny that I told Mrs Noble to *piss off*. Twice.'

Bardy's not sure it's wise to put so much venom into the two words.

'I would like to apologise for my choice of words…'

How did Pia get Tay to agree to that?

'…but the language I used demonstrated the frustration I was feeling at my work situation and came about because of Mrs Noble's behaviour towards me. Specifically, bullying by Mrs Noble and her contact with one of my clients thereby breaching company guidelines and undermining my position in the team.'

Tay takes a deep breath, and keeps reading. 'I would also like to state that my position was made worse due to the lack of support that I have received from HR.'

Jonathan stops picking.

He goes to speak, but Tay talks over him. 'I have here a list of times and dates on which I spoke to HR.' She flicks a quick look at Jonathan. 'I have noted my questions and their responses.' Tay starts to fumble for the sheets. Bardy takes them from her. These people are not going to see her hands shake. He passes papers over to Jonathan and Jan, and keeps one for himself.

Tay reads it out. It itemises the times Tay asked for Jonathan's help. Firstly to explain to the team that she had to go to college and that she wasn't skiving off and missing any dates. His response was that she should just ignore it. Then on a number of occasions she asked Jonathan to provide more training for the team on Excel as she was being called upon to constantly help people with spreadsheets. It seemed no one even asked politely anymore, it was assumed her role was spreadsheet support. Jonathan had said he would look into it but that budgets were tight. Nothing was done. The next item makes Bardy want to get hold of Jonathan by his badly tied tie and throttle him. It relates to a date when Jonathan found Tay alone and upset in the corridor. In her statement she records that she asked for his help as Karen had told her that her mother was a piece of shit and that Tay might not know who her dad was, but anyone could see who her mother was. His response apparently was to tell her to just try and get on with them better and especially not to upset Karen. Finally there is the date on which she asked Jonathan whether Karen was allowed to just take over the client she was dealing with, Mrs Willis. She had asked if she could speak to Mrs Willis. Tay's record stated that Jonathan had said that it was far easier to let Karen do what she wanted, and that it was against GDPR rules for Tay to contact Mrs Willis. She had asked if he could contact Mrs Willis. He had said he couldn't.

'This is nonsense... you're making this up...' Jonathan splutters.

Jan holds up her hand. 'I think we will want to come back to discuss these very serious points. But before we do that do you have any questions, Tay?'

Tay looks around helplessly, 'Well, only it's about that list. He did do all of that. He can't say he didn't.'

Bardy can feel Tay losing it. She's been amazing. But she can see where this is heading, where it has always been. Her word against theirs. She doesn't have anyone in the team who will stick up for her. They are going to want evidence and that's what they don't have. Bardy stands. He has their attention. He isn't sure what he is going to say, just anything to stop them looking at her, seeing her vulnerability. 'Jan, Jonathan. I would like us to take a break now. This is a difficult situation, especially for Tay.

Could I ask you to leave the room for just a few minutes so I can talk to Tay privately.'

They look surprised, but after glancing at each other Jan says, 'I can give you five minutes.' She checks her phone and continues. 'Jonathan would you get some water for the room.' Jonathan obviously hadn't thought Tay important enough to provide the normal meeting room refreshments.

As the door closes behind them, Tay starts to shake, shivering violently. Bardy puts his arm around her. Not their normal style. But then he's never been in a disciplinary before. Never wants to be in one again.

'Look, we can't prove anything but we can ask some questions. Just get it into Jan's mind that it might not be as clear cut as Jonathan is saying. God he's a prize prat.'

'Told you,' Tay says, trying to smile.

His phone vibrates. It's Pia asking how it's going. He types quickly. *We need a bloody miracle.* Then he sets about logically working through what questions it is best to ask. He knows it will be repeating the points Tay has already made, but maybe it will hammer them home. He just hopes Tay holds it together. He wishes he could ask them for her, but Pia said it should come from Tay. Said it would make her stronger. *For fuck's sake.* He wishes Lou was here with his big stomach. Clemenza would know how to deal with these people.

They set about making a list. Before they are ready Jan and Jonathan are back. Is it his imagination or is Jonathan looking flushed? Has Jan had a go at him? Water is provided. Bardy takes some. Tay doesn't. Probably wise. Might spill it over herself. Or throw it at Jonathan. He just hopes Tay can read his list of scribbled questions.

Bardy begins. 'Tay is now going to ask some questions. While these might not constitute evidence for her case, I think they cover such serious issues that at the very least they warrant *proper* investigation.' He glances at Jonathan and looks meaningfully at Jan.

Still nettle green. Bardy still doesn't know what that might mean for Tay.

'Tay?' Jan prompts. Bardy sees that Jonathan is looking much more focused, has a pad out and is making notes. Bardy does the same. Team Tay.

Tay begins, a little croaky but she is no longer shaking, 'I would like to ask Jonathan, did I ask you to give the team extra Excel training?'

'Yes, but it's not as easy—'

'Did I ask you to explain to the team about my absences due to attending college? Training that is required by law.'

Jonathan risks it. 'No I think you might be misremembering that.'

Tay throws Bardy a helpless look.

'Go on Tay,' he says quietly.

She takes a breath. 'Are my college and work records good?'

Jonathan looks more confident, 'Well, as to that, you have been doing well, but of course there are the incidents with a colleague which you have now admitted to, which led to this disciplinary hearing.'

Tay's voice rises with her level of frustration, 'But that's because she called me—'

There is a knock on the door. They all turn. A young woman stands in the doorway. 'Yes, Angie?' Jan asks crossly.

'I'm sorry but this woman has—'

Pia peeps past Angie. She looks tiny, dwarfed by the younger woman. 'I am so sorry to interrupt. Normally I wouldn't dream of doing this.' As she steps forward she looks both hesitant and embarrassed. 'It's just I am here for Tay. I have something she might need.'

She sounds like a mum who has forgotten to give a child their sports kit.

'Can't it wait?' Jan asks, clearly irritated. She glances at her phone.

Nettle green deepening as if in shadow.

Jonathan just stares at Pia, slack-jawed.

So does Bardy but for completely different reasons.

What is she up to?

'It is just that Tay did mention that she can present evidence in this... er... meeting. Have I got that right?'

'Yes,' Jan says briefly.

'And I thought she might need this.' She has a sheet of paper in her hand.

'Well, fine, give it to her then,' Jan snaps.

Pia limps into the room, wincing in pain.

'Pia! Are you okay?' Bardy is on his feet. So is Jonathan. As Pia clutches at the tabletop for support Jonathan pulls out a chair for her.

'Thank you so much. Do you mind?' she asks Jan.

'What?' Jan is thrown.

'Would it be alright if I sat down?

'Of course,' Jan says to the woman who is grimacing in pain.

Pia sinks into the seat and looks earnestly at Jan and Jonathan. 'I do know that this is very unorthodox. This is a very important meeting. Tay did ask if I could come too. I think she really wanted me here for moral support. She's very young, you know. But Bardy did explain it could only be one of us.'

Now they look like Tay's anxious parents.

'But since I'm here now, might I stay? Or I will go if you really think that's best.' Pia tries to rise.

'Well, I think we're nearly finished,' Jonathan concedes. And Pia beams at him, sinking back into her chair. Bardy suspects Jonathan sees this family reunion as the end of his questioning. Plus, Jonathan is still staring at Pia in open admiration.

Did he look like that?

'Well, alright, but please can we get back to the subject we are discussing,' Jan insists. She nods at Angie, who closes the door.

'Jonathan, please take down this lady's full name for the minutes.'

Jonathan sits and looks at Pia, head tilted enquiringly.

'I am Pia...' Then comes a surname that is guttural and completely incomprehensible. She smiles blandly at Jonathan. 'Normal spelling,' she says helpfully.

Jonathan looks like a confused sheep.

Jan has clearly had enough. 'Tay, please continue with your questions. Jonathan, make sure you get all of this down. If you can.'

Tay has now stopped staring at Pia and is reading what Pia

handed her. Bardy pushes his notes closer to Pia so she can catch up on what has happened so far.

Tay then reads her next question. 'Jonathan, did I ask you whether it was okay for Karen to take over my relationship management of Mrs Willis?'

As she asks this, Pia is quickly scanning Bardy's notes.

'You may have mentioned it, but you are the newest member of an experienced team and as such I would hope that you would be grateful for any help that is offered.'

'But am I still her contact?' Tay asks and Bardy thinks she looks tearful. Sounds almost pleading. He had hoped Pia's appearance might have given her a boost.

Jonathan checks something on his laptop. 'Yes, you are still her relationship manager,' he admits.

Tay starts to cry. Quietly at first and then with noisy sobs, covering her face in her hands. Bardy had no idea Mrs Willis meant so much to her.

Pia strokes Tay's back.

Jan looks again at her phone and then tries to pin a sympathetic expression to her face. 'Perhaps we should leave it there for today…' she begins.

Pia nods sympathetically at her, still patting Tay. 'Yes, perhaps we should. We could come back tomorrow and start all over again.'

From the look on Jan's face, Bardy is sure she is horrified by this prospect and that she is mentally reviewing her diary and where else she needs to be. She clearly thought this meeting would take half an hour at most.

Tay has stopped sobbing now but still has her head low. She

mumbles something, Pia leans in to hear. Tentative but helpful, she says, 'Tay suggests maybe if I were to read her questions for her then we could get this all sorted out quickly?'

It is only then that it strikes Bardy that he has never seen Tay sob like this.

What was it Pia had written on that piece of paper?

Tay, head still down, pushes the questions over to Pia.

'Yes, well, thank you. Let's try and wrap this up and not cause Tay any more distress,' Jan agrees.

Pia sits up straight in her chair. 'Jonathan,' she begins, 'if as you have just confirmed, Taylor Drakos was the relationship manager for Mrs Willis, why would you tell her she could not contact her?'

Jonathan looks confused. His brain not catching up with the change happening in front of him.

'Well I thought... Karen... um Mrs Noble said...'

'Jonathan, we have established that Taylor Drakos is Mrs Willis's relationship manager. Can you explain why Mrs Karen Noble appears to have taken over the account with no reference to anyone else in the company? She is neither Taylor Drakos's line manager, nor is she the designated relationship manager.'

'Well, she is really experienced—'

'So, for example should Mrs Noble decide to access, say my details, or anyone else's details on your CRM system she would be able to do so, and contact them and nobody would be any the wiser?'

'Well that wouldn't happen.'

Pia pauses. 'But that is *exactly* what has happened.' She turns briefly to Bardy. 'Please make sure you are making comprehensive notes of this, Mr Shakespeare.'

He starts scribbling even more furiously. He says under his breath, 'We're very formal today.' There is the tiniest twitch by Pia's mouth.

Oh, she's enjoying this.

Jonathan's large glasses are starting to slip down his nose.

Pia continues, 'Mrs Noble said Mrs Willis wasn't happy. Obviously she made a record of that complaint against Taylor Drakos. This would be company policy as outlined in your published statutes. Could we see a record of that?'

'Well, it was just a conversation... she said she wasn't happy.'

'But surely Mrs Noble will have recorded such a serious complaint and you would have noted the reporting of this to you? I am correct in believing that would be following company protocol?'

'Well, it wasn't quite like that... it was... well we tried to keep it informal. Not make a big deal of it.' Jonathan seems to find inspiration. 'It was to help Tay...'

Bardy feels rather than sees Tay flinch.

'We often try to deal with things informally so that they don't get blown out of proportion.'

'Ah, I see. Have you made a note of that point Mr Shakespeare?'

'Yes,' Bardy says. He almost adds, 'M'lud'.

'Jonathan, when Taylor Drakos asked you to contact Mrs Willis to confirm that she was indeed dissatisfied with the service she provided, did you do so?'

Jonathan shakes his head.

'Why was that?'

'Well Karen, I mean Mrs Noble said—'

'We seem to be hearing a lot of what Mrs Noble says. One would almost imagine she was in charge here.' Pia looks directly at Jan and leaves that hanging for some moments.

Jan stares back, the question *who the hell are you?* written like a neon sign above her head. She knows she has been out manoeuvred. She said Pia could stay. She agreed she could ask Tay's questions.

Pia turns away, 'Jonathan…'

He jumps.

'I would now like to take you back to the beginning of this complaints process. When someone makes a complaint isn't it company policy that the first recourse is for this to be dealt with informally so that things do not escalate. Mr Shakespeare, could I ask you to read back over your notes.'

Bardy is on it: '…*we often try to deal with things informally so that they don't get blown out of proportion.*'

Tay looks up briefly. 'Yeah, he said that.' She nods at Jonathan then ducks her head down again.

Jonathan is sweating now.

'Did you in fact try to resolve this informally?'

'It just wouldn't have worked, Tay would only have sworn at her again.'

'Yet, today we have seen that Taylor Drakos is prepared to apologise for her language, despite—' Pia flashes a look of ice at Jan '—having the provocation of being bullied and left unprotected as a vulnerable young person by those whose responsibility it is to care for her.'

'You don't know she was bullied.' Jonathan is getting desperate. Bardy is pleased to see that Jan is looking horrified.

Deep nettle green now. Almost the colour of ivy. He hopes she realises much of this is her fault – however busy she has been, Tay deserved better.

'I just don't think it would have worked,' Jonathan declares in desperation.

'So, the policy of informal conflict resolution as laid down by the company that you are employed by, does apply to the other 5043 employees around the UK and Ireland but in your case, you can implement that policy at your discretion?'

'It's not like that.'

'Isn't it?'

'Did you find Taylor Drakos crying in the corridor and did she tell you that Mrs Noble had said to her that her mother was a piece of shit and that she might not know who her dad was, but anyone could see who her mother was?'

Bardy sees Pia place her hand on Tay's back as she says this. He also watches Jan bow her head. So she should.

'She could have made it up, to get back at... Mrs No—'

Pia doesn't so much as cut across him, as mow him down.

'Why would anyone willingly tell another human being such a personal and hurtful thing unless they were desperate and needing help?'

Jonathan looks anywhere except at Pia or Tay.

'Jonathan, do you ever use social media when assessing the suitability of a candidate?'

'What?' Jonathan looks totally confused by this change of direction. 'I'm sorry I don't understand.'

'I will repeat the question. Is it company policy for HR to

use social media? By which I mean information that is in the full public domain.'

'Well no. I mean, yes. It's quite a contentious area.' Jonathan seems to be regaining some little confidence now they are back in the heartland of HR. 'It would only be used in exceptional circumstances.'

'Such as?'

'If there was real concern that someone was likely to damage the company's reputation, or it was extreme views or behaviour.'

'Like bullying?'

'Well, I mean, I don't know…'

'But isn't bullying considered gross misconduct worthy of instant dismissal?'

'Er… yes, I suppose.'

'*It is.*'

Bardy is shocked to hear Jan speak.

She adds, 'May I ask what you are getting at?'

'You may,' Pia replies more pleasantly. She turns to Jan. 'A cursory search of Mrs Noble's social media revealed that she was dismissed from her previous post for bullying, five years ago. She obviously will not have revealed that to you but even a rudimentary interrogation of her past employment would have exposed it. In addition she was happy to post her views about her previous company online and the thread of comments revealed the reason and also her quite illuminating opinions of those who stood up to her. I shall be sending you a link.'

Jan looks confused. 'How do you—'

'I already have your email addresses,' Pia assures her.

Finally, Jan asks Pia the question that Bardy knows has been drilling into her brain for that past fifteen minutes. 'Who *are* you?'

At this point, Tay looks up. 'She's my friend.'

Pia grins and squeezes Tay's hand briefly. 'I sure am, lovely.'

Pia turns to Jan and Jonathan. 'This is what we require. Firstly, a full investigation into Tay's allegation of bullying against Mrs Noble. This must include anonymous testimony thereby protecting other members of the team who Mrs Noble may also be bullying. Should the outcome be as we expect, it will be up to you to deal with Mrs Noble as you see fit. Tay however will require a written apology from the company and that this spurious complaint be removed from her record. She will also re-engage with Mrs Willis as her rightful relationship manager. HR will implement further Excel training for the team, and will communicate in a clear and open way what the law is regarding young people attending college and why the company supports this further education.'

Jan just nods. Bardy thinks she doesn't have any other option. She has stopped looking at her phone. He has the first glimmer of hope that this woman will do right by Tay. Nettle green. Red ochre. Complementary colours.

Jonathan on the other hand looks like he would like someone to shoot him.

Pia goes to rise. She hands Jan and Jonathan each a card. 'You may not have heard of me, but you will certainly have heard of my firm. I am here today as Tay's friend. However, if I hear that as a result of today's meeting Tay is subjected to any emotional abuse or discrimination then I will be back, not only as her friend, but as her lawyer.'

'Shall we?' she says to Tay and Bardy.

As Pia heads to the door, her limp has completely disappeared.

A bloody miracle.

Chapter 29

Kate

The smallest worm will turn, being trodden on

They are in the Angry Beaver, all gathered around Tay. She looks embarrassed and flushed, but Kate thinks she is more relaxed than she has ever seen her. Relief she supposes. She is even having a pint of cider. She is perching on the back of a sofa, Pia beside her. Pia looks radiant and is quietly smiling. The story of the meeting has been told and re-told. Linda repeating it loudly for Leonard's benefit. Leonard proclaiming, 'Oh, well done. Well done!' Jack has come along with Satya, which at first Kate saw as a good sign but they have barely spoken all evening. Jack is talking to Bardy, while Satya's asking Pia about her company and her work. Lou just beams at Tay (when she's not looking). Tay catches him at one point and Kate hears him say, 'What? *What?*' His belligerence fools no one.

Two things happen at once: Hana walks in one door of the pub and Simon walks in the other. For a ridiculous moment

Kate feels like she is in a sliding-doors type of film. Simon is with two other men. Hana is on her own. Neither notice Kate and she is glad of the breathing space to calm down. Leonard is talking at her and so she just focuses on his face, nodding, and lets his words wash over her. It is only as she looks up that she sees Linda studying them. The memory of the words come back to her: *I think I am going to be spending the rest of my days with a boring, selfish old fart.* She wishes she could do something for her. She genuinely would hold Leonard down while Linda put his hearing aids in, if it would help.

Over Leonard's shoulder she sees Tay spot Hana. She puts her pint down and walks over to her. Hana wraps her in a huge hug. Blimey, Hana must mean a lot to her. Kate can tell that Tay isn't the sort of girl who likes to hug. Kate has one of those. Jess and Ellie: big huggers. Bella: prickly pear. She glances at Bardy and sees such a look of longing that she is swept with a massive wave of sympathy. Whether the look is because of Hana's relationship with Tay, or because he finds it so hard to be around his ex-wife, Kate has no idea. She touches Leonard on the arm and says loudly, 'I'm going to get another drink. Would you like one?'

'No, no, I'm the designated driver.'

Kate smiles at him and heads for the bar. She is joined a moment later by Simon. Had she timed it for when she saw him moving that way?

Maybe.

'Kate, we must stop meeting like this.' He shakes his head. 'I can't believe I actually said that.'

'Me neither.' She grins.

'Look I'm no good at this. Never was if I'm honest. I keep mentioning supper but we haven't done anything about it. Can I just take you out sometime? I don't even know if this is how it's done anymore.'

Kate suddenly realises she has no idea if this man is married, divorced, single or a bigamist. It is so long ago since they met. One thing her brief foray into online dating taught her was, it is best to ask – which is not the same as believing you will always hear the truth. 'Did you ever get married?'

'Twice.' He looks at her. 'Now I don't know whether to say I'm really not that bad. Two divorces. What's wrong with him? But if I say that you'll think I'm trying too hard. The man doth protest too much.'

They are both laughing now.

'I told you, completely useless. Never going to get laid again.'

Oh, I don't know.

He flushes. 'Did I really say that?'

'It's, *the lady doth protest too much.*'

They turn in unison towards the voice.

Bardy is standing behind Kate's shoulder queueing for a drink.

'Sorry, didn't mean to overhear, it's just that quote. It's from *Hamlet.*'

'Oh, thanks mate,' Simon says, glancing at Kate and raising an eyebrow.

Before Kate can do or say anything, Bardy moves away, heading back to where Hana and Tay are standing. He seems to have forgotten to buy a drink.

'Do you know him?' Simon sounds baffled.

'Yes… er, I don't know what that was about.'

Simon glances towards his friends. 'I've got to go. But could we go out?' Before Kate can answer he appears struck by a thought. 'I don't know if it's your thing or not but I've got a couple of tickets that my sister can't use, in a week or so to see the new production of *King Lear* in London. It's not *Hamlet*,' he laughs, throwing a look at Bardy, and Kate likes him just a little bit less, 'but it could be fun.'

She doesn't think anyone has ever called *King Lear*, 'fun'. But a night out in London with Simon? She has been planning to go to London to look at some art galleries, to study some oil paintings close up. She could do both. 'That would be great. If I'm free I would love to.'

Simon shakes his head. 'Now if you say you're busy I'm not going to know if you were ever seriously considering it.' He smiles at her and walks back to his table.

She gets her drink and wanders over to Pia who is with Jack. Satya is now talking to Lou. 'Jack's been telling me about the band he was once in. It sounds like it was a wonderful time.'

Jack shrugs, 'It was.'

'Do you play now?' Kate asks.

'No. When Satya started her company we sold our flat and moved into a small rental she... we... sold all my guitars. Didn't have the room. Needed all the money we could lay our hands on.' He continues with a desperate attempt to sound more upbeat, 'But hey! It worked.'

They all fall silent, Jack staring into his pint.

Kate feels so sorry for him but has no idea what to say. She turns to Pia, 'It sounds like you were amazing today.'

Pia glances at Jack. But he is still gazing into his drink. She leans closer to Kate, 'I nearly didn't go in. I mean it was totally unprofessional.'

'But?'

'I had found the social media posts and the comments and I thought Grace would have done it. She would do anything for her friends. For me,' she adds, sadly. Pia smiles very gently, more hesitant than the firebrand that Bardy and Tay had described. 'And I know she will never know about it, but in a funny way I wanted to make her proud.'

'Is there any chance the two of you…'

'No. Grace really is seeing someone else now. A doctor.'

'Ah.'

Kate wants to say more. Something consoling? But she is also intrigued, she has a feeling there is something that Pia isn't telling her. She glances at Jack, but he is still staring into his pint – miles away. She asks, 'Did it worry you, getting involved in Tay's stuff. I don't know why but I thought you seemed a bit reluctant to go there at first.'

Pia stiffens beside her.

Has she said too much, gone too far?

Eventually Pia says, 'It isn't always that easy. You think you are going to do some good, but… sometimes it's a mistake to get too involved.'

Had Pia once got her fingers burnt helping someone? Kate waits. But it seems that Pia doesn't want to say more, and Kate is perfectly sure she shouldn't push it.

In silence they watch Tay who is still talking to Hana and Bardy. Kate thinks they look like a family. 'I did want to give

Tay a fighting chance, I hate it when the little ones get trodden on,' Pia adds.

Jack has now finished his pint and is also watching the 'family' group.

'You've known them a long time, haven't you?' Kate says.

'Seems like forever. Still miss Tom, he's been my best mate since primary school.'

'It's a shame Bardy and Hana...' Kate can't finish, feeling it might be tactless to talk of broken marriages.

Jack unexpectedly gives a small laugh.

'What?' the two women demand.

'Those two do make quite a team. Tom always said it was like being brought up by a botanist and a gardener.'

'Really?' Pia enquires.

'Yeah.' Jack is smiling now. 'Hana can't get enough of studying you. I mean the woman finds everything interesting. And don't get me wrong, she really is fascinated with what you have to say. We used to love hanging out there, especially as teenagers, when pretty much everyone else gave us the go-by.'

'And Bardy?' Kate asks.

'Gardener Bardy. Oh, he gets stuck in and gets his hands dirty. Lot of love in that man.' Jack looks at her, as if recalling where he is. 'Better get a move on,' he says, putting down his empty glass, 'got to get back to the babysitter.'

They all gradually start to drift away. Kate would like to have a word with Bardy but he is sitting in one of the pub's worn armchairs with Hana perched on the arm. They look like a couple. She likes Hana, said a few words to her earlier, but she doesn't want to intrude on this. Whatever this is. Hana puts her hand on Bardy's shoulder and Kate is thrown by how painful this feels. She thinks of what Jack said.

Maybe the team's getting back together?

She can't bring herself to join them to say goodbye, so she goes in search of Linda. Pia and Tay have already left. Having said goodbye to Linda, Kate is just heading down the short corridor to the back door of the pub, when she hears Bardy's voice. He is hidden in the stairwell.

Then comes Lou's voice. 'You don't *have* to do that, you know.'

Leonard's voice follows. For once just a murmur.

Why are Lou and Bardy out here with Leonard?

'*You want to do what?!*' This from Bardy.

There is silence and then Lou and Bardy start laughing.

'I'm sorry mate. I didn't mean to...' Lou can't finish.

Bardy, still laughing. 'Leonard, trust me. You *really* need to tell Linda.'

It is the last thing Kate hears as she disappears out of the back door.

WEEK 5

The old brick windmill stands with sails spread as if welcoming the latecomers. The first of these migrants had arrived in April, now in early May they are back in numbers. The swallows come closest to the sails, flying like a child would scribble; erratic, chaotic, joyous. The house martins swoop lower collecting mud from the puddle at the windmill's feet, while the swifts fly about them all, tracing broad sweeping patterns in the sky.

Chapter 30

Bardy

An honest tale speeds best, being plainly told

They are back in the lifeboat station and the warmer, muggy May weather has been broken by a sudden storm. Wind is lashing the building, rain pummelling the big window. The run from the car park had been a dash that left them dripping. Coats are now hung from spare chairs and they are gathered around the main table, lit by a pool of yellow light. A good place to gather.

All except Tay.

'Out with her mate Uzma tonight,' Bardy tells them.

Bardy doesn't mind. Smiled when he got the text. Friendship comes hard to Tay. And now there's Uzma. This group too. Sometimes you only need a start. He glances at Lou, who is on his way to the kitchen with Linda, cake tin in hand. She has brought coffee cake, he has brought Italian pastries. Like an old married couple. Which makes him turn to Leonard.

'Have you told Linda?'

'Well, I've not really had the time. It's been a busy week with one thing and another.'

Silver bright Kate comes straight out with it, Satya and Pia listening in. 'Told Linda what?'

Silver bright Kate who is going out with that big blond prat. Or is *he* the prat? *The lady doth protest too much.* FFS!

Plus, he's the prat who had looked at Pia like... well like that prat Jonathan.

So many prats. They could form a band.

He turns to Pia who is asking, 'Is there something you are not telling us, Leonard?' So soft now, gentle. A twinkle. But boy, does he want this woman on his side when the going gets tough.

Leonard's blustering continues until the others are back.

'Linda, Leonard has something to tell you.' Bardy pushes him to the edge of the cliff and holds him there.

'Leonard?'

Bardy is surprised how concerned Linda sounds. The woman who wants to run her husband over. Linda continues to pass around cakes and coffees, but her eyes are on her husband. And Leonard only has eyes for Linda.

It is as if the rest of them don't exist.

Is this love? Is this what it really looks like? Not as in the films, or even in most of the books he's read. How many times have this couple looked at each other over the years? How well they must know each other's eyes, their changing light and expressions.

'Leonard?' Linda sits down, coffee forgotten.

'I don't want to paint.'

Linda laughs. It is propelled by relief. What had she been expecting?

Leonard looks at his laughing wife and glances helplessly at the man who pushed him to the cliff edge.

'What do you want to do?' Linda knows there is more.

Leonard pauses. They all wait. The rain on the window his drumroll.

'I want to write a musical.'

'*Oh Leonard!*'

Bardy never knew that name could be said with such delight, enthusiasm and – you can't deny it – sexual promise. *Blimey, Leonard.* Hidden depths.

Now they are all joining in with enthusiasm. And Leonard the composer is off.

'I've always wanted to but I just didn't have the time, or I thought people might think it was beyond me, or laugh at me.' But it is Leonard who is laughing with the relief of his confession.

'What's it going to be about?' Satya asks.

'I have this idea of a story of a middle-aged man who is running a big factory making something boring like… oh… extruded plastic. All whistles and big chimneys – an industrial setting. I can see the stage set. He is not happy but keeps going to make sure his family are provided for. Here I am imagining some darker scenes, thumping tunes, machinery whirring. Then there is his walk home to his family and that moment before he opens the door.'

Leonard is now leaning forward with enthusiasm. 'Now comes the family scene, warm and happy, this man really loves his family. But there is a hidden sadness. He is keeping this secret from them.'

'Oh Leonard,' Linda's voice cracks.

He pats her hand. 'No, it's alright. It has a happy ending.'

'Does it?' She doesn't sound so sure.

'The man's wife realises he isn't happy and she says he should do whatever he wants to do. Now that's a very poignant scene. I have the song for that one already.' Leonard is nodding and smiling.

Bardy glances around, everyone looks dumbstruck.

'Then – and this I think has the chance to add in some comedy – we see the man trying out new jobs. He tries to be a painter, but he's really bad at it, and his father laughs when he sees what his son is doing. Tells him he's no good and should go back to running the factory…'

Bardy hears the next, whispered, 'Oh Leonard,' from Linda. He doubts Leonard does. Still no hearing aids.

'So the man goes on to try all sorts of things. He could join a circus, try to start a newspaper,' Leonard glances at Lou, 'become a baker and set up a cake shop. Lots of possibility for colour and humour. Each scene change could see the man reinvented, but failing.'

'He could be a guitarist in a band,' Satya suggests. But Bardy notices she isn't smiling.

'Oh, great idea.' Leonard has started making notes. 'I am thinking quick scene changes. Lights fade and we open on a new scene, then another. The set miraculously altered. The man could become mixed up with who he is, to create more comedy.'

'What happens in the end?' Pia asks.

'Ah.' Leonard looks a little crestfallen. 'I haven't really got that far.'

'But it has a happy ending?' Pia sounds anxious.

The hardnosed lawyer who wants to believe in happy-ever-after.

'Oh, yes!' Leonard proclaims. 'It's just I haven't come up with the right thing yet.'

'You will, dear,' his wife tells him.

'You don't think it's ridiculous me thinking I can do this at eighty?' he asks.

'Not at all,' they chorus.

Linda takes his hand. 'I was once with a woman who was dying, she was very old, it was definitely her time. She told me she had one big regret. She said that had she known she was going to live to 101 she would definitely have learnt the piano when her grandchildren suggested it on her sixty-sixth birthday. She always wanted to play and never did. So you see.'

They all did.

'Blimey, Leonard, I think you've stolen the show. Anyone else want to say what they're up to? Lou? Thinking of writing a play?' Lou's hand is still bandaged.

'No. I'll leave that to you, mate.'

Bardy wonders if Lou guesses he still hasn't actually written a word of a short story.

'I've been collecting driftwood. Think I might make something from that.'

'I like that idea,' Kate says.

Lou looks embarrassed. 'Well, we'll see.'

'Kate? Are you really interested in that tall tosser?'

Luckily this only sounds in his head, although he does manage, 'Kate?'

'I'm experimenting with colour. Hana was really helpful, so

thank you for that Bardy. I am just mixing different shades at the moment. So in some ways it feels like I've gone backwards. But in lots of ways it doesn't, if that makes any sense.'

Pia leans forward. 'Can you paint on fabric?'

'Yes,' Kate responds, 'especially on natural fibres. What are you thinking of?'

'My quilt,' she replies, 'my huge quilt. I think the stitching is getting lost. So I wondered about adding something extra.'

'I think that's a lovely idea.' Linda. Mellow plum.

'Come round and I will show you which paints work,' Kate offers.

'Great, so who's next, Satya?' Bardy suggests.

Satya pulls out her tablet and holds it up. 'I've been thinking about how most of us find it hard to find the time, or give ourselves permission to do this.' She smiles at Leonard. 'Anyway, I've been thinking about that.' She starts to flick through photos of paint boxes, brushes in colourful pots, fabric tied in bundles, crayons, pastels and piles of sketchbooks. Each is a study in its own right and filled with colour. A poem starts to form in Bardy's mind, about old paint dried on the tip of a well-used, well-travelled brush. *Burnt sienna*.

Satya continues, 'It occurred to me that over the years I've bought so much stuff like this because I love the colours, the idea of them. Even the textures.' She points to a photo of a box of chalky pastels. 'In a way it reminds me of starting my business. I began with make-up – all those colours and the feel of them, glossy and matt, liquids to powders. And I learnt about them. How they were best used, the chemistry behind them.' She looks at Bardy. 'And it wasn't just work, it was fun. So when I look at all these,' she gestures to her images, 'I think what I wanted to capture is the promise they bring, of maybe being able to create something. Even if the reality is that I keep buying them and they sit around and I don't know what to do with them.'

'All-the-gear-but-no-idea,' Kate says.

They all look at Kate.

Especially Bardy. Not great. Unlike her.

Kate flushes. 'I'm so sorry Satya, I didn't mean it quite as it came out. It was just a saying I heard once.'

Bardy has heard it too. Hana. What did Kate and Hana talk about? Hana had said she liked Kate but she hadn't been exactly enthusiastic. Then she had been different with him in the pub. Kept close. What was that about? He tries to concentrate on what Satya is saying.

'No, it's alright, Kate it's true.' Satya nods.

'I do love the photos,' Kate responds, 'I think they really capture something.'

They all make noises of agreement. Linda adds, 'I feel like that when I see beautiful spices. I might not know quite what to do with them.' She chuckles. 'And can't usually be bothered to find out, but I can still enjoy looking at them, smelling them. I agree, Satya, you can enjoy the promise of them.'

Mellow plum merging with the blue of lapis. Reassuring.

'Same with me,' Lou unexpectedly adds, gesturing with his bandaged hand, 'something about having the tools, seeing the gouges lined up. Pleasing.'

Bardy realises he felt the same seeing Hana's palette of oil paints. Those splatters of colour. Something satisfying and also beguiling. Even to the non-painter, like him.

'Who's next?' Bardy asks.

'How about you?' Leonard suggests.

Non-painter. Non-writer.

Bardy looks at him and eventually finds some inspiration. 'I'm thinking about a short story that is a love story. Bit unexpected.' He pauses, looking at Linda and Leonard, before continuing. 'Just don't know the ending yet.'

'Oh, very good,' Leonard chortles. Confessing to Linda seems to have given Leonard a new lease of life. From Lockdown King to Musical Maestro. A man with a love story.

And what about my own love story? Fat chance. Hana is going to New Zealand, despite that hand on his shoulder that had made him think... he has no idea what. And silver bright Kate is with a tall good-looking bloke who makes her laugh.

Still a prat.

He will end his days with Lou, the baker in a pink spotty pinny.

'Linda? How about you? Still planning on that short story?' Bardy eventually asks.

Linda looks towards the rain-soaked window. 'Perhaps not.' She smiles very slightly. 'I thought I might try painting birds.'

'*Really?*' This from Leonard.

'And maybe Leonard,' she continues loudly, 'you might like to take us all out on a birdwatching trip?'

'Indeed I would!' Leonard enthuses, rubbing his hands together. 'Oh, I know just the spot.'

Linda looks around at them. 'Kate it might help with your painting and Pia with ideas for your quilt. Satya, you could take photos and Lou you can look for new bits of driftwood.'

Linda turns to him. 'And who knows Bardy, you might even find your happy ending.'

They are all getting coats on ready to dash back through the rain. Bardy watches Kate. Should he say something? It is then he sees Kate beckoning Pia and Satya. They gather around her. He moves a little closer, ostensibly to tidy the chairs, and catches Kate saying, 'I've had an idea…' but he hears nothing more. However, a few minutes later Pia and Satya laugh. They all glance towards Linda and Leonard.

Lou appears beside him. 'What is it mate?'

Where does he even begin? As usual Bardy feels like he is living in an alternative universe – feeling he is missing something – and that even in his own world, nothing much is making sense.

'Pint?' Lou suggests.

Bardy nods, gratefully.

Jon and Lou. He'll take that.

And it's so wet, they might even see an otter.

Chapter 31

Kate

O, beware, my lord, of jealousy:
It is the green-eyed monster which doth mock

The weather has cleared and while it is still overcast the air feels balmy. They are all gathered outside Pia's house. A good place to leave cars and bikes. Kate was pleased to see Tay arrive with Bardy. Pia has invited them for coffee and cake afterwards and Linda is already talking about cake. This followed on from Kate's suggestion that on their next group outing they might like to come to London with her to look around some galleries. Everyone seems enthusiastic and Linda is telling them about her friend's approach to looking at art.

'She says the best way to go round a gallery is to find a painting you love, a painting you hate. And then go and eat cake.'

'I like it, I think we should do that and then talk through what we chose,' Satya suggests and Pia nods.

'Would you be able to come?' Kate asks Tay, knowing it is likely to be a mid-week trip. Ideally when she is going to see *King Lear* with Simon. She could meet up with Simon afterwards. She hasn't seen him since the pub, but they have been texting.

Tay nods. 'I guess so. Jan told me to take off whatever time I need.' She smiles, and Kate thinks it makes Tay look younger somehow. 'They binned her off, you know.'

'What, that woman who was so awful to you?' Linda asks eagerly.

'Yep. They got security to walk her to the door. She was mouthing off at us all.' Tay is really grinning now.

'How have the other women been?' Kate enquires, slightly worried.

'They're not so bad. Shit at spreadsheets, but they are getting some help with that.'

'Have you heard what's happening to Jonathan?' Bardy asks.

'Nah, but he had to write me an apology.' Tay says gleefully. 'Twat.' She turns to Pia. 'Is Noy coming with us?'

'No, I think he might disturb the birds.' Tay looks disappointed and Pia adds, 'Brenda's looking after him, but he will be here when we get back. Have you ever had a dog Tay?'

Tay looks at her like she's mad. 'You're joking me! Toni wanted one of those handbag dogs but Bardy stopped her. It would have been dead in a week. Would have forgotten to feed it or left it in the pub. Or some dickhead she was with would have kicked the shit out of it.'

The casualness of this retelling horrifies Kate and makes her want to hug Tay. Hard-shelled, spiky Tay. She thinks of Tay walking into Hana's embrace. There really must be something pretty special about Hana.

'Right, are we ready?' Leonard emerges from around the tail end of their car. He is wearing camouflage gear, has binoculars slung over his neck and has a telescope and tripod strapped to his back. It is clear he is in a very good mood. 'Off we go,' he calls and he heads off down the path that leads along the water's edge and across the fields to the bird reserve. He has already told them which hide they will be visiting and got them all the relevant day pass. He and Linda have lifetime membership.

Kate glances at Pia and Satya who nod at her meaningfully. She hopes her idea might work. But who knows? She sees Bardy watching them but he quickly looks away.

Oh Bardy.

She likes Simon. He makes her smile. She is genuinely looking forward to going to see *King Lear* with him… but…

Her thoughts are interrupted by Bardy who catches up with her.

'Kate, I've been meaning to say, look, I'm sorry about the other night. The *Hamlet* rubbish I was talking. Sorry. Seems like a nice bloke. Lou said…'

'What did Lou say?' And why does she feel Bardy hadn't meant to say that bit?

'Oh nothing. Seems to know… Simon, is it? From way back. Says he's not so bad.'

Why the hell have Lou and Bardy been discussing Simon? It is none of their business. Kate is suddenly angry with Bardy. The Bardy who couldn't even speak to Pia, because he fancied her so much. The Bardy who was getting oh so cosy with Hana in the pub.

'He *is* really nice,' Kate responds.

'Yes, well, yes that's what I'm saying,' Bardy says, flustered. 'Have you known him long?'

'From way back, but he's been living abroad, in Dubai.'

'Ah, must be good to meet up again. You and he are…'

'Bardy, what are you on about?' She continues before he can answer, 'Look, he's a friend. Someone who wants to get to know me better.' Why had she said that last bit? A dig because he hadn't been interested in her?

'I bet he does,' Bardy mutters to his boots.

The phrase *you want your Kate and Edith* comes to her. Except Pia or Hana was Bardy's equivalent of Edith. This fuels her anger. On top she heaps her frustration. She wants to shout at him. *Why didn't you see me Bardy? Why didn't you like me?* Even now she is willing him to tell her that she might mean something to him. That despite the hair, the scar that she fears will brand her as damaged and ugly, that she *is* attractive to him. That he could desire her. She dips her head to hide the sudden tears.

Bardy continues to walk looking at his boots.

Then Kate thinks of Alice, her dragonfly bright sister. She lifts her head. Fuck it. She's worth more than this. 'It's been really good to meet him again. I hope we can arrange this trip to London to the galleries and I might spend a bit more time there. Simon's taking me to see the new production of *King Lear*.'

Now he does look up. 'But that's my favourite play.' Without another word, Bardy stomps off to join Lou and Tay.

Kate wants to lift her head to the sky and scream. Long and very loud.

She picks up her pace to catch up with Pia and Leonard, bypassing Linda and Satya who appear deep in conversation. Kate hopes Linda can work some of her magic, and ease what is troubling Satya. She must have seen it with her own boys, partnerships or marriages that hit rocky patches. Then she hears the words 'mission statement' and her heart sinks.

When she reaches Pia and Leonard, Pia is asking, 'So what is the difference between a twitcher and a birder?'

'I'm sorry. What was that?'

Pia repeats it more loudly.

Leonard adjusts his binoculars around his neck. 'Now birders, they are not just about ticking species off a list, like your twitcher. More of a genuine interest in birds I always feel. And the liberties some of those twitchers take, invading people's gardens, gearing themselves out in all the latest army gear. Ridiculous!' says the man in camouflage trousers.

'Oh, I see,' Pia says, solemnly, eyes twinkling.

Soon Leonard is leading them along a broad bank that runs perpendicular to the sea. Either side of the bank are a series of wide expansive pools. These lie between reedbeds and broader flatlands, intersected by rivulets. Kate thinks Hana is right, everything reflects everything. Each strand of water carrying the reflection of the sky deep into the marshland. And everywhere there are birds. An erratic scuttering of small birds explodes from the reedbeds nearby and in the pools are the waders and the ducks. Kate is not surprised Leonard thinks this is a 'good spot'. It reminds her of an African waterhole – there are so many species gathered here. Leonard may not be a twitcher but there is no doubt that he is excited by each bird he sees: the curlews, redshanks, shelducks and ruffs.

'I've even heard there's been a sighting of a long-billed dowitcher,' he exclaims happily.

Kate looks at Pia and Satya and nods. They nod back.

'What's that all about?' Bardy says quietly making her jump. She just shakes her head. 'Wait and see.' It seems he has recovered from his... whatever it was.

And so has she.

It seems impossible to hold on to annoyance, and even her grief, when standing here listening to the wind and the birds. She thinks again of Alice, feeling the air on her face. She looks up, taking in the sky above her. Breathing it all in.

Despite whatever is going on – or not going on – with her and Bardy, Kate knows she has much to be happy about. That she should be grateful just to be standing here, with these people.

And for the first time in a long while, Kate finds that knowing this *does* make it so.

Chapter 32

Bardy

To sing a song that old was sung

'Now, quietly now.' Leonard beckons them to follow him along the broad wooden walkway that leads to the bird hide. Bardy thinks they must look like mismatched ducklings hurrying behind. Leonard lowers his hand to indicate no one should talk as they approach the door.

With a loud slam the door opens, banging back on its hinges, and nearby a flock of ducks takes flight. 'I still don't see why we can't have brought the dogs,' a woman declares loudly to her companion. 'They could have had a great time in those ponds.'

Tash is back among them. Not that she's spotted them, yet. Then she does.

'Oh.' She nudges the big man next to her and gives him an, 'I'll tell you later' look. 'Not much to see,' Tash proclaims as she passes them. As the couple disappear around the bend in the walkway, Bardy hears a burst of laughter.

'Well!' Linda ejaculates. Mellow plum now deep purple.

However, there seems to be one advantage to meeting up again with Tash. She has cleared the hide for them. As they step inside they have the place to themselves. 'Oh excellent,' Leonard declares speaking just above a whisper, 'now take a seat everyone.'

A series of wooden benches are placed in front of slats that have been raised to enable them to look out over the pool. Leonard starts to set up his telescope and hands his binoculars to Linda. Bardy has to give it to Len, the view is wonderful.

Could he call him Len?

He glances at the man adjusting the eye piece of his telescope. Nope. Leonard Bernstein was not a 'Len'.

'This is an amazing spot,' Bardy says, squeezing on to a bench next to Tay. He's pleased she came. She has even brought a small sketchbook. So has silver bright Kate. And Linda, the bird painter.

The broad pool in front of them shimmers with the occasional gust of wind and then settles, the surface flecked with smaller ripples caused by the movement of the feeding birds. Above the water, swallows and house martins dart and swoop. Tash clearly has no idea what she is talking about, the pool is teeming with birdlife. Leonard points out the different species to them, the avocets, little ringed plovers and dunlin, as well as teal and shoveler ducks. He invites them to use his telescope when he gets a particularly interesting bird in his sights. 'I'm sure they said there was a dowitcher around here,' he mutters.

Kate looks up at him. 'I can see why you love it here, and love the birds.'

Leonard looks pleased. 'I do have to say, Kate, that I am very taken with the idea that as the land changes below, the birds keep flying over it all, migrating, year after year. Following the old paths, singing the old songs.'

'That's very poetic, Leonard,' Bardy comments.

'Are all these birds part of the migration?' Satya asks.

'Oh no,' Leonards replies, 'some of the species are real home birds and never want to move far...'

He knows that feeling. He supposes it is the same for Leonard and Linda. Tay? No, he hopes Tay *does* move on. Even just for a while. He glances at her. Head down busily sketching an avocet.

'...others are passing through, and then decide to stay...' Leonard continues.

Is that Kate? Possibly.

Hana? But she didn't want to stay. Had already stayed too long.

I really loved you... but then yes, Bardy, I did want more.

What about Satya? She may have Indian heritage, but she was born in Norfolk, the daughter of a doctor and a businessman. Has based her own business here too. Yes, Satya is a home bird. Like Jack.

Leonard looks at them over the top of his telescope. 'Now, some are exotics who become home birds. Definitely not from around here, perhaps they got blown off course, but decided to stay.'

Lou leans back on the bench, so he can see Pia. 'There you go, we're the exotics.'

Leonard is now in full flow: 'So those are the home birds,

then we come on to the migrants. You have the seasonal migrants who stay a while, and then the passage migrants who are passing through on their way north or south.'

'And that's what you like so much?' Kate asks.

Leonard nods. 'And it can get quite exciting when the eruptive migrants appear.'

'Oh, people often think I'm one of those,' Satya says.

'What?' Leonard looks puzzled.

'A disruptive migrant.'

'No, no.' Leonard looks distressed. 'I said *eruptive* migrant. That happens when food might be scarce elsewhere in the world and the birds come here to swell the numbers for a while.'

'Makes sense,' Tay says, looking up from her drawing.

'And the other birds accept them?' Pia asks.

'Usually,' Leonard nods.

Pia looks thoughtful and Bardy wonders if she is thinking about her human rights work with refugees. Were people always as welcoming to migrants as the birds?

Leonard is suddenly distracted by the vibration of his phone. 'It's the bird group. Definitely a dowitcher around.' He picks up the binoculars that Linda had put down when she started sketching.

'How do we spot the dowager?' Kate asks.

'*Dowitcher*,' Leonard repeats slowly, eyes peering through the binoculars.

'I think a *dowager* bird would be quite grand,' Pia comments.

'Dowitcher,' Leonard says, patiently, 'I can see the mistake you're making.'

'Any sign of that dowager?' Satya asks, innocently.

Bardy has no idea what is going on but he can detect the women's suppressed mirth.

Leonard, shakes his head, momentarily lowering his binoculars. 'It's—'

'Is that the dowager, there Leonard?' Pia asks, pointing vaguely into the distance.

'It's a d—'

Kate interrupts him. 'You know the bird I really like, that's the prattling cole, but I hear they're quite rare.'

'You mean a *pratincole*,' Leonard insists.

'Yes, the prattling cole isn't seen much around here,' Pia says, seriously.

Leonard looks to Linda for help, but Bardy sees she has her eyes fixed on Kate, a slight smile on her face. Eventually Linda says, 'Kate, you know which bird I've always wanted to see – that would be the spotted cake.'

Leonard turns on his wife. 'What are you talking about? Cake? *Cake*? It's a spotted *crake*.'

Satya adds her bit. 'Even more than the dowager and the spotted cake, what I'd really like to see is…'

'Would that be the black-tailed gobshit?' Lou enquires.

Oh, very good, Lou.

Bardy thinks Leonard's head is going to spin. 'Black-tailed *godwit*, pratincole, spotted *crake* and it's a DOWITCHER,' he almost shouts.

Satya ignores Leonard. 'No Lou, not the black-tailed gobshit, but the fluffy-backed tit-babbler.'

Most of them are laughing now. Leonard looks totally confused.

'But they live in Thailand!' Leonard blurts, he looks around. 'I don't understand.'

For a moment they ignore him. 'Is there really such a bird?' Pia asks, grinning.

'Oh, yes, I looked it up. Great name,' Satya says.

Kate now turns to Leonard, and Pia and Satya also gather around. Bardy glances at Linda who says nothing but sits back to see how things unfold.

'Leonard,' Kate says loudly. 'Isn't it really, *really* annoying when someone can't understand what you're saying?' She pauses, 'So we are asking you, in fact begging you, for your sake and ours...' Pia and Satya join in '...*please wear your hearing aids.*'

Leonard throws an anguished look at Bardy and Lou.

They both shrug. *You're on your own mate.*

Besides, they're both laughing.

'It isn't as simple as that and they're not always comfortable.'

'Wear your hearing aids, Leonard,' the three women chorus.

'But they make me feel old,' Leonard pleads.

'WEAR YOUR HEARING AIDS, LEONARD,' they repeat loudly, and the others join in now.

'You're ganging up on me,' Leonard says, peevishly.

'Do you want me to get angry with you?' Pia asks. She is still laughing but there is a glint of something hidden.

Leonard looks away quickly. 'Linda?'

His last resort.

'*Please*, Leonard,' she says softly. And even if he doesn't hear, he understands.

Still Bardy can see him wavering.

'Don't know how the fuck you're going to write a musical if you don't,' Tay offers, looking up briefly from her drawing.

'Oh,' Leonard says, as if he hasn't considered this.

And Bardy feels sure the next time he sees the composer he will be wearing his (bloody) hearing aids.

On the walk back to Pia's house, Bardy falls in with Pia and Lou. The exotics.

'Good job back there,' he says, nodding towards Leonard.

'Kate's idea, she thought it would be interesting to see how he felt when we kept mishearing.' Pia smiles slowly. 'Having your Kate and Edith… pasta bake…'

'Ah, yes,' Bardy responds.

'So, Bardy, you home bird, are you okay hanging out with us exotics?' Before Bardy can answer, Pia says, 'Lou, do you ever mind being an exotic?'

He appears to consider this. 'No, I've always liked being Italian, even if it made me a bit different.'

'But then you had the Mafia on your side,' Bardy murmurs.

'I do sometimes wish I felt a bit more like a native,' Pia admits.

They are passing through countryside now and pause to look up at a church that is at the top of the field beside them, swifts soaring above it. The flint and brick walls look as if they are growing out of the terracotta, stone-strewn field.

'You are more at home than you know,' Lou suggests, gesturing to the field.

'I am sorry, I don't follow you,' Pia says.

Nor does Bardy.

'Look at all that flint, the countryside's scattered with it.'

Bardy and Pia nod. To Bardy this flecking in the soil and in the buildings is just one of the things he loves about North Norfolk.

'All that flint came from Scandinavia, was carried here by the glaciers that moved over this land when we were linked to Europe.'

'Pre-Brexit then,' Bardy suggests.

Lou snorts, but ignores him. 'When the glaciers melted they left the flint here.' He turns to Pia, with a grin. 'You're like the Scandinavian flint – tougher than you look.' He then nods towards the field. 'But meant to be here. This is your home now. Just like the flint.'

Pia smiles a little mistily at him. 'Why thank you, Lou.'

Yeah, well done, Clemenza.

But then geography had always been Clemenza's best subject.

Chapter 33

Kate

With hair up-staring – then like reeds, not hair

The wind has picked up and by the time they get back to Pia's house Kate is conscious her bristle-brush hair is even more on end than usual. They bundle inside and Kate heads for the boot room where she knows there is a loo and a mirror. Emerging a few minutes later, she finds Pia and Linda studying photographs that line the corridor leading to the stairs. She can hear the others above in the big living space, exclaiming at the view.

Linda is looking at a photograph of a younger Pia on a march through some city. 'Pride?' Linda asks.

'Um. That was in London, I forget how many years ago.'

Leonard appears beside his wife. 'You need to come and see this view Linda. Beautiful house,' he adds to Pia. Then he catches sight of the photograph. 'Linda goes to Pride every year.'

'*Do you?*' Pia and Kate exclaim.

'Oh yes. Well, since about 2010.'

They start to mount the broad wooden stairs to join the others.

'Do you mind me asking why you go?' Pia says.

'Well, that would be because of jury service,' Linda replies. 'My goodness, Leonard you were right, it is a wonderful view.'

'Jury service?' Kate asks, perplexed.

'Um, yes, let me help you,' Linda offers, and they head towards the kitchen area. Leonard returns to studying the view. 'I was called for jury service, and one of the other people on the jury was a young girl. Well, I say young, maybe mid-twenties. Certainly, younger than the rest of us. Lovely girl. We started talking about festivals, our boys were heading off to one that weekend. She ended up telling me about going to Pride, and she said that sometimes people like me went.'

'Like you?' Pia quizzes her.

Linda smiles, 'I think she meant because I was "mumsy". She said women like me went along to give out hugs. Some of the people who went to Pride had been ostracised by their families and many really just wanted a hug from their mum.'

'Oh, Linda.' Kate's eyes are swimming. It reminds her of something. 'Alice came out to my parents when she was about eighteen. Mum was fine…' JoJo Rose. God, she had almost forgotten her painting past. It comes as a shock to be reminded of it.

'So your mum was fine… but?' Pia asks.

'Well, I don't think Dad was. I didn't realise until Alice was ill and she told me that was the reason she stopped coming home so much. She said he used to dodge hugging her, pretend he was busy with something, get her a drink, take her bag upstairs. Anything rather than touch her.' A second memory comes to Kate. With it comes guilt. She pushes against it, forcing it back into the place where it lives.

'That's sad,' Linda comments. 'How were your parents?' she asks Pia.

'I can't even remember telling them. I think it isn't a big thing in Denmark. But I still like to go to Pride sometimes. Do you still go?'

'As long as there are people who need a hug, I shall keep going,' Linda says, placidly.

'I think we all need hugs.' It is the hesitant, tentative Pia.

Linda pulls Pia unceremoniously into an embrace and then reaches out an arm to include Kate. Kate feels bundled up in cashmere, warmth and the faint scent of magnolia. She hears Linda murmur, 'Thank you for Leonard's bird lesson.' She smiles and rests her head on Linda's shoulder feeling suddenly sleepy but also hugely grateful to have met these women.

'Can anyone join in?' Lou asks, and looking up, the others are watching from behind the counter that faces into the room. Satya beside Lou, watching the three of them.

'Enough of this,' Linda says briskly giving both Pia and Kate's backs a final rub, 'time for coffee and cake.'

They are sitting on the horseshoe of grey sofas, coffees and an assortment of Danish pastries laid out on the table in front of them. Pia has just produced a bottle of white wine which Satya, Linda and Kate have accepted a glass of. Pia and Tay are talking in more detail about Tay's work. All seems so much better and Tay has nearly finished her college course. The others have been discussing the proposed trip to London and decided the National Gallery would be a good place to start and then maybe to take in the Portrait Gallery as well.

There is a sudden scrabbling sound and Tay is instantly on her feet heading towards Noy who appears at the top of the stairs. He dances around her while Tay makes a fuss of him. Brenda follows shortly after, 'Oh, he likes you, don't you Noy Boy.'

'Brenda come in and meet everyone,' Pia says, from the sofa.

Brenda joins them, still clutching a lead and what looks like an orange woolly hat. Pia makes the introductions, but Kate can see she is eyeing the hat with misgivings. One of Brenda's or a new knit for Noy?

'Would you like a coffee or a glass of wine?' Pia offers.

Brenda looks longingly at the wine. 'No, no, I don't want to disturb you all.'

'Well if you're sure—'

'Nonsense,' Linda interrupts, budging up on the sofa and she starts to pour a glass for Brenda, also pushing the depleted plate of pastries towards her.

Brenda beams at them and as she sits down Noy jumps up on the sofa to settle between her and Pia, very much at home. Kate is not at all sure Pia is pleased to be sharing what is clearly her and Noy's usual spot. Tay slumps on the floor next to Noy's head and helps herself to another pastry.

The Noy fan club.

She notices that Tay has her arm and shoulder near Pia's legs, almost touching, and it strikes her that since the disciplinary meeting there has been a bond between the two of them.

'Well, this is very nice, and you are all artists, you say?' Brenda sips her wine and nibbles on an iced pastry.

Bardy explains about the group. 'Do you paint or write, Brenda?'

'I did try doing some paintings of flowers once. I wasn't very good. My husband Brian said he'd seen better at the local primary school.'

'Maybe he just didn't appreciate your particular style,' Linda suggests, kindly.

'Oh, no,' Brenda responds, 'Brian knows much more about art than I do, and he said I shouldn't bother as I was never going to be an artist. I think he's probably right, he says I'm not a creative person.'

Kate frowns at her acceptance of these unkind comments, and she wonders what else Brian has opinions on. It prompts her to say, 'But you are creative Brenda, you knit.' Kate avoids looking at Pia as she says this.

'Do you?' Linda enthuses.

Kate sees Brenda glance uncertainly at Pia. 'Well, yes, I do. It's something to do as I watch TV or when Brian is out with his fishing pals, which he is rather a lot.'

'What do you knit?' Linda asks.

Brenda glances at Noy who is now nuzzling into Tay, happily having his ears stroked.

'Oh, this and that.'

But this is not good enough for Linda, she starts to ask Brenda about the jumper she is wearing and before long the two of them are discussing the diagonal basketweave stitch and the reverse stockinette.

Kate leans her head back on the sofa and half listens as the others form knots of conversation. Lou and Leonard talking local council politics; Pia and Satya chatting about a new Netflix series; Tay listening in.

Bardy's voice brings her back to the room. Was she falling asleep? 'Kate, would you like me to top your wine up?'

She must have been half-dozing. She smiles at him sleepily and his look reaches out and holds hers. His eyes are grey, but there are flecks of brown she hasn't noticed before. And still they look at each other. The moment stretching on.

Oh, I see you Bardy.

And Kate knows he sees her. In their gaze everything else falls away. The questions, the what ifs. She can't name what is left but she knows with complete certainty she will remember this moment even when she is a very old woman and is finally weary of life.

Linda's rich laugh makes them both look away and Kate is left reeling, dizzy and feeling somehow bereft. 'But these are wonderful,' Linda is saying. She seems to be studying something on Brenda's phone.

Brenda glances nervously at Pia who is still chatting to Satya. 'They're just a bit of fun. I had all this wool to use up.'

'What's that?' Tay is now leaning in looking.

There follows a very un-Tay like gurgle of laughter. 'They're beaut!' She pats Noy some more. 'You're a superstar dog.'

This does attract Pia's attention. Kate isn't sure what is coming next but she knows it's not going to be good.

'Noy is the perfect model,' Linda comments, laughing. As she holds out Brenda's phone to show the others, Brenda makes an ineffectual grab for it. She is too late. They are now all looking at photos of Noy modelling a series of fetching outfits. A jester whippet in gold and blue with extravagant pompom buttons. A clerical whippet, sombre black coat with a white dog collar, and black beret. Kate puts her hand over her mouth and stifles her laugh. The others are less successful.

There is Noy in a woollen coat of 3D flowers – complete with a cupcake hat. And finally, a green and red dinosaur whippet with knitted spines down his back. In all the photos Noy is looking pathetically patient, but as before when Kate saw him in his cerise jumper, his brows are drawn together into a 'why me' expression.

Most are laughing now, including Kate. It's Noy's expression that set her off.

But Pia is not laughing. Nor is Brenda.

Brenda looks pleadingly at Pia. 'It was only a bit of fun. I didn't take him out in them after you…'

'Is this your Instagram account?' Pia's voice cuts through, her face rigid.

'Yes, but it's a private account.'

'You will take those photos down straight away.'

Brenda nods, her round, good-natured face flushed. Kate abruptly stops laughing. She thinks Brenda is close to tears. 'I didn't mean any harm.'

Linda hands her back the phone, looking stricken. She clearly thought Pia already knew of the whippet knits. The rest of the laughter slowly fades.

'Brenda, I am very conscious of how much you like Noy and

I am grateful for all you do. But he is not your dog. And I will not have him made to look ridiculous by you.'

Brenda winces. And for some reason Kate thinks of her husband, Brian.

Brenda scrambles to her feet. 'No, I'm very sorry. I'll get rid of it all. Nice to meet everyone.'

But Pia hasn't finished. 'And please stop calling *my* dog, Noy Boy.'

'No, no, of course,' and Brenda all but runs for the stairs.

Before anyone can say anything Tay is on her feet and after her. From halfway down the stairs comes the sound of muffled conversation.

'I cannot believe she did that!' Pia declares, eyes flashing, face flushed.

There is complete silence.

'Blimey Pia.' This from Lou.

She whips around to him, 'What?'

He holds his hands out, shaking his head, 'Nothing. Your dog. Your rules.'

Kate glances at Bardy, but he is looking anxiously after Tay. His face relaxes and turning she sees Tay re-emerge at the top of the stairs. Noy goes to move off the sofa to join her, but Pia clicks her fingers together smartly and loudly. Noy sinks back down.

Tay approaches and looks around at them all.

'Sit back down here,' Linda says, soothingly. 'Now anyone for the last pastry? Pia, you really must give me the recipe for that… what did you call it… kransekage?'

Tay ignores Linda, and looks down at Pia, a frown on her

face. 'Look, I know you love Noy, and he's your dog, but at the end of the day it *was* funny. She wasn't doing any harm. And you...'

'And I what?'

Kate has never heard Pia's voice like this. No hesitancy, no softness. Just a honed edge. Was this what she was like in that meeting?

'She's not like that twat Jonathan, but you're treating her like she's rubbish. She's not...' Tay can't seem to find the words. She turns abruptly to Bardy. 'Can we go?'

He's on his feet in an instant. 'Right. Okay. Look... anyway... well, great trip, Leonard. Thank you, Pia.'

Pia doesn't say anything. She's just looking at Tay. What is it? Shock? Hurt?

Kate thinks back to their conversation in the pub – or rather non-conversation. She had walked away that evening wondering what it was that had made Pia initially reluctant to help Tay. Did something happen to Pia? She doesn't think it's family, Pia always talks about them with great warmth. Grace? She had clearly been hurt by her last relationship. Or was there some case that had affected her? Maybe caused her to form a shell around her. Now Tay has got in under her guard, and despite the anger and biting comments to Brenda, there is no doubt about it, Pia is upset by Tay's words. Shocked even.

Satya's phone buzzes. 'Oh, that's Jack and the boys downstairs.' She sounds relieved. Pia goes to rise. 'No, don't worry. Got to rush. Thanks everyone. See you at next week's meeting.' Satya throws a final look at Kate, and Kate is conscious that something has upset her. Not Brenda. Is it Jack and the boys? Then why does she get the feeling it has something to do with her? Before Kate can even finish this thought Satya is heading after the retreating figure of Tay.

With a helpless wave of the hand, Bardy follows suit, leaving Kate, Lou, Leonard and Linda with an indignant Dane and a yawning, oblivious whippet.

Chapter 34

Bardy

When the battle's lost and won

Satya is looking for a fight. He can see it, and it starts, even before Bardy has had a chance to say hello to Jack.

Jack who is the green of toy soldiers.

He knows who he'd put his money on.

'For God's sake Jack, look at the state of them and the car!' Satya is standing by the open door of a 4x4 staring in, Jack beside her.

From inside he hears, 'And great to see you too Mum.'

Bardy looks for Tay. She is waiting where his car is parked near the road. She is staring into space. Even from here he can see her face is white and pinched.

Jack tries to head Satya off. 'So what! We've been having a great time. And it's only a bit of mud. It doesn't matter.'

'Yeah, but you won't be the one clearing up the house when there's mess absolutely everywhere. It's always me.'

Oh, this woman really wants a fight.

Bardy is taken back to the classroom. Satya was bright, no doubt about that. But sometimes she just wanted to get stuck in. Too much pressure at home, he'd always thought. Be a doctor. Be a lawyer. He'd learnt early on, don't go head on. That way, one of you has to lose.

Satya with her phone blatantly on display. Every bit of her willing him: *Come on then, sir.*

'Do you want to put that phone in your bag, Satya? Or shall I take it to the office?'

The illusion of choice. Plus the real fear her phone will be confiscated.

Phone goes in bag. If he'd demanded the phone – stalemate. What was he going to do, wrestle it from her? But Satya would still have given him *that* look. The look she is now giving Jack.

'You have no idea how much work I've got on at the moment. How much extra work *you* make! We still haven't got a mission statement sorted...'

'Will you shut up about the bloody mission statement. You haven't even said hello to the boys. Why can't you just be pleased to see us? Why are you always having a go at us?' Jack is shouting now.

Satya matches him, 'Because you don't help me! You lot do what you want, having a great time. I'm left working all the bloody time. I don't even feel part of my company anymore.'

'You've done exactly what you wanted to today, haven't you? Hung out with these guys?' Jack seems to clock Bardy. 'Sorry, mate.'

Bardy shakes his head, as if to say, no you go on. Not sure if he should step in. Or just head home with Tay.

'I don't feel part of anything anymore! I'm not really needed anywhere. Don't you understand how that feels? Us. My work. This!' Satya throws her hand back towards Bardy and the house. The others are emerging from the doorway, stepping uncertainly into the war zone. Bardy sees Kate. And he sees something else. The memory of a hug and a thank you from Linda that had included Pia and Kate but not Satya. He wonders if she minded. Of course she had. The latecomer.

Jack glances at the growing audience, but Bardy feels that he needs to get this out. He hisses, 'And you think this is always easy?!' He keeps his voice low, but Bardy can feel the frustration. 'Maybe there are times when I've had a shit day, maybe I want more, but it's always about you and the sodding mission statement. And it doesn't make any sense anyway, it's a load of pretentious crap...'

From inside the car a lone voice says, 'Sorry, Mum but the man's right. Total bullshit.'

Oh, not helping.

Satya opens her mouth, but before she launches into whatever she was going to say she becomes aware of her growing audience. She appears to stutter on her unuttered words, then turning, she marches to the passenger seat and gets in, slamming the door. Jack throws Bardy a look of wretched helplessness, latent anger and apology. It's quite a look. And he too gets in the car. He closes his door softly. Point made. And he starts the engine. As the car disappears out into the road the others spread out on the drive. Everyone is looking at everyone else. Nobody is saying anything.

Lou nods at him and heads off towards Tay.

Clemenza just keeping an eye on things.

Leonard breaks the silence. 'Right! Home Mrs Cowland. Thank you, Pia. See you all soon.'

Kate approaches Bardy. 'She felt left out, didn't she?' Before he can answer she continues, 'I didn't think. It just happened. And she was brilliant with…' she nods towards Leonard who was getting in his car.

'I think it's more than that, Kate. It's work, it's family. That wouldn't have mattered if she wasn't feeling shit about all that.'

She nods and pauses for an infinitesimal moment as if deciding, then she leans in and kisses him on the cheek.

His surprise is washed away in a wave of silver. His skin shimmers with the sense of her. It's like being immersed in a bath of liquid light, sinking, twisting, then floating. Kate breaks away and it is as if someone has pulled a giant plug.

What the fu…

How could he ever get used to…

All speech has gone.

He just wants to kiss her. Hold her.

Sex would probably kill him.

But what a way to go.

'Bardy, are you okay?'

'Yes, whoa. Yes. Um do you need a lift?'

Kate laughs. 'It's okay I've got my bi—'

Her words are cut off by Tay's scream.

Bardy spins towards the sound, his brain registering

incomprehensible images. Lou punching Tay in the chest. His big body spinning. Tay falling on to the drive. A black bonnet of a car appearing from nowhere.

Then it is screeching. Tyres. Something else. Screaming.

A car sliding. A thud and Lou is down.

Things change gear. Or maybe it's the car. Screaming revs and the car is off. He sees a face. Passenger. Ash white. A boy.

Then all is white. The sensation of swirling snow. A storm. He can't seem to see or grasp what is unfolding. His mind filled with clouds of white mist. Impossible to define what has happened through the colour flooding his mind.

Then he is running. Around him noise, shocked voices. Movement.

He reaches Lou's body as Tay does. She is struggling for breath where Lou pushed her. But she has crawled to him, crouching. A wounded animal. The noise she makes is of an animal in pain. Her anguish centres him. He has one arm around her, one hand on his friend's thigh. His leg twisted beneath him. Blood on the tarmac by his head.

Then they are there.

Linda at Lou's head.

Leonard in the road. Stunned, staring after the car, but already moving forward to direct traffic. Kate appears and gently lifts Tay, holds her close. Both shaking. Pia is on her phone. Precise. Clear. And all he can do is place both hands on his best friend. Fingers splayed. It feels like prayer. Maybe it is. He watches as Linda checks Lou's breathing. Pulse. Then her hands patting over Lou's body. Calm.

He wants to scream. *Is he dead?* Then Lou's hand twitches under his.

Linda looks at Pia. Questioning.

'They're coming.'

'Good.'

Leonard standing firm. But no longer speechless. 'Did you see that! The speed they were going. Hit him on the side. Didn't stand a chance. And just drove off! Didn't stop! My God! How is he Lindy?'

'He's out and losing blood.'

'Is Tay okay? Did you see that, he pushed her out the way.'

Linda nods but doesn't take her eyes off Lou.

Pia is back. He didn't know she had gone. She has a first aid kit which she is ripping open. Linda selects. Quickly. Tearing open packages.

'What can I do?' He is surprised to hear his own voice.

Linda flicks him a look. Then eyes back on Lou. 'Hold this against that cut on his leg. And press firmly.' Linda holds a pad against Lou's head. Sitting back on her heels. Breathing hard now.

The white is swirling, thick like a blizzard. Tay breaks from Kate's hold and crouches beside him. Hand on his back. Knees in the gravel. He reaches for her red ochre and lets it pulse with his racing heart. Holding out against the white fear.

As he hears her whispered, 'Don't die, please, don't die,' he also hears the sirens.

Chapter 35

Kate

A good heart, Kate, is the sun and the moon

Kate sits with her phone in her lap. She is still wearing the clothes she wore for their walk. It is 3.15am and she is in her kitchen looking out over the creek. Moon on the water, full tide, stiff breeze swaying the boats on their moorings. They shift as she shifts unable to settle.

Bardy had gone with Lou in the ambulance and now all they know is that he is in ICU, Bardy with him. Leonard and Linda had taken Tay home with them. The paramedics had checked her over, given her the all-clear. Kate is not sure whether Tay is still with them, or with her mum, Toni. Maybe she is with her friend… Uzma? She hopes so.

There have been a few messages. Leonard had been straight on to a friend in the police. It seems the car that hit Lou had crashed further up the road. The driver, a man the police knew well – older, forties – seemed to like to hang around with a younger crowd. He had been thrown clear, but the passenger, a seventeen-year-old – also known to the police – had been trapped in the wreckage. Kate wonders what has happened to this boy.

Pia and Satya have been texting her. Satya shocked with their news. No fight in her now. Pia particularly anxious about Tay. Upset they had fallen out? The messages are sporadic. But what is there to say? Just checking in on each other. Reassuring one another: the ambulance came quickly; Lou was still breathing; Linda was there, she knew what she was doing.

But the blood.

Kate has a flashback of Linda and Bardy standing to make way for the paramedics. Hands, clothes, streaked with blood.

She gets up from her chair and starts pacing. She walks into the hallway, grabs her coat and is out the front door before she even knows where she is going.

The nurse reminds her of Linda. Unflappable, quietly humorous. They might be chatting in the door of a coffee shop or garden centre, not the doorway of ICU. Kate has been explaining about Lou and the hit and run. 'I didn't really mean to end up here. I was just driving around.'

'Of, course, come in.' The nurse points the way. 'He's stable but unconscious, and don't worry if he comes round and sounds confused. It's often that way with a head injury. They come and go.'

Lou going.

Kate experiences a sick weakness.

'But he'll be okay?'

How often have people pleaded with this woman for the promise of life?

'You just go and see him. We are doing everything possible. There may be staff coming to check on him, sort out his meds and make sure he's comfortable. So just be conscious to give them space if they need it. Not to crowd them.'

She nods encouragingly at Kate. She can't read anything in the nurse's look as much as she wants to believe it signifies something positive.

Lou is lying in a small room of three beds. The other two beds are empty. Bardy is sitting beside him with his back to the door, holding Lou's hand. All the machinery and paraphernalia seem familiar yet totally alien. Too many hospital dramas. Then come the memories. Oncology. Chemotherapy. The 'home touches' well-meant but jarring, opening the door on her fear. Kate stays half hidden by the doorway, unable to go in. The sight of Lou's inert hand in Bardy's more than she can bear. She shouldn't be here.

Bardy is talking softly. 'Tay's text me. She's at Leonard and Linda's. Leonard went to fetch her friend Uzma and they're putting them both up for the night. God, bet that's five star. She'll never want to go home. She's fine though. Said you punched like a girl.' Bardy pauses, shifts position.

How long has he been here? Should she offer to get him coffee? But still she can't move. Cannot drag her eyes off that hand in his.

Kate is taken back to visiting the 9/11 museum in New York. So many images of hands. Hands over mouths registering shock. She recalls putting her hand over her mouth the instant the car hit Lou. Do we try and keep the shock inside of us? So pointless. Then comes the reaching out of hands. Images of hands, covered in dust and blood, holding strangers' hands. She thinks of Ellie sitting on the sofa with her. Her hand clasped in hers as she fought the waves of sickness. Who was the last person to hold her hand?

Pia.

They had stood beside each other on the drive as the ambulance drove away and instinctively reached for each other's hand. All thoughts of anger and arguments carried away on the marsh breeze. Kate can recall the feel of certain hands. Her girls. Each different. Even the memory of Doug holding her hand when her dad died comes back to her. The chemo nurse, patting Kate's arm. Warm and worn. Alice. Freckles on the back of her hand. And at the end so thin, and brittle in Kate's hand. Bird-like. This brings with it so much regret that Kate has to lean on the door frame. Propped up as she is engulfed in pain, and also guilt.

Bardy is speaking softly. 'Linda moves fast for a woman of her age. Bloody hell mate, she was with you almost before you hit the deck. The paramedics were impressed. They've all been texting. Not sure if I'm supposed to use my phone. So not really replying. But they're all thinking of you. Gina and Mark are on their way. Mark should be here soon. Gina's getting a flight first thing.'

Oh it must be bad. The family are coming. She *really* shouldn't be here.

She spots Bardy's reaction before she sees Lou move in the bed. Bardy's back snaps straight, leaning forward. Lou groans beside him. She can't see his eyes, but Bardy is now talking directly to him. 'Welcome back, mate.'

More groaning.

Kate hears the rasping, whispered. 'Tay?' The urgency within it.

'Mate, she's fine. Said you punched like a girl. But you got her clear. Shame you weren't faster on your feet. But you're in hospital now. The kids are coming.'

'Fuck. That bad?'

Bardy's laugh is croaky. But he doesn't answer.

How bad is it? Have the staff told him anything?

Kate hears an exhale of breath through the beeping of the monitors. 'Tina.'

'I know, mate.'

'God, I miss her.'

'I know.'

Then, after a long pause. 'Tell me one more time. You know what I mean.'

It seems Bardy does.

She sees his back relax and softly, quietly he speaks.

'Tina was citrus orange. The orange of sliced fruit nestling in a glass of ice. Sun beating down. Warm and fragrant. Zesty too.'

He pauses.

'Go on,' a whisper from the bed.

'She was the citrus orange of the sunshine in the Mediterranean, the orange that lingers on your skin late into the evening and that reaches into your bones warming them.'

'That's a beautiful orange.'

'Sure is, Lou.'

'And that's how you saw her?' Lou a little fretful and anxious now.

'You know it was.'

A sigh from the man in the bed, and Kate doesn't need to see it to know both men are crying.

She creeps away, feeling she has trespassed on something private. She isn't sure what Bardy was talking about. Did he associate Lou's Tina with a colour? It certainly seemed so. All she knows is that she can still feel the warmth emanating from the friendship and love between these good men.

WEEK 6

The terns are back filling the sky and settling in clusters on the shingle shoreline. When the wind is strong they appear to hang motionless in the air. Wings tipping, this way, that way as if trying to regain balance. Trying to hold on.

Chapter 36

Bardy

The worst is death, and death will have his day

He sits on the bench on one of the pathways that dissect the area around the hospital. There seems to be no logic to these walkways, a labyrinth. But the staff still come and go, walking with purpose and the sure knowledge of where they are going. He is oblivious of the drizzle, just wonders vaguely why they put a bench here in such an odd spot. For people like him who had lost the ability to move on and who just needed to sit and stare?

Everything is cancelled.

The group meeting.

The trip to the gallery.

Luigi's: Closed.

Finn's café: Closed.

He wonders if Kate is still going to see *King Lear*. It hardly seems relevant. It all ends in death anyway. That's the truth of it.

A life lost.

He looks up and sees Tay and Hana walking towards him. He is conscious of wondering how they found him. He would get up, but he is too damn tired. He has no idea how long he has been in the hospital, how long he has been on this bench.

They sit either side of him. Tay close but not touching. Hana taking his hand.

Chapter 37

Kate

What is the city but the people

Kate wonders if it takes a tragedy to sift out all the irrelevant particles that clog our lives. The shock shaking out the small irritations and worries, until they fall around us to be trodden underfoot. If we did look down, Kate thinks, we would be surprised to see them lying there.

I was worried about that!

She remembers this from the deaths she has known and wonders how long it takes for the cogs to start turning, once more sucking up the niggles of life. Clarity only lasting for days or sometimes weeks. Or is that piercing vision of what really matters unrealistic? Like a shaft of sunlight, or a rainbow? Not the stuff of everyday life.

Kate sits with Pia and Satya in her kitchen. Satya has been talking about Jack and the boys. Honestly. How hard she finds it. Of course she loves him, and my God, after what has happened, she and Jack had wanted to draw their boys to them, hold them tight. But it is so hard sometimes. They can't seem to see each other's point of view. Each thinks the other has it easier. And the worst of it is, every time she gets cross with Jack and the boys, she feels guilty. And there is this endless conversation with herself about how she has every right to be pissed off. She seems to be doing everything. Including a load of household stuff. Is looking after the boys really that big a deal compared to what she does? Then she remembers the times she has been the sole parent in charge and just how bloody hard it is. So this makes her feel guilty all over again… and so it goes on.

Where do they go from here?

Who knows.

'Have you seen Bardy?' Satya asks.

Pia and Kate shake their heads.

'He is still spending a lot of time at the hospital or with Gina and Mark, Lou's kids.' Kate does know this.

'But he is going to be okay?' Pia sounds anxious. '…Lou?'

Kate does manage a smile at this. An exotic worrying about a fellow exotic.

'Lou is doing really well.'

Satya looks up. 'When you first called I thought you were going to say…'

'That it was Lou?' Kate finishes.

Both women nod.

Kate recalls the phone calls, the wary silence before she had told them about the young boy brought into ICU from the car wreck. He had died a few days later from a heart attack when his body went into shock.

'Had he taught him?' Pia asks.

'For a bit, and he knows the family.'

'He was at the same school as our eldest,' Satya tells them. 'Everyone's so shocked. He was only seventeen. He was expected to do well in his exams, but he just started hanging out with the wrong crowd.'

'Linda knew a bit more because of Leonard's contacts in the police. The older guy who was driving, preyed on boys like him,' Pia informs them. 'I think they have enough to charge him with manslaughter. He was well over the limit when he flipped the car.'

Pia looks off into the distance. 'I once knew a young man who died of a heart attack, after his body...'

She doesn't finish but turns to the two women beside her. 'He was an Iranian refugee – an asylum seeker. I find it helps if I say refugee.' She shrugs, 'If I start talking about asylum seekers, especially if it's a young man, people can jump to conclusions.'

'Disruptive migrants?' Satya suggests.

'Oh, yes,' Pia nods, before continuing. 'It was early on in my career and I thought I could change the world.' She passes a weary hand over her eyes and attempts a smile.

'What happened to the boy?' Kate asks, wondering if this is what is behind Pia holding herself apart from people sometimes.

'He had come here after many months of walking, hitching and jumping trains. Eventually he hid under a lorry. His father had been killed in Iran, tortured to death because he was a Christian. Arash had been at university studying physics. His English was good, which is why he chose to come to the UK. He thought if he could make a new start he could then bring his mother and sisters over. He was terrified leaving them behind, worried what the authorities would do, but he thought it was his only chance. He had already been locked up for a while by the police, but he thought if he disappeared they would leave the women alone.'

'What happened?' Satya asks.

'He was taken into a hostel and from there things just dragged on, month after month. He tried to keep in touch with his family, but it was hard. He knew they were struggling and being watched by the authorities. He wasn't allowed to work, but he took some jobs on the side to try and send them cash.' Pia looks up, 'That's when I got involved. When he was caught.' She shakes her head. 'I knew he had broken the rules, but at that stage I honestly thought I could make them see sense. At the hearing the judge asked about his time with the police. We showed them photographs of his back and buttocks – the scars from the torture. But the judge said they could just be bad insect bites.' Pia shakes her head. 'I just couldn't believe it.'

'Did they send him back?' Kate asks.

Pia shakes her head again. 'They didn't have to.'

Kate sees the tears sparkling in her friend's eyes.

'We appealed – oh, time and time again. But eventually that was it. He thanked me politely for everything I had done. And the next night he threw himself off the top floor of a multistorey car park. He didn't die immediately... it was his heart in the end.'

'Oh, Pia.' Both women move closer.

'He left me a letter. He just couldn't face going back, but

more than anything he felt such shame at letting his mother and sisters down. Arash was only nineteen.'

Kate takes Pia's hand.

'And the thing I can't forgive myself for is that I gave him hope. I had been so sure I could make a difference. Like it was a game. I have always been competitive, but now I was playing with a young man's life. So after that I changed.'

'You grew a tougher skin?' Kate suggests.

Tears are running down Pia's face. 'But now I worry I am like that judge. I don't believe he was a bad man. He had just seen so much and… I have seen it before… people get inured to what they deal with day in day out.'

Kate thinks of Grace and her comments about Pia.

Satya leans in, taking Pia's other hand. 'You did everything you could.'

'Did I?' Pia wonders aloud. She shakes her head. 'I am sorry, I didn't mean to say all of that. It was just this young boy dying…'

'His brother was Finn, you know the guy who runs the coffee shop and volunteers for the RNLI,' Satya says, tears in her eyes.

Pia and Kate nod.

It is a town where most people know someone you know.

Somebody is always going to be somebody's brother.

Chapter 38

Bardy

We that are young
Shall never see so much, nor live so long

He sees a face. Passenger. Ash white. A boy.

Bardy cannot shake the image. Sleeping or waking.

He had bumped into Jack in the street and he had hugged him close. A surrogate son. The absence of Tom and Ned piercing him. He has spoken to them both. Ended up telling them not to drive too fast. Make sure their cars' brakes were checked. They had ridden the wave of his anxiety like the surfers they are and at the end, when he told them once again, to be careful, Ned said, 'It's cool Dad, Mum rang us.'

Hana has been there for him, and for Tay who was shaken more than she would admit. She has cooked for them both, watching him as he walked around in a daze. *So* tired. God, he has spent hours by Lou's bedside. What does he think is going to happen? If he takes a day off, will his friend die too?

Jack had talked about how Satya and he had gathered up the boys, hugging them close. There was no doubt they had been upset. The whole town is. Bardy had asked how he and Satya were. Jack had given a helpless shrug.

So Bardy walks around thinking about love and family and balance. But he doesn't reach any conclusion. Or not one that will help him. Just thinks of a boy's face.

Ash white.

He remembers him working on the checkout at the local Co-op – straight faced, asking Mr Shakespeare for ID when he bought beer. He'd done okay in his GCSEs. Thought he might like to try for an apprenticeship somewhere.

You'd think he'd be used to it by now. He isn't the first youngster Bardy has known to die. It's seeing the shock on his friends' faces. The look on his brother's face. You just don't expect life to end when you are that young. Think you can live forever.

And what can you say? Not a lot. But better to turn up clutching the wrong words than turn away from the bereaved like somehow it's their fault.

Bardy pushes open the garden gate and walks up the path that leads to Finn's flat.

WEEK 7

The long-billed dowitcher forages in the shallows of the pool, small and plump with modest plumage, it does what it does best, plunging its long beak deep into the soft mud. From inside the hide comes the rustle of excited birders.

Chapter 39

Kate

A ministering angel, shall my sister be

'The dowitcher's back.' Linda looks up from where she is weeding.

Kate smiles slightly. She has come around the side of the house to the garden, as Linda had suggested when she asked Kate to call over for coffee.

Linda gets to her feet, unbending slowly and stretching. 'I'm getting too old for this.'

'Is Leonard back at the hide?'

'Oh, yes. He will be gone for hours.' Linda doesn't sound too distressed by this prospect.

It isn't long before they are sitting together on a bench, legs stretched out. Tray of coffee and cake on the small table in front of them. The garden of grasses is sheltered and warm in the mid-May sunshine. Kate tips her head back, watching the birds overhead. A buzzard wheels slowly in the blue sky.

'Have you heard from anyone?' she asks Linda.

'I was going to ask you the same... Bardy?'

'I think he's doing okay. I think it really upset him when that young boy died.'

'The lad in the car?'

'Yes.'

'You've seen him?' Linda enquires.

'No, I spoke to him on the phone.'

'And how's Lou doing?'

Kate brightens. 'Better. He is on a normal ward and they are letting him out tomorrow. No lasting damage, just an awful lot of bruising. His kids have gone home.'

Linda smiles. 'So it will be back to Bardy and Lou.'

And Hana. She seemed to be there a lot when Kate had been in touch with Bardy.

Linda continues, 'Leonard told me they are definitely charging the driver. He was drunk and I think he was showing off to the lad in the car.'

'God, that is so sad. Pathetic too.'

'Have you heard from Pia and Satya?' Linda asks.

'Yes, we've had coffee a couple of times.' Is she imagining it or are they already returning to the old ways? Maybe not Pia so much. Telling Kate about the refugee she couldn't save seems to have softened Pia somehow. But Satya? After talking a bit about the issues she and Jack are facing, she seems to have shut down again. She's not sure talking about it has really solved anything.

Kate grins suddenly, as she remembers something. 'You're not going to believe this, but Pia's joined Brenda's book club.'

'*Really?*'

'Yep, she didn't exactly say she'd apologised to her but she did say she wanted to get to know her better.'

'Before you know it Pia and Noy will be wearing matching Brenda knits,' Linda suggests.

'I'd pay to see that,' Kate laughs, 'still, I think Tay being upset really made an impression. It did make me think that Pia and Tay are a bit alike. Both can be reserved but also quite tough.' For a moment she thinks of telling Linda Pia's story, but decides it isn't for her to tell.

'Uzma was nice,' Linda muses.

'Her friend?'

'So chatty and she teased Tay a lot. You wouldn't have thought they would have got on, but I think she is so over the top, she makes Tay relax.'

'Is Tay okay though? I was worried when she saw Lou get hit.'

Linda sighs. 'Oh I think Tay has seen an awful lot worse than that.'

'Her mum?'

Linda nods.

Sitting in the warm sunshine and eating apple cake, Kate thinks maybe she should tell Linda about JoJo Rose. On the other hand, it feels like it couldn't matter less, so why bother? Instead she says, 'This really is a beautiful garden, Linda.' The more she looks the more she sees it isn't just grasses, but subtle, grey, blue and white foliage and flowers planted in swathes, almost like waves washing the pale stone pathways. The walls are placed to give protection from the wind, but also to allow glimpses of the sand dunes beyond.

She doesn't think she has ever seen a garden so suited to its environment.

Linda looks around. 'It's early days but it's coming on.' She laughs, 'Bardy would be proud of me. It is the one thing I don't rush and I am quite happy to see how things naturally emerge and develop.'

'A creative gardener,' Kate suggests, smiling.

'And what about you and Bardy?'

Kate is startled. 'What?! There is no me and Bardy.'

Linda tuts. 'The two of you are as bad as each other. Well, how about the man from the pub? The tall one.'

'Oh, I don't know. When Lou was still in ICU it didn't seem right to go to London with him.'

'And now?'

Kate has absolutely no idea, so shrugs. Simon had said he understood. But had he been a bit short with her? He definitely was texting less.

Linda changes tack, and Kate is grateful. 'I wish Leonard had a friendship like Lou and Bardy's.'

'Does he have many friends?'

'More than you would think,' Linda replies, chuckling.

'I like Leonard,' Kate protests.

'I know. And you girls did such a good job. He really is making an effort with his hearing aids. Keeps telling me how good they are now.' Linda raises her eyes to heaven.

'I didn't tell you I saw Lou and Bardy at the hospital, the night it happened. I think I didn't know what else to do. In the end I didn't go in but I heard Bardy talking to Lou.' The image of Bardy holding Lou's hand comes back to her.

Why does she want to cry?

She knows why.

Kate can't speak for the threat of tears.

'What is it?' Linda sits up straighter on the bench.

How can she have thought JoJo Rose was what she wanted to talk about? It was always this. This guilt. Letting her sister down.

Kate makes an effort to speak. 'It brought back the night Alice died. And how I wasn't there for her at the end. I keep coming back to that thought.' Kate looks up at the now empty sky. 'Alice never seemed to ask anything of me. Maybe because I was so much younger. The one thing I tried to do for her was to be there for her at the end. When she got ill and...'

'Yes, I know you had her moved to be near you. You didn't let Alice down, Kate.'

'How can you say that when I wasn't there for her at the very end? I had gone out with friends for the night and we ended up back at a friend's house, talking.' Kate can feel the tears forming in earnest.

'But you saw her a lot, I am sure of that.'

'Yes, but I didn't get there in time. I'd fallen asleep and they'd left me on the sofa tucked up under a blanket. So, it was a while before I realised the hospice had called.'

'Oh, Kate, some people need to die on their own. They cannot do it with their loved ones around them. For Alice, maybe your pain would have been too much for her, maybe she wanted to spare you that. Alice might have been trying to give you a final gift.'

'But I wanted to help her, I wish I could have comforted her.

For her to be alone, with no one to hold her hand. It breaks my heart.'

'Oh, my poor girl, Alice wasn't alone. Someone did hold her hand,' and with this Linda reaches out and enfolds Kate's hand in her own.

Kate can feel the warmth, the dry skin, the plumpness of it, and she understands this is the comfort her sister would have known. She leans her head against Linda's shoulder, and lets the tears fall. With her other hand Linda gently strokes Kate's arm, just as she had stroked her sister's as the last breath left her body in a slow, sad sigh.

Chapter 40

Bardy

We've seen better days

'And I thought it was wood turning that would ruin your good looks.' Bardy helps settle his best friend in a chair in the corner of Lou's sitting room.

'That bad?'

'He's joking you,' Tay interjects, putting a cup of tea down within easy reach. She adds, 'But I'm not goin' to lie, you sure look shit.'

Lou's laugh is cut short. 'Bugger, that hurts.'

'No bones broken though,' Linda says, settling a cushion behind his head. 'There now.'

'Thanks Linda.'

'Are you okay with that, or do you need a hand?' Bardy asks Pia and Satya who are unrolling a large white screen from a tatty looking box. 'It's a bit ancient but I think it should be okay.'

'Oh, I think we've got it,' Satya responds drily.

'Sorry,' Bardy murmurs. He guesses a top lawyer and an award-winning entrepreneur might just manage to put a screen up.

Kate glances up from where she is attaching her laptop to a projector and gives him an understanding grin. Silver bright Kate. Those eyes. He'd never really looked into them until that time at Pia's. Now he doesn't want to stop.

As Lou was in no fit state for a day in London, Kate suggested they bring the art gallery to Lou. On the group chat the instructions were to choose one painting they loved. Linda had added: *And then we eat cake.* She has done them proud, a coffee and walnut, an orange and lemon brûléed bundt plus a white chocolate, cardamon and damson cake. She thought they might help Lou with his recovery. And no one was arguing with Nurse Linda.

Surveying the cakes laid out on a low coffee table, Lou suggests that Bardy get some wine and glasses. 'There's a couple of nice bottles of Barolo I've been saving,' he adds, nodding towards the cupboard in the corner.

But Bardy is still looking at Kate.

And what is even better, silver bright Kate is looking at him.

'Mate,' Lou interrupts, 'wine?' Bardy knows from his expression that his best friend sees right through him.

'Where's Leonard?' Bardy asks as he starts to sort out glasses and bottles.

'He's got a meeting at the art gallery, something to do with the council and possible funding. I think it was that,' Linda responds. 'He should be here soon.'

Kate looks up. 'That's good, I know they are really worried and when I bumped into Nate, the manager, he said he'd hit a problem with the Constable exhibition he was planning.'

'What exhibition is that?' Satya asks.

'He was hoping to get a small number of Constable paintings, ones he painted of Norfolk and Suffolk, to help publicise the fact that the gallery has lost funding and to put a bit of pressure on the owner not to sell the building,' Kate replies.

As if on cue the doorbell rings. Lou automatically goes to rise, then wincing, thinks better of it. 'You stay where you are,' Nurse Linda tells him, 'I'll let him in.'

'Good meeting?' Kate asks as Leonard emerges into the room.

'I'm afraid not,' says the man with the discreet hearing aids. 'The council just don't have the funds and the owner still wants to sell the building. Plus, Nathan thinks he will have to pull the plug on his exhibition. Just too many problems.' He turns to Lou, 'Now how are you doing? You're looking very well.'

Even Lou joins in the laughter, whimpering, 'Please don't make me laugh.'

Bardy passes him a glass of wine. 'That might ease the pain.'

They are now settled in chairs or on the floor facing the white screen, Kate kneeling by the projector which she has placed at one end of the coffee table. Linda starts to cut cake and pass it around.

'Before we visit Kate's art gallery, shall we have a quick catch up. The MACKL competition is already open, but we've got another two weeks to get our entries in,' says the man who hasn't written anything.

Bardy can tell by their faces they have completely forgotten about the reason they get together. What is he going to do when it's all over? He senses a looming loss.

And what about the rest of his life?

Plus, why is Hana being different with him?

Too many questions.

Satya is first. 'I'm working on something new.'

'Great.'

'But I don't want to talk about it.'

'Okay,' Bardy says slowly. Has this got anything to do with her and Jack? He hasn't liked to ask how things are.

The next surprise is Tay. 'I'm working on something too. But I don't want to talk about it either.'

'Right. Anyone else?'

The others are more forthcoming: Leonard has a few good songs written, but he hasn't worked out the ending for his musical; Kate is getting on much better with her painting; Pia is painting on fabric but hasn't added anything to her quilt yet which she claims is now the size of Denmark. Unsurprisingly, Linda has had enough of bird painting, but she does have another idea. But like Satya and Tay she doesn't want to talk about it. Although she does say cryptically to Kate, 'I could do with a bit of help from you.' Kate looks puzzled, but nods.

He just thinks he is going to be put on the spot when Pia saves him.

'While we haven't been able to meet...' She glances at Lou and smiles softly at him. *What a woman of contrasts she is.* 'I have spent a little time with Brenda. I think I was rather rude to her. For which I have apologised.'

She glances at Tay. Tay barely moves, but it is enough. Pia smiles. She is forgiven.

'We have come to a compromise. I will choose the wool and

together we will think about the designs. Brenda is a very fast knitter and Noy is a superstar model.'

She glances at Tay again, who nods. 'Real.'

Satya pipes up, 'You could start an online business. Beautiful Scandi designs in neutral natural fibres.'

Ever the entrepreneur.

Pia continues, 'Brenda also asked me to join her book club. I found the meeting I attended very interesting. I had been thinking of our group, and missing you all. And I ended up asking if anyone in the book group was creative. Apart from a woman called Amanda, who did a lot of different things, and felt we were all creative in some way, everyone else said no. Even Brenda.'

Pia looks around earnestly. 'And this is what I found so interesting. When I asked some more, pushed them—' she half-smiles at Bardy '—not like a lawyer, but because I really wanted to know, I discovered so much.'

They all wait expectantly.

'One woman wrote poems on her phone…'

Bardy looks up from pouring out more wine for people.

'She had a difficult relationship with her daughter I think. I didn't pry, but she said this poetry helped her. Another woman then admitted that at family gatherings she was always asked to do the speech and so she wrote a poem for that person. And *then* the woman next to her said she has written a poem about each book that the book club had chosen to read. So there you had it, three poets on one sofa.'

But Pia hasn't finished. 'Then Sunita, a scientist, admitted she painted. And when she showed us the images on her phone, they were just beautiful. Well, this reminded a woman called Vix of how much she loved making her Christmas door wreath.'

Satya lets out a small sound between a sigh and a cry.

'What is it?' Linda asks in concern.

'Oh, nothing.'

After a pause, Pia continues, 'One woman, I forget her name, once won a competition for a short story about an ancient tree in the Highlands, which locals know is a wishing tree...'

He wishes he'd thought of that one.

'...and another said she designed gingerbread houses. Then they told me about Brenda.'

'Her knitting?' Kate asks.

Bardy is thinking of her flower paintings. And a man called Brian.

'No, they didn't even know about that. Although at the end of the evening I did suggest Brenda show them all Noy's outfits.' She winces like Lou had done when he laughed.

'Anyway, the women in the group told me that two of them had lost their husbands, and what Brenda did was to take one of their husband's shirts and make a teddy bear from it.' Pia cannot help adding, 'It is perhaps not something I would have liked, but for these women it gave them something to hold at night that brought great comfort.'

Pia looks at Tay now. 'I think, perhaps I did not take the trouble to get to know Brenda. She is a very kind woman and I do not think she has a very easy life with this Brian.' She adds, reflectively, 'It also occurred to me talking to her friends that perhaps sometimes we also underestimate ourselves. All that creativity and everyone saying they weren't really good enough, or only doing something for a special family party or for Christmas.'

She looks at them all now, tentative, hesitant. 'I was wondering if for our next group outing, perhaps we could have an evening of music at my house? Leonard could play us some of his songs, I have a piano. And I could cook a Danish meal for you all.'

She is met with noises of full approval. Especially from Leonard the composer.

'And I wondered if it would be alright with the group if I were to invite Brenda.'

More noises of agreement.

'We could dance. Your sitting room would be a great spot for a party,' Linda exclaims.

'Do you like to dance?' Kate asks, and it's a while before he realises she is talking to him.

'You askin'?'

She grins. 'You dancin'?'

He has a sudden image of Lou and Tina dancing. Lou surprisingly light on his feet, swinging Tina around. And there was no doubt, Jon and Lou always had the best moves at the school disco. One of the very few things that won admiration from their peers. He glances at Lou, thinking of the painting he has chosen for Kate's gallery.

'That's a date,' he says to Pia. But all he is thinking of is dancing with silver bright Kate.

He turns to her now.

'Right, over to you... Kate's gallery is now open.'

Chapter 41

Kate

The clouds methought would open and show riches

'Leonard, I think you should go first, bearing in mind what we were talking about earlier.' The large screen is suddenly filled with the image of Constable's painting, *The Haywain*, a horse and cart depicted halfway across a shallow stream, surrounded by Suffolk countryside.

'Could we draw the curtains a little,' Pia suggests, and Tay obligingly closes them. The room is now almost dark and the painting stands out rich and clear on the screen.

'Ah, wonderful,' Leonard enthuses. 'Do you want to know why I chose it?'

'That would be good,' Kate agrees.

'I think you probably have guessed I'm quite a traditionalist. So this is a classic English painter, showing us a part of the world I love. And just look at that sky, those clouds,' he enthuses.

'Sort of painting I like too,' Lou tells Leonard.

'I hope the gallery does get some Constables, and they get some publicity. It would be a shame if it had to close,' Satya adds.

'Linda, how about you, which painting did you choose?' Kate asks. She already knows and loves Linda's choice. It is by another famous painter, this time the Dutch artist, Vermeer: *Cavalier and Young Woman.*

The screen is now filled with a painting of a girl smiling at a young man in a large extravagant hat, he has on a red coat with ruffled sleeves. The light from the window falls on the girl's face. The man has his back to the artist.

'Now this reminds me of when we went to Amsterdam to see the Vermeer exhibition. It was a wonderful weekend.'

'It was indeed,' Leonard agrees, and Kate thinks how much nicer it is, now that he can hear most of what is being said.

Linda continues, 'When we were looking at this painting some American academics were in front of us and, my goodness, how they went on about the supposed love affair between the two of them. In the end I just had to interrupt them.'

'She did, you know,' Leonard chortles.

'It seemed to me that they didn't really know much about the two figures, in fact nobody did. So I just said, "Excuse me, but she's his older sister."'

'What did they say?' Bardy asks.

'Well quite a lot as it turns out, but eventually they asked me if I was an art historian and I said no, I was a retired nurse. They had quite a lot to say about that too, but eventually, when I could get a word in edgeways, I told them that I was also a sister and that when my younger brother joined the police and came home for the first time in uniform that is just how I looked.'

They all gaze at the woman in the painting. And Kate sees it. A girl gazing with love and pride, but also a fleeting smile of suppressed humour. An expression of, 'just look at *you* all grown up'.

'What did the academics say?' Lou asks.

'Oh, they went on and on. I think it rather upset them. But we didn't stay around to listen. We wanted to go for a coffee and to smoke some dope.'

Kate chokes on her wine.

'Only medicinal, of course,' Nurse Linda says, eyes gleaming.

They are all laughing now. Even Lou who is clutching his side.

'More wine?' Bardy suggests.

Most agree and as he tops up glasses, Kate wonders which image she will show next.

Bardy's.

She is intrigued by his choice. An abstract in all shades of orange, with the hint of leaves within the design. It takes her back to the words she overheard in the hospital. She selects the image, and the room is filled with a rich orange glow. There is no mistaking the look on Lou's face. Surprise and also – there is no hiding it – love.

Bardy looks at Lou as he speaks. 'This is by a lad I used to teach. Went on to study English at Cambridge, although it's fair to say he was equally good at art. In the sixth form he did a series of paintings inspired by the poet, Rilke. This one is based on his poem, *Dance the Orange.*'

Even in the gloom Kate can see that Lou is transfixed.

'I chose it because it has given me the idea for a short story. It is going to be about a man who sees certain people in colour. Not their skin, or hair – just that his mind is flooded with a colour when he looks at them.' Bardy's voice falters. 'There will be a woman he meets, a friend, who is warm and generous. A woman who this man sees as the colour of Seville oranges, plucked from the trees, bursting with zest and life, and scented with sunshine.'

Kate sees Lou wipe a tear away.

'Is that you, Bardy? Is that how you see people?'

She hadn't meant to speak, but something suddenly makes sense. She is conscious of the shock on Bardy and Lou's faces. There is a heartbeat of silence and then Bardy coughs, 'No, just a story Kate. Nice idea though.'

But now he won't meet her eye.

'Okay,' she says, slowly, 'who's next?'

Tay and Satya follow quickly one after the other. Tay chose a Banksy, an image of a seagull left on the wall of a house in Suffolk. She says the bird reminds her of living here, but it shows how messed up things get. People tried to steal part of the wall and the owners were told by the council they had to spend thousands guarding the art twenty-four-seven. In the end they had to have the wall cut away. 'How fucked up is that,' Tay concludes.

Satya goes for a Picasso, *The Guitar Player.* She says very little about her choice and Kate is left wondering if her feelings about her own guitar player are as complex as the deconstructed shapes in Picasso's painting.

After this, Linda declares, 'Time for coffee and a loo break, I think.' She heads to the kitchen with Leonard in tow. Bardy flicks one of the side lights on, illuminating the room in a gentle light and then follows them. Is Bardy avoiding her?

This makes her think of Simon. Is he avoiding her too? Not many texts and only vague mentions of meeting up. She can't decide if he is pissed off with her for not going to London, has lost interest or is simply busy. Thinking about Simon makes her feel like a teenager, excited and uncertain. But trying to interpret hidden messages in his texts just makes her feel exhausted.

As people move around, Kate reflects that it is nice to see Lou, Pia and Tay chatting. Pia had told her about Lou saying she was like the Norfolk flint. She thinks he has a point. She goes to sit beside Satya on the sofa.

'How are things?'

Satya swats the question away like it is too much effort to answer. Eventually she says, 'I liked what Linda said about the Vermeer painting. I've got a brother too. When I saw him all dressed for his wedding, I couldn't help smiling like that. He looked amazing, so grown up, but I kept thinking of the little boy playing cricket.'

Linda and Leonard are back with fresh coffee and a pot of tea. Satya drifts away to cut more cake. Kate wonders if she is exhausted, going around in circles, but nothing really changing. And she is not sure she has any answers that would help her – apart from feeling that Jack and Satya seem good together. Despite the fights.

The lights are dimmed once more, and Kate puts her own choice up. The screen is filled with billowing light, and glorious, gentle colours. 'This is a painting called *Sewing the Sail* by the Spanish artist, Sorolla.' A group of women are shown working on a huge white sail, the fabric flowing down the painting. They are under a veranda surrounded by flowers. Painted in an impressionistic style the picture is luminous: bright sunshine plays across the sail, yet under the veranda and in the edges of the garden the light is dappled. 'Sorolla was known as the master of light.'

'I can see why,' Leonard comments.

Kate nods – she thinks Sorolla must be her favourite artist. The light in the painting is extraordinary. Kate looks at it, head slightly on one side. 'He often painted outside, his paintings of the beaches near Valencia are filled with people and life and are just wonderful. You can still see the sand caught up in the paint.'

'Why didn't you choose one of those?' Pia asks.

'I think because of Alice.' She looks at Linda.

'Go on,' Linda tells her.

Kate can feel the others watching her. The lamps may be off and curtains drawn, but the painting on the screen has lit the little group. 'My sister Alice died when she was fifty-eight.' Kate can feel the stir of sympathy in the room. 'All her life she was a great campaigner. She never shied away from things that were difficult and she really did do her best to help.'

Kate hears a murmured, 'Real,' from Tay. She is taken back to watching *The Life of Pi* with Alice. Two sisters, one who wanted to see the story, one who was brave enough to look at the pain. Kate thinks her sister was one of the bravest people she ever knew. Maybe she *had* chosen her own time to die, thinking she was sparing her younger sister.

Kate blinks her tears away. 'I do love Sorolla's paintings of the sea but I chose this because Sorolla also painted the things others didn't. He was a campaigner in his own way. He painted children who were suffering from inherited syphilis, women prisoners and here, the sailmakers. They would have had a hard life. They weren't the type of people who would normally feature in a painting.'

'So a homage to Alice,' Pia says.

Kate smiles. 'Yes, and because, well, it is the most awe inspiring and beautiful painting.' She gazes at the image in front of her, as do the others.

'I think I'm getting somewhere with the colours in my paintings, but how to ever capture that light.' Kate half-laughs, thinking of the view from the lifeboat station, the evening light playing over the broad stretch of sand as the sun sets. 'I know I will never be able to paint like this.'

'I'm never going to write like Shakespeare,' Jon Shakespeare comments, 'but it's good to know there were people who could write or paint like this.'

'That's what I thought too,' Kate replies.

'It is a beautiful painting, Kate,' Lou says, sitting back in his chair as if taking it all in.

'Yeah, okay, no one can paint like Sorolla.' Tay struggles to say the Spanish name but keeps going, all now looking at her. 'But no one else can paint like Kate. Only you see it your way.'

'Well said, Tay,' Leonard approves.

'At the end of the day, it is what it is,' Bardy murmurs.

Kate catches the muttered. 'Oh fuck off Bardy,' from Tay. But she can also hear the laughter.

Leonard looks around slightly confused. His hearing aids are good. But not that good.

'So, there you have, the master of light,' Kate concludes.

The final painting is Pia's choice, *Summer Evening at Skagen Beach* by Krøyer. For Pia it is also about the light.

She explains, 'I was fascinated by that point at the horizon, where the sea and the sky merge, it is what my mother calls a liminal space, a threshold of sorts between worlds.' Pia shakes her head. 'I am not sure I believe what my mother does about people crossing over from one world to another.' She smiles. 'But,' she continues slowly, 'when I gaze at that space, the haze between ocean and sky, I do feel suspended and I wonder...'

They all sit in silence for a while, until Tay's phone buzzes. She jumps up, 'Gotta go. Uzma. See ya.' And she's gone.

'Oh, to be able to move that fast,' Linda murmurs as she hauls herself to her feet and starts clearing plates and glasses. Bardy puts on the light and he and others go to help.

From his chair Lou calls, 'That was great, Kate. Thank you.'

'I know it wasn't the same as London...'

'Better!' Lou exclaims, 'No crowds, or going on the underground.' He raises his glass of wine, still half-full. '*Saluti, grazie bella*.'

'What painting would you have chosen?' Kate enquires, smiling. She hadn't asked Lou for a choice, conscious he was settling in after hospital.

He glances towards Bardy, who is struggling to get the screen back into the box. 'You might want to ask Satya to give you a hand with that.' Lou suggests.

Bardy swears.

Lou looks up at Kate. Back to paintings. She knows what he is going to say, so says it for him. 'You loved *Dance the Orange*.'

Lou smiles wistfully.

'*Always.*'

WEEK 8

An old wooden boat lies lopsided, slats sinking into the mud, the marsh reclaiming its broken bones. Beside it two gulls fight over a scrap of fish, neither giving ground in a tug-of-war. For once mouths too full to speak. Others make up for it; all around is a cacophony of birdcalls. And from the reedbeds comes the booming of the bitterns.

Chapter 42

Bardy

A bright particular star

'Lucky guess?' Bardy suggests.

Lou and Bardy are in Luigi's – newly re-opened – trying to work out how Kate knew about Bardy's... talent? Affliction?

'You've not told anyone else?' Lou presses.

'Nope, only you and Hana.' Hana's laughter had put paid to that. Lou hadn't mocked him. Just pursed his lips and nodded. Same as with his surname.

'Doesn't really matter how it happened,' Lou concludes. He follows this up with, 'You've got a bit of a thing for her.' This hangs suspended between statement and question.

Bardy shrugs.

'And Hana? You've been seeing a bit of her.'

Bardy shrugs again. No clue what is happening there. Just

a feeling Hana is building up to something, but never quite getting there. Just glowing deeper yellow.

'You're sure, you and Kate...?'

He wonders if he should tell Lou about silver bright Kate. But what's the point?

'No good. She's going out with that bloke.' He adds, 'The one you like so much.'

'No mate, just said he wasn't such a tosser as you were saying.'

Yeah, he had been pretty vocal about that. But that was after the 'lady doth protest too much'. Was feeling bruised. Wanted to kick something. Or someone.

'Look at that.' Lou nudges Bardy in the arm.

From where they are sitting – it is early and the café isn't open yet – they've got a clear view of the street. Simon is walking on the opposite side of the narrow road.

'It's like one of those...' Lou struggles.

'Those tossers,' Bardy suggests, helpfully.

Lou snorts. 'No, you know, one of those coincidences, but more like, you think it and then it happens. Tina had them all the time.'

Bardy's thinking about Simon flying back to Dubai, but he's not sure that's going to happen anytime soon.

'Better get opened up.' Lou rises slowly from the chair. Most of the bruising has faded but Bardy can see some movements still give him pain.

'I'll do it.'

He is at the door when Pia and Kate appear from the other direction. They meet Simon, framed on the opposite side of the road by the café window. Bardy opens the door slightly, then sidesteps so he is out of direct view. Behind the counter Lou sidesteps the other direction. They glance at each other stifling their laughter. Never far from ten-year-olds.

'Told you, one of those thingys Tina was always on about.'

Bardy hushes with a raised hand. He's trying to listen. Maybe Simon will mention when his flight is.

'Hi Simon, how are things?' Kate, airy. Interested? Couldn't care less?

'Ah great to see you Kate. We need to get another date in the diary.'

'This is my friend, Pia,' Kate responds. Avoiding a date? Or just being polite?

Simon isn't staring at Pia like most prats do, Bardy will give him that. But he is staring at Noy. 'God, dogs in jumpers. You don't see that in Dubai.'

Bardy thinks it's not too bad today. More tasteful Aran than dinosaur or vicar.

Simon lets out a loud guffaw. 'Looks like he could do with a good meal. I always think those dogs are more like rats.'

And that is it.

Pia's face registers her outrage. But Kate's expression is the one that he will replay in his mind. The thing is, they've all grown to love Noy. He's one of the gang. Bardy thinks he might even write a poem about the colour of the scales that fall from a woman's eyes. He's thinking of an off-white, cream. Bit like the colour of an Aran jumper.

He has his back to the window, grinning at Lou, fist clenched to punch the air, when the door opens.

'Bardy?' Pia says, sounding confused.

He spins around, arm still outstretched.

She doesn't come all the way in. Behind her he can see Kate and Simon on the opposite side of the street, having what seems like an argument. Voices strident, but subdued.

Good.

In fact, fucking fabulous.

'Kate and I had coffee with Satya yesterday, and I think she'd really like to host our musical evening at hers. I talked to Leonard and he's happy to bring his keyboard. So Satya is going to message everyone their address. Tonight at 8pm and she's going to do food.' Pia grins. 'I think it might be a bit of a party.'

Bardy turns his half-finished air punch into an awkward thumbs up.

But he doesn't care if he looks an idiot.

He is an idiot who can dance.

Bardy, Lou and Tay arrive together, and with them is Tay's friend Uzma. Bardy has been trying to play it cool. Not bearhug the short, smiley girl who doesn't stop talking and who clearly – despite the teasing – thinks Tay is awesome. He's gone into friendly teacher mode, nudging the conversation along without bombarding her with questions. It seems Uzma works in underwriting and is doing pretty well. She is four years older than Tay but looks incredibly young. 'I'm thinking of having my ID tattooed on my head I have to show it so often,' she grins.

'I keep telling her she'd look awesome with a tat,' Tay responds.

'I'll get one, if you get *I love Jonathan* tattooed on your arse,' Uzma teases.

'Only place for it,' Bardy suggests as he rings the doorbell. Earlier Tay told him Jonathan has been given a formal warning and someone has been brought in over him.

Satya and Jack's house is at the top of the town, not far from Lou's café. It is a double fronted Georgian house with a navy door, facing on to a large green surrounded by similarly sized houses. There are also a few smaller, brick cottages along with a number of pubs and restaurants. The green is edged with large shady trees and is a popular spot for dog walkers and in the summer, picnickers. Tonight there are very few people out. After a spell of nice weather it has turned cold. Just in time for half-term, Bardy had heard one visitor comment testily. But it seems the pubs and restaurants are doing brisk business and the lights showing through the windows either side of Satya and Jack's front door, glow warm and inviting.

Bardy is taken back to the afternoon of looking at paintings. The glow of that lamp light. The virtual gallery had worked. Good idea of Kate's. Silver bright Kate. He can feel his pulse quicken as Satya opens the door.

'Come in,' she smiles.

Things better with her and Jack?

As she ushers them through the broad hallway and takes coats, Tay introduces Uzma. They then follow her down the corridor. Bardy hangs back slightly. 'How are things?' he asks Satya quietly. Keeping it vague.

She gives him a quick look. 'We've called a truce for this

evening. Jack got the boys to clear up the basement and I promised I wouldn't nag if it wasn't perfect.' She adds defiantly, if untruthfully, 'I *don't* nag.' She perks up. 'Anyway, come and see. They made a real effort.'

As they pass the kitchen there is the sound of laughter – the boys – and the murmur of conversation and chords from a piano from further in the house. 'We are down here,' Satya tells them, pointing to a half-open door at the end of the hall. 'All the others have arrived.'

They descend a flight of narrow stairs into a large room that runs the length of the house. Bifold doors the width of one end look out onto what Bardy suspects is a sunken garden. There are small rectangular windows at the other, at pavement level. At this end of the room old sofas and chairs are scattered in a rough circle. Around the walls are hung a number of posters, Bardy recognises a couple from Jack's old band, and also big colourful abstract paintings. Ikea or made by the boys? Fairy lights have been looped over these and a large table to one side of the room is loaded with food and drinks. The others are gathered around Leonard's keyboard which is set up at the far end of the room. Jack is sitting on a bar stool, with a guitar, his foot up on a chair. He is reading music over Leonard's shoulder. He is clearly in his element. Bardy glances at Satya. Is her expression a bit softer when it rests on him? Maybe.

Linda hails them. 'Leonard's got his ending.' She is wearing a mellow plum-coloured dress. It is as if she knows.

Kate is in jeans and a shirt threaded with silver.

Perhaps she knows too.

He knows this is nonsense, but somehow it gives him hope as he steps forward. 'Spill the beans, Linda.'

Leonard is rattling out a jaunty tune with an attractive repeating melody, Jack following him on guitar.

'Very catchy,' Lou says.

As Satya gets drinks for them and refills for the others, Tay introduces Uzma and Bardy greets Linda, Pia, Brenda and silver bright Kate. Brenda is looking nervous, Noy keeping close to her side. It is as if he knows. Intelligent dogs, whippets. Slim. Just the right size. Not like a rat at all. Bardy goes over to talk to Brenda.

'Good to see you again.' He smiles.

'They're very talented,' Brenda returns, sipping her glass of fizz, other hand stroking Noy's head. Jack, who is focusing on keeping up with Leonard, gives Bardy the briefest of nods. Nice to see the lad smiling. Much more like Tom's school friend who used to hang around their house. This makes him think of Hana. This hanging around they've been doing since Lou's accident is strange. A weird limbo. What did Pia call it, a liminal space? Maybe it's a liminal time. Part of him wants her to go. Part of him wants her to stay. Forever.

Leonard finishes with a flourish and bows self-consciously to the enthusiastic applause. 'So, what's the ending of the musical?' Bardy calls, glad to be back to whatever is happening right now.

'Ah, it came to me the other evening eating a trifle.' He smiles fondly at his wife.

Hearing aids seem to be doing their stuff.

'You tell them, Leonard,' Linda encourages.

'Well, the trifle got me thinking how much I like jelly.'

'Jelly?' they chorus, except Tay and Uzma who are a duet of, 'You're joking me.' They then fall about laughing. Tay giggling.

You're joking me.

'Yes,' Leonard continues undaunted, 'it occurred to me that most things have been franchised: ice-cream, burgers, cupcakes, sandwiches, frozen yogurt – all been tried. I've got my main character giving a few of them a go, after he gives up running the factory. No luck of course, until his young son says he wants a jelly for his birthday shaped like a rocket. Well, they can't get one anywhere. Not even a mould for one. But our hero is an expert in extruded plastic, so he knows just what to do. He makes the mould and his wife makes the jelly. Soon they realise you can make pretty much any shape out of jelly, and in any flavour.'

'Sweet or savoury,' Linda chips in. She laughs. 'And we should know, we have been trying them out. Orange jelly lobsters, blackberry and lemon jelly dinosaurs and a rather large reclining jelly nude.'

'Milk jelly. Delicious,' Leonard says, winking at his wife.

Hidden depths, Leonard.

'We've also been experimenting with jelly shots and cocktails, and we've brought a few for you to try,' Linda says, nodding towards the table.

'So is this *real* or just for the musical?' Satya the entrepreneur queries. Bardy thinks her eyes are glistening with interest.

'Oh, just research,' Leonard replies.

'It sounds fun,' Pia says.

Linda raises her eyebrows. 'Oh it has been. You would be amazed what you can do with jelly.'

Too much information, Linda

'So, the musical?' Lou prompts, now settled in a comfy armchair, sipping a large glass of red wine.

'Ah, the musical. The man sets up a jelly empire, a chain of shops. Hugely successful. Even supplying the royal family. Jelly shaped like palaces and carriages.'

'I love it,' Kate enthuses.

'Have you got a name for the musical?' Pia asks.

'Oh yes,' Leonard cries and he launches into a rousing, bouncing tune. '*Wobble*.'

Jack joins in and to everyone's surprise, Pia moves beside them and starts singing the words over Leonard's shoulder.

Blimey. Amazing voice.

Kate is at his elbow. Arm just touching his. Silver shimmers doing untoward things to his mind and body. She is laughing, 'You know the ridiculous thing is I can imagine this in the West End. I think I'd actually go and see it.'

'Not *King Lear*?'

Too much of a dig?

'Not a chance!' She glances at Noy who is now sandwiched on a far sofa between Tay and Uzma. 'You know Simon called Noy a rat!'

'No, *really?!* Did he?'

He risks it.

'Tosser.'

'He certainly is,' Kate agrees.

And Bardy kicks back, floating in her silver light.

Chapter 43

Kate

That which hath made me drunk, hath made me bold

The party is in full swing. And that is definitely what this is, *a party*. The lights have been dimmed and only fairy lights illuminate the middle of the room where people are dancing. At the far end of the room a few of the exhausted rest – Noy keeping them company – before hitting the improvised dance floor again. Even Lou is gently pulled to his feet by Pia, for one track. The music is a random selection, usually preluded by someone crying, 'Oh, oh, we need to listen to this one.' Tay and Uzma's choices left Kate bewildered but laughing. And shattered – she had tried to copy their moves. They all had. Bardy was the most successful. *Who knew that man could dance?*

She danced with everyone, but something keeps pulling her back to Bardy's side. And for one track he had held her. Close but not too close. And all she could think of was getting closer. For a while Jack, Leonard and Pia had entertained them with old dance numbers – Linda's choices. And Lou had once again been pulled from his chair and he had guided Kate around the room, safe in his expert hold. Somehow, she hadn't been surprised Lou could dance. *But Bardy.* There wasn't anything flamboyant about his moves, just that man had natural rhythm.

She is watching him now, dancing with Linda. Tucked on the sofa with Pia, both hugging their knees.

'I have been reading about the Finnish boys who can dance,' Pia tells her.

'The what?'

'It's this book I am reading about psychology. They recorded that the men in Finland who danced when they were boys, turned out to be more socially adept and more thoughtful people in later life.'

'Really?'

'Um… I think maybe Bardy and Lou were boys who danced.'

Kate doesn't say anything but just watches Bardy, as he spins Linda around.

'You like this man, don't you?'

'Um.'

'You should do something about it.'

Kate doesn't know how to answer this so instead asks, 'Have you heard anything from Grace?'

'No. But…'

'But, what?' Kate perks up.

'There is a woman at Brenda's book club who I rather like.'

'*Really!*'

'Oh, Kate, I feel so badly that I did not take Brenda seriously.

She is such a kind woman and has really interesting friends, and I think she has a lot to put up with from her husband, Brian.'

Kate is sure of it, but now wants to know about the woman in the book club, 'So, this woman...'

'She's a history professor at the University of East Anglia. Half Spanish, half Mexican, she is an expert on the role of women in fascism.'

'Franco?'

Pia nods. 'And much more besides.'

'Interesting... and you and she?'

Pia leans towards Kate, nudging her slightly. 'A bit like you and Bardy.'

'Which is?'

'Circling each other,' Pia laughs, 'both afraid to make the first move.'

Leonard appears, pulling both of them up to dance. Kate watches Bardy, now dancing with a reluctant but laughing Tay and an enthusiastic Uzma. What a change in that girl. The girl who hugs Hana. What is happening there? Bardy had been as reluctant to talk about Hana as he had been when she asked him about seeing people in colour. On everything else the conversation flowed – in fact was effortless – just those two subjects seemed to be no-go-areas. Does it matter? She wishes it didn't.

Maybe he'd talk about it in bed?

Kate grins to herself. The wine talking? Or a perfect way to stop circling? Something certainly seems to happen when they touch. It sounds corny. But it's true. Sparks fly.

The pace slows, and Kate is grateful to collapse on the sofa again, this time next to Satya and Brenda who are deep in conversation – about knitting of all things. All the others gradually settle. Bardy beside Lou and Linda on the other sofa, Tay and Uzma squished into one armchair, Pia in the other, Leonard standing behind her sipping a beer. Jack re-appears after checking on the boys and nods to Pia to join him at the other end of the room. He is carrying some sheet music. He flicks the sound system off and stepping back to give Pia the limelight, he starts to play. It is an old Bruce Springsteen classic, a slow ballad. Kate's thoughts flit to Bazza but soon are banished by the pleasure of listening to Pia's voice and Jack's accompaniment – on the guitar and at times with husky vocals.

Beside her Kate sees Satya rest her head on Brenda's shoulder. The older woman pats her arm.

'He bought that guitar with the boys,' she hears Satya say. 'We sold all his guitars years ago. He said it was okay, in fact he suggested it. We just didn't have the space and he got a job with a social media company so was working all hours.'

Kate shifts in her seat so both she and Brenda are bent towards Satya. 'Why didn't he say he really did mind?' She struggles to sit up straight, and Kate realises Satya is a little drunk. 'We didn't have *any* money. So for Christmas I knitted him a hat. He loved that hat.' Satya is crying now and Kate glances at Brenda who just nods and keeps patting Satya's arm. 'I knit him a new hat every year, it's a bit of a joke, but it's a tradition. It means something.' Satya slurs, 'It's always his favourite present. And I love doing it. It's often the one bit of creating I get to do. Jack's hat.' The slurring is getting worse now because of the tears. 'Sodding mission statement,' Satya mutters. She looks intently at Kate. 'Why didn't he say he minded about the guitars. He bought that one with the boys. Didn't even tell me.'

'Maybe it was a surprise?' Kate suggests, gently.

'I asked him, and all he said was he didn't have to run everything he bought past me.' Satya is shaking her head now, slowly, from side to side. 'That's not what I meant.' She slumps with her head back on Brenda's shoulder and Kate and Brenda exchange a look over her head.

'Marriage,' Brenda mouths, quietly, 'never easy.'

The song finishes, accompanied by a round of applause and Jack starts on a Springsteen rock anthem. Pia now on backing vocals.

From the other sofa, Kate sees Linda beckoning her. She struggles up and moves over. 'I've been meaning to ask, Kate, would you help me with something?'

'Of course.'

'You made me think of it when you came to the garden. But I think I need some drawings.'

'Of course,' Kate repeats, intrigued.

Linda nods. 'We'll have coffee.'

The music flips back to a soundtrack. Back to dancing.

Leonard materialises and pulls Linda on to her feet.

'Love the idea of *Wobble*,' Kate calls to him above the music as he whisks his wife away. She instinctively looks towards Bardy but his seat is empty. Everyone is heading to join Leonard and Linda, except Satya, who appears to be sleeping, head on the arm of the sofa.

Kate realises she needs a drink. Probably a soft one would be best. Those jelly shots and cocktails are amazing, but with those and the wine, she should probably slow down. Especially if she thinks she and Bardy…

And there he is. Framed in the doorway to the stairs, talking to Jack.

And beside them, Hana.

What is she doing here?

Next Jack is pulling them both onto the dance floor.

Helping herself to sparkling water, Kate has ample opportunity to see how well Bardy and Hana dance together.

It is as if they were made for each other.

Kate is so tired. Tired of dancing. Tired of smiling like she means it. This is the most exhausting. She has been avoiding Pia. But Lou caught her eye and she read sympathy and something else in his look. *Does everyone know?* She feels exposed and stupid. Hana has stuck to Bardy, like – well, like a long-lost wife.

How can she have been thinking of asking him home with her?

Thank God the party is breaking up. She didn't want to be the first to leave. Too obvious. But she has no problem being the second. She knows she won't feel this bad in the morning. She knows the drink isn't helping. She has grown to love these people. But now all she wants is to be alone in her cottage looking out at the creek. That ever changing, indifferent, but endlessly reassuring band of water. She glances at Noy.

Maybe she should get a dog.

It now seems everyone is leaving at once. A cascade of hugs, thanks, collecting coats, reversing to collect forgotten items. She is one of those, slipping back down the steps to get her bag.

In the flickering fairy light Bardy and Hana are alone on the dance floor.

Something hangs in the air.

A question?

Or is it just the look between them that has suspended movement. Stopped all speech.

Then Hana is leaning into Bardy.

For a heartbeat she thinks he will step back.

Then she realises he is holding Hana's hands.

In the next that he is kissing her back.

She stops breathing. Total stillness. Total quiet. She cannot bear them to look up and see her. Her pain, foolishness, everything, stripped open, laid bare for their inspection. For some reason she thinks of the first time she saw her scar. The dressing had been removed, the bruising still evident, but fading. She was home in her bedroom, Jess making tea downstairs. She had stripped and held her breasts, arms crossed over her chest. She had been stoic, grateful. She knows she is not a vain woman. Which is why the sudden wave of sadness and vulnerability that overcame her had shocked her.

Now, she knows she needs to protect herself. She is already planning her retreat on tiptoe back up the stairs. Fast forwarding to the spare key hidden in the shed. Her bag can wait. And if she forgot to put the spare key back, as she sometimes does, she would rather sleep in her car. No, she won't have those keys either.

A night in the shed won't kill her.

Staying here, watching this, might.

Chapter 44

Bardy

The course of true love never did run smooth

Bardy is out on the beach and the surroundings perfectly suit his mood. If he looks one way the sun is shining turning the town in the distance rich terracotta. Looking the other, there is a purple bruise of a rain cloud. A confusion of weather. And he knows if he stands staring out to sea for much longer he is going to be caught by the tide and then he really will be fucked.

What the hell is he going to do?

Even he realises to answer, 'I don't know', just isn't good enough.

But the one man he wants to talk to is out of bounds. Wouldn't be fair.

Lou, do you think I should sell up and move with Hana to New Zealand?

He hadn't seen it coming.

Blind as Gloucester in *King Lear*.

What an idiot he's been. Knew something was coming, but not that. He had kind of been expecting the kiss. Even he'd noticed Hana was hanging around a lot. Being... oh, Hana didn't do 'nice', but being Hana at her best. Making him laugh. Thought it was because of 'that Kate of yours'.

He can't go there.

The dancing with Hana had brought it all back. Those nights in Botswana when they first met. A group of teachers, so young it was ridiculous anyone let them teach their children. But hanging out together, impromptu music and dancing. And that kiss was good. Everyone else had gone. He just leant into her golden yellow.

He looks towards the horizon. That liminal place. A threshold.

Is home a place or a person?

The water is now submerging his boots. Pulling his feet out is an effort that nearly makes him fall. Then he is off striding towards the lifeboat station. Better to get there under his own steam than have them called out to the man stuck waist deep in water, staring out to sea, wondering what the fuck to do.

It's the boys. That's what gets him. The chance to be a family again. How does any landscape weigh against that? Is home a place or *people*?

They had stopped before sex. Somehow that felt all wrong. But the kissing? Familiar and odd all at once.

God, he wants to talk to his best mate.

Then there is Tina. The orange that warms the heart and the bones of a man and makes his best friend cry with the loss of her. Was she wrong?

Thinks you could do better. Hana was kind of hard.

But Tay? Tay who walked into Hana's arms.

That red ochre girl. He dodges her shards of rust. Gets frustrated by her switches in mood, her language, her time keeping. But he trusts her like few others. His closeness to her – that close, but no closer – was hard won and is one of the things he is most proud of. But that girl, that exceptional girl, saw Hana as a person she could trust. She walked straight into her arms and hugged her right back.

Why is he even thinking like this? Trying to understand his ex-wife. Understand the roots and branches of the woman. Like there is some equation he can do, this versus that, which will give him an answer. The truth is he wasn't enough for Hana in the end. It wasn't just about the place. Would a different continent make any difference? How much has this change been brought about by 'your Kate'. Hana jealous.

And what does he want?

Your Kate and Edith? He almost smiles.

It's that or cry.

He does want Kate. Silver bright Kate. Extraordinary. No doubt about that. And there was hope there too, the possibility of exploring so much together. If she could be persuaded and didn't run a mile – a fresh start.

But New Zealand. His family again. A different sort of fresh start?

But what about Lou and Tay?

How can he leave Tay after promising he was staying?

He can't imagine what he would say to Lou... 'You remember me apologising for being a twat for talking about

New Zealand. And not giving a toss about how you might feel? Well, I've changed my mind.'

No, not a conversation he wants to have.

As the rain starts to fall, Bardy walks on oblivious.

Only when he reaches the town does he realise he is soaked to the skin. He glances down into the creek, unsure what he is expecting.

An otter?

God, he wishes he could talk to Lou.

Chapter 45

Kate

For death remembered should be like a mirror

Kate is running hard. It is all she can think to do. Sitting still certainly doesn't work. But this pounding in rhythm along the old sea wall, stretching her muscles, her heart racing at least stops her from hitting something. She is sad and angry and most of all frustrated. Furious with the frustration of not being able to conquer what she feels now and unable to subsume the eruption of pain from the past. Her parents' deaths, her failed marriage, the weight of carrying this and bringing up the girls. Those teenage years. Doug buggering off to be Dougie. She, hanging on, keeping up the pretence of calm, not wanting to scare the girls with her rage and fear. Then Alice and the cruel joke of the same disease stalking her. The loss of Alice the hardest to bear. Still unable to understand why one sister lived and one had died.

Kate stops, and leans over, hands on her thighs, panting. She recalls Linda's words: *it is like asking, why isn't the sun the moon? It just isn't.* This does help. As her breath slows something eases. There really is no reason why someone dies and someone lives. For the first time she feels the logjam of her guilt shifting.

Beyond tears, Kate spins on her heel and turns for home. Her renewed movement builds momentum, dislodging her guilt further and allowing her grief full flow. And now she thinks of Bardy. The man she likes so much. A man who in some way or another seems to see in colour. A good man. But never destined to be her man. She wishes she had held out, not let him in. Then it would be easier.

The closer she gets to home the more Kate feels like she is now running back over trodden ground. No longer running away but returning to something. She knows exactly what she wants to paint. Has the bones of the painting already. She can see the finish of it in her mind as clearly as the sweep of the creek in front of her which is taking her home. For the first time she understands what Alice said: 'Katie you need to show what no one else sees.'

It is a story she is going to tell. It was always going to be that. But it will also evoke all that she feels in that liminal space between sea and sky. For it is there that she now knows she can find her sister and paint her own pain. For once not turning away. This will be for a sister who left before saying goodbye. That was Alice's gift. Kate's gift will be this painting. Doing what her sister told her to, 'Paint how you see the world, Katie.'

Now she is ready to acknowledge her deepest grief, she realises that by expressing it she will find hope. She thinks this is something her sister had always understood.

A final gift from Alice.

As she turns on to the path that leads to her cottage she can see the end of a car poking out from her driveway. She recognises it at once.

Linda has come to see her.

WEEK 9

The great-crested grebes carry their young on their backs, both parents playing their part. The young are striped and look like miniature fairground zebras gliding across the water. Other birds are more independent, the young avocets able to feed themselves as soon as they are hatched. For now migration is over, and the birds are staying. Until the weather and winds change and then they will be off once more.

Chapter 46

Bardy

Love looks not with the eyes but with the mind

They are back in the creaking beach chairs. Golf umbrellas and fleece blankets protection against the drizzle. It is 4.16am. Bardy had texted. Lou had answered his cry for help. As he knew he would. Bardy excuses himself, everyone knows 4am is a low spot. Defences down. More people die at that time than any other. He'd read that somewhere.

They are circling. A settling before the real business starts.

Bardy: 'You're back wood-turning then.'

Lou, self-conscious: 'More like a bit of sculpture. Doubt I'll enter it for anything.'

Bardy: 'But you'll show it at the exhibition?'

Lou: 'I'd forgotten that.'

It was a tradition that the group always put their work on display for a weekend before entering it for the MACKL prize, and anyone in the town could come and have a look.

'Yep. Nate said we can use the gallery. Might be our last chance.'

'It's really closing? Shame. What about the Constable exhibition or whatever?' Lou asks.

'Not sure it's fully decided, but in the end he only secured the loan of one painting. A minor one of clouds. I've seen it. It's good and definitely looks like Norfolk. But Nate thinks it will take more than that to get the press interested.'

'So this new bloke will turn it into flats?'

Bardy nods.

Lou's chair creaks beneath him as he reaches for the thermos in his bag. 'Tea?'

'Look!' Bardy whispers.

On the bank in front of them, not three metres away is an otter. Body sleek and shining, even in the early morning drizzle. It runs like an undulating wave for a few moments, before pausing, studying them, then slipping back into the water with barely a splash.

'Well! Would you look at that,' Lou says, sitting back.

They smile at each other. Both nodding.

Bardy knows it's time. Both do.

'Hana's asked if I would come to New Zealand with her. Make a fresh start.'

Lou blows out a breath and putting his umbrella aside concentrates hard on pouring tea. After a while, nodding, he says, 'Well, that would be good, wouldn't it? Be there with the boys.' He passes Bardy a cup. Face composed. Body solid, shrouded in a fleece blanket. Only his hand trembles slightly.

'I don't know what to do, mate.'

'How come?'

'Of course I want to be with the boys and I think I never really got over Hana.'

'But?'

Does Lou sound hopeful?

Was this really such a good idea?

'I'd miss this,' Bardy says simply.

'What! Getting up at the crack of dawn as some bugger's texted you? Sitting in the rain drinking lukewarm tea? Arses about to end up in the mud?' Lou's chair creaks ominously.

'We did get to see an otter.'

'Of course there is that.'

Bardy can detect his best friend's laughter.

Lou sips his tea before saying, 'Seriously mate. Family first.' He looks Bardy full in the eye now. Clemenza, reassuring, saying it how it is.

'I keep coming back to what Tina said.'

'Should never have told you that,' Lou replies, shaking his head.

'Nah, it's alright. Just wish I could talk to her.'

'You and me both, mate.'

Bardy would like to hold his best friend's hand. But they don't do that. Unless he's in hospital and you think he might die.

How can he leave this, leave this man?

How can he not?

'Then there's Tay,' Bardy says.

'Ah, yes that would be hard on her. But she's getting on with stuff. She and Uzma make quite a team.' Clemenza coughs. 'And I'd keep an eye.'

'I know you would. That wasn't quite what I meant.' Bardy sips his tea. It really is disgusting. He thinks of the café. Bacon sandwich and a large Americano. His usual. God, he'd miss that.

'What did you mean about Tay? I'm not a bloody mind reader.' Lou lets some of his hurt show.

'It's the way Tay hugs Hana. Trusts her completely.'

'Mate, not being dense here, but isn't it more the way you feel when you hug the woman?'

He hasn't thought of that. How does it feel? Good. Familiar. But also odd. He did have doubts and what about…

'And what about Kate? Thought you two might make a go of it.' Lou reads his mind and plays his trump.

'She's silver, you know.'

Lou nods. 'I can see that.'

That's why he loves this man. He gets it. Never laughs at him. Well not when it comes to the important stuff.

'I don't know if Kate would even be interested.' Bardy knows he is playing for time rather than compliments.

'For fuck's sake!' Lou exclaims.

'What?'

'You need to get on with whatever you're going to do.' Lou stares off into the distance.

He should never have contacted Lou. It hadn't been fair.

'She saw you, you know.'

'What? Who?' Bardy is struggling to keep up.

'At Satya and Jack's. Think she went back down for something. I was behind her on the stairs. You and Hana. *You know.*'

'Oh fuck!'

'Yeah, quite. Made myself scarce. Didn't want to make her feel worse.'

'Was she upset?'

'What do you think, mate.' Lou now sounds angry.

'Right. Right. You're right, I need to get my shit together. Make a decision.'

Bardy can feel the big man beside him relax slightly, soften.

'Look, I can see it's hard. You and Hana have history, the boys. Family. But it will only work if you and Hana are solid.'

And are they? Yes and no.

Bardy wonders if life would be easier as an otter.

'And what did you mean about Tay?' Lou rewinds.

'It's just Tay doesn't trust many people. And yet with Hana she's different. I can see that, and it does make a difference. Tay sees what is special about Hana. And that counts for something. Then I think... sorry mate... that Tina must have been wrong.'

'Well, you can't ask Tina,' her widower says, 'but you can talk to Tay.'

Chapter 47

Kate

Smiling at grief

She may be late, but she comes into the exhibition smiling. Talking to Linda had helped so much. So, she and Bardy may not make a thing of it. She suspects he will be off soon to New Zealand. To his family. And who can blame him? She thinks it will be easier when he has gone.

Anyway, she has her home, her friends and *her* family. Ellie has messaged that she will be home for Christmas, Bella always planned to be back in the autumn and Jess called last night and she and Matt are expecting a baby. So much to be grateful for. Happy about. And now there is also her art.

She looks around at the gallery. She can't wait to see what everyone has done. There are a few people already milling around the exhibition. God, is that Tash? She is obscuring Kate's own painting. She wants her to step aside so she can see how Nate hung it. She glances around. He really has done them proud. Linda approaches and wraps her in a hug. 'That's the ticket. Chin up. Tits out. Leonard is about to start.'

Before Linda finishes speaking the space is filled with one of the tunes from Leonard's musical, *Wobble*. No singing this time, but a lovely melody. It reminds her of the party. And as if on cue, there is Bardy turning to welcome Lou. He catches her eye and raises his hand. Apologetic? Embarrassed? Tash steps aside and she has a clear view of her painting. So does Linda. 'It really is something Kate, you must be very pleased with it.'

Kate links her arm with Linda's and squeezes it, not speaking. She doesn't think she could.

The painting, which she has called *Migration*, shows the creek in the foreground but the majority of the painting is of the marsh and the sky. Most of the landscape is in the natural colours of the lowlands but she has chosen colours that Alice would have worn for highlights: ochres, turquoise and purples. Just like the splashes of colour Alice had sewn into Kate's clothes. Despite everything, she *is* grateful to Hana for her advice on colour. It is the marsh, but it is her re-imagining of it. In the space where sea and sky merge are the birds. A crescent sweep of what might be geese, with one exotic – the focus. The birds are on the move, and there is a sense in that liminal space between the world of water and the expanse of air, of the birds being on a threshold. The story is of an exotic who crosses over but who leaves the world changed.

'The light is beautiful,' Linda comments.

'Thank you.' Kate will take that. It is what she is most proud of. And looking at this image just makes her want to paint more. Another gift from the sister who she loved so much.

'Come and see what I have done with your drawings,' Linda says, tugging on her arm.

Pia and Brenda are already there admiring Linda's entry. 'Of course it won't be finished,' she tells them.

'But you can see from the drawings what it will look like. It's a seed, isn't it?' Brenda comments.

'Yes, a seed head exploding.' Linda points to Kate's drawings. 'It's going to be a garden sculpture. I did do metal work years ago on one evening course, but I will definitely need some help to finish it.' So far Linda has the stalk and the beginnings of the seed head. 'I've got to work out how to do the seeds, I want to capture them as if they are flying out.'

'I like it very much,' Pia says. 'You will have to have a grand unveiling when it is finished.'

'Any excuse for a party,' Linda agrees.

Bardy and Lou join them, and Kate feels her face flushing. She notices that Lou stands close to her, and she is grateful to the big man.

'This is great, Linda,' Bardy says, 'it really is going to be wonderful.'

'Well, I thought you would approve,' Linda laughs. 'I am trying to capture an instance, a fraction of time, but I am taking my time about it. I think the garden gave me the inspiration. I never seem to rush my gardening. You can't get impatient if things don't do everything all at once.'

'Perfect,' Lou says. 'And Kate, I have to say your painting is incredible.'

'Yes, it's fantastic,' Bardy echoes. And Kate finally looks at him. There it is, the held look. The falling away of everyone else.

But she has finished with wishing for him to choose her. That way only leads to pain and feelings of inadequacies. She glances back at her painting. It sustains her and suddenly she needs to tell these people, these friends something. 'I won't actually enter it for the competition though, because—'

Uzma bounces up, cutting her off mid-sentence. 'Have you seen Tay's drawing? You gotta see this.'

'I thought she hadn't done anything. I mean it didn't matter.' But even as Bardy says this, Kate knows that he had been disappointed.

'Not gonna lie, she was late. But come and see. You're gonna love it.'

They follow her across the gallery, dodging the growing crowd of people.

Nathan is hanging a large, framed charcoal drawing. 'Look okay?' he asks Tay over his shoulder.

'Yep.'

'It's stunning babe,' Uzma exclaims. She grins at Bardy. 'See. Said you'd like it.'

Kate glances at Bardy's face. She thinks he is trying very hard not to cry. Tay has created a charcoal drawing of Bardy sitting on a chair. Maybe a sofa? He has his legs crossed (ah, tricky – the need for life drawing). He is looking sideways as if at someone beside him. There is a small white card beside the picture with the title, *Close*. This doesn't make sense to Kate, but when Bardy reads it, he no longer pretends he isn't crying.

Eventually he manages, 'Thank you, Tay.'

For a moment she thinks Tay might hug him, but turning,

they both see Hana approaching. 'That's fabulous Tay. The frame worked out well, didn't it?'

'Yeah, thanks for the help,' and Tay gives Bardy a funny sort of nudge as she walks past to Hana who puts an arm around her shoulders.

'Nice one,' Hana says.

Kate sees Bardy watching them. She can't read his expression, any more than she can name what she is feeling. Hopeless? Moved? Confused? She is just conscious that Lou and Linda seem to have sandwiched her between them and takes comfort from that.

'Now we need to show you Pia's piece and Brenda has done something really rather wonderful,' Linda says.

At least this distracts Kate. 'Brenda's entering something?'

'Oh, I don't know about that but come and see. And then coffee and cake,' Linda suggests and Kate is happy to be led away. First stop is Pia's exhibit.

'Wow! I mean, Wow!'

'You like it?' Pia, tentative, hesitant.

'It's fantastic,' Kate says and means it.

Pia's quilt is now a narrow band of quilted, rectangles. Rather than one enormous quilt 'the size of Denmark', it forms a strip of quilting that stretches almost the full length of the wall. Each rectangle is quilted but also painted with the colours of the marsh. Images, or rather hints of birds seem to have settled within it and some are suspended in the fabric above what appears to be a horizon. Kate thinks that the sheer scale of it makes it a true North Norfolk quilt. It is set off well by the white gallery wall that seems to add to the feeling of a vast space.

'It's good, isn't it?'

Kate turns to find Nate beside her. 'It made me think we could have done a textile art exhibition. It's not something we've done before. But ah well.'

'You're going to be closing?'

'Looks that way. You need to come and see Constable's clouds before you leave. Small...' He nods towards Pia's exhibit. 'Much smaller than this, but you still get the sense of space.'

'What will you do?'

'No idea. Might take a tip from Bella and go travelling.'

Kate rubs his shoulder. 'Something will turn up.'

'You think?' Nate doesn't sound convinced.

'Sorry to interrupt, but you need to see Brenda's contribution,' Linda urges.

This does make Nate grin. 'Yeah, go and have a look.'

Kate can't tell exactly what it is from a distance – something knitted? But as she gets closer she starts to laugh. Brenda has knitted each member of the group, including Noy. There is Linda, plump in a purple dress with beads, Leonard complete with knitted piano. Kate is on a knitted bicycle, hair sticking up. How the hell did the woman knit a bike? She even has Jack playing guitar. 'I love it, Brenda,' Kate enthuses. 'But where are you?' As she says this she wonders where Jack and Satya are. Their knitted versions may be here, but she hasn't seen them in person yet.

'Well, I didn't like to put myself in. I mean I'm not really one of the gang.'

'Oh, but you are, Brenda,' Pia insists.

Brenda colours with pleasure. 'Well, I did actually do one, but I didn't like to put it out.'

'Oh, you should,' Linda says, persuasively.

Brenda reaches into her large shoulder bag and pulls out a knitted figure wearing a knitted purple and pink suit. The figure is seated in a squishy armchair and appears to be knitting something. A matching dog's outfit? Kate hides her smile.

Pia takes it from her and places it with the other figures.

'What did Brian think of them?' Kate asks.

'He couldn't understand why I was knitting such rubbish. Or why his tea was late.' For a moment Brenda looks despondent, then looking at the three women she continues, 'So I told him to make his own tea.'

'You did?' Kate grins. 'How did that go down?'

'He got a bit angry and then went to the pub. So I was able to get on with what I wanted in peace.'

Pia looks concerned. 'You're not frightened of him, are you Brenda?'

Brenda looks surprised. 'Oh, no, Brian's not a violent man.' She pauses reflectively. 'Just a very boring one. And between us I don't think he's all that bright. I've always looked after the bills and finances, and he really has no idea of all the accounts we have. He really wouldn't have a clue if I left him.'

'Are you thinking of leaving him?' Linda asks.

'I hadn't been, but maybe things need to change a bit.'

The three women surrounding Brenda glance at each other. Kate wants to laugh.

'And there is always the life assurance,' Brenda continues, a twinkle in her eye. 'Brian has no idea how much I have him insured for.'

Chapter 48

Bardy

For where thou art, there is the world itself

'Is Satya here?' Jack comes into the gallery at a run.

'No, is she okay?' Bardy asks, concerned.

Jack draws a deep breath. 'No, nothing wrong, just thought I was late and would get a bollocking. Ah, great, Linda's got cake.' He claps Bardy on the shoulder and wanders off to where Linda and Leonard are now serving teas and coffees. Leonard let off his piano duties for a while. There is quite a crowd. He's not surprised, Linda has made some great cakes. He's already had one of her chocolate and chilli brownies. He knows a few faces. Some retired teachers, Tash is there with a big bloke he presumes is her husband. And Simon. Which makes him immediately think of Kate. Is he with someone? Seems to have a brunette hanging on his arm. Moving on or trying to score a point knowing Kate would be here?

Tay and Uzma pass him, heading towards where Hana is

standing. He doesn't feel like joining them but touches Tay on the arm. 'Could we talk later?'

'Yeah,' she says briefly. She adds, 'Thought you were writing short stories, like, you know, the girl who surprised the world.'

'Thought I'd give the poems about colour a bit of an airing.'

'No offence, but about time.'

'You knew?'

'Hana told me once about your colour thing.'

He's not sure how he feels about that. Before she moves on Tay asks, 'Do I have a colour?'

He nods. 'Red ochre.'

She frowns. 'Is that good?'

'It's bloody beautiful.'

And who thought Tay could blush? She punches his arm as she moves on. It's not a hug but he'll take it.

Bardy looks around the rest of the room. Pretty good turnout. He must start talking to people about next year's group, try and recruit a few. This brings him up short. Will he even be here? He doubts it. His decision is pretty well made. Tom and Ned. Family, Clemenza had said. He hasn't said as much to Hana. But it seems she has taken it rather for granted. Started talking about dates. He sees Kate with Lou. Nothing but a chasm of pain looming that way. He turns away to smile at Pia who has come up beside him.

'You are a fool. You do know that. You choose a woman who left you, didn't bother with you for years, over Kate?'

'Whoa. Has Kate said something?'

'No, Linda. Bardy, you are out of your fucking mind.'

He has never heard Pia swear before.

'Oh, babe!'

They both turn to the cry. Jack and Satya are standing close by them, beside Satya's photographs: *Details of a Guitar*. Close up images of parts of a well-used guitar. All black and white. They remind Bardy of a jazz club he once went to.

Jack and Satya are standing a few metres apart. The cry had come from Jack.

Satya is carrying a guitar. Bardy is pretty certain it is the guitar in the photos.

'How did you? Where the hell?' Jack isn't making any sense as far as Bardy can tell. But Satya seems to know what's going on.

'I knew it was your favourite, so I tracked it down. Took bloody ages, and the bloke was an old sod. Racist, and so mean, mean as a… well as a really mean fucker.'

English composition had never been Satya's subject.

'But I got it!' She holds it out triumphantly to her husband.

'Oh babe!' he says again and takes the guitar reverently in his hands and holds it, looking down at it. Without looking up, he says, 'I know we're shit. We don't help you like we could and we leave you out of stuff sometimes.'

'Oh, babe,' this time from Satya.

'We all think you're incredible. I just think sometimes you might need the boys, but you don't really need me.' The last part is almost a whisper.

Satya gets up close to her husband. A beloved guitar between them. 'You're right, I don't need you Jack.' He looks up, startled.

She has her palms open. 'Why does a woman always have to

need a man? And you're right, I am incredible; I know women aren't supposed to say it but I'm a bloody good businesswoman.'

'Mission statement,' her husband murmurs, and Satya laughs. 'I'll give you that one.' She takes the guitar from her husband and looks around. Bardy steps forward and takes it from her. Now she is up and close to Jack, the man she has adored since she was fourteen. 'I don't need you, Jack. But I *choose* you. How much better is that? And I will never stop wanting you and choosing you and loving you and all that shit.'

No, terrible at English composition. But Bardy is welling up again.

What is it about these people?

Jack pulls Satya to him and wraps her in his arms. And there they are locked together, snogging like they are back in the cupboard off the sports hall. Bardy wonders if there are any new stories left to be told in the world.

'I like your poems. The ones about colour.'

'What? Oh, God Kate, I'm so sorry,' he blurts. Then stops. He has no idea what to say to her. Just wants to look at her and go on looking at her. She puts her hand on his arm. Which only makes him feel ten times worse. Waves of silver now washing over him, then ebbing. Not creating the normal feeling of exhilaration, just a sense of something precious lost. Kate glances at Satya and Jack still locked together, his hands in her hair.

'That's good' she says, and sighs, looking directly at him, 'and the other stuff, that's okay too, Bardy.' She says brightly, 'Jess is going to have a baby. I'm going to be a granny.' And she lets go of his arm. The loss of her touch feels like a burn.

'Kate... I don't know...'

'I think Lou's sculpture is really good too. I'm not sure what it is or how he got the driftwood to hold together like that but I like it. Looks like it would be good in a garden. Perhaps it could go in Linda's garden. Linda's met a blacksmith, she's been getting some tips from him. I bet he ends up helping her.' She stops abruptly. 'Sorry. Going on a bit.'

Leonard bustles up beside them. 'The mayor's here.'

'The what?' Bardy tries to refocus. 'Sorry. Right, got it. With you.'

'Why's the mayor here?' Kate asks.

Bardy hurries off with Leonard. 'You'll see.'

Chapter 49

Kate

Truth is truth

The mayor has been talking for some time.
Community project.
Wonderful effort.
Encouraging local involvement.
The crowd are getting restless. Kate can hear Tash's voice from somewhere in the room; querulous. There are a couple of people she knows from work, listening more politely. And Simon seems to have put himself and the new girlfriend directly in her line of vision. Coincidence? Kate isn't feeling particularly good about herself – but she doesn't think so. The woman beside him looks nice. Kate hopes she's not a dog lover.

'...and the winner for best newcomer goes to Kate Oliver for her magnificent painting, *Migration*.'

It takes a few seconds for the words to penetrate. Then

Linda is pushing her gently in the back, whispering, 'Go on. He wants to give you something.'

Kate looks around helplessly. She can't accept this. She had no idea there was going to be a prize. What the hell is she going to do? Everyone is clapping and waiting. Maybe take it, get it over with, then explain. She heads to the front. Shakes Bardy's hand which feels weird. He looks confused. Has he spotted her eyes pleading, trying to tell him something? Then she is shaking hands with the mayor. Sweaty. Him or her, she isn't sure.

'Speech,' someone calls.

She looks down at the small plaque she has been handed. And finds she just can't look up.

'Kate?' She hears Bardy's troubled enquiry.

'Best newcomer? That's a good one.'

If the room hadn't just gone silent, watching and waiting for Kate to speak, maybe no one would have heard. As it is, people are turning to Simon, and his girlfriend's voice is clearly discernible. 'What do you mean?'

Simon looks around. Kate is now watching him. All she thinks is: *get it over with*.

'Well, Kate is JoJo Rose. Spent years painting. I mean, hardly a newcomer.' Simon sounds almost apologetic. He is looking around at the crowd. He won't look at Kate.

'But you said you'd never sold anything?'

Bardy.

Kate instinctively looks to Linda.

Shocked. And worse, Leonard looks horrified.

Then there is an outbreak of talking.

JoJo Rose? Blimey.
I used to have a few of her prints.
I've still got one of her aprons.

Tash, strident, outraged. 'Well that's a bloody cheek. I'm an accredited sculptor and they threw me out. That's cheating. I always thought that JoJo Rose stuff was tat anyway.'

'I'm really sorry,' Kate manages to say above the noise, 'I didn't mean to accept this. And I wasn't going to enter my painting. It was just that…'

Her mind is too full of things she cannot share with these people. If it was just the group, she might stand a chance. But not here, not now.

She pushes the plaque back into the mayor's hands.

'I'm sorry I lied.' She directs this at Bardy.

He just stares back. His face blank.

She throws a look at Pia. Her friend is frowning.

Kate blindly pushes through the crowd. She sees Nate open mouthed. A last glance at Satya's photos and she is in the foyer and heading for the door. She is brought up short by a smiling Hana. 'Great painting, Kate. Is Bardy still in there?'

'What? Oh, yes.' Kate's heart is racing. The delay killing her. She wants to be gone.

'Brilliant.' Hana holds up her phone. 'I think I've got a friend who wants to buy his flat.'

It only needs this. Without another word, Kate dodges Hana. By the time she is on the street she is running. She thinks she hears a voice calling her name. Lou? But she cannot stop. All she can think about it being alone by the creek.

* * *

Kate sits in a hollow looking down at the bones of an old boat that lie exposed in the creek bed. The yellow gorse is a prickly neighbour shielding her from view. She feels like she has been running forever. Her heart is aching, but she is not sure that is from the exercise. Ahead of her is the landscape she loves. The creek at low tide, a flickering, flowing ribbon filled with June sunshine.

Everything reflects everything.

Beyond this is a carpet of sea purslane and sea lavender stretching to the thin line of indigo that is the sea. Above it all is *that* sky. She thinks of Pia's quilt. It really did capture the breadth of this land. The waders scouring the exposed mud and sandbanks remind her of Leonard.

She will find a way to apologise. In the gallery she had felt her shame reflected back from the bright white walls.

Everything reflects everything.

Here in this huge open space, nature tells her that nothing matters that much, and this brings her some sense of peace. Anything is possible.

Well, maybe not everything.

Kate closes her eyes and tips her head back so her face catches the sun. She rests her head on the sandy bank behind her. She is sheltered, but above her, all is wind and the sound of the birds.

The migrants here for a while raising their young.

Family. Even with the birds it counted for so much. She remembers Leonard telling her that an avocet will fake a broken wing to draw prey away from its young. She can't blame Bardy for wanting to be with his boys. Wanting to be with Hana? Well, that is a different matter. She left that good man for nearly five years. Broke his heart.

Kate has an image of Tay walking into Hana's open arms. She feels that this does count for something. That this weighs with Bardy in some important way.

But does Hana really love Bardy?

Who knows.

To be or not to be... in love

Does *she* love Bardy?

No.

But she knows she could.

It would be as easy as sitting in a hollow, falling asleep in the sun listening to the birds.

Chapter 50

Bardy

Action is eloquence

Tay and Bardy are on a bench on the quayside, ice-cream cones in hand. Mint-choc-chip for Tay. Vanilla for Bardy.

'Who's JoJo Rose?' Tay is asking. 'Can't see what all the fuss is about.'

'It was years ago now. A range, a bit like Cath Kidston, but teacups covered in flowers.'

'Doesn't sound like Kate to me.'

Bardy doesn't think so either. Was it really her? Why hadn't she just said? That does worry him. Why hide it?

'She'll have her reasons.' Red ochre now a mind-reader. He greedily takes in the colour. Trying to store it in his mind, even though he knows it doesn't work like that.

'Have you seen her?' Tay asks, nibbling now at the cone.

'Not yet.'

'She'll be feeling shit.'

'She's not answering texts.'

'I am on the group chat, you know,' Tay eye rolls.

'Yeah, well Linda came to see me.'

'About Kate?'

'Sort of.'

Tay grins. 'She rip into you?'

'Oh yeah.'

'Good.'

'Thanks.'

'Well, no offence, but you are a complete arse sometimes Bardy.'

'Yep. Don't worry, Lou said the same.'

Tay eases up. 'Look we do all get it. Family and all that.'

'You understand?'

'I'm not thick, Bardy. Toni may be shit, but I could always see what you lot had.'

'Which was?'

'Proper family stuff. When I was little I used to pretend that we would discover I was really related to you and Hana.'

'Oh Tay. You do know we love you.'

'Oh, fuck off.' She feeds her last bit of cone to a passing seagull. 'So what's this all about? The *I want to meet. I want to talk*. Got things to do.'

She never could sit still for long.

'Okay. Why is it you hug Hana?'

'And not you?'

'I guess. And it's okay. We're cool the way we are.' He points to the gap between them on the bench. Close but not too close.

'You really want to know?'
Bardy nods.
So Tay tells him.

Ten minutes later she bounces up from the bench. Bardy is still staring out beyond the fishing boats to the channel leading to the sea. He shakes off his preoccupation and rises.

'I guess this is goodbye, then,' Tay says.

Bardy can't speak.

Tay nudges him. 'Go on, you know you want to.'

He opens his arms and she walks into his hug. He can feel her skinny arms hugging him back and it is pure red ochre. And he had been right; in that beautiful ruby colour there is so much hope.

Chapter 51

Kate

And by and by a cloud takes all away

Kate knew she was being a coward not looking at her phone messages, so when she hears someone knocking on her door she thinks it might be Linda, worried. Pia even. She does not expect Bardy.

For a ridiculous instant she thinks of simply closing the door in his face, then Linda's words come back to her. 'Chin up, tits out.' So she smiles as best she can and steps back to let him in.

'How are you doing Kate?' Bardy asks.

For some reason his concern irritates her. 'I'm not ill,' she replies sharply. She sighs. 'Come into the kitchen and I'll get us some coffee, or I've got some white wine open.' She suddenly realises this might be easier over a drink.

'That would be good,' he answers cautiously, as if worried she might snap at him again.

Even before the wine is poured she starts. 'I'm really sorry about the JoJo Rose stuff. There are good reasons why I didn't mention it. Well, things that were important to me. But I should have just come clean once I got to know you all. And I was never going to enter that competition.'

'Okay,' Bardy says, slowly, taking a glass of wine from her. 'Would you tell me? I mean, you don't have to.'

She looks at him, and suddenly this all seems so pointless. Best get it over with. They are still standing by the fridge. It hardly seems worth asking him to sit down. He can then tell the others. Then he can pack up his flat and catch his flight.

So she explains about her parents and Alice and her dad's new wife Maureen.

She had expected Bardy to understand. She will give him that. She had even imagined him being sympathetic. She hadn't expected him to laugh.

'That's bloody brilliant. So everywhere Maureen went she saw your granny's china and your mum's name. Plus she must have known you were raking it in.' He looks conscience stricken, mentioning the money. But for the first time in days Kate grins, and gestures around her. 'Well, it bought me this.'

'Blimey.'

'Look, it was good while it lasted, but I'm not particularly proud of those paintings.'

'As Tay would say, it is what it is,' Bardy remarks.

'Or was what it was.' Kate smiles. 'How is she? I thought her drawing of you was so good.'

'She's okay. I've just been saying goodbye to her.'

'Ah.' So another reason for this visit. A farewell. It is

happening so fast. Maybe that is for the best. Kate looks out across the creek and draws its magic to her. She can do this.

'Yes, wanted to say goodbye as she's moving with Uzma to Leeds.'

'Oh! Oh... that's sudden.'

'Yes, Uzma is taking over from someone who was rushed into hospital, going to be months before... Oh sod it Kate I don't want to talk about that. I want to talk about us... well, if you... oh bollocks... I'm doing this all wrong. You might not like the idea of an us... and think I'm an arrogant sod, coming here after everything... and oh fuck it,' says the man who writes really rather beautiful poetry.

He takes a deep breath. 'I'm not going to New Zealand with Hana.'

'You're not?'

He gazes at her and shakes his head. 'Couldn't.'

The intensity of his eyes holds her and all she can do is look back at him. She wonders what his eyes see.

Everything reflects everything.

He is the first to break the gaze, looking down at his glass of wine as if surprised to still find it there.

'Say it,' she says, softly.

'What?' He looks up, quizzical.

'Go on say it,' she insists.

There is the flickering of a smile.

'Oh, Bardy, don't tell me you haven't thought it. You're Jon *Shakespeare*. It's one of his best lines. My favourite.'

He laughs, puts his wine down, spilling most of it, but he gets her hand and pulls her to him, holding her tight.

'Come on, kiss me, Kate.'
So she does.

They are sitting in the kitchen looking out over the creek. They have finished the little bit of white wine that Kate had and opened a bottle of Champagne. It seemed to suit their mood.

'But the boys?' Kate is asking. She finds she cares about them. Not a lot about Hana.

'Linda said something interesting. And Lou.'

'You've been talking to them about all this?' Kate feels herself flushing, then wonders why. They must all have known how she felt. How she feels.

Bardy isn't going to New Zealand. She glances out towards the creek and the clouds clear letting in the sunshine. She thinks what a truly beautiful day it is.

'What did Linda and Lou say?'

'Well, Linda's got two boys and she said that they move on. Their own families are where they're at. And that they might not want me muscling in trying to make it all about how it used to be.'

Oh, thank you Linda.

'Good point,' Kate says, thinking of her own girls.

'I'll visit my boys of course, and they're both doing pretty well so I'm sure they'll come back for holidays, and we'll still FaceTime a lot, but I don't think they necessarily need me on their doorstep.'

'It's weird isn't it the way you say, "my boys" and I say "my girls" even though they are grown up. Sometimes halfway round the world. Completely their own people,' Kate reflects.

'I know it's not like it was, when my girls needed me but they are still… so much part of me…'

'Like your heart,' Bardy finishes, simply.

Kate smiles softly and nods.

'And you mentioned Lou said something?' she asks.

'He said that none of it would work unless Hana and I were really solid.'

Another good point. *Thank you, Lou.*

'And you're absolutely sure you're not?' She needs to know.

'We were and I think I kept trying to live in the past. But she left, Kate, for good reasons. I guess I missed what we had so much that I couldn't see that I wanted different things too. And when she came back and could see I liked you and well…'

'Have you told her you're not going?' Kate thinks of Hana, organising the sale of Bardy's flat.

Bardy nods.

'What did she say?'

He looks pensive, and a little sad. Kate tries hard not to feel jealous.

Bardy isn't going to New Zealand.

'I think she was sort of expecting it. Had been rushing things along, to stop us having the sort of conversation we needed to.'

'And you've done that now?'

'Yep, and it's okay. She's gone back to Wales and then will fly out to New Zealand from there.'

She can't read Bardy's expression.

'What?' Kate queries.

'She said something odd just before she left. I didn't really get it. We'd been talking about Tay and about her drawing. Tay's plans to go with Uzma to Leeds, and how her work are trying to help find her a role.' He is momentarily distracted. 'So they bloody should. Anyway we were chatting about that, and local things, like the gallery closing, just ordinary stuff. I was waiting with her for her taxi to the station and she said she had a gift for me.'

'What was it?'

'Well that's it. It was just the name of an artist. One I'd never heard of.'

He tells her, and Kate hasn't heard of him either.

Bardy's phone buzzes. 'Ah, that's the group chat. They want to know how I got on.' He grins. 'What shall I say?'

'Tell them they're bloody nosy and that I want nothing to do with you,' Kate laughs. 'No, say to come over. It would be good to see them. I'd like to explain everything to them too.'

While Bardy is busy texting, Kate stretches and fills up their glasses. She looks down at him. Oh, yes, she could definitely fall for his man.

What does she mean? *Could* fall for him.

'They're all coming.' He pauses, and looks at his phone again. 'Oh, except Tay, she and Uzma are busy packing.'

This reminds her of something. 'Bardy, does it really bother you that Tay hugs Hana, but not you?'

'I got one, you know,' he says, proudly, and Kate feels her heart swell a little for him.

'What was the hugging all about? I kept thinking it meant something to you.'

Bardy sips his Champagne. 'It did. You're right. I felt like if Tay did that it really showed what an exceptional person Hana was, and that I would be an idiot to let her go.'

'And?'

'Well, she is exceptional,' Bardy agrees.

'Jack once told me that Tom said it was like growing up with a botanist and a gardener.'

'Did he?' Bardy laughs.

'He said that Hana takes a real interest in people and that is all genuine. It's not fake.'

Bardy nods again.

'What I don't get,' Kate continues, 'is what's this got to do with Tay?'

A shadow passes over Bardy's face. 'She has had a pretty tough time. I can't bear to think of some of it. It isn't really Toni's fault. She had no role model and struggles with addiction. Bad choices in men too.'

'I know that one,' Kate says jokingly, looking significantly at Bardy.

Bardy smiles, but shakes his head. 'No. I mean *really* bad, Kate.'

'So is that why Tay wouldn't hug you? Because you're a man?'

'Partly,' Bardy acknowledges. 'But mainly it was because I cared too much. Like you say, I'm the gardener, Hana's the botanist.'

Kate shakes her head, not understanding.

'The thing is Tay has had to deal with so much crap, from a really young age. And it is a huge amount to deal with emotionally. And what she told me is sometimes she wants to be hugged by someone who isn't weighed down with more emotion. If they feel sorry for her or are upset, she somehow feels that is also her fault and it is all too much. She just sometimes wants a break from it.'

'And Hana doesn't care?' Kate is confused.

'It's complicated. She is very fond of Tay. Is incredibly interested in her. Would do anything for her. But she's not torn apart by some of the stuff that Tay has had to deal with.'

'And you are?'

'Oh, yeah,' Bardy says, wearily.

'So much easier to hug Hana?'

'Tay tried to describe it as friends with benefits, which didn't quite work. But it made us laugh. And I got it.'

So does Kate.

'She is amazing to be able to express all that.'

'Incredible girl, Tay. Red ochre.'

'What?!' Kate spins around to look closely at Bardy. 'So the colour stuff is real?' The doorbell sounds in the hall. 'Don't think I've finished with you, Bardy,' she says as she heads for the door.

From behind her she hears a muttered, '*Oh I do hope not.*'

Chapter 52

Bardy

The quality of mercy is not strained,
It droppeth as the gentle rain from heaven

They are all gathered around Kate, chairs borrowed from around the house. More wine has been opened and Kate has just finished telling them about JoJo Rose. She ends with an apology for lying to them.

Bardy thinks Pia is spot on when she says, 'There is absolutely no need to apologise, Kate.'

Bardy glances around at them all: Linda and Leonard sharing a window seat, Pia, Brenda and Satya on kitchen chairs. Lou in a larger wicker chair. *Being Clemenza*. The man looks happier than he has done for days. Couldn't leave his best mate – mad idea. Then there is silver bright Kate beside him. Only Tay missing. But he has a message from her for Kate in his pocket.

'So, Kate we have something we want to say to you,' he declares.

She looks at him in surprise.

Bardy can see the others nodding their encouragement. They've discussed this, well most of it. 'Now it's time to actually enter the MACKL competition…'

He sees Kate wince at the mention, and he takes her hand, interlacing his fingers with hers.

Silver, like pure electricity ripples up his arm.

Bardy tries to concentrate. 'We decided as we will no longer be meeting up like we used to, that we should form a new group.'

Linda leans forward eagerly. 'None of us could bear not to keep this going.'

'Indeed not,' Leonard echoes.

Bardy grins. 'And this group is going to have a name.'

Kate looks puzzled. 'What is it?'

Pia continues, 'We are going to be called the *King Lear* Liars.'

'*The what?*'

'The *King Lear* Liars,' Lou repeats. 'Because Kate, you are not the only one. We all lie.'

'Plus we wanted a name that reminded us of how we all met, you know, how Shakespeare wrote all those plays in quarantine,' Satya adds.

Bardy can see the confusion on Kate's face, but nods reassuringly. He turns to the others. 'Go, on then, confession time. Who's going to go first?'

It is the Danish lawyer who raises her hand and covers her eyes with the other one. She then lifts her head, and looking at Linda says, 'I have lied to you all. But particularly to you, Linda.'

Linda shakes her head, smiling but uncomprehending.

'I don't actually bake anything. I have no idea what I am doing in my kitchen and I have barely ever used my Aga.'

Linda starts to laugh. 'But how do…'

'I order all my cakes from a Danish bakery in London.' Pia puts her head in her hand, but Bardy can see she is laughing.

They all are.

All except Brenda.

'Oh, Pia, I've lied too!' Brenda exclaims.

'My goodness, what is it?' Pia's laughter turns to concern.

'Well, I did take down the photos of Noy in his smart new outfits, but not before other friends shared them and well…'

They all wait, Pia looking anxious.

'It seemed other people did like them and I have quite a few orders in. So I have used his photos to show people the full range of designs.'

'People want to dress their whippets like that?' Pia sounds more astounded than angry.

This seems to give Brenda confidence. 'Oh yes, I have orders in for four jesters, two floral coats, six vicars and *ten* dinosaurs.'

'*Really?*' Pia appears stunned.

Brenda nods. 'You don't mind?'

Pia smiles at the neighbour who is now her friend. 'No, I don't mind, Brenda. But I do have to say… you English are so strange.'

Over the laughter, Kate tugs on his hand. 'Bardy, tell me, have you been lying?'

He takes a deep breath. 'Yes,' he declares, looking around at them all. 'The short story I was telling you about – well, that *is* me. I do see certain people in colour. It's a weird sort of synaesthesia.'

There is an outcry of exclamations and questions. Only Lou sits quietly, Clemenza looking a bit smug. Bardy goes on to explain about how his mind is flooded with colour, but only with certain people.

'So who here do you see in colour?' Satya asks.

He looks at her. 'You are the blue of lapis lazuli.'

'Oh.' The small word a mix of surprise and delight. 'How lovely.'

'It is,' he tells her. 'Linda you are mellow plum.'

Linda nods contentedly. 'Very nice.'

'And me?' Pia asks tentatively.

Bardy shakes his head, hating to disappoint her. 'It only happens occasionally, only some people. And I have no control over it,' Bardy assures her.

'Do you see me as a colour?' Kate asks quietly.

'No,' he replies.

'Oh.' He sees her face drop.

Lou laughs and Kate glances at him. 'Tell her,' Lou says.

'What?' Kate asks.

'Kate, you are pure silver.'

'Oh, really, the colour silver?' She pauses. 'But you said I wasn't a colour.'

'Not a colour, you are pure silver light.'

'Aah.' Kate's sigh is echoed around the room.

'And with you, my mind is only flooded with it when I touch you.'

'Really,' Kate exclaims. Then her eyes start to shine, with something that gets his heart racing. 'Oh, *REALLY*!'

Everyone is laughing again, but Bardy doesn't care, silver

bright Kate is looking at him, and it dawns on him – he's not going anywhere. He is staying right here. A home bird.

'Tell them about Tina,' Lou says softly.

Bardy looks at Lou. 'You sure?'

He nods.

'Lou's wife Tina, was the citrus orange of the sunshine in the Mediterranean, the orange that lingers on your skin late into the evening and that reaches into your bones warming them.'

But Lou is frowning now, shaking his head.

'What is it mate?' Bardy wouldn't have mentioned Tina. But Lou had asked.

'I've lied too,' Lou says, clearly distressed. 'I was going to say something else, but really this is my biggest lie.' He is talking directly to Bardy now, oblivious of the others. 'I feel terrible. I told Tina that there could never, ever be another woman for me.'

'And?' Bardy can't imagine what is coming next.

'I've been chatting online to a woman from Norwich called Lisa and she suggested we meet for a drink.'

'Oh, mate. That's okay.' Bardy is flooded with relief.

Lou is now looking around at everyone.

Linda – mellow plum – is the first with reassurance. 'Of course it is. A woman as wonderful as Tina would have understood.'

'I don't know,' Lou says, rubbing his thighs in his distress.

'Well, she wouldn't want you to be on your own for ever. I am certain of it.'

'I know it, mate,' Bardy assures him.

Lou's hands still. 'You think it would be alright to meet her then?'

There is a loud chorus: 'Of course.'

Lou looks shaky. 'Thanks, maybe I will go, she seems really nice.' He nods at Linda. 'She used to be a nurse too.'

'Oh, Lou, I think that was really brave, so I'm going to try and do the same.' Linda sounds far more serious than normal. She looks directly at Lou, but Bardy sees her take Leonard's hand. 'I was going to tell you all something pretty unimportant, but I think I need to say this. And I'm sorry I haven't told you this Leonard.' She turns to her husband. 'I've got to go into hospital. It's a procedure on my heart. I think it is going to be okay. But I didn't tell you Leonard, because…' Linda is looking down at their hands clasped together. 'Well, because I have always said I wasn't frightened of dying.' She looks up at them all. 'And that's a lie. I find I am really rather scared.'

The whole group move forward in their seats towards Linda. All eyes on Leonard. He has his head bent over his wife's hand.

'Leonard?' Linda says, quietly.

'Well, Lindy. I have always said I am a man who would never read someone else's letters. But I find out now that was a lie too. When I saw a letter from the hospital addressed to you, I read it. I'm very sorry, but there it is.' He sits up straighter. 'I just thought you would tell me when you were ready. And, you see, I was right. But in the meantime, I have researched this condition, and there is a very good success rate. I've talked to a private heart specialist, but he said really the NHS is the best place to be. And well, he is very optimistic. And so my dear, sweet love, you mustn't worry. I will be there with you every step of the way.'

'Oh Leonard,' Linda, says. She is crying now and it seems Leonard is too.

Bardy thinks they probably all are.

What is it about these people?

'I'm sure it will be okay,' Pia says, and Linda smiles mistily at her.

Blimey. He hadn't expected all of this.

He takes Tay's note from his pocket. Now might be the time for this.

'Tay can't be part of our new group as she is moving with Uzma to Leeds. But she did want me to read out this to you, Kate.'

'Oh, that is good. Moving to Leeds.' This news seems to have done much to restore Linda's normal good humour.

Bardy reads:

'I lied when I said I was sorry for telling ratty Karen to piss off. Twice. I meant it. Twice.

Love Tay x'

Bardy looks around – who else? 'Satya?'

'Oh, mine's easy. I lied when I told Jack that I didn't think the mission statement was a load of crap.' She laughs, shaking her head.

'What are you going to do?' Pia asks.

'Not sure yet. Well, I know I am going to come up with my own mission statement if I decide to have one at all. But mainly Jack and I are talking about what to do with the company. I think either I will stop trying to be a big global player and stick to what we do best, or I'll sell it and start something else.'

'A jelly empire,' Leonard suggests, blowing his nose on a big white handkerchief.

'There are far stupider ideas out there,' Satya laughs.

Bardy sits back in his chair. 'So there you have it, Kate. We are all liars.' He turns to her. 'Will you join the *King Lear* Liars?'

'Of course I will.' She smiles. 'I think it's a wonderful idea.' She continues, pensively, 'But if we aren't all working towards the creative competition, what are we going to be doing?'

'Well I've been thinking about that.' Bardy leans forward. 'I think the first thing we should do is campaign to keep the gallery open.'

'I think that is a splendid idea,' Leonard says. 'Do you have anything in mind?'

'Well I do actually,' Bardy says.

Dare he suggest it?

He thinks it is what Hana had meant when she gave him that artist's name as a gift.

'So out with it, stop sitting there looking all mysterious,' Lou demands.

'It's to do with the Constable painting.'

'The trouble is just one minor work from Constable won't get the press's attention,' Kate says, sadly.

'Well I have an idea… of what might…' Bardy starts. 'No, let's keep it for our first meeting. I'll tell you then. For now I think we should toast our new group.'

Kate grabs the bottle of wine and tops up glasses.

Bardy looks at all these people – his friends: the home birds, the exotics and he thinks of Tay, now a migrant heading north. But hopefully a seasonal visitor.

He stands and raises his glass. The others follow suit.

'I give you, the *King Lear* Liars.'

* * *

The others have left and Kate and Bardy have moved outside to watch the sun go down over the creek. Kate has gone inside to fetch a jumper. It is a beautiful evening, but the chill is setting in. Bardy's not feeling the cold. But then he's not feeling anything – except shock and awe that this amazing woman likes him.

As he waits he gets out his phone and reads up on the artist, Sean, that Hana told him about. It's a great story. Makes him laugh. He thinks again of the gallery. Everyone said one obscure Constable painting wouldn't attract the press. But this? Could the *King Lear* Liars pull it off? Maybe if Nate were to turn a blind eye...

He puts his phone away and watches a seabird flying low over the water. He's not sure of the breed. He needs Leonard. What was it Leonard said about some seabirds... the petrels and the gannets? Not so much home birds or migrants, more like nomads. Natural travellers. Perhaps that is what Hana really is. A traveller. Well, he knows he's a home bird. No doubt about that. He squints into the sun. But no reason why he can't be a traveller now and again. New Zealand. And short trips. A visit to Leeds could be good. He and Lou could make a day of it.

He thinks back over the evening, the lies, but also their achievements. How far everyone has come. He's glad he finally got his poems out there. Maybe he will approach a publisher? Who knows. And Leonard's musical, *Wobble*! Kate was right, he really can picture it on stage. More than anything he is pleased Leonard is no longer comparing himself to his brother. And Pia seems to have thrown off worries about her family and stopped pigeonholing herself as *'creative as a stone'*. Satya had said something interesting as she was leaving tonight too: she and Jack are turning their basement into somewhere to paint, sew, perform music… anything creative really. So, the awesomely impressive businesswoman is learning to play. Satya also said she didn't want all the paints, crayons and brushes she's bought over the years stuck away in drawers. A bit like the photos she'd taken of them. She wants them out, to be enjoyed even if sometimes it is just looking at them – the promise of them. He guesses a bit like Linda and her spices. And what about Linda learning a bit of patience and realising things can take time. Never thought he'd see that. Remembering her garden sculpture makes him think of Lou. He smiles. Wonders how the drink with Lisa will go. He's pleased for him. And pleased that he is now happy making something that he just likes to look at. Not yet another bowl for his green salads. He grins to himself, thinking of Mr On-there-like-that.

Kate emerges from the house. Kate the artist. She certainly was that. He is a bit in awe of her talent. What was it about him and artists? Their love of colour? But with Kate it was all about the light. And her painting showed that.

She joins him on the bench at the water's edge and they sit watching the sunset. The birds calling all around them. It is full tide and the expanse of water in front of them is sparkling in the rays of the dipping sun.

Maybe this is what sex with Kate will be like? Sparkling?
He's willing to find out.
Still hopes it doesn't kill him.
Kissing her had certainly been something else.
But not what he had expected.

He reaches out and pulls her to him, the last of the sun's warmth on his arms as he wraps them about her. She leans into him and she tilts her face to his.

He murmurs in her ear, '*Come on, kiss me, Kate Oliver.*'

Six little words.

And there it is.

It isn't just Kate who is shining. With this incredible woman kissing him, he, Jon Shakespeare, a sixty-four-year-old retired English teacher, in that moment, shines glorious and luminous. Gardener Bardy, a simple man who has never, in his heart, travelled far from home, a man with a lot of love to give – he is alight.

He is golden.

A good heart, Kate, is the sun and the moon – or rather the sun and not the moon, for it shines bright and never changes, but keeps his course truly.
If thou would have such a one, take me…

Epilogue

All's well that ends well

BREAKING NEWS:
A painting by the acclaimed British artist, John Constable has been stolen from a gallery in North Norfolk. The curator of the gallery, Nathan Spencer, said the painting had been exhibited as part of a campaign to save the gallery from closure. The gallery has been on the same site for over 150 years and Mr Spencer said the threatened demise of the well-loved art space was of great concern to the people of the town. The new owner of the building, Mr Jordon Boyce, is thought to have plans to develop the site for luxury apartments. Mr Boyce, an IT specialist with companies in Norfolk and London, was unavailable for comment. The police have asked members of the public to contact their helpline with any information.

BREAKING NEWS:

A ransom demand has been received for a John Constable painting stolen from a gallery in North Norfolk. The ransom note, received by a local community paper from a group using the initials KLL calls for the gallery to be saved from development and that in addition, Mr Jordon Boyce, the owner of the building, auction a pair of his underpants to raise awareness of the gallery's plight. This is thought to be a move reminiscent of the theft in 1972 of a Lowry painting by John Durkin, a Middlesborough man who campaigned for galleries to be open on Sundays to allow working-class people to visit. Mr Durkin also demanded that the mayor auction his underpants, which the mayor duly did. While arrested and fined for his crime, in the long run Mr Durkin achieved his aim of greater accessibility to the arts. John Durkin's son, Sean Durkin, has since gone on to be a successful artist. His works are known for including a figure of a policeman and a burglar hidden within the paintings. Mr Jordon Boyce, who has plans to develop the gallery as luxury apartments, was unavailable for comment. It is not known if he has any plans to auction his underpants.

BREAKING NEWS:

A happy ending in the saga of the John Constable painting that was stolen from a North Norfolk gallery. The painting has been returned, undamaged, and the gallery has been saved from closure. Nathan Spencer, the gallery's curator, said he was delighted by the public's response to the news of the theft, including several celebrities who offered to auction their underpants. It also brought the gallery's plight to the attention of grant givers, and it is rumoured that the gallery will be receiving lottery funding. Mr Spencer said he could not comment on that at this time, but that claims that the painting never left the building are unfounded. He was able to reveal that the owner of the building, Mr Jordon Boyce, has accepted an offer to sell the well-known historical landmark to a local business owner. The unknown benefactor wishes to remain anonymous, their only stipulation being that the gallery should ensure information headsets are always compatible with hearing aids.

Police say they are no further forward in discovering who was responsible for the theft.

Bibliography

Colour by Victoria Finlay
RSPB Handbook of British Birds by Peter Holden and Tim Cleeves
The Secret Lives of Colour by Kassia St Clair
Conscious Creativity by Philippa Stanton
The Artist's Way by Julia Cameron
Creativity by John Cleese
The Creative Act: A Way of Being by Rick Rubin
Sorolla: Painted Gardens (Rizzoli)
Sorolla: Spanish Master of Light (National Gallery)

Acknowledgements

This book was inspired by my love of North Norfolk. I would particularly like to thank my brother Stephen and sister in-law Judith, who spent many hours explaining the history of the landscape and in particular educating me about the bird life. Leonard eat your heart out! Thank you also to Nigel Done for bringing so much to this book: advice on flora and fauna; thoughts on colour and living a creative life; supplying the wonderful bird drawings in the book; and for being a great travelling companion – even on a bike! This book is dedicated to the three of you, with my love, and I hope we can go back together very soon.

Those who know this region will spot that I draw upon Wells-next-the-Sea, Cley and Salthouse. However, I never name them specifically, as I took liberties and changed aspects of their landscape to fit my story. I hope that I am forgiven and that readers feel I have stayed true to the spirit of the area. I would like to thank Jessica Curtis who guided me on working and living in North Norfolk, and with thanks to Dr Jane Chick for sharing her wonderful holiday home. Many pages were written at her table looking out over the creek at Wells. I would also like to mention the Holt Bookshop and thank them for their support. Nothing beats a good independent book shop!

Much of the story I wanted to tell is rooted in my experience of what it is to be creative – and also, what it is to struggle. I write and I paint. I find writing a whole heap easier. When it comes to picking up a paint brush, I have encountered all the problems experienced by my cast of characters. The thoughts that limit what I am prepared to stick at or even try, were echoed in the many conversations I have had with others about creativity. I would like to thank everyone who shared their stories with me: Belinda Toor and the team at Harper Fiction; Tanera, my agent – the Christmas hat knitter; all the many book clubs who spoke to me, but especially Victoria Barnes and the Year 2 Book Club in Bath. There are too many conversations to mention in detail, but I would particularly like to thank the beautician who, while painting my nails, told me about her love of photography and of how her husband sold his guitars when they came to the UK. I am just sorry I didn't take down your name.

The idea for a book about a creative competition began when a friend told me about *The King Lear Prize*, an initiative started in lockdown to inspire creativity in the over 65s. I was intrigued by the association with Shakespeare and this was a launch pad for my writing. But the group and prize I describe in my book are purely fictitious and I have no link with *The King Lear Prize*. Nor do the *King Lear Liars*! But I would like to thank *The King Lear Prize* for starting me on a journey towards what would become *Six Little Words*.

In addition, I sought out many people asking them to share their advice. Everyone was very generous, and their thoughts and wisdom helped shape Kate and Bardy's story. So, a big thank you to:

Carolyn Corlett and Jenni Richards from the South West Art Courses in Sherborne, for your help with oil painting, colour mixing, pen and ink drawing, and textile art. Plus what it is like to run art courses. I would highly recommend a visit!

Chris Brickell on the delights and dangers of woodturning.

Tabbin Almond on dealing with and surviving breast cancer.

Jo Ovenden on what it is to be a teacher (and a very good one too).

Anna Ovenden and Josslyn Marshall for reminding me of what it is like to be seventeen.

Fiona Oliver on running community groups, whippet knits and for introducing me to the art of Sean Durkin. What a wonderful true story that is.

Georgia and Jon Kay on living with a whippet.

Martin Gordon on creativity and attending art college.

Hilary Cowell on HR. And please forgive me and Pia for taking liberties!

Dijana Rakovic from Counterpoint and Jane Russell KC on dealing with some of life's toughest issues, including those facing refugees.

Isabella Thordsen Bell on what it is to be Danish and living in the UK.

Pippa Bell on art and liminal spaces.

Annie Hughes on end-of-life care and your approach to interiors.

Lily Done on adding those special extras to clothing.

Michael Warren for attempting to teach me the piano.

The Royal Shakespeare Company for their excellent online resources.

And not forgetting, Neil Oliver, for a poem celebrating the joys of camping!

As ever I would like to thank my agent Tanera Simons and the team that support me at Harper Fiction. You do a wonderful job! Specifically; my editor, Belinda Toor; Vicky Joss in marketing; Libby Haddock in PR; Holly Martin and Harriet Williams in sales. Plus I would like to thank Ellie Game for the cover design.

And finally, thank you to my early readers who always give me encouragement and friendly advice. Anne Heywood, Sonja Eyre, Pippa Bell, Merle Benson and Jo Ovenden.